HIS TRUTH
IS MARCHING ON

HIS TRUTH IS MARCHING ON

A WWII Novel

Robert Vaughan

WESTBOW
PRESS

A Division of Thomas Nelson Publishers
Since 1798

visit us at www.westbowpress.com

Copyright © 2004 by Robert Vaughan

Published by WestBow Press, a division of Thomas Nelson, Inc., Nashville, Tennessee 37214.

Publisher's Note: This novel is a work of fiction. All characters, plot, and events are the product of the author's imagination. All characters are fictional, and any resemblance to persons living or dead is strictly coincidental.

Scripture quotations are from the King James Version.

Library of Congress Cataloging-in-Publication Data

ISBN 0-7852-6185-0

Printed in the United States of America
1 2 3 4 5 6 — 07 06 05 04

This book is for my wife Ruth
Words are not enough to express my love

Prologue

Harmony Baptist Church
Gulf Shores, Alabama
October 22, 2004

The parsonage was situated on the Gulf beach, some three miles west of Harmony Baptist Church, on Fort Morgan Road. When Hurricane Hannah hit, there was no mandatory evacuation, so the Reverend Carl Baumgartner did not leave his house. He did try to get Jenny to go to Mobile to stay with her parents, but she said she had no intention of letting him ride out the storm alone.

During the night the Gulf roared with a thunder that could be heard even over the banshee howl of the wind. Trees bent sideways, and the rain slashed against the house, which shuddered but did not break before it. Only the hurricane shutters kept the windows from being blown out.

The next morning Reverend Baumgartner awakened to a bright, blue, sunny sky and a calm sea. But the dunes had been flattened by the storm, and the beach was covered with black seaweed that had been churned up from the Gulf.

Concerned about how the church had withstood the hurricane, Carl drove down for a look, even before breakfast. Fort Morgan Road was not closed, but the flotsam of the storm—sheet metal, porch furniture, plywood, trash cans, palm fronds, and bits and pieces of unidentifiable brightly colored objects—lined the road.

Then as he turned into the parking lot of Harmony Baptist, his heart fell when he saw the damage. Although the main structure of the church was unaffected, the storm had wreaked havoc on the fellowship hall. The walls still stood, but the roof was gone. Inside, the kitchen was a mess. Water and mud covered the floor, and tables and chairs were strewn about. The surviving bulletin board had been cleared of every posting but one.

> Loaves and Fishes Dinner
> Sponsored by the Men's Prayer Group
> Friday Night
> Bring a side dish.
> (Remember, the Gospel accounts
> make no mention of tuna casserole.)

Underneath, someone had penned, "Does this mean I can't bring lobster?"

Carl picked up one of the coffee makers that had blown into the parking lot. He was holding it aloft when a bright red Jeep SUV drove up. A lean and spry driver emerged. Reverend Baumgartner didn't know exactly how old Dewey Bradley was, but he knew that Dewey had fought in World War II, so he figured he had to be in his eighties. It said something for Dewey's personality, though, that while other men his age were driving full-sized sedans, Dewey drove a vehicle that was typically associated with much younger men.

Dewey walked over to stand beside Carl and survey the damage. The two men stood in awed silence for a moment before Dewey spoke.

"Any damage to your house?"

"No, thank God. What about you?"

"We came through it in fine shape. We were without power for most of the night, but it's been restored." Dewey shook his head. "A shame about this."

"Yes, especially since we just built it and it is underinsured."

"Well, when you live on the coast, this is always a possibility," Dewey said.

"I know. Still, I . . . ," Carl started, then stopped. He pinched the bridge of his nose. "I had hoped we would be spared this, at least until we could get the insurance brought up to date. The congregation was so proud of the new fellowship hall. Losing it is going to be a devastating blow."

Dewey put his hand on Carl's shoulder. "We've lost our hall, Carl. We haven't lost our fellowship."

Carl pointed to the bulletin board, where only the single flyer remained. "The Loaves and Fishes Dinner. That was to have been our first event in the new hall," he said. "I guess we won't be having it now."

"Oh, but clearly God intends for us to have it," Dewey said. "Otherwise, the hall would have blown away along with everything else."

"But how can we have it now? Where can we have it?"

"Jesus had His fishes and loaves dinner on the side of a hill. We don't have a hill, but we do have a parking lot."

"Dewey, you are indefatigable," Carl said. "How do you do it?"

Dewey walked over to his Jeep, then he turned back. "The Lord will give strength unto his people, Carl. It's not just a platitude such as, 'When the going gets tough, the tough get going,' or 'Keep on keeping on.' Psalm 29:11. 'The Lord will give strength unto his people.' It is the core element of my life."

Carl watched Dewey drive away. Had anyone else quoted scripture to him, a minister of the gospel, Carl would have considered it patronizing, and he would have been offended. But he took no offense from Dewey Bradley. He had known Dewey for many years now, and he marveled at what a remarkable life this man had led.

Litchfield, Illinois
November 27, 1941

The late fall rains had stripped the trees so that the leaves lay sodden in the gutter while the bare limbs rattled dryly against the gray November sky. On this Thanksgiving Day, most of the businesses in the little town of Litchfield were closed for the holiday, and the streets were nearly deserted.

On the east side of town, Shackleford Jackson stadium formed a natural bowl scooped in the earth and built up with steel and wood. Today, the stadium held its ten-thousand capacity for the thirty-sixth annual Thanksgiving Day game between Litchfield College and Washington University. It had been a close game, and the cheering and stomping of the students rocked the stadium's upper tiers, causing it to live up to its appellation of "Shaky Jake."

With one minute and twenty-two seconds remaining, the right end for Washington U broke free, took a pass from the quarterback, and streaked, untouched, down the left side of the field. The point-after try sailed wide, but the touchdown had put the St. Louis team up by six points. In the stands on the opposite side of the field, red-and-green pom-poms waved as the Washington U supporters cheered loudly.

During the break between the extra point try and the kickoff, Warren Sapp, the coach of Litchfield College, called his team together. The young men gathered around their coach, focused on him with determination. Their faces were bloodied and bruised, indicative of the ferociousness of the game.

"Dewey," Coach Sapp said to his quarterback, "don't throw an interception, and don't get sacked. If you can't find a man open, throw the ball away, or if you see you can pick up several yards and get out of bounds, do that. Receivers, when you get the ball, if you know you can't go all the way, get out of bounds. We've got to work the clock."

"All right, Coach," Dewey said.

Behind the players a sea of blue and orange surged as the Litchfield student body and fans cheered their team on.

The Bearcats hurried onto the field to receive the kickoff. Dewey waited on his own 10-yard line, and he watched as the ball made a high, end-over-end arc toward him. He caught it on the 15-yard line, then broke to the right. Don Mitchell made the block that allowed Dewey to turn the corner into the corridor of blockers, and suddenly Dewey realized that he had a chance to go all the way. He ran down the corridor his teammates had provided for him, staying close to the out-of-bounds line so that, even if tackled, he would be able to stop the clock.

He avoided the defensive backfield and crossed the goal line. Seconds later, the point-after try was good. The scoreboard now read Litchfield Bearcats 21, Visitors 20.

Litchfield stopped Washington U cold on the next four downs, then ran the clock out to secure the victory. The crowd's roar remained loud and sustained as the thirty-three blue-and-orange-clad young men left the field in triumph. Across the field from them, those in red and green trudged toward the visitors' locker room, feeling the bitter disappointment of having seen victory slip from their grasp.

Inside the Litchfield locker room, the young men whooped and cheered and banged on the locker doors. Then, in unison, "Bearcats, Bearcats, rah, rah, rah!"

"Men!" Coach Sapp shouted to get everyone's attention. "Men!" He climbed onto one of the benches so he could see all of his players. He had a football in his hand, and he held it over his head.

"Listen up, guys. Coach is talking!" one of the seniors shouted. The celebration quieted as the players, some of whom had stripped off their shirts and pads, turned toward the coach.

"Men, you won a great victory here today. Two times you were behind on the scoreboard, but you never gave up!"

The team cheered again.

"I wish I could give a game ball to every one of you, but I can give it to only one. And I think I've made the right choice when I say—"

"Bradley!" Don Mitchell shouted. "Give it to Dewey Bradley!"

"Bradley!" the other players said, taking up the chant. "Bradley! Bradley! Bradley!"

Coach Sapp held his hand out toward the men and waved them quiet.

"Well, now," he said, "it just so happens that Dewey Bradley is the one I chose." He handed the football to Dewey. "Dewey, the game ball is yours. You earned it, Son, not only in my eyes, but in the eyes of your teammates."

"Bradley! Bradley! Bradley!" the other players chanted.

With a broad smile, Dewey accepted the ball.

"Say something, Dewey!" one player shouted.

"Yeah, give us a speech! No, wait, what am I saying? You're going to be a preacher. You'll wind up giving us a sermon!"

The other players laughed.

"From what I know of most of you guys, a sermon wouldn't hurt you," Dewey said. He held up the ball. "I thank all of you for making this season special. And I thank God for giving me the opportunity to come and play football with such a great group."

Unity Rankin stood just outside the dressing room, waiting for the players to come out. Full of life and with a nearly perfect figure that blended womanly curves and girlish innocence, Unity had light brown hair, shot through with sunbursts of gold, so that in certain light it appeared almost blonde. Her eyes were hazel, with flecks of silver, and her skin was smooth and clear.

As she knew he would be, Dewey Bradley was one of the first players to come out of the locker room, and smiling, she waved at him. He hurried over to her.

"Did you bring the car around?" he asked.

"Yes, it's right over there." She pointed to a yellow 1937 Chevrolet.

"What time is it?"

"It's a quarter 'til four."

"Come on. If we hurry, we can be there for the start."

"Oh, heavens, we wouldn't want to miss the start now, would we?" Unity teased. "Miss the start, and you miss half of the event. When you're watching a cross-country race, all you see is the start and the finish."

"Not so," Dewey said. "There are three places in the park where you'll be able to see them come by."

Hurrying to the car, Dewey drove away from Shaky Jake, headed toward Litchfield's Walton Park, where the Thanksgiving Day Cross-Country Meet was being held. Eight schools, including Litchfield College, fielded teams in the meet.

"Anybody who runs like this does it because he loves it, not for the glory," Unity said as they drove toward the park. "I mean, nobody ever comes out to watch a cross-country meet except family."

"And that's a shame too," Dewey said. "Cross-country runners are much better athletes than football players. And Lee is one of the best in the country."

"Lee Arlington Grant," Unity said. "What is it he says? He's named after the two most famous generals in American history, plus all the heroes of Arlington National Cemetery."

"Well, his father is a colonel in the army, and his grandfather and great-grandfather were generals."

"And he's in the last year of seminary." Unity laughed. "I'll bet his father likes that."

They found a parking place near the start, and when they got out, they saw a rainbow of colors as the cross-country runners were loosening up. Blue and orange for Litchfield, red and green for Washington U, blue and white for Westminster, black and gold for the University of Missouri, black and orange for Greenville College, crimson and white for Southern Illinois, red and black for Southeast Missouri Teachers College, and blue and yellow for Murray State.

Lee Arlington Grant, lean and sinewy, was pushing against a tree. Seeing Dewey and Unity approach, he smiled.

"I caught your winning touchdown," he said. "Great game."

"Yeah, now all you have to do is come in first here, and Litchfield can sweep the day."

"Our first three runners should do all right," Lee said. "But the field gets pretty tight when you get farther down. We've got to get a good finish from four and five if we expect to win."

"Ahh, you can do it," Dewey said.

"Runners to the starting line!" the meet director called through a long megaphone.

"Well, it's that time," Lee said.

"Good luck," Dewey called to him.

Lee hurried over to the starting line, where he crowded in with his teammates and all the runners from the other schools. There were a handful of people lining the racecourse.

"Ready!" the starter shouted.

The runners leaned forward.

The starter fired the pistol, and the runners surged away from the line. When they ran past Dewey and Unity, they were still tightly packed, and Lee was in the first third of the pack.

They ran to the far end of the park, then disappeared behind the pine trees on the other side of the small lake.

Those who knew about cross-country races, and this course in particular, knew exactly where to go next, and Dewey and Unity moved into position, where, in approximately six minutes, they would see the runners come by. They waited.

"Here comes the first one!" someone called.

On a distant hill, they saw a runner in green.

"It's a Wash U runner!"

"That has to be Joe Thomas," Dewey said. "If there's anyone in this race who can beat Lee, it's Joe Thomas."

"There's Lee!" someone called.

Lee was the next one over the hill, running about fifteen yards behind Joe Thomas.

Thomas ran by them, blond, thin, his hair bouncing as he ran, his mouth open, his arms bent, his lean, muscular legs propelling him forward with an easy grace. Lee was next, a mirror image of muscular grace and form. The next nearest runner was about forty yards behind them, the first of a group of seven. Ten yards behind that batch, an even larger pack ran.

"We have five runners in the top twenty," Dewey said. "If we can hold that, we can win the meet."

Moving to the next spot on the course, Dewey and Unity waited about four minutes to watch the runners come by again. The first two runners, Joe Thomas and Lee Arlington Grant, stayed in the same relative position, but they had opened up an even larger lead over the next group. The next batch had thinned to only four runners, and from there on, they spread out in a long line.

The third time around, Lee had closed on Joe, but he had not been able to pass him. No group of runners followed them now. A rather long trail of men appeared, their faces gaunt with the strain of the race.

Dewey and Unity hurried to the finish line to be able to see the end.

"How long, do you think?" Unity asked.

Dewey glanced at his wristwatch. "We should see them any moment now," he said.

Dewey no sooner had the words out of his mouth than someone shouted, "There they are!"

"Dewey! Lee is in the lead!" Unity gasped excitedly.

"Come on, Lee! Come on!" Dewey shouted.

Lee did hold the lead, but only by a yard or two, and Joe Thomas ran close behind. Even from where he stood, Dewey realized that Lee wasn't going to be able to hold him off. Lee struggled, whereas Joe loped easily. About twenty-five yards from the finish line, Joe maneuvered from behind Lee, put on a kick, then went ahead. As they crossed the finish line, Joe pulled away.

The two runners passed on through the chute, then stood at the end, bent over, their hands on their knees, their faces glistening with sweat. Looking at each other, they smiled, shook hands, then came back to cheer their teammates through.

Litchfield's first four men came through in good shape. It was the fifth runner they were worried about. He had to improve by two positions in order for Litchfield to win. The other Litchfield runners scooted down the course to yell at him, to tell him what he had to do. As he came down the stretch toward the finish line, he made a heroic effort, passing first one and then the other, just before they entered the chute.

"That's it!" the Litchfield coach shouted. "That will give us the win!"

After the race the runners congregated in the park for a bit, reconstructing the race, congratulating one another, and meeting friends and family.

Lee walked to the car with Dewey and Unity. "You coming to the chapel Thanksgiving service tonight?" Lee asked.

Dewey replied, "We're driving down to Sikeston, Missouri, to spend the weekend with Unity's folks."

"Sounds nice," Lee said.

"What are you going to do for the weekend?" Unity asked.

"Stay here."

"Oh, that's right. Your folks are in Hawaii, aren't they?" Dewey said.

"Yes. My dad is stationed there at Wheeler Field."

"Would you like to come home with us?" Unity asked. "I'm sure my folks wouldn't mind."

Lee smiled. "No. Thanks for the invitation, but I'm helping with the service at Holy Spirit this weekend."

"Okay, but you know that the invitation is always there."

"I know," Lee said.

"Can we give you a ride back to the dorm?" Dewey asked.

"No, thanks. My gear is in Charley's car. I'll ride back with him. Thanks a lot for coming to the meet. I appreciate that."

"I'm always there for a teammate. Can't wait to run track together again in the spring," Dewey said. "You ran a good race today, Lee."

"It was my best time ever for this course," Lee said. "But Joe Thomas was something, wasn't he? He flew by me like he had wings on his feet."

"Lee, come on!" one of the other Litchfield runners called.

"I've gotta go. You folks have a nice weekend," Lee called, trotting across the park toward the green '32 Ford, where three others of the victorious Litchfield team waited.

"Are you all packed to go?" Dewey asked as they climbed back into the car. "Or do we need to stop by your dorm?"

"No, I put the suitcase in the car before I came to Shaky Jake," she said. "What time will we be there?"

Dewey looked at his watch. "About nine tonight, I would say."

"Good. That's not too late."

There was very little traffic as they left town. All the football traffic had long dissipated, and most people who had Thanksgiving engagements had already gone. Unity's parents had planned to have their Thanksgiving dinner the following day in order to accommodate the football game.

"I think it's neat," Unity said.

"What's neat?"

"You and Lee are the two best athletes in the school. And you are both going to be ministers of the Lord. That proves that ministers aren't sissies."

"Unity!" Dewey slugged her playfully on the shoulder. "Sissies? What a thing to say! I happen to know that your father was a very good baseball player when he was younger."

"I'll say. The Philadelphia Athletics wanted him to play for their team. But he wanted to preach the gospel."

"Would you call him a sissy?"

"No, I was saying that Daddy, you, and Lee are the opposite of that."

"I've never been of the opinion that we needed proof," Dewey said.

"I know, I know, I was just . . . I don't know what I was just doing. Let's listen to the radio, shall we?" she asked, reaching for the dial.

It took a moment for the radio to come on, then it whistled and screeched as she turned the dial, searching for a clear station. Finally they heard an announcer's clear voice.

"NBC presents the distinguished clarinet playing of Artie Shaw and his orchestra here in the Blue Room of the Hotel Lincoln in New York City. And now to start things off is 'I Can't Believe You're in Love with Me.'"

Night fell, and Dewey turned on the lights. The twin beams stabbed into the darkness ahead of them, illuminating Highway 3. The interior of the car glowed dimly from the instrument lights and the radio dial.

A half moon hung big and yellow just above the eastern horizon, and it reflected softly off the tin roof of a barn. Dewey put his arm on the back of the seat, and Unity shifted over to be close to him. He pulled her even closer and wished somehow that he could preserve the moment forever.

Litchfield, Illinois
December 3, 1941

The place was called the Bearcat Den because its customers were almost exclusively Litchfield students. It served hamburgers, hot dogs, barbecue sandwiches, french fries, onion rings, ice-cream confections, and an assortment of soft drinks. The booths encircled a dance floor, and at the back of the place a jukebox blared. The walls and booths were painted in blue and orange, and a collage of old football and basketball programs, photographs of past players, and even a few football jerseys and basketball shirts dating back before the Great War covered every available square inch of the walls.

"How can you do that?" Unity asked.

"How can I do what?" Dewey asked as he took a big bite from his second hamburger.

"How can you eat like that and not get fat?"

"It's called wind sprints," Dewey said.

"What?"

"Wind sprints. It's a particular form of torture designed by football coaches. You run, stop, run, stop, and run again until you can hardly stand."

"Yes, but football season is over now, and you're still eating like you did when you were doing . . . what is it you called them? Wind sprints?"

"Ahh, I don't eat all that much," Dewey said. "It just looks like it to you because you don't eat at all. I mean, your mother made that wonderful dinner, and you hardly ate any of it."

Unity said, "That's all right. You ate enough for both of us."

"It was nice of your parents to invite me down for the weekend. And to hold up on Thanksgiving dinner until we could be there to celebrate with them was especially thoughtful of them."

"You paid for it by preaching at Daddy's church on Sunday," Unity reminded him.

"It was gracious of him to allow me to do it," Dewey said.

"I think he just wanted to see what kind of preacher you were going to be, to see if you would be able to support his daughter."

Dewey reached across the table to take Unity's left hand. The diamond on her ring finger sparkled in the subdued lighting.

Like Dewey, Unity was a senior at Litchfield College. Studying to be a teacher, she had met Dewey not in school, but at Trinity Baptist of Litchfield, the church both attended while they were in school.

They had been going together for two years. Then, over the Thanksgiving weekend, while Dewey was a guest in the home of Unity's parents, he asked her to marry him. Unity accepted the proposal to the great delight of her father, the pastor of the First Baptist Church of Sikeston, Missouri. He was particularly pleased that his daughter had chosen to marry a man who was studying for the ministry.

Don Mitchell walked by their booth on his way to the jukebox. Seeing them holding hands across the table, he smiled at them.

"Hey, if you two lovebirds are going to get all cuddly like that, maybe you would prefer to be alone. You want me to run interference for you, Dewey? Clear out the place?"

"As big a horse as you are, I believe you could do it," Dewey said.

"I was just doing my bit for the old school," Don teased. "Hey, Mark White is in town. Did you know that?"

"Mark White? Professor White's son?"

"Yeah, he's right over there holding court in the corner booth," Don said. "He's in the army."

"Really. I thought he would probably be teaching at some college by now."

"Teaching in a college? Why would you think that?"

"He's a brilliant man. Have you read his book?"

Don smiled. "No, but I've heard about it. It's one of those high-brow books, isn't it? I mean, no pictures? What's the name of it?"

Dewey laughed. "*Man's Heavenly Quest.* It's a good book, but you're right, it doesn't have any pictures."

"You know what, Dewey? You've got that book in the car," Unity said. "Why don't you ask him to sign it?"

"Hey, that's a good idea," Dewey said. "Excuse me, I'll be right back."

Dewey hurried out to his car, retrieved the book, then returned. He and Unity walked over to the booth.

Mark White, in uniform, was indeed "holding court," as Don had put it. One coed was sitting with him, two more were across the table from him, and a couple of fellows, wearing orange sweaters with a block letter *L* in blue, stood nearby. Mark looked up as Dewey approached, and before Dewey could say anything, Mark stuck his hand out.

"You're Dewey Bradley, aren't you?" Mark asked.

"Yes."

"I saw the game on Thanksgiving. Great game, and your run at the end was one of the best runs I've ever seen."

"These guys helped set up the blocking wall," Dewey said, indicating the two young men who stood near the booth. "And Don Mitchell opened the corner for me so I could get into the seam."

"You're being modest," Mark said. "But it was still a good game and a great run."

"Thanks. I wonder if I could get you to—" Dewey held out Mark's book, and seeing it, Mark interrupted him.

"Don't tell me you are one of the twenty-seven people who bought my book?"

"Now, who is being modest?" Dewey replied. "I happen to know that the book did very well, and it got a great review in *Time* magazine."

"And in the *Pilot Town Sentinel*," Unity added.

"The *Pilot Town Sentinel?*" Mark asked.

"My father owns the paper in my hometown," Dewey said. "I reviewed your book in that paper."

"Did you, now? Well, I thank you for that, Mr. Bradley," Mark said.

"Would you autograph the book for me?" Dewey asked, handing him the book and a pen.

"It would be my honor and privilege," Mark said, taking the pen. "But, tell me, how did a book on theology happen to catch the attention of a football player?"

"I'm planning to enter the ministry after I graduate."

"Really?" Mark asked, looking up from the book. "Have you always wanted to be a preacher?"

"I think so," Dewey said. "What about you? Have you always wanted to be in the army?"

"No, not really. I'm still trying to decide what I want to do. I majored in philosophy and theology, and I found the subjects fascinating, but you don't just hang out a shingle that says, 'Mark White, Philosopher.' So, I joined the army to fly. I thought that might be something interesting to do while I made up my mind."

"So, you're a pilot?"

"Not yet," Mark said. "But I have applied for aviation cadet training." Mark inscribed the book, then handed it to Dewey.

To Dewey Bradley, athlete, scholar, and gentleman. I've no doubt you will do well in service to the Lord.

Mark White

"Thanks." Dewey held up the book. "And I promise you, when I get my church, this book will have a place of honor in the library. Oh, and good luck in flying school."

"Thank you," Mark said.

When Dewey and Unity returned to their booth, Don walked over to them again.

"Did you get your book signed?"

"Yes," Dewey said, showing it to him.

"That's nice," Don said. "Say, I'm about to go feed the jukebox again. Tell you what, in honor of the occasion of you two getting engaged, I'll pick something out just for you. What would you like to hear?" He held up a coin. "I've got my nickel, ready to go."

"How about 'String of Pearls'?" Unity suggested.

"'String of Pearls'? You've got it," Don said.

The music started, and several stepped onto the dance floor.

Dewey raked a couple of French fries through a glob of catsup, then made a face when he put them in his mouth. "They got cold," he said and picked up more.

"You're still going to eat them?" Unity asked. "How can you do that?"

"I paid for them," Dewey said. "I don't like to see them go to waste."

"They look awful," Unity said. "Dewey, where do you think we will live?"

"I guess it all depends on where I can get a church," Dewey answered. "That will be the governing criterion. I mean, let's face it. You'll be able to find work as a teacher, no matter where we go."

"I hope it's a town about like this one," Unity said. "This is just about right, not too small and not too large."

"I agree," Dewey said. "I think a town this size gives you a chance to find a church that is like an extended family. But it's always difficult to make it at first, especially when you're young. We'll have to pay our dues."

"Oh, speaking of church, don't forget that this Sunday, after service, Reverend Owens has invited us to his house."

"Is the good reverend going to feed us?" Dewey asked as he took several slurps of his vanilla milkshake.

"Is he going to feed us? You're awful!" Unity laughed, reaching across the table to slap him playfully.

As Dewey jerked back to avoid her hand, he spilled some of his milkshake onto his plate.

"Now look at what you've done," he teased. "You've made me get snow on my French fries."

Blockade near Slutsk, Russia
December 3, 1941

The whole world was covered with snow. Gunter Reinhardt didn't think there could exist as much snow as he had seen this winter. An infantryman in the German Wehrmacht, he stood in the trench that had been scraped out of the snow and held his hands over the small fire. The fire did little to push away the minus fifteen-degree temperature, but the trench did protect him from the wind.

Although he was only a private, Gunter was the grandson of a general and could quite easily assess the situation of the German army. And in his assessment, things weren't going well.

The Germans were outnumbered and fighting on the enemy's home soil. Wehrmacht soldiers were freezing to death, and those who weren't dying were suffering from frostbite and other exposure problems. But it wasn't only the men who suffered. The bitter cold affected guns and machines as well. Ice jammed up the tank tracks, and the fuel and oil congealed in the vehicles. The telescoping gun sights were useless, and even had they worked, many of the guns were frozen so solid that they couldn't be fired.

Suddenly, Ernst Fikuart jumped down into the trench and, dropping a few items in the snow, hurried over to the fire.

"Ohhh," he said, rubbing his hands together. "I have never been so cold. You know, a man could freeze to death in this weather."

"Yes, well, many already have," Gunter reminded him. Gunter pointed toward the little bundle. "Blankets, I hope?"

"Blankets, yes, from the Führer himself," Ernst replied.

Gunter smiled. "You don't say. From the Führer himself? Herr Hitler has come here to the Russian front to hand out blankets?"

"Oh yes, he is here," Ernst insisted. "'Here, Ernst, you brave boy,' the

Führer said to me. 'I know that you and the other brave boys out here might be just a little cold. So, you may have my blankets. I have no need for them. After all, I am warm and comfortable in my house in Berlin, eating wurst, and drinking hot coffee with cream and sugar.'"

"I have heard that the Führer is a vegetarian," Gunter said. "So, how is it that he told you he was eating sausage?"

"I think he just wanted to make me feel good," Ernst replied. "He wants all his soldiers not to think about being cold or hungry, so he told me about all the good things he has to eat and the warm house he lives in. That way, he believes I will forget that I am cold and hungry. Yes, that must be it. The Führer just wanted to make me feel good."

Although Ernst had started in jest, it was difficult for him to keep the bitterness from his voice.

Gunter laughed, but then cautioned, "You had better not let any of the officers hear you talking like that, Ernst. They will think it is defeatist."

"Oh, I'm not worried, Gunter. After all, your grandfather is a general, is he not?"

"Yes, but how does my grandfather being a general keep you from being worried?"

"Because if I get into trouble, I know you will get me out of it. Is it true that your grandfather offered you a commission?"

"Yes, it is true."

"And you turned him down?"

"Yes."

"You are crazy."

"Perhaps. But I look upon my being in the army as a service to my fatherland, not as an occupation. When the war is over, I will finish my schooling and become an engineer."

"I still say you are crazy," Ernst commented. "Even if you do not wish to stay in the army, it would be much better for us if you were an officer."

"For us?"

"Of course. We are friends, aren't we?"

"Yes, but if I were an officer, we wouldn't even know each other."

"I knew it. Give you a commission and the first thing you do is start acting like all the other stuck-up officers. 'I'm an officer now, Ernst. I don't even know you.' I can't believe that you, my dear friend, could so quickly and easily forget me. And after I saved your life in Poland too."

"You saved my life in Poland by relieving yourself in the bushes."

"Yes, and while you were waiting for me, a shell blew up the bridge we were about to cross. If I hadn't stopped, you would have been killed."

"You would have been too."

"That's not the point. The point is that, unlike you, I don't forget my friends."

Gunter laughed again, then wrapped his arms around himself in an effort to keep warm. He looked toward the little bundle Ernst had dropped on the snow-packed floor of the trench. "I wish those really were blankets," he said.

"They aren't blankets, but we can use them like blankets," Ernst said. He opened the bundle and handed some crimson-colored material to Gunter. "Here, my friend. What do you think of this?"

"What is this?" Gunter asked.

"These are drapes that I tore from a window," Ernst explained. He picked up the other piece of cloth, then wrapped it around himself. "Use it like this," he suggested. "It will make a fine blanket."

A sound like an empty boxcar rolling along a railroad track surrounded them. Without further word, the two soldiers dived to the bottom of the trench and lay there in the snow, with their heads buried in their arms. The incoming artillery shell burst near the lip of the trench and had the effect of collapsing the sides of the trench on them.

Gunter felt himself buried beneath the avalanche of snow. The little fire he had started earlier was extinguished at once, and Gunter and Ernst were so covered with snow that, had their folded arms not made a very small pocket for their faces, they would have suffocated.

Gunter struggled against the snow and, after some effort, managed to dig himself out.

"Ernst!" he called. "Ernst!"

He saw a little piece of red, part of the drapery Ernst had wrapped around himself. Digging frantically, Gunter managed to extricate his friend.

"Thanks," Ernst said, gasping for breath when Gunter finally dug him up.

The two men found a part of the trench that had not been collapsed, and they sat there somewhat protected from the ongoing bombardment. They were wrapped in the ersatz blankets of crimson drapery, but because the coverings were totally inadequate to the task, they shivered almost convulsively against the cold.

The artillery rounds continued to rain down upon them, and though occasionally one of them burst close enough to send shards of smoking shrapnel whistling overhead, none of the others were as close as the first had been. After a bombardment of about fifteen minutes, the artillery barrage stopped.

Ernst looked toward where their little fire had been. It was so covered with snow that none of it could be seen. "Have you any matches left?" he asked.

"No. Have you?"

"No. Maybe we can find a fire somewhere and borrow a burning brand," Ernst suggested.

"I will look for one," Gunter offered. "You dig up our old one so we will have something to burn."

Crawling up from the collapsed trench, Gunter began his quest. It was easy to see where all the Russian shells had fallen. The snow was dug up and colored black by the powder of the detonation.

Most of the rounds had fallen harmlessly, but one had found its mark with devastating effect, landing in a hole that had been occupied by four men. All four soldiers were killed, and the red of their blood made an uncommonly bright contrast to the black and white of the shell-pocked snow.

The German army, which had moved so swiftly and victoriously across Russia during the summer, was now bogged down by what the soldiers were calling General Winter. Nature did what the Soviet army could not do, and the German advance had been halted in its tracks.

The problem was that the German high command, anticipating a quick victory, had not brought winter gear with them. Thus, all but a very few of the soldiers were still in their summer uniforms, and they had no coats or blankets. Some supplies were getting through, but with the arrival of each supply shipment, the soldiers found not coats, blankets, or food for the men, but fuel for vehicles that could not negotiate the frozen roads, and ammunition for artillery pieces that could not be fired.

Gunter found a few men gathered around a fire that had not been put out by the bombardment or had been started anew.

"I need to borrow some fire," he said, putting a stick into the fire until it caught.

"You may borrow some, but be sure you bring it back," one of the soldiers joked, and the others laughed.

Cupping his hands around the tiny, flickering flame, Gunter returned to the trench he shared with Ernst. By now, Ernst had dug up the old fire and cleaned off the wood. Gunter held the flame to one of the pieces of wood, and the fire caught. When the flame died down to sparks, Gunter and Ernst got on their hands and knees and began blowing hard, fanning the sparks into renewed flame. Finally, the fire took hold, and Ernst was able to toss a few additional pieces of wood onto it.

"Good fire, Ernst. This is nice," Gunter said.

"Who would want to be back in Germany when we have such a wonderful fire, eh? Oh! And something else!" he said. He looked around. "Where is my kit?"

"It is still buried under the snow."

"Help me dig it up," Ernst said. "I have some bread and cheese."

"Bread and cheese? How did you come by such marvelous things?" Gunter fell to his knees and began helping Ernst dig through the snow.

"It was for the officers," Ernst said. "Of course, I shouldn't tell you such a thing. When you were an officer, you didn't even know me."

"I was never a . . . ," Gunter started, then he laughed. "Never mind."

"Ahh, here it is," Ernst said, pulling his snow-covered kit from the hole. Opening it, he took out a paper-wrapped package. In the package were a loaf of bread and a hunk of cheese. He divided his bounty equally, giving half of it to Gunter.

Ernst took a bite. "This is good. You officers know how to eat."

"Ha, I'll show you how much we do know," Gunter said. He pulled out his mess kit, then put the bread and cheese into the skillet.

"What are you going to do?" Ernst asked.

"I am going to have a hot meal," Gunter said, holding the bread and cheese over the fire.

"Yes, what a marvelous idea!" Ernst said.

The two men held their kits over the fire until the cheese began bubbling. Then, leaning back against the bank of snow, they ate their meal.

"Gunter," Ernst asked as he popped a bit of hot bread into his mouth, "what do you think the poor people are doing right now?"

"Why, they are envying us, of course," Gunter replied as he licked melted cheese from his fingers.

3

Litchfield, Illinois
December 7, 1941

E xcellent sermon this morning, Reverend Owens," Dewey said. "I really liked the idea that you don't have to know the gospel, chapter and verse, to share it with others."

Reverend Owens chuckled. "St. Francis of Assisi once said, 'Share the gospel with others, and if necessary, use words.'"

Dewey laughed.

"I'm glad you enjoyed it, Dewey, but you don't have to butter me up. I believe Lucille would have offered you another piece of pie anyway."

Lucille Owens laughed and looked across the table at Dewey. "Would you like another piece of pecan pie?"

"Oh yes, ma'am, thank you," Dewey said. "But your sermon was a good sermon," he added.

"What about you, Unity?" Mrs. Owens asked as she cut a generous piece for Dewey.

"Oh, thank you, but I couldn't eat another bite," Unity said.

Dewey and Unity regularly visited with the Reverend E. D. Owens and his family. Reverend Owens was pastor of Trinity Baptist Church. Because of the college in Litchfield, Trinity had a very active college student program.

Reverend Owens had two children, Johnny, age twelve, and Beth, seven. Johnny was a big sports enthusiast and had insisted that he get to sit next to Dewey.

"Dewey, are you going to play basketball for Litchfield?" Johnny asked.

"I don't think so, Johnny," Dewey said. "I think my athletic days are about over. I'm going to be busy for the rest of my senior year, trying to find a church."

"But we need you," Johnny said. "And you are a real good basketball player, almost as good a basketball player as you are a football player."

"Johnny, there comes a time when a young man has to put aside some childish things so he can plan for his future," Reverend Owens said. "And I think that time has come for Dewey." Then to Dewey, he asked, "How is your search for a church coming? Do you have any leads?"

"I'm not really searching yet," Dewey said. "I plan to start in earnest as soon as the final semester gets under way. As you know, Unity's father is pastor of First Baptist in Sikeston, Missouri, and he is looking around for me."

"That should help. If you would like, I have a few friends I can contact as well. I've heard you preach, and I know your heart. I don't think you'll have any trouble at all finding a church, though you might have to start as an assistant pastor somewhere."

"Yes, sir, I'm aware of that, and I'm perfectly willing to do so," Dewey replied.

"Well, what do you say? Shall we have our coffee in the living room?" Lucille invited.

"Can I help you, Mrs. Owens?" Unity asked.

"Of course you can, dear. You can carry the tray."

In the living room, Johnny went over to the large console radio and turned it on. He fiddled with the dial until the little green tuning eye showed that the radio was receiving the strongest signal. The song "Chattanooga Choo-Choo" was playing. Smiling, Unity stood up and, pretending that she was holding a microphone, began lip-synching with the words. Suddenly, the song stopped, and everyone looked toward the radio.

"Johnny, did you do something to the radio?" Mrs. Owens asked.

"No, ma'am. I didn't do anything," Johnny said.

After a few seconds of silence, an announcer came on.

"Ladies and gentlemen. We interrupt this broadcast to bring you a special news bulletin. We have just been informed that Japanese air and naval forces have attacked the American base at Pearl Harbor. Pearl Harbor is located near Honolulu in the Hawaiian Islands. As the Hawaiian Islands are an American territory, this is tantamount to an attack upon the United States itself. Informed sources tell us that President Roosevelt will, in all likelihood, ask Congress for a declaration of war."

"What does that mean?" Mrs. Owens asked.

"I don't know," Reverend Owens replied. "But I don't think it's good."

Episcopal Diocese of Central New York
January 8, 1942

Lee Arlington Grant, wearing vestments but, as yet, no stole, approached Bishop Edward Coley, who was sitting in his chair near the Holy Table. Father Malcolm Peabody made the presentation.

"Reverend Father in God, I present unto you this person to be admitted to the order of priesthood."

Bishop Coley looked at Lee, then at Father Peabody.

"Take heed that the person whom you present unto us be apt and meet, for his learning and godly conversation, to exercise his ministry duly, to the honor of God and the edifying of His church."

"I have inquired concerning him, and also examined him, and think him so to be."

The bishop then began questioning the candidate.

"Will you maintain and set forward, as much as lieth in you, quietness, peace, and love, among all Christian people, and especially among them that are or shall be committed to your charge?" the bishop asked.

"I will so do, the Lord being my helper," Lee replied.

"Will you reverently obey your bishop and other chief ministers, who, according to the canons of the church, may have the charge and government over you, following with a glad mind and will their godly admonitions, and submitting yourself to their godly judgments?"

"I will so do, the Lord being my helper," Lee answered.

"Almighty God, who hath given you this will to do all these things, grant also unto you strength and power to perform the same, that He may accomplish His work which He hath begun in you, through Jesus Christ our Lord. Amen."

Lee knelt before the bishop, who, standing, put his hands upon Lee's head.

"Take thou authority to preach the Word of God, and to minister the holy sacraments in the congregations where thou shalt be lawfully appointed thereunto."

Following the ordination, a reception was held in the parish hall of the church.

Discovering that he had enough hours to graduate, Lee had left Litchfield College at the winter semester break, then returned to New York for his ordination. He had selected Endicott Peabody as his sponsoring priest because Peabody was the son of the founder of the Groton School, the private academy where Lee had attended high school.

The Episcopal Women's Club had gone all out for the reception, providing cookies, cakes, canapés, coffee, and punch.

Lee stood with Father Peabody and Bishop Coley, greeting the parishioners as they came through a receiving line to congratulate him. Most didn't know him, for this had never been his church, but because of his Groton School connection, it was the quickest and easiest route to ordination.

"I understand you are going into the army," one of the older men asked as he came through the reception line.

"Yes, sir," Lee said. "I've applied for and have been accepted by the Chaplain Corps."

"Well, I'm sure Iron Mike will be proud of you."

"You know my father?" Lee asked.

"I'm Colonel Refern Hicks, U.S. Army retired. I do, indeed, know your father. We flew mail together back in the twenties. Do give your father my regards, will you?"

"Yes, sir, I will," Lee said.

After Lee had greeted everyone, he went over to the hors d'oeuvres table and filled a little plate with selections. Then he moved close to a window to watch the swirl of people as they gathered around the table or collected in little conversational groups. The bishop approached him.

"Father Peabody told me of your military background," the bishop said. "Father, grandfather, great-grandfather. And now you are joining that long and distinguished line."

"Yes, sir."

"I'm sure your father must be very proud of you."

Lee chuckled. "I'm afraid that remains to be seen," he said.

"Oh? And why is that?"

"I had an appointment to West Point," Lee replied. "But I gave it up to go to a small religious school. My father was very unhappy with that decision."

"But you are going into the army now," the bishop said.

"Yes, sir, I am. I suppose some sense of military obligation remains within me because, though I had no intention of entering the service, I felt called to do so, once our country entered the war. And I feel that I can fulfill that obligation as an army chaplain. I'm not sure my father will see it that way, though."

"But your father is a Christian, isn't he?"

Lee was silent for a moment before he answered. "Let's just say that Christianity isn't something he lets stand in the way of his duty."

"Then I shall pray for him," the bishop said. "And for you."

"Thank you, Bishop. I will need all the prayers I can get," Lee said.

Litchfield, Illinois
February 11, 1942

The guest preacher at Trinity Baptist's Wednesday night prayer service was the Reverend Otto Rodl, recently arrived from Germany. In his introduction of Rodl, Reverend Owens described how Rodl, who had been saved by the Southern Baptist Missionary ministries, escaped from Germany.

"In Germany today, there are fewer than 150,000 worshipers in the free Protestant churches, including Baptist churches," Owens said. "Today, many of those men, women, and children are being rounded up. Reverend Rodl was slated to be a prisoner of the Nazis, but in a daring escape that would make an exciting adventure novel, he managed, with God's help, to get out of Germany."

After thanking Reverend Owens for the introduction, Rodl addressed the congregation. He told them how the Nazis had attempted to take over all the churches of Germany, uniting them under something called the German Christian Faith Movement.

"My dear friends, Christianity is in great peril of being eliminated from Europe," Rodl began. "If Nazism is not defeated, if Hitler is not stopped, he will have done what Satan has been unable to do for the last two thousand years.

"Hitler has ordered that all Christians stop being Baptists, Methodists, even Lutherans, and unite under something he calls the German Christian Church. But don't let that name fool you. There is nothing Christian about the German Christian Church.

"Here is what they are advocating. First, they want to completely abolish the Old Testament. Then, they want to rewrite the New Testament, changing the very words our Savior spoke. In that way, they will make it appear as if Jesus is more interested in the Aryan concept of blut und erde, that is, blood and soil, than in the salvation of the soul.

"Listen to what the Reich Minister for Ecclesiastical Affairs, Dr. Hans Kerrl, said."

Rodl began to read: "'The National Socialist Party stands on the basis of positive Christianity, and positive Christianity is National Socialism. National Socialism is the doing of God's will, and God's will reveals itself in German blood. Traditionally, Christian theology has tried to make it clear that Christianity is based upon one's faith in Christ as the Son of God. That makes me laugh. No, Christianity is not dependent upon that doctrine. True Christianity is represented by the party, and the German people are now called on by the party and especially by the Führer to a new Christianity, a real Christianity. And Adolph Hitler is our savior, and the herald of a new revelation.'"

Rodl looked up from his document and studied the faces of the congregation for a moment before he continued.

"My friends," he said, "all over occupied Europe, two hundred million of your brothers and sisters in Christ have seen their religion perverted or taken from them by the heresy that is taking place in Germany now.

"Hitler's anti-Semitism is well known. Hundreds of thousands, perhaps millions of Jews, not just in Germany, but throughout Europe, have been put in concentration camps. The treatment they are receiving there is brutal beyond description, and there are well-documented reports that these aren't just concentration camps, but are actually death camps.

"What is less well known is Hitler's anti-Christian doctrine. Those Christians who have stood up to him, such as the Reverend Dr. Martin Niemoeller, have found themselves in those same concentration camps.

"Albert Einstein, the world's most famous scientist, German born but now residing here in the United States, said, 'Being a lover of freedom, when the [Nazi] revolution came in Germany, I looked to the universities to defend it, knowing that they had always boasted of their devotion to the cause of truth; but, no, the universities were immediately silenced. Then I looked to the great editors of the newspapers whose flaming editorials in days gone by had proclaimed their love of freedom; but they, like the universities, were silenced in a few short weeks.

"'Only the Church stood squarely across the path of Hitler's campaign for suppressing truth. I never had any special interest in the

Church before, but now I feel a great affection and admiration because the Church alone has had the courage and persistence to stand for intellectual truth and moral freedom. I am forced to confess that what I once despised I now praise unreservedly.'"

Once again, Rodl looked up from his prepared text to address the congregation directly.

"Your country managed to stay out of war until you were bombed by the Japanese, but on the day following the Japanese attack, Hitler declared war on the United States. War is not a good thing. I believe that God weeps when He sees His children engaged in such wholesale slaughter. But I tell you now that I, and millions like me, gave thanks to God that America entered the fray. Surely, with the United States allied with the rest of the world, the evil that Hitler has spread across Europe will be lifted."

After the sermon that evening, the congregation met in the church basement, where they had a reception for Reverend Rodl. Several asked him to describe the adventures of his escape to them, and he did so, with great relish. Others asked what it was like to live under Nazi dictatorship, and he described that just as vividly, telling of hearing the sounds of police cars during the night, or the staccato rhythm of hobnailed jackboots as storm troopers marched down the street.

Though many were gathered around Rodl, there were several other conversational groups as well, and in one, Unity was telling several of her friends about her upcoming wedding.

"We will be married in June," Unity said. "Mom is already planning the wedding."

"What colors are you picking?" one of the girls asked.

"The colors are going to be lavender and white," Unity said.

"Oh, that will be beautiful."

The girls wanted to know every detail about the wedding: the dress, the decorations, the cake, honeymoon plans.

"We haven't talked about a honeymoon yet."

"Is your father going to perform the ceremony?"

"Absolutely," Unity said. "Why, he would be crushed if he didn't."

Somebody else said something, and everyone, including Unity, laughed. But as her eyes searched the room, looking to reestablish contact with Dewey, she was surprised to see that he wasn't talking to Reverend Rodl or even Reverend Owens. He wasn't talking to anyone. Instead, he was at the very back of the room, his back to everyone else as he looked out through the high basement window, staring into the darkness beyond.

"Excuse me," Unity said to the others.

She walked through the room, speaking to those who spoke to her, until she reached Dewey. She had never seen him looking so preoccupied, and she felt a little twinge of worry. Was he having second thoughts about the wedding?

"Dewey?"

Dewey turned toward her and smiled, though even the smile was pensive.

"Hi," he said.

"Is anything wrong?"

Dewey shook his head. "No, nothing is wrong."

Unity breathed a sigh of relief. "That's good," she said. "From the way you were just standing here, staring through the window, I was imagining all sorts of things."

Dewey smiled. "You mean like, am I having second thoughts about getting married?"

"Yes, something like that," Unity said with a little laugh.

"Don't worry about anything like that," he said. "You aren't going to get rid of me that easily."

"Well, I would hope not."

"What did you think about what Rodl had to say tonight?" Dewey asked.

"I thought it was awful, I mean, what all those poor people are having to go through in Europe. Can you imagine someone coming in the middle of the night, breaking into your house, and taking the whole family, father, mother, and children, off to concentration camps?"

"Yes, I can imagine it," Dewey said. He looked back through the window into the darkness. "I can imagine it very vividly. In fact, I can't get it out of my mind. And that's what's bothering me."

"What do you mean?"

"What Hitler is doing over there is terrible," Dewey said. "And anyone who calls himself a man of God has the obligation to fight it. But
do you think he intends to stop with the Jews? After he gets through
with them . . . or perhaps, listening to Reverend Rodl, even as he *is*
dealing with them . . . he is also starting on others, beginning with any
Christian who won't join that perverted German Christian Church he
has started."

"I know," Unity said. "It is really awful."

Dewey took a deep breath, then turned toward Unity. He took both
her hands in his and looked her right in the eyes. Something about the
expression in his eyes frightened her, and she felt her stomach turn.

"Here is the thing, Unity," he said. "I can't just stand by and watch
this."

Unity was puzzled by his statement, and she screwed her face up in
confusion.

"I don't understand," she said. "What do you mean you can't just
stand by and watch?"

"On Thanksgiving Day I played in a football game," Dewey said. He
pinched the bridge of his nose. "I can't believe how important it was to
me for us to beat Washington U."

"Yes, and we did win, thanks to you," Unity said.

"You don't understand, do you? While I was playing in that stupid,
insignificant football game, people were being starved, beaten, and
worked to death in concentration camps all over Europe."

"I know, and it's awful," Unity agreed. "But the fact that you were
playing football has nothing to do with what is happening in Europe."

"That's just the point," Dewey replied. "I have nothing to do with
what is happening in Europe."

Unity shook her head in confusion. "Dewey, I don't understand.
What are you trying to tell me?"

"I'm going into the army," Dewey said.

"You've been drafted?"

"No," Dewey said. "I'm not waiting for the draft. Tomorrow I'm going
down to the post office, and I'm going to volunteer."

"Tomorrow? Well, will they give you time to graduate?"

Dewey shook his head. "I'm not going to graduate," he said. "At least, not yet. I'll finish school when the war is over."

"What? Oh, Dewey, no!" Unity said. "You can't do that. We've made plans. This will mess up everything."

"Darling, how many people all over the world do you think have made plans, only to have those plans changed by this war?"

"But that's different," Unity protested. "Their plans were changed for them. What you are talking about is changing the plans."

"We can still get married," Dewey said. "I mean, nothing has really changed."

"Nothing has changed?" Unity asked. Unable to hold back the tears, she could feel them stream down her face. "You have just turned my life upside down, and you say nothing has changed?"

All the time Unity was talking, she was working hard to take the ring off her finger.

"Well, you are wrong," she said, putting the ring in his hand. "*Everything* has changed."

Dewey looked down at the ring, then up at her, but she had already turned away from him and was walking quickly toward the door.

"Unity, wait!" Dewey shouted, hurrying after her.

Dewey followed Unity through the door and up the steps.

"Unity, wait! Please wait!" Dewey called to her as he saw her walking not toward the car, but back toward the campus.

"Leave me alone!" Unity called back over her shoulder.

"Well, at least let me take you back to the dorm! It's cold!"

"Leave me alone!" Unity repeated.

4

Schweinfurt, Germany
February 17, 1942

K arla Maas stood at the window, holding the curtain to one side as she looked out.

"Will this miserable winter never end? It is snowing again," she said. "Can you believe that it is this close to spring, yet still it is so cold?"

Karla's mother, Olga, was sitting in a rocking chair knitting woolen mittens. She held the mittens out to look at them.

"If it is miserable here, think of our poor soldiers on the Russian front," Olga said.

Beside Olga Maas's chair, a fire roared merrily, supplied with coal that Viktor managed to bring home from the factory. Officially they were supposed to have a fire only four hours per day, but Olga openly and without apology violated that law. She kept the fire going twenty-four hours a day, though she did bank it all night. Karla's father was plant manager for FAG Kugelwerks, the huge ball-bearing plant that employed more Schweinfurt citizens than any other place of employment.

"Why don't the generals just go ahead and capture Moscow?" Karla asked. "Surely, there are places in Moscow where one can get warm."

Olga chuckled. "Dear, don't you think they would have captured Moscow by now if they could?"

"What are you saying, Mamá? That the Russian army is better than our army?"

"No, dear, of course I'm not saying that. But the only thing the papers tell us is that our army has 'dug into winter positions.' That doesn't sound very encouraging to me. It sounds to me that we are just hanging on."

"But wouldn't the newspapers tell us if it was bad?"

"The newspapers aren't always right, are they?" Olga said. "The newspapers all said that America would not come into this war. Their people have no will to fight. I think that is the way it was put."

"Oh, pooh, I'm not worried about the Americans. They are too busy with the Japanese to ever come to Europe to fight."

Olga laughed. "So, when did you become the military expert?" she asked.

"I never read the newspapers anyway," Karla said. "The casualty reports depress me so." She picked up the paper and opened it, then began reading, picking one report at random.

"In a hero's death for the Führer, there died on January 22, in Russia, Sergeant Willy Pfaff, my husband and the father of our three children."

Karla put the paper down. "There is an entire page of such notices," she said. "Oh, Mamá, do you think Gunter is safe?"

"There, I think these will keep his hands warm, don't you?"

"Mamá?" Karla asked again. "You didn't answer me."

"Child, we can only pray that your young man is safe," Olga said. "Every day that you do not hear otherwise is a day God gives you. Be thankful for that."

From outside the house, they heard the sound of automobile tires rolling on snow.

"Oh, Papá is home," Karla said brightly.

Olga walked over to look through the window and saw a black

Mercedes pull into the circular driveway and stop at the front porch. Privately owned automobiles were not all that common, but because of Viktor's position as head of the ball-bearing plant, he had a car.

"You're right. It is your father," Olga said. She glanced toward the clock on the wall. "I wonder what he is doing home so early?"

Viktor exited the car, then stamped his feet on the front steps before coming into the house, bundled in winter wear.

"Olga," he scolded as soon as he came inside, "it is too hot in here."

"Nonsense. You're too hot because you just came in from the cold. And you have your coat on. It's actually very comfortable."

Viktor took off his wrap and hung it on a freestanding coatrack. When he turned around, he saw his wife and daughter staring at him. There was concern on their faces.

"What is it?" he asked. "What is wrong?"

"You are home early," Olga said. "Have you bad news for us?"

Viktor saw the intense worry in his daughter's face and knew that she was concerned for her fiancé. He smiled to put her at ease.

"Relax," he said. "As far as I know, Gunter is fine."

Both Olga and Karla breathed a great sigh of relief.

"Thank God, he is all right," Karla said.

"But I do have bad news," Viktor continued. "Nothing that affects us directly, but bad news nevertheless."

"What is it? What has happened?" Olga asked.

"Lübeck was bombed by the British last night," Viktor said. "The entire town was burned to the ground. Many killed, and more than fifteen thousand are now homeless."

"Turned out of their homes in weather like this?" Olga said. "Who would have thought the British so evil?"

"Yes, well, the point is, Schweinfurt may well become a target someday," Viktor said. "After all, we do furnish most of the ball bearings for the war production."

"Oh!" Olga said, putting her hand to her mouth. "I never thought about it before, but that is true, isn't it? You are in danger every time you go to work now."

Viktor chuckled quietly, shook his head, then wrapped his arms around Olga.

"Don't you understand, Olga, my love?" he asked. "It isn't just me. It isn't just the factory. When they bomb a city, they bomb the entire city. I fear you will be in as much danger here, in our own home, as I will be at the plant."

"Oh!" Olga said. "But somebody must do something! Surely, the authorities are doing something, aren't they?"

"Yes, they are doing something. They have moved in several more antiaircraft batteries, at both Conn and Ledward Kasernes. Although I'm told that unexploded antiaircraft shells falling back to the ground can do almost as much damage as the enemy bombs."

"Then why put them here?"

"Well, we can't let them just bomb us with impunity," Viktor said.

"No, I suppose not."

"They are also bringing in radar to protect us."

"What is radar?" Olga asked.

"Oh, Gunter told me about radar," Karla replied. "It is something that can detect enemy bombers long before they get here. It tells which way they are coming from, where they are, and how fast they are approaching."

"Yes, that is what it does, though I have no idea how it does it," Viktor agreed.

"And it is said that they use women with the radar, sending messages to our antiaircraft batteries and to our interceptor bases. Our brave fighter pilots can be guided right to the bombers."

"That is true," Viktor said.

"I should like such a job."

"Would you really?" Viktor asked.

"Yes. I feel so useless, sitting at home and doing nothing. Gunter is in Russia, fighting for the fatherland. I think I would like to do something as well."

"Then I shall talk to the authorities for you," Viktor said.

"Oh, Viktor, isn't such a job dangerous?" Olga asked.

"No more dangerous than if she stayed at home every day," Viktor said.

On the Russian front

The engineers had brought a bulldozer and used it to open a grave in the cold ground. It sat beside the hole with its engine rumbling because they were afraid that if they shut it down, they wouldn't be able to start it again.

A pile of corpses lay beside the hole, some killed in artillery barrages, but most dead from the cold. They were frozen into the same positions they had been when they died so that now they looked like twisted pieces of grotesque sculpture.

Even more grotesque was what they were wearing, for they had all made some attempt to keep warm and were wrapped in tablecloths, civilian coats, colorful quilts and blankets. One was even wearing a woman's coat, gold colored, complete with bangles and beads. Gunter's eyes were drawn to a splash of crimson, and he fought the lump in his throat as he saw Ernst among the others.

"Lieutenant," one of the burial detail called to the officer in charge of burying, "we can't move them. They are frozen to the ground."

The lieutenant stroked his chin for a second, then looked toward the bulldozer driver. "Push them into the hole," he ordered.

"Lieutenant, they are our comrades," the bulldozer driver protested.

"Push them into the hole," the lieutenant said again.

Reluctantly following the lieutenant's orders, the driver climbed back onto the bulldozer and drove it around behind the bodies. Lowering the blade, he started forward. The bodies began to break apart, but because they had been dead for a long time, and because they were frozen solid, there was no blood.

The driver pushed them all into the hole, then made a few more scrapes to make certain that everything was buried. After that, he pushed the dirt over the top. After a moment or two of work, there was nothing left but a patch of bare, track-marked dirt in the snow.

"All right, that's it. You can all get back to your holes," the lieutenant said.

"Lieutenant, aren't we going to say anything over the grave?" one of the soldiers asked.

"Why? They're dead, aren't they? What good will that do?"

"If you don't mind, Lieutenant, I think we should say a prayer," Gunter said.

The lieutenant looked at Gunter. Ordinarily, he would have reprimanded a soldier who questioned him, but he knew that Gunter's grandfather was Colonel-General Jakob Reinhardt, and that fact intimidated him enough that he gave Gunter more leeway than he would give any other private.

"Very well, pray if you must," the lieutenant said, resenting the fact that he, an officer, could be intimidated by an enlisted man.

"Our heavenly Father, we commend the bodies of these, our comrades, to the ground, in the sure and certain hope for the general resurrection on the last day, and the life of the world to come, through our Lord Jesus Christ.

"Amen."

"Amen," a few other soldiers said.

Gunter walked away from the mass grave and returned to the hole he had shared with Ernst. Ernst had been alive last night. He complained of the cold, but then, he had complained of the cold every night. This morning, Ernst had not woken up.

Army Chaplain School,
Fort Benjamin Harrison, Indiana
March 20, 1942

Lee sat at his desk in his room in the BOQ. It was the last week of Chaplain School, and he was filling out the assignments request. He heard a light knock on his door.

"Come in. It's open," he said.

"Good evening, Lee."

Recognizing the voice, Lee turned and stood at attention. His visitor was the school commandant, Chaplain Colonel Ken Cumbie.

"Colonel Cumbie," Lee said.

Colonel Cumbie made a sitting motion with his hand. "Please, please, sit," he said. "And may I?"

"Yes, sir, of course," Lee said. There were only two chairs in Lee's room, the hard desk chair, where he had been sitting, and an only marginally more comfortable stuffed chair that was near the window. "Please, sit there," Lee said, offering the more comfortable of the two chairs.

"Thank you," Colonel Cumbie said.

"Would you like a Coke? There's a machine in the hall."

"No, no, nothing, thank you. Lee, you know you are being selected as most outstanding student for this class, don't you?"

Lee shook his head. "No, sir, I wasn't aware of that."

"I don't know how you could not be aware. You were head and shoulders above everyone else in the class, especially in your physical training and in the military courses."

"Well, I have somewhat of an unfair advantage in that department," Lee said. "I come from a military background."

"Your great-grandfather was a brigadier general on General Sherman's staff during the Civil War, your grandfather commanded a regiment during the Spanish-American War, and your father flew with the Hat in Ring Squadron during the world war."

"Yes, sir, that's true."

Colonel Cumbie chuckled. "As you can see, I've done my research."

Lee nodded, but said nothing.

"That explains your superiority in the military subjects. But the sergeant in charge of physical training tells me that after a day running, you sometimes go out and run on your own. Is that true?"

"Yes, sir. I was a cross-country runner in college, and I find that running helps me to think."

"Which, no doubt, explained why you were number one in your class in academics," Colonel Cumbie said.

Again, Lee was silent because he had no idea how to respond to such praise.

Colonel Cumbie pointed to the papers on Lee's desk. "I see you are filling out your assignment preference sheets."

"Yes, sir, I am."

"What are you requesting?"

"I want to go where I can do the most good," Lee replied. "Wherever our men are being sent into harm's way."

"What if they are mutually exclusive?"

"I beg your pardon?"

"What if where you can do the most good is not necessarily where our men are in harm's way?"

"I don't understand, sir," Lee said.

"Lee, chaplains have the unique opportunity to connect soldiers and family members to God on a daily basis. As spiritual leaders, chaplains help young men become effective soldiers in body, mind, and spirit. Do you believe that?"

"Yes, sir."

"Do you also believe that, with the rapidly expanding army, there is a tremendous need for more chaplains?"

"Yes, sir, I do."

"Good. Then I'm sure you will understand why I have asked the War Department to assign you to me, to help in training new chaplains."

"Colonel Cumbie . . . ," Lee started to say, but the senior chaplain held up his hand to still Lee's protest.

"I understand your desire to go into the field," he said. "But consider this. The very mission of the Chaplain Corps, the mission you just subscribed to, can be multiplied many times by increasing the number of chaplains in service. And you are uniquely qualified to serve in that capacity."

"Colonel, I—"

"I will make a deal with you, Lee. I don't have to make deals. You know I can have orders cut that will keep you here whether you want to stay or not, but I will make this deal with you. If you will stay through the first few cycles, say, about six months, I will let you go. Your country needs you, Lee. By doing this, you will bring God closer to the soldier, and the soldier closer to God."

"Of course, if you are going to put it like that, I will stay," Lee agreed.

5

Camp Shelby, Mississippi
March 23, 1942

A powerful mine exploded just in front and slightly to the left of Dewey, causing his ears to ring and flashing its heat against his face. Mud, water, tiny shards of gravel, and burning bits of guncotton rained down on him as smoke from the blast drifted off through the gray rain-washed air. Just inches above the advancing platoon, machine-gun bullets cracked loudly in their deadly transit.

Dewey looked at the others around him. Like him, they were wriggling on their bellies through explosive charges, maneuvering across a machine-gun-raked muddy field, sliding under concertina wire, rolling over logs, and trying to maintain their weapons in firing condition while keeping themselves below the kill zone. When he looked toward the far side of the field, he could see the four machine guns. Terrifyingly, he also could see the winking glow of tracer rounds flashing just overhead.

"Only twenty more yards," Dewey gasped, measuring the distance between himself and the objective. "Please, God, only twenty more yards! Help me get through this!"

The image of twenty yards on a football field flashed through his mind, and he compared running through tacklers to machine-gun fire and explosions. "And I thought it tough to gain twenty yards against SIU," he said through clenched teeth.

He flinched at yet another explosion. The concussion of this one was great enough to knock his helmet off. Frightened, he scooped it up and replaced it, barely cognizant of the liquid mud that ran down over his ears, matting his hair and oozing under his shirt. He took a deep breath, made several more desperate snakelike lunges forward, then clambered over the last berm.

Checking the machine guns, Dewey saw that his last rush forward had carried him far enough beyond them to take him out of their field of fire. Instead, the bullets were whipping across those unfortunate souls behind him who were still mired in the slime and mud of the open field. Wearily he stood up, and holding his rifle at high port, he ran as fast as he could toward the point where they were to rendezvous.

Reaching his goal, he belly-flopped onto the wet grass, where he lay gasping for air, painfully aware of every heartbeat as it drummed inside his chest. Behind him, the machine guns maintained their hammering fire while out in the field, the explosions continued.

Dewey had been the first one through, and after getting his breath, he sat up to watch the others negotiate the infiltration course. One by one, other men joined him until finally the field was clear.

"Cease fire! Cease fire!" a voice shouted over the loudspeaker.

Abruptly the guns stilled.

For a long, breathless moment, there was dead quiet . . . an unearthly quiet when contrasted to the din of just a few seconds earlier. In the distance Dewey could hear a train, its peaceful, commercial sound incongruous with his surroundings.

"Congratulations, men! You have just successfully completed the infiltration course. Everybody in the trucks. We ride back to the company area," the instructor said.

Cheers erupted. Dewey stood up and saw a dozen other mud-caked apparitions rise from the earth to congratulate one another while wide, happy smiles spread across mud-spattered faces.

Most of the men were so exhausted that when they returned to the barracks, they took off their muddy uniforms and lay on the floor alongside their bunks. José Montoya, who had the top bunk just over Dewey, was one who did that, and he lay on the floor, using his helmet liner as a pillow.

Dewey went to his locker, got out a change of clothes, towel, and soap, then started toward the shower.

"Man, how do you even have the strength to move?" José asked.

"Don't you know? We're jocks," Travis Logan said. "Wind sprints, right, Dewey?"

Dewey smiled, then gave Travis a thumbs-up. "Right," he said.

"Yeah, well, you're lying down too. Why don't you have as much energy?" José asked.

"Oh, I was just a high school jock," Travis said. "Dewey was a college jock."

"Pienso que usted está lanzando toro a este niño Mejican," José said.

"Come on, José, you know I don't speak no Mex," Travis said.

José laughed. "It is Spanish, not Mexican. And I think you don't speak no English that well, either."

"What did you say in Mexican, uh, I mean in Spanish?"

"He said he thinks you are throwing a little bull at the Mexican boy," Dewey said.

"You speak Spanish, Dewey?" José asked. "I didn't know that."

"I had two years of Spanish in high school," Dewey said. "But I wouldn't say that I speak it."

As Dewey headed for the shower, he heard Travis call out to the others in the barracks. "Hey! Does anyone know what we're having for supper tonight?"

"Yeah, I know. Alphabet was by the mess hall a while ago," Roberto Sangremano answered. "He says we're having pork chops."

"Pork chops? That's good," Travis said.

"Ha, like you wouldn't eat anything," José challenged.

"Liver," Travis said. "I won't eat liver."

"What about last week?" Roberto asked. "We had liver last week, and you scarfed it down pretty well."

"Well, yeah, okay, I'll eat liver. But I don't enjoy it," Travis said.

Only a couple of other men were in the shower, which was good, because it meant Dewey wouldn't have to wait for an empty showerhead. He turned the water onto full and stood under it for a moment, letting the stinging little sprays of water begin to soothe his aching body.

Dewey was used to football practice and thought he knew what it was to work out and have a sore, aching body. But nothing in football had prepared him for basic training. He felt as if he were building up hurts that would take a year to go away.

A few minutes later, showered and changed, Dewey left the barracks and walked down to the orderly room. Stopping by the bulletin board, he checked the duty rosters and groaned when he saw that he had KP the next Wednesday and guard duty next Saturday.

Just down from the bulletin board, at the back end of the orderly room building, the top half of a Dutch door opened, and the mail clerk appeared.

"Mail call! Mail call!" the mail clerk shouted. The entire company spilled out of the barracks then, gathering around the mail room as the young, bespectacled corporal stood just inside, calling out names and passing the letter through the open window.

"Haverkost, J."

"Here."

"Tinker, R."

"Here."

"Cooper, P."

"Here."

"Montoya, J."

"Here."

"Sangremano, R."

"Here."

Dewey stood with the others, waiting for his name to be called. His parents had been very good about writing him.

Dewey's mother, Julia, filled the pages with her small, neat script, giving him all the news of the family. His cousin Charley had joined the navy. Aunt Amanda had gone to work in the shoe factory. Uncle Clyde bought a new Oldsmobile, saying that there was no telling when they would start making cars again, so he needed a good one to get him through.

Green Bradley, Dewey's father, was editor of the *Pilot Town Sentinel* in Pilot Town, Tennessee. Although it was only a weekly, Green's editorials were often picked up by newspapers across the state. Green's letters to Dewey, written in broad strokes, were almost like his editorials. To some, Green's letters might be impersonal, but they weren't to Dewey. Julia often chastised Green, saying that he was incapable of social discourse. As long as Dewey could remember, his father's conversations were but verbal editorials. He had opinions about everything and shared them with anyone who would listen.

Green's last letter to Dewey had railed against a proposal for a general sales tax for the duration of the war.

There is a great movement throughout the land for a national sales tax to be added to the income tax and the state and local taxes we already pay. And yet, the same Congress pushing this idea recently provided themselves with a generous increase in salary and an even more generous retirement pension. The incontrovertible fact of the matter is that sales tax is not an equitable tax. It hits hardest those who can least afford to pay.

Since coming into the army, Dewey had also received mail from Coach Sapp, from one of his theology professors, and from his teammate, Don Mitchell. But in the six weeks he had been at Camp Shelby, he had not received one letter from Unity.

Dewey had written Unity three letters since he arrived, and he vowed that the third letter he sent her would be the last if she did not reply.

I will make one final effort to explain to you why I did what I did. I'm not comparing myself to the apostles of Jesus, but what made those men of biblical times turn their backs on their lives, put down everything, and follow the Lord? It was a calling that they could not deny.

That is what I had, Unity, a calling that I could not deny. I know it is hard for you to understand, but I feel that God has led me here. And I cannot turn my back on that.

I love you, Unity, and I know that I always will love you, no matter what happens. But I will not ask you to wait for me until this war is over because nobody knows when it will end. I do pray, however, that you will understand this commitment I have, and that you will find a place in some small, secret chamber of your heart to hold and to remember the love that was ours.

If you choose not to answer this letter, I will know that you wish to put this part of your life behind you. I will respect that and honor your wishes. I wish nothing but the best for you.

The mail clerk continued to call out the names, each shouted name happily responded to as the soldier stepped up to get his mail. "Sta. . . Stac. . . uh. . . S-T-A–K–O–W–I–A–C!" he said, spelling out the name.

"Hey, Alphabet, that one's for you," one of the soldiers called, and the others laughed.

"It's pronounced Sta-ko-viack," a soldier said with the tired resignation of someone who has had to pronounce his name for a lifetime. He reached up as the letter was handed to him.

"Weintraub, A. Weintraub, A. Weintraub, A. Weintraub, A."

"Here."

"Hey, Aaron, are all those letters from Hollywood stars?" Roberto Sangremano asked.

"They are starlets, not stars," Aaron Weintraub responded good-naturedly. "They aren't stars until my father makes them stars."

Aaron Weintraub's father was Eli Weintraub, a film director who had won an Oscar for his picture *The Other Side of Memory*.

"Man, wouldn't you like to have an ol' man like that? Every beautiful girl in the country would be coming on to you, trying to get you to get your papa to make her a movie star," Travis Logan asked.

"Hey, Aaron, is that really the way it works out there in Hollywood?" José Montoya asked.

"That's the way it works," Aaron said.

"Bradley, D," the mail clerk called. "Bradley, D. Bradley, D."

"Whoa, Dewey, you got three letters," José said.

"Yeah, and he's not even from Hollywood," Travis added.

"Dear sir. About that bill you owe us," Roberto teased, and several laughed.

Dewey waited as the letters were passed back to him.

"Hey, wait a minute, guys!" Roberto said. He held one of Dewey's letters under his nose. "This is no bill unless bill collectors have started putting perfume on their envelopes."

"Here, let me smell that," Aaron said. Taking the letter, he held it under his nose and sniffed. "Ahh, yes, this is a clear, sensuous, wooded perfume that is full and voluptuous with overtones of organic musks and Chinese osmanthus along with intense and suggestive scents of vanilla, orchid, and cinnamon, combined with oriental sandalwood to form a mellow, lasting fragrance. Yes, I would say that the young lady who mailed this letter is quite serious."

"Ooh, la, la!" Haverkost said.

"Dear Dewey, I love you so much!" Cooper said.

Dewey wasn't being singled out. Mail call was generally a happy event, and the good-natured teasing among the men was part of it.

He felt a sudden surge of excitement. Was there really perfume on the letter? His mother certainly didn't put perfume on her letters. Could it be a letter from Unity?

He reached forward eagerly as the little white envelopes made their way, hand over hand, until they reached him. One was from his mother, one was from Reverend Owens, and . . . yes! One of the envelopes was perfumed, and it was from Unity!

Dewey took the three letters back to the barracks with him, then lay on his bunk to read them.

Outside, he could hear the bugle playing mess call.

"Soupy, soupy, soupy, soup without any beans, soupy, soupy, soupy, we don't know what meat means!" Travis Logan was singing along with the bugle call as he came walking back from the shower. He stopped at the foot of Dewey's bunk.

"Hey, Dewey, you goin' to chow?" he asked. Though he had on trousers, he was shirtless. His hair was still wet, and a towel was draped around his neck.

Dewey chuckled. "You look a little better now than you did the last time I saw you."

"Yeah, I feel better too. José said we're having pork chops. You coming?"

"I'll be there. I want to read my mail first."

"Did you . . . ," Travis started.

"Yeah, I did," Dewey answered with a big smile. He had shared with Travis his frustration over not getting any mail from Unity.

"All right!" Travis said. "Uh . . . you don't think it's a Dear John, do you?"

The smile left Dewey's face. "What? I don't know," he said. He held up the letter and looked at it. "I really don't know."

"Let me see the letter," Travis said. "I don't need to read it. I can tell just by holding it."

Dewey chuckled. "You're full of it." He handed the letter to Travis.

"Whoa, this letter is perfumed," he said.

"Yes."

Travis handed it back. "I don't even have to hold it. My boy, you don't have to worry about a thing. Never in the history of the United States Army, and that's going all the way back to when Robert E. Lee fought against the Spartans with Caesar's legions, has there been a Dear John letter with perfume."

"I hope you're right."

"I know I'm right," Travis said. "Now, come on, read it, and let's go to supper."

"Give me a minute," Dewey said. "I'll be along."

"Okay, I'll hold you a seat."

Travis and everyone else in the barracks left for supper, leaving Dewey alone in the barracks.

The barracks, Dewey's temporary home, was a long, narrow, two-story, cream-colored building. He was on the bottom floor. In the two-tiered bunk, Dewey had the bottom; José Montoya, the top. The bunks were made up head to foot, meaning that Dewey slept with his head to the wall, but the men in the bunks on either side of him slept with their heads to the center aisle.

The center aisle separated the bunks on the left side of the bar-racks, which was Dewey's side, from the bunks on the right. A series of support poles ran down each side of the aisle, marking its perime-ters, and hanging from each pole was a number-ten can that had been painted red. On each can, printed in the interrupted yellow letters that were the result of using a stencil, were the words, PUT BUTTS HERE. The cans were half-filled with water as a precaution against smoldering cigarette butts.

Floating dust motes glowed as bars of late afternoon sunlight stabbed in through the windows. Dewey lay on the rough texture of the olive-drab blanket and held the letter for a long moment, somewhat hesitant about opening it. Slowly, Dewey opened the envelope and pulled out the letter.

Dear Dewey,

Please forgive me for not replying before now, but I've had a lot of thinking and praying to do, and I've come to the conclusion that I have been selfish and immature.

If you felt the call to do something about the war, then of course you must answer that call. I respect and admire you for that. It was wrong of me to question you, and very wrong of me to add any anguish to what you are already having to go through. I beg that you forgive me for being so childish.

You said in your last letter that you wanted me to reserve a small chamber of my heart so that I might hold on to the love that was ours. I can't do that because a small chamber isn't large enough. My love for you fills my entire heart. Please tell me that it is not too late for us.

With all my love,
Unity

"Yahoo!" Dewey shouted at the top of his voice.

Travis was standing in the chow line when he heard the yell, and he turned to José, who was right behind him. "What do you think, José?" he asked. "It sounds like Dewey's back on track with his girl."

6

Canby Hall,
Litchfield College
March 27, 1942

Unity was sitting at the desk in her room, studying for an exam. At least, she was trying to study. The mail wasn't supposed to be up until noon, but most of the time they had it up by eleven-thirty. Since this was a free hour, Unity had taken a chance that it would be there. She had already gone downstairs twice to see if the mail had been put up yet, but it had not.

"Haven't you ever heard the expression that a watched pot never boils?" Carol, her roommate, asked.

"Yes."

"Well, a watched mail slot never has mail," Carol said.

"Oh, don't tell me that, Carol. I will die, just die, if I don't hear from him. Oh, I was so foolish to treat him the way I did."

"Don't worry. He still loves you," Carol said.

"How do you know?"

"Are you kidding? From the time he met you, he never even saw another girl."

"I hope you're right."

"I'm going to get a Coke. Do you want one?"

"No, thanks," Unity said. "I really do need to study."

It was unseasonably warm, and through the dorm window, Unity could see the students walking around on campus in shirtsleeves. The redbud and dogwood trees were ablaze with their red, pink, and white blooms, and they and the yellow forsythia made the quadrangle particularly beautiful. She found the view much more interesting than the book she was supposed to be studying: *Curriculum Development for Elementary Grades.*

"Unity?"

Unity turned toward the door of her room. Carol was standing there with a big smile on her face.

"What is it?"

"Forget what I said about a watched mailbox never having mail." She held up a white envelope. "It's from Dewey," she said.

"Oh!" Unity screamed, jumping up from her chair and crossing the room quickly to grab the letter.

"What does he say? What does he say?"

"Wait a minute. I don't even have it open yet."

Unity took the letter out and began reading it. Almost instantly her eyes welled with tears.

"Oh no," Carol said quietly. "Unity, I'm so sorry. I wouldn't have—"

"No, no!" Unity said, shaking her head and smiling broadly. She wiped her eyes. "These are tears of joy, Carol. He still wants to marry me."

Camp Shelby, Mississippi
March 30, 1942

Those men who were scheduled for KP, or kitchen police, were told to see the charge of quarters (CQ) before turning in the night before and tell him where they could be found. That way the CQ runner would be able to find them when he came through the barracks in the predawn darkness.

"I'm barracks number twelve, bottom floor, fifth bunk on the left, bottom bunk," Dewey told the CQ.

The CQ, who was a corporal, put the information in his duty log. "Tie a white towel on the end of your bunk closest to the center aisle so my runner can find you in the morning," the corporal ordered.

"I will."

That night Dewey sat on his footlocker shining his boots. On one of the bunks across the aisle, a penny ante game was in progress, and the men who were playing laughed or groaned according to how the cards were falling.

"Yes! Yes! There's my second king! Two cents!" one of the men said.

"I'll see your two cents and raise you two cents," another said.

"You're bluffing."

"Call or raise."

"All right, I call. That's four cents to you, Haverkost."

"Too rich for my blood. I'm out," Haverkost said.

Travis, who was sitting on his own footlocker, was shining his boots as well. The top lid of the shoe polish was filled with water, and Travis had a sock over his hand. Dipping the sock into the water, then into the polish, he used his fingers to make tiny, shining swirls on the toe of his boot.

"You got a car, Dewey?" Travis asked. He held his boot out and looked at it. It glistened a golden brown.

"Yes."

"What kind have you got?"

"It's a '37 Chevrolet. Yellow, with four doors."

"Oh, then it's not a V-8?"

"No."

"What you ought to do is get yourself one of those Ford V-8s. Those things will really run."

"My Chevy is fast enough."

"Yeah? How fast is it?"

"As fast as the speed limit," Dewey replied.

"Oh, man, you are so straight. I'll bet you never speed, do you?"

"Seldom, if ever," Dewey agreed.

"If I had a car, you wouldn't even see my smoke. I'd be up and down that highway so fast . . . vroom!" he said, imitating a fast-moving car.

"You don't have a car?"

"No, not yet," Travis said. "Heck, my pa doesn't even have a car. He has a pickup truck, though. He said a farmer needs a truck more than he needs a car."

Travis's father was a sharecropper on a cotton farm just outside Blytheville, Arkansas. One of the reasons Dewey and Travis had become friends was that they were from the same part of the country. Blytheville, Arkansas, wasn't that far from Dewey's hometown of Pilot Town, Tennessee. In fact, the Pilot Town Rivermen played football against the Blytheville Chicks. Though he had not gone on to college, Travis had played high-school football for the Chicks, and he could remember playing against Dewey and Pilot Town.

"In fact, I put you on your rear end," Travis told Dewey shortly after they made the connection. "I remember it because we were all told what a hotshot player you were, so I got a big kick out of tackling you."

Dewey chuckled. "Well, you weren't the only one," he said. "Believe me, over my years of playing football, a whole lot of people put me on my rear end."

"You were good, though," Travis admitted. "I'd say you were far and away the best I ever played against."

"Well, thank you, Travis, I appreciate the compliment."

Dewey held his boots out and looked at them. Satisfied with the shine, he put them under his bunk. They were issued two pairs of boots and were supposed to alternate them from day to day, with one pair left on display, alongside their shined shoes, on the floor just under the bunk.

The pair Dewey had just shined were the boots that would stay under his bunk tomorrow. He didn't even bother to shine the others. There was no sense in wearing shined boots for KP.

"Want to go over to the PX for a while?" Travis asked.

"No, thanks," Dewey replied. "I've got KP tomorrow. I'd better get to bed early."

"Oh, yeah, I forgot. Well, no hard feelings, but I'm glad it's you and not me. I hate KP. I mean, I really hate it," Travis said. He stood up, stretched, then reached for his hat. "I tell you what. I'll drink a beer for you," he offered.

"I don't like beer," Dewey said.

"Well, then you won't mind if I drink yours?"

"Not at all," Dewey said.

"I wonder where José is. Hey, any of you guys seen José?"

"I think he's down to the dayroom shootin' pool," one of the card players said.

"Shootin' pool? That's not good. Next thing you know, he'll be hangin' around pool halls. I better go get him," Travis said.

After Travis left, Dewey tied a white towel to the foot of his bunk. Then stripping down to his underwear, he crawled into bed. It was an example of how much his lifestyle had changed that, even with all the barracks lights burning brightly, the noise of the poker game across the aisle, and the sound of a couple of guys singing at the far end of the barracks, Dewey was able to go to sleep without difficulty.

"Bradley?" a voice said. Dewey felt a hand on his shoulder. "Are you Private Bradley, D?"

Dewey was in the midst of the best and most restful sleep, the sleep that grows deepest in the last hour before dawn.

Slowly Dewey came out of his slumber. He lay there for a moment, reconnecting with the world he had abandoned the night before. Opening his eyes, he saw the CQ runner's flashlight shining in his face, and he covered his eyes against its painful glare.

"Are you Private Bradley?" the runner asked again.

"Yes," Bradley replied. "Could you shine your light away, please?"

"Yeah, sure," the CQ runner said easily. "You got KP."

"Yes, I know. Thanks."

The CQ runner left, and Dewey sat up, afraid to stay in bed any longer for fear he would go to sleep again. He could hear the heavy breathing and light snoring of the other soldiers in the room. Looking across at Travis's bunk, he saw that he had the pillow scrunched up under his head. He looked very comfortable, and Dewey wished with all that was in him that he could just crawl back into his own bunk and go back to sleep.

Steeling himself, he stood up and made his bunk in the dark, knowing that Travis would square it away for him when he got up later on. Dewey dressed and walked across the company quadrangle toward the still-dark mess hall. The dew on the grass dampened his boots, and from the distance he could hear the lonesome call of a whippoorwill. In the vaulting night sky above, the stars were shining as brightly as diamonds on velvet. Though it would get hot during the day, there was a slight chill in the air at this predawn hour, and he shivered against the cool.

Ahead, on the side stoop of the mess hall, he could see the orange-red gleam of the end of a cigarette. It glowed a little brighter as the smoker took a puff. When Dewey got closer, he could see the smoker, who was one of the other KPs, sitting on the stoop. Dewey felt a little disappointed. If he had been first to arrive, he would have been able to sign up for dining room orderly. DROs bused the NCO tables, kept the milk machines full, and the dining room floors mopped. It was the easiest job on KP, and because the KPs got to choose their jobs in the order of their arrival, the first ones there always chose DRO.

The lucky soldier this morning was Ron Stakowiac.

"Good morning, Alphabet," Dewey said. The name wasn't pejorative. In fact, Stakowiac even took some pride in being called that. "I'm addressing the DRO, I presume?"

"Ha," Alphabet said. "Some may look at me and think they are seeing a DRO. But they would be making a big mistake. What they are actually seeing is the mâitre d' of Chez Mess Hall."

"Of course you are. And I'm not some KP pulling front sink duty. I am the sous-chef," Dewey said. "Good to meet you, Monsieur Mâitre D'."

"And it is good to meet you, Monsieur Sous-Chef," Alphabet said, continuing the banter.

They saw the dark forms of two more men moving through the shadows. "Who is that? Can you tell?" Alphabet asked.

Dewey stared into the dark. "Looks like Aaron Weintraub and Roberto Sangremano," he said.

A few seconds later, Aaron and Roberto arrived.

"Cook hasn't opened the door yet?" Aaron asked.

"Not yet."

"Hey, Alphabet, you got a smoke?" Roberto asked.

"Let me ask you somethin', Roberto," Alphabet replied. "Have you ever bought a cigarette in your life?"

"Yeah, sure I have. And I got some in my footlocker right now," Roberto answered. "I just forgot to bring 'em, is all. I'll pay you back."

"If you pay back all the cigarettes you've bummed in the last few weeks, you'll need a trailer truck just to haul them in here," Alphabet said, but he tapped the bottom of his pack of Camels, making four cigarettes slide up, with one a bit higher than the others. Roberto took the proffered cigarette, put it in his mouth, then leaned forward to light it from the glowing end of Alphabet's smoke.

"Hey, Aaron, what do you hear from Hollywood?" Alphabet asked. "Is your dad going to put me in the movies?"

"You know, Alphabet, I had everything all set for you," Aaron said. "But when it came time to put your name in the credits, they ran out of letters, so Dad had no choice but to call the whole thing off."

The others laughed.

"Ain't that just my luck, though?" Alphabet replied good-naturedly.

Roberto had just managed to finish his smoke when the two cooks arrived. The head cook unlocked the door, and they all went inside. It was dark in the mess hall, but the cook turned on the lights in the kitchen, illuminating the stove, sinks, work tables, coffee makers, and large refrigerator that had sat dormant through the night. The KPs signed up for their jobs, Alphabet taking DRO, and Dewey taking front sink.

The first thing Dewey had to do to get ready for the day's work was to carve up a few bars of lye soap. He did that, then dropped them in a number ten can, into which several holes had been poked. Using a wire bail, he then hooked the can onto the faucet so that it would be ready when needed.

"KPs, come have your breakfast," one of the cooks called, and the four privates stopped what they were doing and lined up at the serving window.

The cook had broken eggs onto one end of the large griddle, and they lay there in four pairs, eight of them, white with bright yellow centers. Bacon sizzled at the other end. Skillfully, the cook flipped the eggs over, then served them as the men held out their trays.

Dewey got a couple of pieces of toast from the toaster, then stopped in front of the steaming and aromatic Silex machine. The glass tube was filled with a rich brown liquid, indicating that the coffee was brewed. Dewey drew a cup, then poured in a stream of milk from the canned milk. Taking his tray and coffee over to the first table, he joined the other KPs in eating breakfast. At that moment it was warm, quiet, and almost pleasant as the four young men were gathered in this place and at this time.

"Any of you guys ever think about fifty or sixty years from now?" Aaron asked.

"What? What do you mean?" Roberto asked.

"Well, think about it. Here we are, soldiers in the greatest war in history. Fifty or sixty years from now we'll be telling our grandchildren about this."

"Ha," Alphabet said. "You mean sixty years from now I'm going to say," he made his voice creak, imitating an old man, "Grandkids, you know what I did in the great war? I pulled KP at Camp Shelby, Mississippi."

The others laughed.

"Yes, well, I wasn't thinking that exactly," Aaron said. "But, really, when you think about it, this is part of it too. I mean, someday, we will all look back on this very moment at how the four of us, gathered from all parts of the country, were sitting around this table in an empty mess hall, having breakfast before the rest of the troops arrived. And we'll think, *You know? It wasn't all bad.*"

"That is, if none of us gets killed in the war," Alphabet added.

"Gee, nice thought, Alphabet," Roberto said sarcastically.

"Yeah, well, you do know that it is a possibility, don't you?" Alphabet replied. "I mean, all we're doing here is playing games. The real business of war starts when we get overseas."

"Hey, Aaron, what are you doing here, anyway? Your ol' man is rich and famous. Couldn't he have gotten you some cushy job somewhere?" Roberto asked.

"Perhaps," Aaron said. "But in case you haven't read any of the reports coming out of Germany, the Nazis seem to have taken a special dislike for Jews. So, I'm taking this war personally."

From the megaphone in the quadrangle, they heard the bugle playing reveille.

"Listen to that," Alphabet said. "Most of the time that song wakes me up. Hard to think we've already been awake for an hour."

"All right, KPs, let's move! The thundering herd will be here soon," the head cook shouted. He and the second cook had eaten breakfast at a different table, their rank and privileges separating them from eating with mere KPs.

Aaron joined Dewey at the front sink, and Roberto had pots and pans. Reacting to the head cook's call, they all went to their stations. Dewey started hot water running through the hanging can, and he stood there watching the sink fill as steam rolled up from the building suds. Alphabet passed the trays that the cooks and KPs had used for their breakfast through the window, and Aaron began scraping them off.

Two garbage cans sat in the scuttle area, one for paper, cans, bottles, egg shells, coffee grounds, and so forth. The other can, for uneaten food, was marked EDIBLE GARBAGE.

From the quadrangle, they could hear the sounds of reveille formation.

"Report!" the first sergeant called.

"First platoon, all present and accounted for, sir!"

"Second platoon, all present and accounted for, sir!"

"Third platoon, all present and accounted for, sir!"

"Fall out!"

With the first sergeant's command to fall out, a mighty roar issued from the throats of all the soldiers as they ran toward the mess hall.

Alphabet opened the side door, just long enough to allow the CQ to come in, then he closed it again. The CQ was also the head counter, and he sat at a table just inside the door with a tablet and pencil.

"Okay!" the first cook said. "Let 'em in!"

Once more, Alphabet opened the door, and the men came pouring in. The CQ started his head count, using the method of making four lines, then tying them together with a diagonal.

Just awakened and not yet tired by the day's exercises, the men were full of energy, and they teased one another and laughed and talked about what lay ahead of them. As the number of diners swelled, the kitchen became more and more hectic. What had started as a warm, quiet, and pleasant morning became the hot, loud, and frantic beginning of another day of basic training.

Both Travis Logan and José Montoya stopped by the sink window on their way to their tables to say hello to Dewey and Aaron.

"You guys are looking awful good in there," Travis said, smiling through the window.

Dewey took a handful of soapsuds and tossed them through the window. Travis and José jumped back, but not before being decorated with the suds. Laughing, they moved through the dining room until they found a couple of seats together.

The duty became more chaotic as the morning wore on.

"KPs, keep up with us!" the first cook shouted. "DRO, there's milk spilled in the dining room. Take care of it. Front sink, we need trays! More trays!"

There was a loud noise as a stack of trays fell to the floor.

"Scuttle, get it cleaned up!" the second cook shouted.

"Pots and Pans, get a move on it!" the first cook called.

Aaron got down on his hands and knees to pick up the trays that had fallen.

"Silverware! We need silverware!" the cook shouted. "Pots. I need a clean pot! Pots and Pans man, what are you doin'? You takin' a break back there?"

"Mi piacerebbe rompa il suo collo," Roberto mumbled.

"What's that? What did you say?" the first cook asked.

"I said, how many hands you think I've got, anyway?"

"Better watch your mouth there, KP," the first cook said. "I'll have you on KP for the rest of this training cycle."

"Roberto better watch it," Aaron said to Alphabet as Alphabet brought up some of the NCO trays. "If he gets the cooks mad enough, they really will keep him on KP."

"Yeah, especially if they knew what he really said," Alphabet said.

"You speak Italian?" Aaron asked.

"Yeah. My name is Polish, but my mother is Italian," Alphabet said.

"Well, what did he say?"

"He said he would like to break the cook's neck."

"DRO, what are you standing around gabbing for?" one of the cooks shouted. "Get back out there and get the NCO tables bused!"

"You know," Alphabet said. "Now that I think about it, Roberto had a pretty good idea."

Aaron smiled, then went back to scraping off trays and dropping them in the soaking tub.

For the next several minutes all the KPs worked hard, then suddenly and inexplicably Aaron laughed.

"What is it?" Dewey asked, his arms up to his elbows in hot, soapy water. "What are you laughing about?"

"Six weeks ago Judy Garland was my date for a studio dance." Aaron pointed to one of the garbage cans. "Today I'm scraping uneaten eggs into a garbage can marked 'Edible Garbage.'"

Dewey laughed with him.

7

Camp Rucker, Alabama
April 29, 1942

When reveille blew, Company A of the First Infantry Battalion, Basic Training Brigade, was already awake. Too excited to sleep, the men welcomed the final day of their basic training cycle. From here, all of the companies would be detached from the First Infantry Battalion of the Training Brigade, each company going to a different location.

Dewey's company, Company A, was assigned to Camp Rucker, Alabama, for advanced training to prepare for duty overseas. But before that training, everyone in the company was being given a two-week leave and delay en route. That would give them their first chance to visit home since being in the army.

Blankets and sheets were turned in to the supply room, and the mattresses were stockaded, meaning they were folded into an S shape and put at the head of the bunks, thus exposing the bare springs. Footlockers and wall lockers were emptied. There would be no inspection of the barracks before the men left, but as each would be drawing travel pay, as well as an advance on pay due, he would undergo one final personal inspection when he presented himself to the pay officer.

Pay call was not until 1000 hours, but almost to a man, everyone was ready by 0800. For the first time since they had been in the camp, the men found themselves with two leisure hours, a time when no sergeants were shouting orders at them.

After chow the men sat around on their bunks and footlockers in the barracks, reliving the experiences they had just shared, and talking about their upcoming leave.

"Hey, guys, listen to this letter that the first sergeant has sent to all our folks," Aaron said.

"What?" Roberto said. "What right does the first sergeant have to send a letter to our folks?"

"Just listen to it, Roberto," Aaron said. Everyone gathered around to hear what Aaron had to say.

Aaron cleared his throat, then began to read: "To the parents of the men of Able Company, please do not be alarmed if, at 0530, your son suddenly leaps out of bed shouting, 'Reveille, everyone up!'"

There were a few confused chuckles.

"If he grabs an empty coffee can, paints it red, stencils 'Put Cigarette Butts Here,' then nails it to your wall, have patience with him."

By then, everyone realized that Aaron was teasing, and they laughed aloud. More gathered around to listen to him "read" the first sergeant's letter from a blank piece of paper.

"Immediately after breakfast, do not be alarmed if he asks where he is supposed to put his edible garbage."

"Yeah, like my mom is going to know what edible garbage is," Travis said. They all laughed.

"Hey, you've never eaten my mom's cooking," Tinker said. "It *is* edible garbage."

The laughter was louder.

Aaron continued to read: "Take him outside for something called police call. Yell at him loudly as he walks across the yard, bent over at the waist, picking up items that are too small for you to see."

"Make him fieldstrip a cigarette!" Alphabet added.

Travis got into the act. "If he digs a foxhole in the front yard, then stays out there during the rain, think nothing of it. Simply take him a plate of pork and beans and a canteen cup of very strong, black, three-day-old coffee, and yell at him."

Several more bits of advice for parents were added until the letter was interrupted by the bugle announcing payday.

With a shout of joy, the men rushed out of the barracks, then lined up alphabetically in front of the pay table set up on the quadrangle.

"Hey, Weintraub," Roberto yelled. "It's too bad your name isn't backward. If you were Wientraub Aaron, instead of Aaron Weintraub, you would be number one in line."

"Well, hey, the army changed my name to Weintraub, Aaron," Aaron replied. "I mean, that's the way it is on every piece of paper they've given me. Thank you for calling that to my attention. I think I will go to the front of the line." Aaron started toward the front of the line, but everyone started yelling at him, and with a smile, he returned to the end.

Dewey was at the very beginning of the line, the first of his friends to get paid. After signing the payroll book, Dewey reported to the orderly room, where he picked up his leave and reassignment orders.

With orders in hand, he went over to the sign-out book. For destination, he put Pilot Town, Tennessee. For date of return, he put PCS, meaning permanent change of station. He would not be returning to Camp Shelby, Mississippi.

Duly signed out, he went back to the quadrangle to say good-bye to his friends, who were still standing in line. When he climbed onto the silver-and-blue Greyhound bus, it was the first nonmilitary vehicle he had been on for more than two months. He had never seen anything that looked so beautiful.

Sikeston, Missouri
April 30, 1942

"Soldier? Soldier?"

Dewey woke up with someone gently shaking his shoulder. Opening his eyes, he looked around the Greyhound bus. A middle-aged man was standing in the aisle just beside his seat.

"I believe you said you were going to get off the bus in Sikeston, Missouri?" the man asked.

"Yes," Dewey said. He realized then that the bus was stopped, though he could feel the engine still running through the floor. There was a banging sound from below the bus as the driver opened the luggage compartment. "Thank you," Dewey said. Standing up, he adjusted his tie, sticking it in between the second and third buttons of his khaki shirt. He put on the service cap, the one with the piping of robin's egg blue, then moved toward the front door.

Stepping down, Dewey blinked a couple of times against the bright sun, then he looked toward the pile of luggage, where he saw his canvas duffel bag. He had just started toward it when he heard someone calling out to him.

"Dewey! Dewey!"

Turning, he saw Unity running toward him with her arms open. He met her in the middle and pulled her to him, kissing her.

"Oh, what must people think of us?" Unity said a moment later when the kiss ended.

"Honey, people don't think nothin' of it at all," a plump, pleasant-looking black woman said. "Why, I 'spec' they's soldiers and their wives and sweethearts sayin' their hellos and good-byes all over this country."

"The lady is right," Dewey said, pulling her to him for another kiss.

José Montoya had nearly forgotten how hot it could be in Phoenix. Toward the end of their training cycle, it had started to get hot in Camp Shelby, but the heat there was nothing like it was here.

"But I'm not complaining, Lord," José said, smiling. "No, Sir, I'm back home. You aren't going to hear me complain one little bit."

Picking up his duffel bag, José braced himself to walk from the shade of the car shed out into the bright Arizona sun.

An older Mexican woman was operating a taco stand right across the street from the railroad station. She didn't have any teeth, and she kept her mouth closed tightly so that her chin and nose nearly touched. A swarm of flies buzzed around the steaming kettles, drawn by the pungent aromas of meat and sauces.

José smiled. He hadn't realized how much he had missed tacos. Once, he tried to explain to the others in the company just what a taco was, but they didn't understand him.

José walked up to the woman and smiled at her. "Señora, tendré un taco, por favor," he said.

Working with quick, deft fingers, she rolled the spicy ingredients into a tortilla, then wrapped it in old newspaper and handed it to him.

"Gracias," José said, giving her a nickel.

Eating the taco with his left hand, and carrying his duffel bag on his right shoulder, José walked down the street, taking in the sights and sounds of Phoenix. It was undergoing a transition from a sleepy cow town of the Old West to a bustling city of the future. Trolleys whirred down the dual set of tracks in the center of the street, and cars honked impatiently. The sounds of jackhammers and other power equipment filled the streets with noise and industry.

Finishing his taco, José threw the paper into a trash can, then caught a taxi.

"Tomas and Forty-Fourth," he said as he climbed into the backseat.

"Tomas and Forty-Fourth, sí," the driver repeated, using the Spanish pronunciation. "Usted es soldado para los estadounidenses?"

"I'm not a soldier for the Americans. I am an American soldier," José answered in English.

"I did not mean anything by the question," the driver apologized.

"I know, and I'm sorry I responded in such a way," José said. "I guess I'm a little sensitive. It's just that, I'm an American citizen, native born, but everyone assumes I swam across the river."

The driver chuckled.

"Many of us did, amigo," he said.

José laughed. "Yes, my parents, in fact. They were born in Nogales, Mexico."

José looked through the window as the taxi drove down Central, a wide, pleasant road with a double line of palm trees on either side. It had been only two months since José left Phoenix, but so much had happened in that time that he found himself having to get reacquainted with old, familiar things.

"Here we are, Tomas and Forty-Fourth," the driver said after about fifteen minutes.

"Stop at the service station," José said, pointing to a station on the corner.

The driver stopped. José paid him, then stepped from the taxi.

"I will say prayers and light candles for your safety," the driver said.

"Gracias," José replied.

José stood there with his duffel bag by his side, watching as the taxi driver turned around, then drove away.

The sign out front read HANK'S AUTO REPAIR—WELDING AND CUTTING.

From the shop area on the right side of the service station, José could see the bright flashing lights and hear the snap and pop of an arc welder at work. He walked toward the shop, but put his bag down just outside the garage door to avoid getting grease on it.

In the shadowed interior he could see two men working over a car frame. The flashing arc welder cast everything in bright white and black, and projected huge, misshapen shadows on the wall. Both men had welding masks over their faces.

"You did it!" one of the men said. "I tell you the truth, Jorge, you are the best welder in the entire state of Arizona."

"Just in Arizona?" José said. "And all this time Papá has tried to tell me he was the best welder in the whole Southwest."

Because of the dark glass of the masks, neither of the two men had seen José come in. Raising their masks, both looked toward the door.

One of them, short and with dark features, smiled broadly. "José!" he exclaimed. Putting down the face mask and laying aside the welding gun, he moved quickly through the spare-part and tool-strewn garage to his son.

The two men embraced while Hank Patterson, the owner of the

service station and Jorge's longtime employer, looked on. His smile was almost as broad as that of Jorge. Jorge Montoya had worked for Hank Patterson for many years, ever since he had arrived in the United States as an illegal immigrant.

Patterson could have taken advantage of him, paying him less than fair wages on threat of turning him in as an illegal alien, but he didn't. Instead, he paid him fair wages and even helped Jorge and Juanita get their permanent resident papers. In return, Jorge became not only a very loyal employee but also the best employee Patterson ever had.

José grew up around the garage. He began working there as a small boy, sweeping the floor and picking up the tools. But at an early age, he showed an aptitude for car engines, and by the time he was in high school, he could take a carburetor apart and reassemble it.

"So, the soldier boy is home on furlough, is he?" Patterson asked.

"Hello, Mr. Patterson," José said, extending his hand.

"My boy, I'm as proud of you as your mama and papa are," Patterson said, shaking José's hand.

"Thank you, Mr. Patterson."

"We got your letter saying you would be home," Jorge said. "And all day today, your mamá has been cooking."

"She sure has. I don't know what all she is cooking," Patterson said. "But I went out back, and the smells made me so hungry I couldn't stand it."

"Empanadas, buñuelos, enchiladas, arroz a la Mexicana," Jorge said.

"Mexican rice!" José said. "I was hoping she would make arroz a la Mexicana. She makes the best in the world."

"And sopaipillas," Patterson added. "Don't forget the sopaipillas."

Jorge laughed. "Sí, sopaipillas. Señor Patterson has already had a few sopaipillas, I think."

"I have had many sopaipillas, I think," Patterson said, rubbing his stomach.

"José, since you are here, would you take a look at that Plymouth?" Jorge asked. "It has a problem with the engine that I cannot figure out."

"Jorge, the boy is on furlough from the army. The last thing he wants to do is look at a car engine," Patterson said.

José smiled. "Actually, Mr. Patterson, there have been several times over the last two months when I would have given anything in the world to be working on a car engine. Do you have a shop suit handy? I don't want to get my uniform dirty."

Patterson smiled. "Your old shop suit is hanging up right where you left it."

"Thank you. But first, I would like to see Mamá," José said.

"Yes, go see your mamá," Jorge said. "If I keep you here before you see her, I think she will hit me with a frying pan."

José and Patterson laughed.

One of the most convenient things about Jorge's working at the service station was that the Montoyas lived behind it. José grabbed his duffel bag and the shop suit, then walked out back, through the sand and cactus, to the little white two-bedroom house where he had grown up. Even before he pushed the door open, he could smell the cooking.

"Mamá!" he called, putting his duffel bag on the floor just inside the door.

"José!" his mother shouted happily, running in from the kitchen. She was a large woman, and she pulled him to her more than generous bosom, nearly smothering him with her embrace. "José, oh, my little one," she said as tears of happiness flowed down her cheeks.

José was the Montoya's only child. That fact made him an anomaly among his young Mexican peers, all of whom had multiple siblings. It was not by design that the Montoya family was so small. During José's birth, something had "gone wrong," as Elana said, without further explanation. As a result they could have no more children, so they poured all their love and concern into the one they did have.

After sampling one of his mother's sopaipillas, José took off his uniform, put on his shop coveralls, then went out to the garage to have a look at the Plymouth.

"It was the carburetor," Jorge told Elana at the dinner table that evening. He looked proudly at his son. "And José found it and fixed it in about an hour. It would have taken Señor Patterson and me one whole day to fix it."

"It wasn't that hard," José said.

"For you it wasn't hard."

"But don't forget, you and Mr. Patterson taught me everything I know," José said.

Jorge smiled. "Sí, that is right, isn't it? You are a good mechanic because I, Jorge Montoya, taught you everything you know."

"Jorge, the Lord does not like a man who brags," Elana warned.

After dinner the little Montoya family went into the living room, where José entertained them with stories of some of his adventures during basic training.

"I have written letters to all of our family in Mexico that I know, and I have told them that our José, who is a ciudadano estadounidense, is a soldier," José's mother said proudly.

"Do not say ciudadano estadounidense, Elana. Say American citizen," Jorge corrected.

"Sí," Elana said. "American citizen. And soldier," she added.

Malibu Beach, California

From *Variety:*

Eli Weintraub (two-time Oscar-winning director for *The Other Side of Memory* and *Tea on the Veranda*) has just agreed to direct the motion-picture version of Sean Hanifin's best-selling novel *Gossamer Wings.* Although not yet cast, most insiders say that Errol Flynn is close to inking for the role of Toby McCarthy, the wisecracking pilot of Hanifin's story about the huge transoceanic flying boats.

Diminutive, peach-sundae-cheeked, flaming-haired Marika Fletcher has already agreed to bring to the screen the saucy torch singer, Tammy Tormaine.

Production is being delayed until after Weintraub completes the filming of *Citizen Army,* a mostly propaganda film designed to honor those citizen soldiers who have been drafted.

One such citizen soldier who was recently drafted is Director Weintraub's own son, Private Aaron Weintraub. Private Weintraub is currently in training with the United States Army.

Aaron Weintraub leaned against the fireplace mantel and watched the swirl of people who were guests at his father's party. Although Eli had suggested that it was a welcome-home party for Aaron, Aaron knew that it was actually just one of the regular gatherings Eli had nearly every weekend. The parties were, according to one Hollywood wag, nothing more than "a weekend with Bacchus." Errol Flynn was with Marika Fletcher, giving further rise to the rumor that Flynn was about to be cast in *Gossamer Wings*.

Robert Taylor also was there, as were Gary Cooper, Ronald Reagan, Susan Hayward, and Bette Davis. Also on hand were several people whose names the public would never recognize, but Aaron knew they were the real power elite of Hollywood.

Mingling with the big names and power brokers were the beautiful young and eager people who were just at the start of their own careers. Some, Aaron knew, would go on to be names as recognizable as those of the big stars who were here tonight. But most would return to their hometowns with broken dreams and bittersweet memories of having rubbed elbows with the rich and famous.

"Aaron! Aaron, dear boy, do please come over here," a very glamorous-looking woman called. She held her arm out to Aaron as he approached her. Shelly Castle-Weintraub, at twenty-eight, was seven years older than Aaron. She was also his stepmother, Eli Weintraub's fourth wife.

Shelly had given up a somewhat lackluster movie career that seemed destined to keep her forever in roles of the "other woman." Ironically, she went on to play that part in real life, beginning her relationship with Aaron's father before wife number three was entirely out of the picture.

Shelly was standing with three beautiful young starlets.

"Ladies, I want you to meet our son, the war hero," Shelly said proudly, putting her hand on Aaron's shoulder and pulling him in front of the three young women.

"Thanks . . . Mom," Aaron said, setting the word *Mom* apart in sarcasm.

"Aaron, I just know these ladies want to hear all about your war experiences," Shelly said. "Do entertain them, won't you? Oh, I see that Mr. Flynn is all alone by the bar. We can't have that now, can we? I'd better entertain him."

Aaron watched his stepmother wriggle her way through the crowd as she set out on her errand of entertaining Errol Flynn.

"Oh, my, I'll just bet you have a lot of exciting war experiences to tell about," one of the starlets said.

"Yeah, there are a lot of mosquitoes in Camp Shelby, Mississippi," Aaron said.

"Oh yes, I can remember the mosquitoes from Georgia," a blonde with wide eyes and pouty lips said, not picking up on Aaron's sarcasm.

"Would you ladies excuse me, please?" Smiling his good-bye, Aaron walked onto the back patio, then stood there, looking out toward the ocean. The sun was just setting, and though it had turned the surface of the water into an iridescent blue, it held no promise for a particularly beautiful sunset. The sunsets didn't have to be spectacular, though, to make it one of the most impressive views in all of Malibu Beach.

Like most of the other male guests at his father's party, Aaron was wearing a white dinner jacket. Slimmer and harder than he had been when he left for the army, both the jacket and the pants were too big for him now, and they hung uncomfortably from his newly muscled frame.

It was funny, but throughout basic training, during the hardest parts and especially during the long, lonely nighttime hours of walking guard, Aaron thought about moments like this. Now that he was actually living such a moment, his mind was elsewhere.

The party, the drinking, and the inane gossip seemed trivial to him. In his mind he could smell the cordite of spent powder and hear the bang of rifles on the firing range. He glanced at his watch and realized that back at Camp Shelby right now the barracks sergeants would be turning out all the lights, and the men would be bedding down to the notes of Taps.

"A penny for your thoughts."

He wondered if the other men from the company were going through the same thing. Were they feeling an inability to shut down what had been such an intense part of their lives for the last two months? Where was Dewey Bradley right now? What about Roberto Sangremano, José Montoya, and Travis Logan? Like him, all were home on furlough. But were their spirits still back at the army base?

"Wow, I guess a penny isn't enough. Perhaps I had better give you a dollar for your thoughts."

The voice was female, and it wasn't until she spoke the second time that Aaron realized she was speaking to him. Turning, he saw Marika Fletcher. He smiled at her.

"I'm sorry," he said. "I guess my mind was somewhere else."

"I'd say it was," Marika said. She handed him a glass of white wine. "The bartender said this is what you were drinking."

"Yes, thank you," Aaron said, taking the glass from her. He smiled at her. "I saw you arrive with Errol Flynn. Shouldn't you be with him, trying to talk him into doing my father's movie?"

"Shelly seems to be taking care of that right now," Marika replied.

Aaron glanced back through the wide expanse of windows that opened onto the patio and saw Shelly standing at the bar with Errol Flynn. Both were clearly in the flirting mode.

Aaron smiled. "Yes, mumsie dear seems to have things well in hand," he said.

Marika had just taken a swallow of her drink, and she laughed so hard that she spit some of it out. Aaron came to her rescue, providing her with a handkerchief.

"Mumsie dear," she said. "I'd almost forgotten she was your father's wife."

"Yes," Aaron said. "However, given Eli's record, I'm sure it's but a temporary condition."

"You are awful."

"Not awful, just truthful," Aaron said. "By the way, congratulations on getting the role in my father's new movie."

"Thanks," Marika said. "I'm excited about it."

"Have you read the book?" Aaron asked.

"Not yet," Marika said. "Have you?"

"Yes."

"Did you like it?"

"Yes, very much."

"I've had some tell me that I shouldn't read the book, that I should just concentrate on the script. What do you think?"

Aaron raised his hand. "Don't ask me," he said. "I'm just a simple soldier, doing his duty for God and country."

Marika laughed again. "You're funny," she said. "Do you like being in the army?"

"Do I like it? No, I wouldn't say that I like it exactly," Aaron said. "But I have found it fascinating."

"It has been good for you," Marika said.

"What do you mean?"

"Before you left, you were—" Marika paused in midsentence.

Aaron didn't make things any easier for her. Instead, he just took a sip of his drink and stared at her.

"Well, you know," Marika said. "You were—"

Aaron smiled at her.

"Come on, Aaron, are you going to make me say it? Your father is my director. I have to be a little discreet, after all."

"Honey, don't worry about my father," Aaron said. "You could call me the biggest bum and the most worthless lowlife of all time, and my father would do nothing but agree with you."

"Well, you do have that reputation," Marika said. "Or at least, you did before you left. But now? I think maybe you have changed."

"I've only been back one day," Aaron said. "How would anybody know that I have changed?"

"For one thing, you aren't down there," Marika said. She pointed to the swimming pool where several white-jacketed young men and sequin-gowned young women were drinking, laughing, and shoving.

One of the young women, who had been pushed into the swimming pool earlier, was sitting on a pool-side chair, drinking and laughing, totally oblivious of or perhaps glorying in the fact that her dress had suddenly become much more revealing.

Aaron laughed. "Was I that bad?"

"Don't you remember when you and Judy Garland showed up at a party one time, riding on top of the limo, not in it? And you were drinking champagne straight from the bottle."

"Oh yes," Aaron said. "Well, I tried to drink it from her shoe, but I learned that strapless shoes just won't hold wine."

Marika laughed again. "You were awful," she said.

"As I recall, I talked Judy into doing that," Aaron said. "I believe I said something like, 'Any publicity is good publicity.' So, tell me, how is my studio-arranged girlfriend?"

"What do you mean, 'studio-arranged' girlfriend?" Marika asked.

"Judy was a young actress, seen around town with the son of a top movie director. The whole thing was Maurice Felder's doing."

"Maurice Felder? The press agent?"

"Yes. Did you expect her to date a shoe salesman?"

Marika laughed. "No, I guess not. I've done some of that myself."

"What, dated a shoe salesman?"

Marika laughed again. "No. I mean I have gone on studio-arranged dates."

"Of course you have," Aaron said. "Everyone out here has. This is dream world. It's not until you get on the other side of the screen that you encounter the real world."

"Other side of the screen?"

"Look," Aaron said, pointing toward the Hollywood hills. "Don't tell me that you can't see that great big silver screen over there on the hills? People on the other side see the shadows we project on the screen, and they wonder what we're like. And we pretend to be what we think they want us to be."

"Not all of us, Aaron," Marika said. "You forget, not everyone was born on this side of the screen. Some know what it is like on the other side."

"Indeed, some do know. And that brings up the question about who is worse. Those who were 'to the silver screen born,' or those who have left behind all that was real?"

The smile left Marika's face. "You don't think very much of us, do you, Aaron?"

Aaron finished his drink. "Not much, I'm afraid," he said. "And I include myself in that group."

"You have changed, Aaron," Marika said. "But I'm not sure it's for the better."

Aaron watched Marika walk away, and he felt bad that he had let his cynicism get in the way. He held up his hand once to call her back but said nothing. Instead, he turned back toward the ocean, which was now a black-and-silver pool under the full moon.

8

Sikeston, Missouri
May 3, 1942

T he First Baptist Church of Sikeston, Missouri, was on South
Kingshighway at the western terminus of Greer Street. A brick
building with wide concrete steps spreading across the front, it was an
impressive church, though not as impressive or as beautiful as the
Methodist church, whose graceful dome and Corinthian columns made
it one of the must-see attractions for visitors to the small southeast
Missouri community.

During the announcements, Reverend Phil Rankin introduced
Dewey to his congregation. Dewey, in uniform, sat in the front pew with
Unity, her mother, Margaret, and Unity's friend, Millie Gates. The ser-
mon was on the prodigal son. A couple of times during the sermon,
Dewey got the idea that the good Reverend Rankin had selected the
sermon just for his benefit.

It was quite warm, and during the service, the ushers used long
hooked poles to lower the stained-glass windows from the top and slide

them up from the bottom in order to generate a breeze. With the windows up, the noise from outside came into the church, and Dewey could hear a truck going through its gears as it passed by on South Kingshighway.

After the service several people in the congregation came by to shake Dewey's hand, welcome him to the church, and offer their prayers and blessings for him. Then, Dewey joined the Rankin family for lunch, driving from the church to the parsonage in his own car, which Unity had brought from Litchfield to Sikeston.

"Daddy has a surprise for you," Unity said as they drove to her parents' home.

"What sort of surprise?"

"I don't know," Unity said. "I asked what it was, but he wouldn't tell me."

"Maybe he's going to suggest that we get married right away," Dewey said. He reached over to take her hand. "My next assignment is at Camp Rucker, Alabama, and while we are there, those who are married can have their wives with them."

"Really?" Unity asked excitedly.

"Really," Dewey answered. "Unity, would you consider marrying me during this leave period?"

"Yes!" Unity said. "Oh, Dewey, I would get married this afternoon if we could."

"You won't mind giving up the wedding . . . the lavender bridesmaid dresses, all of that?"

"Darling, the only thing I don't want to give up is you," Unity said. "If you are going overseas, then I think we owe it to each other to spend as much time together as we possibly can."

Dewey squeezed Unity's hand. "You've made me the happiest man in the world," he said.

During dinner Dewey and Unity could scarcely take their eyes off each other. It was all Dewey could do to keep up his end of the conversation with her father, who was asking everything about army life. He wanted to know about the training, the food, the living conditions, and whether Dewey had a chance to go to church during his basic training.

"Yes, sir, I went every Sunday. That is, if I didn't have duty, such as guard or KP," Dewey answered.

"Where is the nearest Southern Baptist church to Camp Shelby?"

"Ah, well, I didn't go to a civilian church," Dewey said. "I went to chapel."

"Was your chaplain a Southern Baptist?"

"We had a different chaplain almost each week," Dewey said. "One of them was Southern Baptist, but we also had Methodist, Presbyterian, Episcopalian. Everything but Roman Catholic. The Roman Catholics have their own chapel."

"Would you say that the army could use more Southern Baptist chaplains?" Phil asked.

Dewey chuckled. "Sure, I suppose so."

"I was hoping you would think that," Phil said. "For that is my surprise."

"More Southern Baptist chaplains is your surprise?" Dewey asked, confused by the comment.

"Well, at least one more," Phil said. Getting up from the table, he walked over to the hutch, opened a drawer, and pulled out a brown manila envelope. He brought the envelope back to the table. "This is for you," he said.

Dewey looked confused. "What is it?"

"It's your commissioning papers," Phil said, handing them over to Dewey. "All you have to do is sign them, then send them back in. When that happens, you will be commissioned as a second lieutenant in the Army Chaplain Corps."

Dewey took the envelope, held it for a moment, then shook his head and handed the envelope back.

"Reverend Rankin, I thank you. I truly do. I know that you must've gone out on a limb to get this for me, but," he paused and took a deep breath, "I don't want a commission in the Chaplain Corps."

"What?" Phil asked, shocked by the response. "Dewey, do you hear what you are saying?"

"Yes, sir."

"But I don't understand. Here is an opportunity for you to do what you have devoted the last four years of your life to doing. And I believe you once told me that you have wanted to preach the gospel ever since you were very young."

"That's true, sir."

"Well, I'm handing it to you. You can preach, and you can be in the army. Unity explained that you felt you had a calling to serve in the military. Well, I can appreciate that. But you also have a calling to serve God, and this gives you the chance to do both."

"I believe that by going into the army to fight against Hitler, I *am* serving God," Dewey said. "And I believe I can serve God better as a fighting infantryman than I could as an army chaplain."

Phil shook his head in frustration and anger. "I don't believe this," he said. He pointed to Unity. "You say you love my daughter, yet this is how little regard you have for her?"

"I do love your daughter," Dewey said. He looked at Unity. "Unity, did you know about this?"

"No," Unity said, shaking her head.

"What do you think about it?"

"Well, what do you think she thinks about it?" Phil asked, speaking before Unity could answer. "Obviously, she would rather have you safe as a chaplain, to say nothing of earning the income of an officer, than to have you serve as a private for practically no pay, with the very real prospect of being killed."

"Unity?" Dewey asked.

The expression on Unity's face was pained, but she took a deep breath, then answered him.

"Dewey, I love you, no matter what," she said. "Daddy is right. I would rather have you safe as a chaplain than risking your life in the infantry."

Dewey started to say something, but Unity held up her hand to stop him.

"But," she continued, "I resigned myself to you being in the infantry, and I realized that I couldn't stop loving you then. Nothing has changed. You are still in the infantry, and I still love you."

"Do you still want to go to Camp Rucker with me?" Dewey asked.

"Yes," Unity answered.

"Go to Camp Rucker with him? What do you mean?" Phil asked. "What are you talking about?"

"I have at least eight more weeks of training before I go overseas," Dewey said. "And in this part of our training, we are allowed to have our wives with us."

"You don't have a wife," Phil said.

"I know. But with your permission and your cooperation, you can marry us while I am home on leave."

"You will not take this commission?" Phil asked.

Dewey shook his head. "No, sir. I can't. I just can't. I hope you understand."

"No, young man. I do not understand," Phil said. He stood up. "I do not understand at all."

Without another word, Unity's father left the dining room and walked through the house. A moment later they heard him slam the door to the study.

"Mama?" Unity said, turning toward her mother. Tears were streaming down Unity's cheeks, and she saw that her mother was crying as well. "Mama, you understand, don't you?"

Margaret tried to speak but couldn't. She got up from the table and held her arms open for her daughter. Unity went into her mother's arms, and they embraced for a while without speaking. Then Margaret left.

"What now?" Unity asked in a small voice.

"Unity, I'm going to go home to see my parents now," Dewey said. "But I want you to think about something. Don't answer me now. Just think about it."

"All right," Unity agreed.

Dewey took a deep breath, then he took both her hands in his and looked into her eyes. "I want you to go to Camp Rucker with me. I need you there with me."

"Dewey, surely you don't expect me to go if we aren't married?" she asked, gasping at the thought.

Dewey shook his head. "No, no, nothing like that," he said. "But if you will agree to it, we can go to Piggott, Arkansas. There is no waiting time there, and we can get the marriage certificate and ceremony at the same time."

"You mean, you want me to marry you without Daddy performing the ceremony? Without even his blessing?"

"I think we will win his blessings in time," Dewey said. "And in time, we can even have him consecrate our marriage. But, honey, we don't have time. We have ten weeks from today. That's not even three months."

"I know."

"Think about it. Pray about it," Dewey said. "Then, wait, let me have a pencil and a piece of paper."

Unity got him the paper and pencil, and Dewey wrote something.

"This is the telephone number at Novak's Drugstore in Pilot Town. Call this number at exactly two o'clock next Thursday afternoon. I'll be there then, and you can give me your decision."

"All right," Unity agreed.

Dewey kissed her. "Tell your mother and father I said good-bye. And try to tell your father that I do understand, and I appreciate what he tried to do for me."

"I will," Unity said.

Pilot Town, Tennessee

Pilot Town was fifty miles south of Sikeston, but on the Tennessee side of the Mississippi River. There was no bridge, but there was a ferry. Dewey drove down to the ferry landing, then turned the big signal board so that instead of showing red, it showed white. By this means he was able to communicate to the ferry operator on the other side of the river that he wanted to come across.

Dewey stared across the Mississippi, which was a mile wide at that point, and was gratified to see that the ferry had come out of its slip and was coming across for him. He was also pleased to see that two other cars came down to wait for the ferry, which would make the trip a little more productive for "Poke" Taylor, the ferry operator.

It took the ferry about fifteen minutes to cross, and Dewey watched until it rammed into the bank and dropped its ramp. Dewey took the heavy hawser from the front of the ferry and looped it around a stanchion on the bank, thus holding the ferry secure. That was usually the task of the ferry operator himself, but Dewey did it because he had done it many times. Over the years of growing up and living in Pilot Town, Dewey had been a frequent passenger on this ferry. More than once, Poke let young Dewey spend the entire day on the ferry with him, crossing and recrossing the river.

The ferry was actually a barge, pushed by a small tugboat. The sides of the tugboat and the barge were covered with old tires, which provided a bumper that protected the two vessels. Glancing up toward the tugboat, Dewey saw Poke climb out of the wheelhouse, then jump down onto the barge. With a big smile, Poke hurried toward Dewey.

"Dewey!" Poke said. "My, my, don't you look fine, though, all dressed up in your soldier suit?"

"Hello, Mr. Taylor," Dewey said.

"Mr. Taylor? That's what you called me when you were a kid. You're a man now, full growed. My friends all call me Poke, and I'm sure hopin' you count yourself as one of my friends."

"Okay, Poke. How is Mrs. Poke?" Dewey asked with a smile.

"Mrs. Poke is fat and sassy," Poke replied. "You home on furlough?"

"Yes, sir," Dewey said. He reached into his pocket. "Is it still a quarter to cross?"

"Not for you, it ain't," Poke said. "Bring your car onto the ferry."

"I can't do that. Not without paying you."

"Sure you can. I've given other boys in uniform free passage. Don't know why I can't do it for you, especially seein' as you're countin' yourself as one of my friends now. Bring your car on."

"When did you get so rich," Dewey teased, "that you can give soldiers free rides?"

"You forget the tire shortage?" Poke asked, pointing to the water-dripping tires that were hanging from the side of the boat. "If I need money, I'll just sell one of the tires. It's like money in the bank."

Dewey laughed. "Thanks," he said. "I'll remember that if I need to borrow money."

Returning to his car, Dewey drove it up the ramp and onto the ferry, then pulled it all the way to the front of the barge. The other two cars, paying a quarter apiece, rolled onto the ferry behind him.

With another wave, Poke climbed back into the pilothouse, backed the little tugboat around on its pivot, then started the other way, pushing the ferry across the river. Dewey got out of the car and walked over to the rail to look down at the brown water of the Mississippi swirling and rolling past the keel. A small branch got caught up in the suction and hung on to the barge for a moment, bouncing up and down in the swirling water. Finally it broke free, then drifted away to continue its transit downriver.

Looking back, Dewey could see the Missouri shoreline slipping away. Looking ahead, he could see the state of Tennessee, mostly green trees from his perspective, as it gradually came closer.

He thought about the events of the dinner at the Rankins' home. He had not handled the situation well. He had been in the army long enough to know, and appreciate, what Reverend Rankin had done for him. It wasn't easy to get a commission, and he knew from firsthand observation how much better living conditions were for the officers than they were for the enlisted men.

Several times during the drive down he had almost turned around and gone back to Sikeston to tell Reverend Rankin that he had changed his mind. He would take the commission and become a chaplain. Once, he even left Highway 61 and sat on the side of the road for several minutes, thinking about it.

But he couldn't do it. More than ever, he felt committed to the path he had chosen for himself or, if he was properly interpreting it, the path God had chosen for him. He would stay in the infantry as an enlisted man.

As the Tennessee shoreline loomed very close, Dewey got back into his car and waited. The ferry made its landing, and the ramp went down. There was already someone waiting to take the hawser and secure the ferry, so all Dewey had to do was start his car. Then, with a final wave toward Poke, he drove off.

Dewey's route through Pilot Town took him down Poindexter Street, past Steinberg's Department Store, Norton's Hardware, Pratt's Five and Dime, Wilma's Café, and finally the newspaper office of the *Pilot Town Sentinel.*

When he noticed the service flag with a single blue star in the window of his father's office, he smiled. His dad hadn't wasted any time letting the town know that he had a son in the service.

Poindexter Street split to go around the courthouse square. On the courthouse lawn stood a bronze statue of a mounted Confederate officer. The Confederate officer's sword was drawn, and he was looking north. Dewey knew, without having to read the inscription, what the plaque beneath the soldier said.

IN HONOR OF THE BRAVE
SONS OF THE SOUTH,
WHO PRESERVED DUTY, HONOR, AND COURAGE
THROUGH THE ANGUISH OF DEFEAT.

Dewey's house was on Fortification Avenue, a broad, paved street that was shaded with towering elm trees. It was a large, old, two-story brick home that sat back on a well-manicured lawn. The porch was deep, and it spread all the way across the front of the house, then wrapped around to the left side, where his mother had planted a beautiful flower garden, which was now blooming in colorful profusion.

A wing of the second story extended from the right side of the house, protruding over the driveway. That wing had been Dewey's room, and the overhang created a carport, under which a dark green Packard was parked. Dewey pulled into the driveway behind his father's car. He didn't honk the horn or give any other sign of his arrival, but even as he was getting out of his car, his mother came running down the wide concrete steps and down the sidewalk to meet him.

"Dewey!" she called, embracing him as he stood just outside his car, the door still open. "Oh, Dewey! I am so happy you are home!"

Julia Bradley squeezed him hard, and Dewey allowed her to do so, hugging her back until she was satisfied with her greeting. Looking just over his mother's shoulder, Dewey saw his father. Green was standing on the porch, halfway between the front door and the top step. He was smoking a pipe, and though not as demonstrative as Julia, he had a wide, pleased smile on his face.

"Hi, Dad," Dewey said, going up on the porch to greet him.

"You're looking good, Son," Green said, shaking his son's hand. "Very good."

"You're looking pretty good yourself," Dewey said.

When they went inside, a little white terrier ran to meet him, rearing up and jumping, trying to get Dewey's attention.

"Hey, Charley," Dewey said, reaching down to pick up the dog. "Have you missed me?"

Charley's stubby tail was wagging rapidly as he slathered kisses on Dewey's face and lips.

"Oh, Dewey, don't let him lick you in the face like that," Julia said.

"Mom, you don't know how many times I've thought about just this very thing," Dewey said. He let the dog kiss him for several more seconds before he sniffed the air. "Mmm, what is that I smell? Is it chocolate chip cookies?" he asked.

"I baked a batch for you," Julia said. "I know how much you love them."

Dewey grabbed a couple of them.

"There's milk in the fridge," his mother said.

"Thanks, Mom," Dewey said, getting a glass from the cabinet.

Dewey took a bottle of milk from the refrigerator, then poured himself a glass.

"How do you feel?" Green asked.

"Great, Dad. I feel great."

9

On the Eastern front
May 6, 1942

H ow do you feel?" the medical officer asked.
"What?" Gunter responded groggily. He looked around in confusion. "Who are you? Where am I?"

"I am Dr. Dostler, and you are in the Sixth Army Field Hospital," the
doctor replied. "Do you not remember being wounded?"

"Wounded," Gunter said. He recalled the sudden searing pain in his
leg. "Yes," he said, the memory coming to him. "Yes, the planes."

"You are a lucky young man."

"Yes, I suppose I am," Gunter said.

"No, I mean you are lucky because you are going home."

"Why am I going home?" Gunter asked. "Is my wound that serious?"

"Not really," Dr. Dostler said. "I expect you will have a full recovery.
But there is a JU-52 flying back to Germany in the morning, and my
orders are to see that you are on board."

"But I don't understand. If my wound is not that serious, why am I going home? I'm just a private. How is it that I have a place on the plane?"

"I arranged it," a quiet voice said, and a man suddenly stepped into Gunter's field of vision. When Gunter recognized him, he gasped.

"General von Paulis!" Gunter tried to get up from the bed, but von Paulis put his hand out, indicating that he should not try.

"Do you feel up to making such a long flight?" von Paulis asked.

"Well, yes, sir, of course. But I don't know why I should be allowed to go home when there are others who are more seriously wounded."

"I am sending you back to Germany with a mission to perform," von Paulis said. "That is, if you are willing to do so."

"Yes, sir, of course I will," Gunter said. "I will do anything you ask of me."

"My information is correct, is it not? You are the grandson of Colonel-General Reinhardt?"

"Yes, sir, I am," Gunter said. "Uh, General, I . . . I don't feel right in being allowed to go home just because I am the general's grandson."

Von Paulis held out his hand and shook his head. "You misunderstand, Soldier. I am not sending you home just because you are General Reinhardt's grandson. I am sending you home because you are his grandson, *and* I need you to speak for me. Though it may already be too late."

"Speak for you?"

"More correctly, urge your grandfather to speak for me," von Paulis said. "For me and for my army. Will you do so?"

"Yes, sir, of course. What do you want me to say?"

"You were here for the winter?"

"Yes, sir."

"Did you watch any of your comrades die?"

Gunter thought of the many men in his company he had seen die during the winter, including his friend, Ernst.

"Yes, Herr General. I watched many of my comrades die," he said.

"The brutal winter is over," General von Paulis said. "Once again, supplies can get through. But we are not getting supplies for the winter to come. The supplies we get are fuel and ammunition, supplies for a victorious army on the advance. We are not a victorious army on the advance. We are an army that is barely holding on, just trying to survive."

"You want me to tell my grandfather that we need winter supplies?"

Von Paulis paused for a moment, then shook his head no. "No," he replied. "I want you to tell your grandfather to convince Herr Hitler to rescind his foolish order demanding that we stand until the last man. Our Führer is determined to see the complete destruction of the Sixth Army. Will you do this for me?"

"Yes, General," Gunter promised.

"The lives of more than a quarter of a million brave men are hanging in the balance," von Paulis said. Turning, he walked away from Gunter's bunk. "A quarter of a million men," he said again, speaking to himself as he left the ward.

Dr. Dostler returned to Gunter's hospital bed and handed him a note. "Private, would you try to get in touch with my wife when you are in Germany? Her name is Helga Dostler, and this is her address in Wertheim."

"Yes, I will," Gunter said, taking the note.

"Tell her that . . . ," Dr. Dostler started, then he stopped in midsentence and pinched the bridge of his nose. "Tell her that . . . ," he started again, then he stopped again. "Well, I trust you will know what to tell her," he finally said.

"Yes, sir," Gunter said.

An orderly came up to the bed then, pushing a wheelchair. "Are you ready for a little fresh air?" the orderly asked.

"Yes, thank you," Gunter said.

The orderly helped Gunter from the bed into the chair. His right leg was in a cast, and it stuck out stiffly before him.

"How did you get the wound?" the orderly asked as he pushed Gunter from the hospital onto a terrace. At least a dozen other wounded soldiers were also taking the fresh air.

"I was on a motorcycle, delivering messages," Gunter explained. "I was strafed by an airplane."

"I didn't know the Russians could shoot that well," the orderly said.

"It was one of our own planes," Gunter said, laughing dryly.

The woman wasn't much more than a girl. Someone had said she was nineteen. Another said she was no more than seventeen. She had light brown hair, rosy cheeks, and big brown eyes. She might have been any young woman Gunter had ever seen, buying flowers in the Schweinfurt platz, walking in the park, or going to the opera. She would have been beautiful in an opera gown because she was even very pretty in the Russian uniform.

"Gunter," she said, looking at him with her deep, dark eyes. "Gunter, why are you doing this?" She reached out to him. "Do not do this, Gunter."

The trapdoor opened, and the girl fell. The rope stopped her short, her head jerked to one side, and she twisted in a slow, one-half turn to the left, then hung there lifeless.

"No!" Gunter shouted.

Beyond the girl's body he could see the hanging corpses of three men and one more woman.

"Gunter," a smiling SS officer shouted to him. He held his hand out. "Come, there are more. You can help us!"

"No!" Gunter shouted.

"Are you in pain?"

When Gunter opened his eyes, he realized he had been dreaming. He was lying on a stretcher, one of eighteen patients. He could hear the sound of the three straining engines as the trimotor Junkers, known as Iron Annie, beat its way through the Russian sky, heading back to Germany. One of the two flight doctors on board was leaning over his stretcher looking down at him.

"I beg your pardon?" Gunter asked.

"You called out," the doctor said. "Are you in pain?"

"No," Gunter said. "I'm sorry. I must have had a bad dream."

"Yes," the doctor replied. "Many of our patients do have bad dreams."

The stretchers were placed in two tiers on either side of the plane. Gunter was on the lower tier, thus allowing him to look through the window. Glancing out, he saw the gray corrugated metal of the wing. At the end of the wing he saw not the familiar white-limned black cross, but a red cross, marking this as a hospital plane. He looked behind the wing, toward the ground one thousand meters below, where he saw nothing but trees and open fields. No towns or villages, not even a house.

He thought about the dream then or, more specifically, what had triggered the dream.

Dismounting from the motorcycle, Gunter was delivering the message from his commanding officer to the major in charge of motor vehicles.

"Captain Berchtold requests six trucks be moved up to Sector B," Gunter said. He handed the paperwork to the major. "Here are the requisition forms, signed by our colonel."

"Sorry," the major said, shaking his head. "I have no trucks to give you."

The major's announcement surprised Gunter because he had driven by the motor pool on the way into the village, and there he saw at least three dozen parked trucks.

"I beg your pardon, Major, but what of the trucks in the motor pool?"

"Those trucks have been confiscated," the major said.

"Confiscated?"

"I do not have to explain myself to a private," the major said angrily. "Go back and tell your captain, he can have no trucks. There are no trucks."

"Yes, sir," Gunter said, coming to attention and snapping his heels together.

Gunter left the major's office, but not content with the answer from the major, he went down to the motor pool. The hood was up on one of the trucks, and a private was working on the engine. Gunter walked over to him.

"What is wrong with all these trucks?" Gunter asked, taking in the parked vehicles with a sweep of his arm.

The mechanic raised up and looked at him, an expression of irritation on his face.

"There is nothing wrong with these trucks," he answered. "I keep them in very good condition. Who said there was something wrong with them?"

"The major said he had no trucks to give my captain," Gunter said. "But clearly there are many trucks here. Since he had none to give me, I assumed they were not in working order."

The mechanic grunted. "It is not because there is something wrong with the trucks," he said. "It is because of the Jews."

"The Jews? I don't understand. What do the Jews have to do with these trucks?"

"The SS has taken over all the trucks," the mechanic replied. "They use them to transport Jews to the railroad stations where they put them on cars to take them back to Germany. How about that? The Jews get to go to Germany, while we must stay in this dung heap of a country."

"Where would I find the SS?" Gunter asked.

"Hah," the mechanic said. "You want to find the SS? Most do not want to be found by the SS, but you want to find them?"

"Yes," Gunter said. "I wish to ask for the use of six trucks for my captain."

The mechanic pointed toward the center of the village. "Go into the village," he said. "Find the best hotels, the best houses. That is where the SS will be."

Thanking the mechanic, Gunter went back to his motorcycle, started it, then drove toward the middle of town. When he reached the center square, a man wearing the black-and-silver uniform of the SS stepped in front of the motorcycle and held out his hand.

"Stop," he said.

Gunter stopped and sat on the motorcycle, holding it up with his foot. He allowed the engine to run for a moment, then when he realized it was longer than a temporary stop, he shut it down.

"Why are you here?" the SS man asked.

"I would like to speak to the SS commandant about some trucks," Gunter said.

"Not now. We have business now."

A truck that was parked in front of Gunter moved then, and when it did so, Gunter saw that there was a gallows in the middle of the square. Several people were gathered around the gallows. Some were villagers, their faces drawn in fear and horror. Others were SS men and ordinary German soldiers. The expressions on their faces ran the gamut from horror to morbid fascination.

"What is this?" Gunter asked the guard. "What is going on here?"

"You will see," the guard replied with a smirk on his face.

From a building close to him, two armed SS men came outside, then stood at the bottom of the steps waiting with weapons at the ready as five prisoners came out. There were two women and three men. The prisoner in front was a woman, young and very beautiful. She was wearing a Soviet army uniform.

"Who are they?" Gunter asked the SS guard.

"They are dead men," the guard replied with a little laugh.

"Dead men?"

The SS guard put his fist beside his neck, pulled it up sharply, then jerked his neck to one side. He made a little sound with his mouth, then stuck his tongue out.

"What did they do?"

"They are Russians."

"Yes, but what did they do?"

"They are Russians," the SS guard said again, as if that simple statement was explanation enough.

The guards marched the prisoners in front of Gunter's motorcycle, less than one meter from him. The beautiful girl in the uniform of the Soviet army stopped for a moment and looked directly at Gunter. Her eyes were large, brown, and deep. But there was no fear in those eyes. Strangely, there was no anger either.

"No," Gunter said to the young woman. He raised his hand and pointed at her. "No, do not look at me."

Amazingly, the girl smiled back at him. It was a small, sad, understanding, and most damning to Gunter, forgiving smile.

The SS guard stepped quickly between Gunter and the young

woman. The prisoners were led to the gallows, then up the thirteen steps. Each prisoner was put into position, and the noose was put over the person's head.

The woman continued to stare at Gunter, the enigmatic smile still playing across her lips.

Gunter wanted to look away. He willed himself to look away, but though he tried as hard as he could, her gaze held him.

An SS officer walked by each prisoner, stopped in front of each one, and spat in the person's face. Then, standing at the edge of the platform, he pointed to someone who was holding on to a lever.

"Heil Hitler!" the SS officer shouted.

The trapdoor opened, and the young woman fell. The rope stopped her short, her head jerked to one side, and she twisted in a slow, one-half turn to the left, then hung there lifeless.

"No!" Gunter shouted.

Beyond the young woman's body he could see the hanging corpses of four more, three men and one other woman. Until that moment, he had been so indifferent to them that he was almost unaware of their presence.

"Now, do you wish to see the commandant?" the SS guard asked.

Gunter didn't answer. His eyes were locked on the five bodies, hanging from the gallows.

"Do you wish to speak to the commandant?" the SS guard asked again, more sharply than before.

Gunter managed to pull his gaze away, and he looked at the guard. It was obvious that what had just happened had no effect whatever on the guard. It was as of little importance to him as stopping traffic to allow a train to pass.

"You look ill," the guard said. He laughed. Without even looking toward them, he pointed toward the hanging bodies. "I know what it is. You see a pretty woman die, and you think it is a waste. Well, let me tell you, my friend, in my business I have seen hundreds of pretty women die. Some of the Jew sluts are very pretty too. But you just have to close your mind to it."

"Close your mind to it?" Gunter asked.

"This is war. You are a soldier. Surely you have seen people die."

Gunter shook his head and pointed at the hanging bodies. "This," he said, barely able to squeeze out the words, "this is not war. This is murder."

The smile left the SS guard's face. "If I were you, I would be careful about making such comments," he said. "Now, do you wish to see the commandant?"

Without another word, Gunter kick-started the motorcycle, opened the throttle to full wide, then swung the motorcycle around. The spinning back tire sent rocks and dirt onto the guard, who shouted in protest, though his shout was drowned by the roar of the motorcycle engine as Gunter sped away.

He was less than ten kilometers away from the village when he saw the two airplanes. Thinking at first that they might be Russian Yaks, he looked closely at them, but when they banked around, he saw by their square-tipped wings and sleek fuselage that they were Me-109s. He paid no further attention to them then and stared at the road ahead.

The noise of the motorcycle engine drowned out all other sound, so he didn't hear the first airplane bearing down on him or the pop of machine-gun bullets as the airplane fired at him. His first indication that something was amiss was when he saw two lines stitched into the road ahead of him, little puffs of rock chips and dust. Immediately thereafter, the first Messerschmitt passed over his head, then pulled up sharply, just in front of him.

Turning quickly to look back over his shoulder, he saw the second Messerschmitt making a pass, flashes of fire winking on the leading edge of the wings. Suddenly, he felt a stinging in his right leg while at the same time he lost control of the motorcycle.

When he woke up, he was in the hospital.

"How do you feel?" the doctor had asked him.

"How do you feel?" the flight doctor asked, stopping by his stretcher and, in so doing, bringing Gunter out of his painful memories and back to the present.

"Fine," Gunter answered. "I feel fine."

"Good," the doctor said. "That is good."

Gunter continued to look out the window as the doctor went to the next patient. "How do you feel?" he heard the doctor ask the patient next to him.

"Fine," the patient answered.

"Good. That is good. How do you feel?" the doctor asked, continuing to the next patient.

"Fine."

"Good. That is good."

"How do you feel?" a new voice asked.

Gunter looked back from the window at this, the second of the two flight doctors who were flying back with the hospital plane. "Fine," Gunter said, looking up at him. "I feel fine."

"Good. That is good," the doctor replied. "How do you feel?" the doctor asked the next patient.

"Fine," the patient answered.

"Good. That is good."

Gunter resumed his vigil through the window as he heard the same question being asked and answered again and again.

10

U nity's best friend in high school had been Millie Gates. Millie worked at the shoe factory, and Unity agreed to meet her for lunch at the City Pig. The City Pig was an aluminum diner with stools at the counter and four booths. It was right across the highway from the shoe factory on the corner of Highways 60 and 61, but everyone referred to it merely as "the intersection."

Unity got to the City Pig a few minutes before noon in order to secure a booth. At exactly noon, the whistle blew. Most who worked at the factory brought their lunches, and they took their sacks or boxes to the lunchroom. Because it was a pretty day, many went outside and sat on the corner under an elm tree. Others went just down the road to Little Man Lamberts. Several came to the City Pig, and Millie was one of the first to arrive.

Millie had dark brown hair, almost sloelike eyes, and an olive complexion. She was an exceptionally pretty girl but seemed unaware of that fact, finding life more of an adventure than a show. She had a very outgoing personality. She was Cayenne, or leader, of the Red Peppers, which was an all-girl pep squad. She made good grades and could have gone on to college but chose not to. About the only two professions available to women that required a college degree were teaching and nursing, and neither of those avocations held any particular interest for her.

Millie once said that a person established the parameters of her acquaintances by picking someone with a strong personality to be her best friend, and someone of equally strong personality to be her greatest rival. For her, Unity was her best friend, and Lucy Fox, a redhead who was beautiful, smart, and gregarious, occupied the position of "greatest rival." Like Millie, Lucy worked at the shoe factory.

"Hi," Millie said as she sidled up to Unity. "Have you ordered yet?"

"No, I was waiting on you."

"I'll order. You want a hamburger?"

"Yes. Want to share some fries?"

"Sounds good," Millie said, stepping up to the counter to give the order, and pointed to the booth where she would be. Then she sat down in the booth across from Unity.

"Whew," she said. "It's been a hard morning. We've got a contract doing shoes for the navy, and we're going full time."

Back when Unity was planning a large wedding, Millie was to have been her maid of honor. In fact, one of the reasons she had chosen lavender was that Millie looked good in the color.

The waitress brought them fountain Cokes, and without lifting the glasses from the table, they leaned over them to drink through straws.

"Have you heard anything from Dewey?" Millie asked.

"I'm supposed to call him at exactly two o'clock today and tell him whether or not I will go to Piggott to get married."

"Are you going to?"

"I'm not sure."

"Don't you love him?"

"Yes. I love him more than I can say."

"Oh, Unity," Millie said, reaching across the table to hold Unity's hand. "If you love him, you should go with him. Elopements are so romantic."

Unity sighed. "I suppose they are," she said. "It's just that for my whole life I've planned on having a wedding, a real wedding. And I know Mom has. If I did this, she would be so disappointed. And Daddy," she paused for a moment, "I don't know what Daddy would do."

"Honey, you've got your own life to live now," Millie said. "Your mom and dad love you. They'll get over it. Believe me, they will."

"Yes, I know they will," Unity said. "But will I?"

"Of course, you will," Millie said. She chuckled. "I must say, though, I was really looking forward to being in your wedding. It was probably the only one I would ever have had a chance to be in, including my own."

"Oh, nonsense. What do you mean by talking such foolishness?"

"Well, let's face it, Unity. I played the field too much before the war started. Now, any man worth having is off in the army or the navy or something." She giggled. "Of course, I could always marry Mr. Keith."

Unity laughed. Charley Keith was the floor supervisor at the shoe factory and the only man on the floor. He was in his forties, short and bald-headed. He wore a bow tie, garters around his shirtsleeves, and always had half a chewed-up, smelly cigar in his mouth.

"Of course, I would have strong competition from Miss Lucy Fox," Millie said.

"Oh, you mean the," Unity patted her hair in an exaggerated fashion, "'don't I have beautiful red hair?' Lucy Fox?"

Millie laughed. "You're awful," she said as their hamburgers and fries were delivered.

Millie took a bite of her sandwich and looked across the table at Unity. Then she smiled. "You're going to do it, aren't you? You've just been stringing me along. You're going to do it."

Unity returned the smile and nodded her head nervously. "Yes," she said. "It's all I've thought about since he went back to Pilot Town. I hate starting our married life this way, but I would hate even more losing him."

"Good, I'm glad for you," Millie said. "You've made the right decision."

"I pray that I have."

Pilot Town, Tennessee

When Dewey went down to the office of the *Pilot Town Sentinel*, all the employees of the newspaper greeted him. Janet Dace, who had been selling advertising for his father for more than thirty years, was the first to speak to him.

"Be sure and check out the paper today, Dewey," she said. "There is a special ad honoring you."

"Honoring me?" Dewey replied in surprise. "What do you mean?"

"Come on, Dewey. You've known Janet your whole life," Tony said. Tony Piper was the Linotype operator. "Anytime she can find some way of squeezing out a few extra inches from our advertisers, she's going to do it."

"It's not like that at all. They enjoyed doing it," Janet insisted. Then she explained to Dewey, "What I did was, put together a very nice quarter-page ad with the cut of a soldier carrying a flag. The copy says, 'For our brave boys in the U.S. Army,' and under the cut it says, 'Congratulations, Dewey Bradley, on completing Army Basic Training.' And all it cost a merchant to get the name of the business included in the ad was two dollars."

"She had fifty takers," Tony said, "including some private citizens. A quarter-page ad usually costs twenty-five dollars, but she's making one hundred dollars from this one."

"I'm not making it. The paper is," Janet said. "And that includes you, Tony Piper."

Tony threw up his hands in surrender. "Hey, I'm not complaining. I'm bragging," he said, and the others laughed.

Dewey went over to the layout table and started reading the lead slugs in the makeup slate. He chuckled. "Listen to this," he said. "Up in Paducah, there was a man named Smith who fed a robin bread crumbs every day. One day the robin turned up on his back porch with a dollar bill in its beak, dropped it on the porch, then flew off."

"Well, you know what they say," Green said. "Cast your bread upon the water, and it shall be returned."

The others laughed, then one of the new employees looked at Dewey. "You can read that?"

"Sure."

"But it's still in the makeup slate. It's backward."

"Oh, heavens, Clara," Janet said. "Dewey learned to read backward before he did forward. He's a natural-born newspaper man if I ever saw one."

"Are you going to come back and work at the newspaper after the war?" Clara asked.

Green, who was looking at the front page of the paper, had just called Tony over to point out a mistake. But when Clara asked her question, he looked toward Dewey to await his answer.

"My father is a wonderful newspaper man," Dewey said. "I could never match him. I've chosen another career field."

"Yes, then you gave that up to go into the army," Green said.

"The army is temporary," Dewey said.

"Yes, well, let us hope it is," Green said as he went back to proofing the front page of the paper.

"Dewey is going to be a preacher," Janet said. "And he'll be a good one. I've known Dewey from the day he was born. No matter what he chooses to do, he will be the best."

From the newspaper, Dewey went down to the corner drugstore, where he bought a vanilla milkshake and sat at a table that was close to the telephone booth. When it was exactly two o'clock, the telephone rang, and Dewey answered it.

"Hello."

"Dewey?" Unity's voice asked hesitantly.

"Hello, Unity."

"Do you still want to go to Piggott to get married?"

"Yes, Unity, I very much want to," Dewey answered. "In fact, I want to do that more than anything I can think of."

Dewey could hear Unity taking a very deep breath.

105

"All right," she said. "If you still want to do this, I'll do it."

"Unity, you have just made me the happiest man in the world," Dewey said. "I love you."

"I love you too."

"Honey, I know this isn't the way you planned it. But people all over the world are having to change their plans right now. And the important thing is, we will be together. For whatever time we have left, we will be together."

"Yes, I know," Unity said. "I'm not having second thoughts, Dewey. I've been thinking about this ever since you left. If this is the only way we can get married, then I say, let's do it."

"You won't be sorry, Unity. I promise you."

"So, what do we do next?"

"I will be there at eleven o'clock tomorrow night. Have your suitcase packed and ready to go."

"All right. I'll hide it outside so we can get to it easily."

"Don't tell anyone we are going to do this, Unity. Not even Millie."

"Don't tell Millie?"

"Don't tell her," Dewey said. "I know she is your best friend and you tell her everything, but don't. One thing they taught us in the army is that the very walls have ears. We have to keep this secret."

Unity debated whether to tell him she had already spoken to Millie, but decided it would be better not to tell him. "All right," she said.

"After we are married, you can write your folks a long letter, explaining everything," Dewey said, continuing with the plans. "And I'll do the same thing with my parents. Then we will pray that they accept our decision, and maybe, one day, we can have your dad bless our marriage."

"Dewey, are you frightened?" Unity asked.

"Frightened? No, I'm not frightened. I'm sorry we are having to do it like this, but I'm not frightened. You'd better hang up now. This is a long-distance call on your dad's telephone bill."

"All right," Unity said. "I love you."

"I love you, and I'll see you tomorrow night at eleven o'clock."

"Eleven o'clock," Unity repeated.

In the back of the parsonage, in the pastor's study, Phil waited until he heard the clicks of both phones being hung up. Then he quietly replaced the receiver of his own phone. He sat at his desk for a long, reflective moment, pinching the bridge of his nose and thinking about what he had just overheard.

He had not intentionally listened in on the call. He had picked up the telephone, intending to call Deacon Virden, but heard that someone was already on the phone. He started to hang it up when he heard Dewey say, "The very walls have ears. We have to keep this secret. After we are married, you can write your folks a long letter, explaining everything. And I'll do the same thing with my parents. Then we will pray that they accept our decision, and maybe, one day, we can have your dad bless our marriage."

He also heard enough to know that Unity would have her suitcase packed and ready to leave tomorrow night, by eleven o'clock.

"Oh, dear Lord," he said, breathing a quick prayer. "Has it really come to this?"

11

Pilot Town, Tennessee
May 14, 1942

Dewey was sitting in the big brown leather chair in the living room of his parents' house. He had his right leg cocked over the arm of the chair, and he was reading a Zane Grey Western novel. His mother came into the room, dressed to leave.

"Mom, you look good," Dewey said.

"Thank you," Julia replied. "Oh, listen, there is some cold chicken in the fridge. Also a nice potato salad and a piece of lemon pie. Just feed yourself supper when you get hungry."

"Feed myself? What do you mean, feed myself? Aren't you and Dad going to be here?"

"No. Your dad and I are going to Dyersburg to visit Amanda. She called today and invited us up."

"You're going to see Aunt Amanda on my last day here?" Dewey asked, a little surprised by her announcement.

"Well, sweetheart, it's not like we're going to have a lot more time to visit now, is it? I mean, you're leaving for your new base . . . where is it? I keep forgetting."

"Camp Rucker, Alabama."

"Yes. You are leaving for Camp Rucker early in the morning, aren't you?"

"Yes."

"Well, then we are only talking about a few more hours, and your father thought it might be easier on me if I had something else to occupy my mind while you are leaving. You know how I hate good-byes."

"Yes, I know. Okay, Mom, tell Aunt Amanda I said hello," Dewey said. Putting his book down, he stood up and embraced his mother.

"You will write?"

"As often as I can," Dewey promised.

Green came into the living room then, carrying a suitcase. "You ready, Julia?" he asked.

"I'm ready."

Green looked at his son. "I know you want to drive your car to your next base," he said. "And I can see why you might want to have the car with you while you are there. Just promise me that you will drive carefully."

"I promise," Dewey said. He followed them out onto the front porch, then watched as they got into the big green Packard and drove away.

After they were out of sight, Dewey went back into the house and settled once more into the big leather chair. On the one hand, it seemed rather odd to him that his parents would leave on this, his last day at home. But as he thought about it, he realized that this might be better. By leaving now, they wouldn't have to wake up in the morning to find that he had disappeared in the middle of the night, without so much as a good-bye.

Yes, as things turned out, it was much, much better this way.

Dewey reached Sikeston just before eleven that night, and he drove straight to the Rankin house. Turning onto Gladys Street, he passed by slowly in front of the house, then turned around to come back. When he came by the house the second time, he turned off his lights, killed the engine, and allowed the car to coast off the street and into the driveway.

Getting out of the car, Dewey closed the door, though not hard enough for the latch to catch and click, but far enough to make the dome light go out. Then he moved silently from tree to porch, then to tree again. Picking his way through the yard, he found himself standing under a giant elm tree along the side of the house and very near Unity's bedroom window.

Dewey picked up a piece of gravel and tossed it lightly against the window screen of Unity's second-floor bedroom. He could hear it thump quietly against the screen.

"Unity?" he called, whispering loudly. He tossed another piece of gravel. The window screen swung out.

"I wasn't sure you would be here," Unity called down to him.

"Are your folks asleep?"

"Yes. Let's hurry before they wake up."

Dewey looked around. "Do you have a ladder?"

"I don't need one," Unity answered. She climbed out of her window, then inched along the ledge until she reached the roof of the side porch. She walked across the roof to the trellis, then climbed down it as easily as if she were coming down a ladder.

"I've been coming down this way since I was ten years old," she said.

"Practicing, huh?" Dewey teased. Dewey met her on the ground, and they went into each other's arms with a long, deep kiss.

"Come on. If we leave now, we can have breakfast in Piggott, get married, and be on our way before noon," Dewey said, starting for the car.

"We need to get my suitcase first," Unity said. "I hid it behind the azalea bushes."

"All right. Show me where it is."

"Right there," Unity said.

Dewey picked it up, then they moved quietly through the shadows, back to Dewey's car. Just before they got there, however, the car door suddenly opened, causing the interior light to come on. And there, standing in the bar of light cast from the car, with his arms folded across his chest, was the Reverend Phil Rankin.

"Daddy!" Unity said with a gasp.

"Reverend Rankin," Dewey said, his voice tight.

"Good evening, Dewey," Phil said. "It was good of you to stop by."

Military Hospital
Schweinfurt, Germany
May 15

Gunter was pleasantly surprised to see that his breakfast was brought to him not by a hospital orderly, but by Karla.

"You are very early," he said.

"Yes," Karla replied as she set his breakfast tray on the little table that would swing out over his bed. "I have the duty today."

"I am told the cast will come off tomorrow," Gunter said.

"That is great news."

"I am also told that I will always have a limp, but considering the alternative, a limp isn't all that bad." Gunter smiled. "In fact, some consider a limp received as the result of a war injury to be a romantic symbol, like a scar from a dueling fraternity. I'm told the girls find that quite attractive."

"Oh, so you want to be attractive to the girls, do you?" Karla Maas asked with a pout. "Well, you can just be attractive all you want."

Gunter laughed. "I only want to be attractive to one girl," he said.

"And are you going to tell me who that girl might be?"

"Why, you, of course," Gunter said. He laughed again and thumped the hard cast on his leg. "Why do you think I went to all this trouble?"

"Why, Gunter, you didn't have to go to all that trouble for me," Karla said. She smiled. "Though since it did get you home from that awful Russia, I am glad it happened to you."

Gunter got a faraway look in his eyes. "There are tens of thousands who aren't back, and tens of thousands more who will never come back," he said.

"But we are winning, aren't we?" Karla asked anxiously. "I mean, all the newspapers say we are winning."

Gunter looked at Karla. In that moment, she wasn't his fiancée; she was merely one of "them." "Them" were those who weren't a part of the fraternity of close-knit men who had served on the Russian front.

Karla and others like her did not understand and could not understand, even if someone explained to them, what it was really like. A screen dropped across Gunter's eyes. Karla didn't see it, but for the moment, she was shut out of the part of Gunter's soul that was reserved only for those who knew and understood.

"Yes," Gunter said flatly. "We are winning."

"Oh," Karla said, breathing a sigh of relief. "You had me worried there for a moment. You know, there has been some defeatist talk going around, rumors about such things as our army retreating in Russia, rumors that we will withdraw from the country this summer. If, as you and the newspapers say, we are winning, I wonder where such rumors get started?"

"I have no idea," Gunter said easily.

"Was it bad there? I mean, the cold and all? They say Russia gets awfully cold in the winter."

Gunter closed his eyes. He saw again the pile of grotesquely twisted and frozen bodies being pushed into an open hole by a bulldozer. Included in that pile was the little flash of crimson that was the window curtain wrapped around Ernst.

"Yes," Gunter said. "It gets cold."

They were interrupted by a quiet rap on the open door of the room, and Gunter and Karla looked toward the sound. They saw a tall, silver-haired, distinguished-looking man standing there. He was wearing a gray uniform with medals and gold braid on his tunic, and a broad red stripe down his trouser legs.

"General Reinhardt," Karla said, standing quickly.

"Good morning, Fraulein Maas," General Reinhardt said. He looked toward the bed and smiled. "And how is my grandson, the war hero?"

"I'm doing fine, General," Gunter said.

General Reinhardt laughed. "General, is it? And not Grossvater? Well, I suppose that is as it should be." He reached out to take Gunter's hand. "And tell me, how did you find Russia?"

"Cold."

The general laughed again. "Yes, cold. I imagine it was."

"Grandfather, I have a message from . . ."

General Reinhardt put his fingers to Gunter's lips as a signal for him to say no more. Gunter looked at him questioningly but said nothing.

"Gunter, I must go now," Karla said.

"Oh, please don't hurry off on my account," General Reinhardt said.

"I must," Karla said. "My duty starts soon."

"Your duty?"

"Karla is a Lichtspucker Mädchen."

"A what? A light spitter girl?" General Reinhardt asked, confused by the term.

Karla laughed. "That is what they call us, yes," she said. "I track enemy bombers when they come to bomb our country, and with a small beam of light, I mark their location on a large map. It helps our Air Defense."

"I see," General Reinhardt said. He smiled and nodded at her. "You are performing a valuable service for our country, Fraulein. I congratulate you."

"Why, thank you," Karla said. She looked again at Gunter. "Do not forget, you are to come to our house as soon as you can. Mamá wishes to cook a good meal for you."

"The entire Russian army couldn't keep me away," Gunter said.

"Let us take a walk," General Reinhardt suggested after Karla left.

Gunter tapped on his leg cast, making a thumping sound. "Walking is a little difficult," he said.

"You ride; I will walk. I will get a wheelchair."

A moment later General Reinhardt and an orderly returned to the room, with the orderly pushing a wheelchair. The orderly helped Gunter into the chair, then got behind him to push.

"I will push him," General Reinhardt said.

"You, sir?" the orderly asked, shocked at the suggestion. "You are a general, and he is but a private."

"I have been in the army for a long time, Orderly," General Reinhardt said. "I can identify insignia of rank."

"But it isn't proper for a general to push a wheelchair."

"I will decide what is proper," General Reinhardt said forcefully.

The orderly waited but a moment longer, then he clicked his heels together. "Jawohl, Herr General," he said.

General Reinhardt pushed Gunter out of the room, down the hall, and through the lobby. They received shocked stares from people observing the strange sight of a general pushing a private. Then when they were well out into the yard, and away from any possibility of being overheard, General Reinhardt set the brakes on the wheelchair. He sat on a low stone wall as he and his grandson began to talk.

"I want to hear from you what it is really like in Russia," the general said.

"Grandfather, the conditions are beyond appalling," Gunter said. "If hell was ice rather than fire, the Russian front would be hell."

General Reinhardt nodded. "I was afraid such was the case," he said. "In the newspapers, of course, and even, I am ashamed to say, in our official briefings, we are told that we are winning in Russia, that victory is within our grasp." He ran his hand through his silver hair. "But I have long had my suspicions that they were not being entirely truthful with us."

"I bring you a message from General von Paulis."

General Reinhardt looked up in surprise. "You are bringing me a personal message from von Paulis?"

"Yes, sir."

The general nodded. "So that's it."

"I beg your pardon?" Gunter asked, confused by the general's comment.

"I wondered how you managed to get out of that place. General von Paulis arranged it, didn't he?"

"Yes. Grandfather, General von Paulis wants you to go to Hitler and ask him to rescind his order that the Sixth Army not be allowed to withdraw as much as one meter."

General Reinhardt stroked his chin for a moment, then sighed. "I can't do that," he said.

"But you must! If you do not, tens of thousands, perhaps hundreds of thousands of our soldiers will die!" Gunter said in alarm.

General Reinhardt held up his hand to still his grandson's protest. "Gunter, do you think I don't know that?" he asked.

"You know that, and yet you will do nothing?"

"I know that, and I *can* do nothing," the general replied. "*Won't* and *can't* aren't the same thing. You don't understand how it is with Hitler. He does not trust any of his generals, except Jodl and Keitel. And they are nothing but his toadies. Even if I went to them, it would go no further. If it did go further, it could well lead to Hitler bringing von Paulis before a firing squad."

"I didn't know that," Gunter said.

"I wish there was something I could do," General Reinhardt said. "I really do."

"I understand."

"I can do this," General Reinhardt said. "I can see to it that you do not go back there. I will put you on my personal staff."

"No, please, don't do that," Gunter said. "I would feel like a deserter."

"If you go back there, you will die or become a prisoner of war of the Russians," General Reinhardt said. "And one is as bad as the other."

"Yes," Gunter agreed. "That is probably true."

"I'll tell you what. I won't put you on my personal staff. I will send you to North Africa. There is fighting in North Africa as well, but our army is well led by my friend Rommel. And," he said with a smile, "I can guarantee you that you won't be cold."

"I won't be cold," Gunter said. He nodded. "All right, Grandfather, if you can send me to North Africa, please do so."

"I will have your orders prepared as soon as I return." General Reinhardt paused for a moment. "Gunter," he said hesitantly, "I think you should know that there are several of us in the army who see Hitler not as the leader of our country, but as perhaps the instrument of its doom."

"Is this something you discuss openly?" Gunter asked, surprised to hear his grandfather say such a thing.

"No, not at all," General Reinhardt replied quickly. "It is a subject that can be discussed only among people in whom you have the utmost confidence. I must caution you not to mention this conversation to anyone."

"I will say nothing, Grandfather."

"Good." General Reinhardt stood and released the brakes on the wheelchair. "We will return now."

12

Sikeston, Missouri
May 14, 1942

For a long moment, Dewey, Unity, and the Reverend Rankin stood in the front yard, looking at one another. The moon was shining brightly, and it made a tableau of black and silver. Finally, Unity broke the uncomfortable silence.

"Daddy, we're going to be married," she said resolutely.

Phil nodded. "Yes, I thought as much."

"Please, Daddy, don't try to stop us."

"I'm not going to try to stop you."

"You aren't?" Unity asked, surprised relief in her voice.

Phil shook his head. "No," he said. "It's obvious that you two love each other enough that you are going to get married no matter what. Even if I could stop you tonight, you would find some other way to do it."

"Reverend Rankin, we didn't want to defy you, but you left us no—"

Phil held up his hand, interrupting Dewey in midsentence. "You don't have to explain to me, Dewey. I understand."

"You understand?" Unity asked.

"Yes."

"Does that mean we have your blessing?"

"You have my blessing," Phil said, "under one condition."

"What is that?"

"I want you to come down to the church with me for a few moments before you leave. I want to have a prayer with you."

"I don't know," Dewey said. "Could you say the prayer here? We don't have a lot of time."

"Please," Phil said. "Just come down to the church first. That isn't too much of a concession, is it?"

"No, of course not," Dewey said. "We'll go down to the church." Dewey held the door open for Unity, then came around to get into the car. By then Phil had already started his own car, and the exhaust glowed red in the light of the Pontiac's taillights. Dewey backed out, and Phil backed out right behind him. Dewey waited on the street for Phil to take the lead, then they headed toward the church.

"Your father wouldn't try any kind of trick on us, would he?" Dewey asked as they followed Unity's father to the church.

"No, what do you mean?"

"I don't know, like trying to delay us until we won't be able to make connections or something like that."

"No. Dewey, I know he is upset with us for the way we are getting married, but he likes you and he always has. He has said many times that I couldn't have picked a better man to fall in love with. He will come around. Actually, I think he already has. That's why he wanted us to come down to the church for a prayer."

"I suppose you're right," Dewey said. "But I wonder why he didn't ask your mother to come with us."

"I don't know," Unity admitted. "Maybe he just didn't want to wake her up."

"Come on, Unity. Not even to tell you good-bye?"

"I don't know," Unity said. "I'll admit, it does seem a little strange."

"It seems a *lot* strange," Dewey said. "Look, if your father is just getting us down there so he can talk you out of it, are you going to be strong?"

"I told you I would marry you tonight, Dewey, and that is exactly what I intend to do," Unity said.

Phil turned north onto South New Madrid Street. Dewey followed him.

"That's funny," Unity said.

"What is?"

"We're going the back way. I was just wondering why."

"Maybe it's the only door he has the key to," Dewey suggested.

"Maybe so."

Phil pulled into the church staff parking lot, right behind the church building. Dewey parked his Chevrolet beside Phil's Pontiac. The reverend was out first, and he waited a moment until both Dewey and Unity were with him. As soon as they were all together, he led them up a narrow stand of concrete steps to the back door entrance.

"I thought we would go in this way," he said. "That way if any patrolling policeman happens by, he won't get suspicious by seeing three people trying to get into the church in the middle of the night."

Dewey laughed. "What if he did get suspicious? It's your church."

"Humor me," Phil said.

"Okay," Dewey said.

The inside of the church was filled with comfortable and familiar aromas—old leather, furniture polish, and candles.

"I thought we would have our prayer in the nave," Phil said. "It seems more fitting to have it there."

"Yes, sir, I agree," Dewey said.

They walked through the pastor's study, then down a long, dimly lit hall toward the front of the church. "We can go in through here," he said, pointing to a door that opened onto the sanctuary.

Suddenly, all the lights in the church came on, and Dewey and Unity were startled to see that nearly every pew was filled with people.

"What?" Unity said. "Daddy, what is this? What is going on?"

"Honey, I have a confession to make," Phil said. "When you called Dewey yesterday, I happened to pick up the phone. It was my intention to call Deacon Virden, but I overheard you two making plans to run down to Arkansas and get married. I knew then that you were serious. I figured I couldn't stop you, so I decided the best thing to do would be to join you."

"Join us?"

Phil pointed to someone in the front row. "That's Judge Craig," he said. "The good judge has granted you a waiver on the wedding license. All you have to do is sign it, and you can be married tonight, right here in this church, in front of God and these witnesses."

"Daddy!" Unity said excitedly. "You mean you will marry us?"

"I will if you will allow me to do so," Phil said.

"Yes!" Unity said, hurrying to her father and throwing her arms around his neck. "Oh yes!"

"Unity, look over there," Dewey said, pointing to the right side of the nave.

Unity's mother and Millie Gates were coming up the side aisle. Millie was wearing a lavender gown of silk and taffeta. Smiling and clapping happily, Millie hurried to embrace Unity.

"Oh!" Unity said, gasping and hugging her back. "Oh, my, I can't believe this! This is all just too wonderful to be true!"

"We were so afraid you might sneak off before we could do this," Millie said.

"Millie, you knew about this? You knew about this and you didn't tell me?"

"I didn't know about it until your mama called me last night," Millie said. She laughed. "So, it looks like I get to be in your wedding after all. That is, if you still want me," she added.

"Of course, I want you," Unity said. "Oh, and how did you get your gown so quickly? It is beautiful."

"I had to go up to Cape Girardeau to find one. It wasn't my size, but Mama helped me with it."

"Oh, Millie, I can't thank you enough," Unity said. The two young women hugged again.

"Honey, wouldn't you like to change clothes?" Unity's mother asked, holding up a box.

"Change?"

Margaret opened the box to show an exquisite white dress.

"Mama!" Unity gasped. "That's your wedding gown."

"Yes. Would you like to wear it?"

"Oh, Mama, yes," Unity said through her tears.

"If we both help, you can get dressed quickly," Millie suggested. The three of them, Unity, her mother, and Millie, hurried toward the bride's changing room in the back of the church.

"Oh, and, Dewey, I have a surprise for you as well," Phil said. "Something I think will please you."

"Reverend, I can't think of a thing in the world that would please me more than you already have. Unless it was that my parents could be here."

Some of the people in the front pews overheard Dewey, and they laughed.

"What is it?" Dewey asked. "Why are they laughing?"

"You folks want to come on out now?" Phil called.

From the choir's vesting room on the opposite side of the sanctuary, Dewey's mother and father came out.

"Mom, Dad," Dewey said in surprise. "You are in on this too?"

"Yes, dear, we knew all about it," Dewey's mother answered as she hugged him.

"Reverend Rankin called me at the newspaper office yesterday," Green said. "Did you really think we would drive to Dyersburg to see your aunt Amanda on the last day you were home?"

"Well, I did wonder about that," Dewey said. "But I thought you might have a good reason."

"We do have a good reason," Julia said. "To see that you start off your married life properly, not by sneaking off like a bandit in the night, but with the bride's and groom's parents present to give their blessing."

"I am glad you're here," Dewey said. "I can't tell you how glad I am."

In the periphery of his vision, Dewey saw someone else coming out of the choir's vesting room. It was another young man who, like Dewey, was in uniform.

"Travis Logan!" Dewey asked. "What in the world are you doing here?"

Smiling, Travis came over to shake Dewey's hand. "Your mom called me and asked if I could come. And after hearing you talk about Miss Unity Rankin for eight weeks solid, I didn't want to miss this. So, I borrowed Pop's truck, and here I am."

"I'm glad you're here," Dewey said. "Oh, and I would be very honored if you would be my best man," he added.

"Yeah, I was hoping you would ask," Travis said.

Reverend Rankin stepped up to the pulpit and held his hands up to address the congregation.

"Folks, I want to thank all of you for coming on such short notice to help my daughter and this wonderful young man and their families celebrate their marriage," he said. He looked at his watch. "It is now eleven thirty-five. I expect we'll be ready to go by about midnight." He chuckled. "I know it is an unusual time to be holding a wedding, but look at it this way. You have to admit that nobody here is ever going to forget this wedding."

The congregation laughed.

"Hey, Dewey, you better give me your ring," Travis said.

"What?"

"The wedding ring," Travis said. "I'm supposed to give it to you to give to Unity. You do have a ring, don't you?"

"Oh!" Dewey said. "Uh, yes, I do. But it's in the car. I wasn't expecting this."

"Yeah, well, don't worry about it," Travis said. "I thought something like this might happen so, like a good soldier, I came prepared." Travis took a ring from his pocket and showed it to Dewey. "You can use this one for now, then give her yours when this is over."

"You bought a ring?"

Travis smiled. "Nah. This is my sister's ring. I borrowed it from her. So, I'll need to take it back to her."

"All right, and thank your sister for me."

Travis shook his head. "I'd better not. She took it off while she was doing chores. She doesn't know I have it."

Dewey laughed.

Looking toward the back of the church, Phil saw his wife on the arm of Deacon Virden, who was acting as the usher.

"Okay, everyone, take your places," he said.

Giving her son one final hug, Julia and Green took their seats in the front pew. Dewey, Travis, and Phil moved to the center of the sanctuary.

Then Deacon Virden escorted Margaret up the center aisle to her pew. When she was seated, the reverend nodded at the organist.

The organist began playing, and everyone grew quiet, then turned toward the rear of the church. Millie, smiling broadly and carrying a bouquet of pink roses, processed up the aisle, then took her place up front. The music changed to "The Wedding March," and all eyes turned toward Unity.

If an angel of the Lord had come down to walk up the aisle, Dewey did not think she could be any more beautiful than this vision of loveliness who was soon to be his wife.

Ozark, Alabama
May 16, 1942

Unity was still asleep when Dewey slipped out of bed at the Mixon Hotel. They had driven straight through to Ozark after leaving Sikeston, sharing the driving so as to be able to make the trip without having to stop.

Dewey dressed quickly, then went over to the window to look down on Union Street for his first glimpse of the little town that would be his temporary home. More correctly, it would be Unity's temporary home because he would have to spend Monday through Friday, day and night, in the barracks on the base. Only on the weekends would he be able to spend time with Unity.

He looked back toward her, unable to believe his luck at having her here with him. He smiled when he saw that somehow she had managed to pull the sheet up from the bottom of the bed so that her feet were exposed. He pulled the sheet down, but without waking up, she worked to get her feet uncovered again.

"Okay," Dewey said quietly. "So, you don't like your feet covered. I guess we'll be learning lots of new things about each other over the next fifty or sixty years."

Today, they would begin their search for a place to live. Being the son of a newspaper man, Dewey decided that the best place to start the search would be the local newspaper. With one last look back at the sleeping beauty who was his wife, Dewey left the room, closing the door quietly behind him.

The lobby had ceiling fans and a lot of white wicker. The wood floors smelled of wax. A bay window at the front of the lobby looked out onto Highway 231. Dewey stepped up to the counter.

"Does this town have a local newspaper?" he asked.

The woman behind the counter looked tightly corseted. Her wrinkled face was heavily rouged, and the dark lipstick was a little out of the lines of her lips. Her blue-tinted hair was piled up on top of her head.

"That would be the *Southern Star*," she said.

"Where could I buy one?"

"Oh, heavens, dear, you don't have to buy one," she said. "I've got the latest issue right here." The woman handed a folded newspaper to Dewey.

"Thanks," Dewey said. "You know a good place for breakfast?"

"Right next door," the woman said. "The Coffee Pot."

Unity was still asleep when Dewey returned to the room. It had been a long eighteen-hour drive from Sikeston, so Dewey let her sleep, knowing that she must be exhausted.

"Dewey?"

Dewey was sitting on a chair next to the window, looking at ads for apartments. He had circled four of them. He looked up when Unity called him.

"Good morning, sleepyhead," he said.

"My goodness, what time is it?"

"Nearly twelve."

"I slept until noon?" Unity said. She sat up quickly, and when she did, one strap of her nightgown fell down, exposing the top of her breasts. She pulled it back up.

"You have every right to be tired this morning," Dewey said.

"Dewey, that's scandalous," Unity said, blushing.

Dewey laughed. "Scandalous? We are married, after all. But I wasn't talking about that. I meant the long drive here."

Unity smiled in embarrassment. "I, uh, was thinking about the driving too," she said.

Dewey laid the paper down, then walked over to the bed and sat down beside her. "Sure you were," he said. Reaching up, he pulled the strap down, this time exposing more than just the top of her breast.

"Dewey, it's broad daylight!" Unity said.

"Uh-huh. And we are married, and the door is closed," he said.

She smiled at him, then pulled the other strap down. "That's true, isn't it?" she said, putting her hand behind Dewey's head and pulling him to her for a deep lover's kiss.

13

TWA Flight 189, somewhere over Kansas
May 15, 1942

A aron Weintraub was sitting in the last seat on the right side of the DC-3, and because the fuselage narrowed here, and because the exit was right across the aisle from him, his was the only seat. He had chosen this seat for that very reason. He was no misanthrope, but on the flight from Los Angeles to Denver, his seat partner had kept up an incessant and exhausting conversation. He was looking forward to a little peace and quiet for this leg of his journey.

Six thousand feet below the TWA airliner the green-and-brown square landscape of Kansas slid by leisurely, its 200 miles-per-hour speed distorted by the optical illusion of altitude.

Shortly after they took off from Denver's Stapleton Airport, the stewardess began serving lunch, and Aaron watched her as she moved down the aisle, deftly balancing herself against occasional turbulence. She was blond, petite, and very pretty.

At first there was something familiar about her, and it took Aaron a moment to realize what it was. She was exactly like the hundreds of beautiful young women who flocked to Hollywood, hoping to cash in on the beauty God gave them.

At the front of the airplane, sitting on the left, were two army colonels, both in uniform. The colonels, who got on the plane at Denver, were obviously surprised to see a private flying commercially. Aaron noticed that when the stewardess served them, one of them questioned her, and by their glance toward Aaron, it was obvious they were asking about him.

The stewardess made some response, then continued through the plane, serving her passengers. Finally, she got to Aaron's seat. Reaching overhead, she took down a pillow and put it in his lap.

"For the food tray," she said. "Coffee, tea, or milk?"

"Coffee, I think. What are you serving for lunch?"

"We have a nice macaroni and cheese casserole," the stewardess replied, setting the tray on the pillow. "Enjoy it, Mr. Weintraub."

"You know who I am?"

"Your name is on the passenger manifest," she said.

"Oh."

The stewardess chuckled, and with a nod of her head, she indicated the two colonels in front. "Your army friends wanted to know who you were. They wondered how a private could afford to fly."

"What did you tell them?"

"I told them you were President Roosevelt's favorite nephew," she said with a twinkle in her eye.

"Works for me," Aaron replied with a little laugh.

The stewardess started to leave, then she turned back toward him. "You don't remember me, do you, Aaron?"

Aaron looked at her in surprise.

"Don't worry," she said. "I'm not offended."

"You should be," Aaron replied. "I don't know how I could forget someone as pretty as you are."

The stewardess laughed, a lilting wind chime kind of laugh. "Oh, heavens, Aaron, Hollywood is filled with beautiful girls, and as I recall, you were always surrounded by them. I believe they thought you might have some influence with your father. My name is Dawes. Betty Dawes. We were—"

Aaron interrupted her. "We shared algebra and English Lit classes. And I believe you were on the staff of the school newspaper. But you were—"

"A brunette?" Betty asked.

Aaron nodded. "Yes."

"Well, the joy of being a woman is, you can have any color hair you want," Betty said, touching her platinum locks. "The chief of stewardesses suggested that I go blonde."

"You make a beautiful blonde."

"Why, thank you, sir. Will you be spending the night in St. Louis?"

"No," Aaron said. "I'm taking a night flight to Memphis. I'll be in the Memphis airport from midnight until six in the morning, then I'll catch a flight to Montgomery. At Montgomery, I'll be taking a bus down to Camp Rucker, Alabama."

"Too bad," Betty said. "I would have enjoyed having dinner with you."

"I would have as well," Aaron said.

Aaron watched Betty as she walked back to the front of the airplane, then he began eating his lunch.

Ozark, Alabama
May 16, 1942

When José Montoya left Phoenix four days ago, he tried to buy a ticket to Camp Rucker, Alabama. But the brand-new army base was only two months old, and the ticket agent could find no such place on the map. However, José's orders indicated that the base was in Dale County, so the ticket agent looked up Dale County, discovered that Ozark was the county seat, and issued a ticket accordingly.

"If it's in Dale County, surely the folks at the county seat will know where it is," the agent explained. "Once you get to Ozark, you shouldn't have any trouble going the rest of the way."

The bus ride took three and one-half days, and when José got off the bus in Ozark, he was tired, wrinkled, and grubby feeling.

José went into the bus stop restroom, where he shaved, washed himself to the degree he could, then put on a clean uniform. When he came back outside, he was surprised to see that the ticket window was closed and nobody was in the station. A small blackboard beside the window announced, "Next bus is to Mobile at six o'clock tonight. Ticket office will open at four."

Glancing at a clock on the wall, José saw that it was just a little after one. Was he going to have to wait until four o'clock to get information on how to get to Camp Rucker?

José picked up his duffel bag and walked outside. It was hot and muggy, and the uniform he had just put on was already beginning to wilt.

A bread truck stopped right in front of him, and the driver called out to him.

"Hey, soldier boy. Are you a-goin' out to the army camp?"

"Yes," José answered. "Do you know where it is?"

"Better'n that, I'm a-goin' out there right now. I ain't got no seat for you to sit in, but you're welcome to ride along if you're of a mind to."

"Yes, thank you," José said, smiling in relief. "Thank you very much."

The truck was open in front, no doors on either side. It had only a seat for the driver.

"You could put your duffel there and sit on it, I reckon," the driver said, pointing to the floor next to his seat.

José put his duffel on the floor, then sat down. The driver shifted gears and pulled away. As they left the bus station they passed an old house, a huge colonial-style home with Corinthian columns. It was grayed, boarded up, and rotting out in some places. It was obvious that no one had lived in the house for many years, but it was equally obvious that, at one time, it had been grand.

To get to the base, which was some distance from town, they followed a narrow road that wound through a pine forest. They drove in silence for a long time before the driver finally spoke. "I was in the last one."

"I beg your pardon?"

"The big one," the driver said. "The First World War. I was in that one."

"What did you do?"

"I was in the artillery."

"I'm infantry," José said.

"You know what we tell the infantry about artillery, don't you?" the driver asked.

"What?"

The driver chuckled. "We tell them that artillery lends dignity to what would otherwise be one of their uncouth brawls."

José laughed.

"You laugh now, but there'll come a time you'll be thankin' the artillery for pullin' your chestnuts out of the fire."

"I'm sure," José said.

When the driver reached the gate, an MP started to wave him through, then, seeing that he was carrying a soldier, stopped him.

"You got orders?" the MP asked.

José showed them to him. "Do you know where this place is that I'm to report?"

"Yeah," the MP said. He looked up at the driver. "You delivering to the mess halls?"

"I sure am."

"Drop him off at Headquarters and Headquarters Company, First Infantry Battalion."

"You got it," the driver said.

Fifteen minutes later the bread truck stopped behind an obvious mess hall. "This here is Headquarters and Headquarters Company," he said. He pointed between the mess hall and the building next to it. "That there building over there is the orderly room."

"Thanks," José said, hoisting the duffel bag to his shoulder.

"Hey, soldier boy," the driver called.

José turned toward him.

"I'm glad to see you Mexican boys is fightin' with us. You take care now, you hear?"

José started to tell him that he was an American, but he just smiled. "Remember the Alamo," he said.

"Yeah," the driver said. "That too."

Shaking his head, José chuckled as he headed toward the orderly room.

Ozark, Alabama
Saturday, July 18, 1942

"The last flies of summer is always the worst," Mrs. Walker said, brushing one away from her face. "They is the fattest and most irritatin', and doggone if it don't seem to me liken they always got somethin' a-stickin' on their feet."

Jolene Walker was Unity's landlady. She told Unity that she was thirty-three, but she could have been between twenty and fifty. She had hair the color of the sunburned grass outside, called wiregrass by the locals, and she wore colorless, shapeless dresses that hung from her gaunt frame. Her skin was weathered and textured, and her bosom was flat.

"I know what you mean," Unity said, brushing a fly away from her own face. "I don't know which is worse, the flies or the heat."

"Oh, honey, the heat ain't nothin'," Mrs. Walker said. "These last few days has been almost like a cool spell a-comin' on us."

Unity was ironing her clothes. She didn't have to iron Dewey's clothes—he had those done at the base laundry—but it was exhausting enough having to do her own. Standing on her feet on the concrete floor of her basement apartment made the chore particularly hard, so much so that she was experiencing bouts of nausea. It had been hot and humid back in Sikeston, but Unity didn't think she had ever experienced as much discomfort as she had lately.

"Oh, I tol' the plumber to pipe you some water down here so's you don't have to go upstairs and tote a bucket down," Mrs. Walker said. "I shoulda done that before I fixed this basement up as an apartment, but all them soldier boys and their wives started a-comin' in here so quick an' all, I just didn't have time to do it."

"Thank you," Unity said. "Having a water faucet down here will be wonderful."

When Dewey and Unity arrived in Ozark, they had two days before Dewey had to report. They thought they would be able to find a place quickly.

They did not. It wasn't until Sunday afternoon, on the day before Dewey was to report, that they found this place. It had no running water, and there was only one electrical outlet, a naked light bulb on a frayed cord that hung down from the maze of pipes and boards underneath the floor of the Walker house. A screw-in receptacle between the bulb and the wire gave Unity a place to plug in a hot plate, and that was all she had to cook on. She was now using that outlet to plug in her iron.

The apartment was furnished with an iron-frame bed, an unpainted table with two rickety chairs, a sofa, covered with a bedspread to hide the tears and stains, and a large old dresser that Unity actually liked. The walls and floors were concrete. The walls had been painted white, but the paint was chipping. Part of the floor was covered by a faded piece of linoleum, gray with irregular black-and-red designs that looked as if someone had spilled a bucket of paint.

"Now, Amon, he raised a fit when I told him I was pipin' water down here and wasn't goin' to raise the rent none," Mrs. Walker continued. "But I told him, what with you bein' pregnant an' all, it just wasn't Christian to make you have to tote your own water."

Unity gasped and looked up from her ironing. "What's that?" she asked. "What did you say?"

"I told him we wasn't goin' to charge one penny more than we been chargin', just 'cause we're pipin' water down here."

"No," Unity said, waving her hand. "I mean before that. Something about me being pregnant?"

"Yes. You know, you got to be careful because you—"

"What makes you think I'm pregnant?" Unity asked, interrupting Mrs. Walker.

Mrs. Walker looked confused. "You mean you ain't pregnant?"

Unity had not even considered the possibility before this moment. "I don't know," she said.

"Honey, when was the last time you had the curse?" Mrs. Walker asked.

"The curse?"

"Your time of the month."

"Oh, you mean my period," Unity said. "Well, it's been . . ." Unity paused to think about it, then she gasped. So much had happened over the last two months that her period had never crossed her mind. But as she thought back on it now, she realized that her last time was before she and Dewey were married, and that was more than two months ago.

"It's been two months," she said in an awe-struck voice.

"Uh-huh, and you been havin' the sickness, too, ain't you?"

"Yes," Unity agreed.

"Honey, I done birthed three of my own," Mrs. Walker said. "And all my sisters has had a passel that I've helped with. If I've ever seen a woman that was pregnant, it's you."

Unity took in a quick breath, then smiled and put her hand to her mouth.

"Yes," she said. "Yes, maybe I am pregnant."

"No maybe to it, honey. You can mark my words on that."

Unity heard a car horn outside and, recognizing it, smiled happily and put the iron down. "It's Dewey!" she said.

"Seein' as you didn't even know you was pregnant, I don't reckon Dewey knows either, does he?" Mrs. Walker asked.

Unity shook her head.

"Uh-huh. Well, I 'spec' maybe I better get on back upstairs," Mrs. Walker said. "You won't be wantin' to share your time with your man with me. Especially seein' as you got somethin' to tell him now."

Not until after the Saturday morning inspections could the soldiers get passes to go into town, and in that, the married men were no different from the single men, who could also get a thirty-six-hour pass good from Saturday noon until Monday morning reveille.

Anxious to tell Dewey the news, Unity hurried up the stairs to greet him. She was happy to see him get out of the car but surprised, and a little disappointed, to see five other soldiers getting out with him.

"Hi, honey," Dewey said. "You remember Travis Logan."

"Yes, of course," Unity said.

"And these fellas are José Montoya, Aaron Weintraub, Roberto Sangremano, and Alphabet."

"Yes, I've heard you speak of all of them," Unity said, smiling as she greeted them. "I'm happy to meet all of you at last. And so, you are the one they call Alphabet?" she asked.

"Yes, ma'am," Alphabet said.

"Nobody can pronounce his name," Travis explained.

"Look, it's not really that hard to pronounce," Alphabet said. "It's Sta-ko-viack."

"Yeah, so you say. But tell her how it's spelled," Roberto said.

"S-t-a-k-o-w-i-a-c," Alphabet said.

"You see why everyone has trouble with it?" Travis asked. "That's why everyone just calls him Alphabet."

"Well, I'm very pleased to be able to meet all of Dewey's friends," Unity said.

"We aren't just friends," Alphabet said. "We are the Double Musketeers."

"The Double Musketeers?" Unity asked, confused by the comment.

"Yeah, you know, like in the Three Musketeers? Well, we're like them, only there are six of us."

"And we're going to have a party this afternoon," Dewey said.

"A party?" Unity said weakly. "Oh, Dewey, I don't know. We don't have . . ."

"Don't worry. We brought our party with us," Travis said. "Show her, fellas."

The men reached back into the car, then brought out five loaves of bread.

"We're going to have a bread party?"

Dewey laughed. "A toast party," he said. "Aaron bought us a wedding present."

"Belated wedding present," Aaron said.

"But like I told him, better late than never," Dewey said. Reaching into the car, he pulled out a toaster. "Ta-da!" he said. "What do you think?"

"Oh no, you shouldn't have!" Unity said. "Toasters are expensive, aren't they?"

"That doesn't matter to Aaron. He's rich," Travis commented.

"I'm not rich," Aaron said. "But my father is, and he provides me with a generous allowance."

"That's . . . very nice of him," Unity said. She looked at the toaster. "And buying us this present is very nice of you."

"What's the use of having money if you can't spend it on your friends?" Aaron asked.

"Come on, let's make toast," Roberto said.

"Okay, come on inside, guys. Let me show you where we live." Taking Unity by the hand, Dewey led the group down the narrow, rather rickety stairs to the basement apartment. "Do we have any butter or jelly?" he asked.

"We just have a little bit of margarine and a little bit of jelly," Unity replied. "It's two more weeks until payday."

"Well, then we'll just have dry toast," Dewey said.

"Hey, nice place," Alphabet said.

Dewey put the toaster on the little counter alongside the hot plate. Then unplugging the iron, he plugged in the toaster.

"Travis, you and Roberto slice the bread," he said. "There's a bread knife in that drawer. I'll toast."

"What about me?" Aaron asked.

"You, José, and Alphabet just sit over there and entertain Unity," Dewey invited.

"Very well. Come, join us, Mrs. Bradley. I shall entertain you with stories of the antics of my Hollywood associates."

"But don't believe a word of any of them," Alphabet said. "They are all lies."

"Of course they are," Aaron said. "How can I make myself the center of all my stories if I don't lie?"

"First two slices coming out," Dewey said a moment later. "The first piece goes to Unity because she is the only lady here, and the other to Aaron because he furnished the toaster."

"Mmm," Unity said after taking the first bite. "I do believe this is the best toast I have ever tasted."

"You haven't even noticed anything different about our uniforms yet, have you?" Dewey asked.

"Different? No, I . . . wait! You have a stripe! All of you have stripes!"

"That's right," Dewey said proudly. "My dear, you are no longer married to a private. You are now married to a private first class."

"That's good, isn't it?"

"I'll say it's good. It means eight dollars more per month," Dewey said.

"You didn't mention our new shoulder patch," Roberto said.

"You have a new shoulder patch?"

Roberto pointed to the patch on his left sleeve. It was a shield-shaped patch, pointed at the bottom. The background color of the patch was olive-drab green. In the middle of the patch was the numeral one in red.

"What does that mean?" Unity asked.

"That means our battalion is no longer just a training battalion," Travis explained. "We are now part of the First Infantry Division. Or soon will be. We'll be joining them when we leave here."

For the next hour they told stories of funny things that had happened during training and of their own pasts. All enjoyed the story of Dewey and Unity's wedding, even Travis Logan's insistence that he had saved the day by furnishing Dewey with the wedding ring he had "stolen" from his sister.

The day wore on, and as the men showed no signs that they were going to leave, Unity became a bit anxious. If they were going to stay for supper, she didn't have enough to feed them, and they had no money to go to the store to buy anything. She didn't want to tell them to leave, but she was hoping they would do so before supper.

Once, during the afternoon, she found an opportunity to speak with Dewey.

"Are they going to stay for supper?" she asked.

"I don't know. I haven't specifically invited them, but I haven't told them not to," Dewey replied.

"Dewey, we don't have anything to give them," she said. "I just barely have enough food left to get us through the rest of the month."

Dewey chuckled. "Well, we could always eat toast."

"I suppose so," Unity said. "But it just upsets me to have guests, in fact, our very first guests, and have nothing to give them but bread. Bread that they brought themselves, I hasten to add."

"Something will come up."

"What?"

"I don't know. Why don't we just leave it in the hands of the Lord?"

"Leave it in the hands of the Lord? Well, that's a testament of faith and all that, but it isn't really very practical, is it? I mean we have five hungry men here, and if they stay for dinner, we will have nothing to offer them."

"Maybe they'll leave before dinner. After all, they are single guys on a thirty-six-hour pass. I'm sure they can think of a better way to spend their time than with some married couple."

They heard someone knocking, and Dewey climbed up the steps to see who it was. When he opened the door, he found Amon Walker, their landlord.

"Mr. Walker," Dewey said. "Hello."

"Dewey, me 'n' some of my friends went a-fishin' this mornin'," Walker said. "And we done real good too. So I had the missus fry up a mess of catfish. I figured that iffen your friends was a-plannin' on stayin' to supper, why, maybe y'all could use it."

"Yes!" Dewey said. "Yes, I thank you, Mr. Walker. That's very generous of you."

"Just a second. I left it on the porch," Walker said. Walker stepped back over to the porch, and a moment later he returned with a roasting pan filled with fried fish. "Jolene says to tell your missus she can just bring the roastin' pan back when y'all are finished with it."

"Mr. Walker, you don't know what this means to us. I can't thank you enough," Dewey said, taking the fried fish from his landlord. He carried it down into the basement.

"Dewey, what is it?" Unity asked. "Who was that?"

"That was Mr. Walker."

"Who is Walker?" Alphabet asked.

"Our landlord."

"Oh, have we been making too much noise?" Roberto asked. "Because if we have, I apologize. You folks have to live here. I would hate to get you into trouble."

"No, it's nothing like that," Dewey said. "Listen, would you guys like to stay for supper?"

"Dewey?" Unity said, packing all her anxiousness in that one word.

"Worry not, Unity. The Lord has provided. Mr. Walker just brought us some fried fish," Dewey said, taking the top off the roaster and showing a large stack of golden-brown, corn-meal-encrusted, fried fish.

"Dewey?" Unity said that night as she and Dewey lay in each other's arms in the iron bed in the almost pitch-black darkness of their basement apartment.

"Yes?"

"How did you know?"

"How did I know what?"

"Tonight. How did you know that the Lord would provide?"

"I wish I could come up with some great theological explanation, but I can't. The truth is, I was as concerned over it as you were."

"You didn't show it."

"I was practicing my male stoicism," he said.

"Well, let me see just how stoic you can be when you learn about something else the Lord has provided."

"What is that?" Dewey asked.

Unity took Dewey's hand in hers, then, raising her nightgown, placed his hand on her bare belly. "In here," she said.

"In here? In here what?" Dewey asked, still not understanding what she was talking about.

"Our baby."

Dewey jerked his hand away from her stomach as if he had touched something hot. "What?" he gasped.

Unity laughed and took his hand, then put it back on her stomach. "What happened to that male stoicism you were so proud of?"

"You're . . . you're pregnant?"

"Yes," Unity said. "Oh, Dewey, isn't it wonderful?"

Dewey was quiet for a long moment.

"Dewey? You are pleased, aren't you?" Unity asked, her voice showing a bit of worry over his reaction.

Dewey took Unity's hand in his. "Yes, honey, it's wonderful," he said.

"I knew you would be pleased," Unity said happily, lifting his hand to her lips to kiss it. "It will be a boy. I know it will."

"Honey, I don't care if it's a boy or a girl. I love you and I will love our child, and that's all that matters."

"Yes," Unity said. "That's all that matters."

That night Dewey lay beside Unity, awake long after she had gone to sleep. He had not planned this, had not wanted to leave Unity with the burden of a baby during his absence. But she was so pleased about it.

He had a secret of his own to share. He wasn't going to tell her until tomorrow, when he could find a way to break it easily to her.

Their attachment to the First Infantry Division entailed considerably more than just sewing on the patch. Their training cycle would end this Wednesday on the twenty-second. They had orders to report to Fort Dix, New Jersey, on Friday, July 31. On Sunday, August 2, Dewey and the entire First Infantry Division would load onto the *Queen Mary* for immediate departure. They were going to Europe.

"Dear Lord," Dewey prayed, "protect Unity and our baby. And if it is Your will that I not return from this war, then I ask that You watch over them, now and forever. In Jesus' name, I pray. Amen."

14

Wertheim, Germany
July 20, 1942

Although he no longer needed crutches or even a cane, Gunter still walked with a slight limp as he moved through the crowd at the railway station. Nestled in the mountains of Bavaria, Wertheim was a very pretty town, the kind of town that used to appear on the travel posters in the offices of shipping lines, enticing tourists to come to beautiful Germany for their vacation.

Gunter pulled the piece of paper from his uniform and checked the address: 2117 Lindenstrasse. Exiting the depot, Gunter thought that it might be a nice gesture to take some flowers to Frau Dostler, and remembering a flower vendor he had done business with before, he walked down to the platz.

It seemed there were fewer kiosks than there used to be. Noticeably missing were the kiosks that sold sausages and cheese. There were still a few flower stands, but he didn't see the one he was looking for.

"Can I help you with something, soldier?" a man asked. The man was sitting on a chair behind a counter that was selling various trinkets, including gold-plated swastikas hanging from chains, buttons with pictures of Hitler, and small Nazi flags. The man, who had only one leg, had his crutches on the ground beside him. And although he was in mufti, an Iron Cross was pinned to his shirt. By his age, Gunter knew that both the wound and the medal had to come in this war, not the previous one.

"Where were you wounded?" Gunter asked.

"In France," the man answered. He laughed, a short, bitter laugh. "We went through France as if we were on tour there. Very few Germans were wounded, but I," he tapped on the folded trouser leg beneath his stub, "I won the prize."

"And the Iron Cross," Gunter said. "You have my respect."

"I saw you limping as you approached the platz. Where were you wounded?"

"On the Russian front," Gunter said.

"I have a brother on the Russian front."

"I am sorry," Gunter said.

The wounded soldier needed no explanation for Gunter's reply. The two exchanged a long, knowing look that could be shared only by those who were members of the fraternity of men who had faced death on the battlefield.

"Your wound brought you home?"

"Yes." Gunter did not explain that his coming home was expedited by the fact that he was Colonel-General Reinhardt's grandson.

"You are the lucky one," the wounded soldier said.

"Yes." Gunter looked around the platz.

"Who are you looking for?"

"There used to be a man who sold flowers here."

"There are many who sell flowers here."

"No, I'm looking for a specific person. He was an old man, tall and thin, bald on the top, but with hair like this." He made a motion with his hands just over each ear, indicating that the hair was bushy. "He was very funny and would make up poetry to go with the flowers he sold."

"Ah," the wounded soldier said. "The Jew."

"Jew? I don't know, he might have been. I guess I never considered whether he was or not."

"His name was Gelbman," the wounded soldier said. "The Jew."

"Has he gone out of business?"

The wounded soldier looked at Gunter suspiciously. "Are you serious?" he asked.

"Yes," Gunter replied, still not entirely following the conversation. He held up the note. "I have been asked to check in on the wife of my doctor in Russia. I wanted to take her some flowers. I wanted to use Gelbman because he would write the poem for me, and I could give it to Frau Dostler, along with the flowers."

"He is a Jew. Do you think that any Jews are still doing business?"

"I know that Jews who are in critical positions, positions where they might be of some danger to our country, have been replaced for reasons of state security," Gunter said. "But this man sells flowers. Of what danger to our country can he be?"

As Gunter stood there talking to the wounded soldier, he didn't see a man in a striped suit and fedora approaching the kiosk. The wounded soldier saw him, though.

"Yes, sir," the wounded soldier said expressively. "I think your mädchen would love to have a golden swastika." He picked up one of the chains and held it so that the little swastika flashed in the midday sun.

"Of course, she might also want to show her loyalty to the Führer by wearing this button with his picture."

Gunter picked up a warning glance in the wounded soldier's eyes and reacted quickly.

"Which is the least expensive?" he asked. "She is only a temporary girlfriend."

"Oh, well, then perhaps you would prefer the flag. It is but fifty pfennig." Then, to the man in the pin-striped suit, he asked, "What do you think, Herr Best? Will this flag be enough inducement for our hero of the fatherland, just back from Russia, to win the affections of one of our fair young women? The *temporary* affections, that is," he added with a broad wink.

Herr Best laughed lecherously. "I think you could have had the Russian whores for nothing, could you not?" he asked. "Yes, I think Russia is a good place for a young man to be."

"Oh, I agree," Gunter said. "You should go there."

The tiniest trace of doubt flickered in Herr Best's eyes, then he chuckled. "Yes," he said. "Perhaps I should." He walked away.

"Gestapo," the wounded soldier said.

"Thank you for the warning."

"You are welcome. A word of advice, my friend? Do not inquire about Jews you might find missing. It isn't healthy."

"Thank you again," Gunter said.

"Do you want the flag?"

Gunter chuckled. "I think I owe it to you," he said. He paid for the flag, but when the wounded soldier started to give it to him, he held out his hand. "No, you keep it. This way you can sell it again."

"Good luck," the wounded soldier said.

Gunter found that 2117 Lindenstrasse was an apothecary shop. On the side of the shop, there was a stairway, and alongside the stairway, a mailbox with the name H. DOSTLER. Gunter looked down at the bouquet of yellow roses he had bought, then squaring his shoulders, he climbed the stairs. In the middle of the door was a twist doorbell with a very small sign that read H. DOSTLER.

Gunter twisted the bell and heard it ring.

A moment later a woman opened the door. She was wearing a pale green dress that looked as if it had been, at one time, the kind of dress a person would wear when going out to dinner or a nightclub. The dress showed considerable wear and tear, obviously long past its prime as a dress of celebration.

The woman was smoking a cigarette, and it hung casually from her lips. A tendril of errant hair blocked one eye. She looked to be in her late thirties or early forties, was probably very pretty at one time, but now looked very tired.

"Ja?" she asked.

"Frau Dostler?"

"I am Frau Dostler."

Gunter handed her the bouquet of roses, and Frau Dostler looked at them with an expression of confusion.

"These are from your husband," Gunter said.

"My husband?" Frau Dostler gasped and clutched at her neck. "Oh, Gott im Himmel! My husband! Is he all right?"

"Yes, yes," Gunter said quickly, concerned that he had unintentionally caused her to think the worst had happened to her husband. "He was very good when I left him."

"You were in Russia?"

"Yes."

"How is it that you are back? I did not think anyone had come back from Russia."

"I was wounded," Gunter said. "Dr. Dostler treated me."

"Please, please, won't you come in?" Frau Dostler asked, stepping back from the door.

"Thank you."

"Would you like some wine? A beer perhaps?"

"A small glass of wine would be nice," Gunter said.

Frau Dostler pointed to a sofa. "Sit," she offered.

Gunter looked around. The dark, massive furniture seemed out of place in what was a rather small apartment. The radio was a large console type, polished wood, upon which sat a bowl of wax fruit. On the wall was a picture of Dr. and Frau Dostler in what was obviously a happier time. Both were smiling broadly for the camera; Frau Dostler had been a beautiful woman. Also on the wall was a picture of Hitler, a rather somber portrait, just his head, floating in a sea of black, with his dark, piercing eyes staring out from the photograph.

Frau Dostler returned minutes later, and Gunter noticed that she had groomed herself somewhat while she was in the other room. Her hair was neatly combed, and she had put on lipstick. The cigarette was gone. She smiled at him as she handed him the glass of wine.

"Tell me about Werner," she said. "How did he look?"

"He looked very well," Gunter said. "Healthy, full of energy and optimism."

Frau Dostler laughed. "That is my Werner," she said. "Always the optimist. Do you think he will be home by Christmas?"

"I . . . I don't know," Gunter answered. He believed he could say, with absolute certainty, that her husband would not be home this Christmas, and there was a very good possibility that he would never be home for any Christmas. But he didn't see any reason for upsetting Frau Dostler now.

"Because, in his last letter, he assured me that he would be," Frau Dostler said. "When you go back, please tell him how much I miss him and how much I love him."

"Yes," Gunter said. "I will tell him that. And, of course, that is the message he has sent to you as well."

The smile left Frau Dostler's face, and her eyes welled with tears.

Gunter looked away, unable to meet her gaze. He hoped that she could not see in his face the truth: He wasn't going back at all.

"The Führer is such a brilliant man. If the generals had only listened to him, I'm sure the war in Russia would be over by now and all our men would be home. I don't know why they won't listen to him."

"I'm sure everyone is doing his best," Gunter said.

"Oh, please, do not misunderstand. This isn't defeatist talk," Frau Dostler said, a hint of fright in her voice. "I am not a defeatist."

"I know that you are not," Gunter said. "If every German had your positive attitude, I'm sure we would all be the better for it."

"Yes," she said, a smile of relief crossing her face. "Yes, I think so too."

They talked for several more minutes, with Gunter lying to her about how abundant food was, and how they managed to stay warm during the coldest part of the winter. He told her little funny stories that made her laugh and spared her the true stories that would make her cry.

"Are you a Christian, Frau Dostler?" Gunter asked. When he saw another flash of concern cross her face, he added, "Because I am. And I thought that, if you were, before I leave, perhaps we could say a prayer together for the safety of your husband and of all our men in Russia."

"Yes," Frau Dostler said, a relieved smile returning.

Gunter stood, and Frau Dostler stood as well. Bowing his head, Gunter prayed aloud: "Almighty and everlasting God, from whom come all things, send down upon Herr Dr. Werner Dostler, his wife, Helga, and upon all our soldiers and their wives and families, and upon those who lead them, the spirit of Thy grace. Pour upon them the continual dew of Thy blessing. Grant this, O Lord, in the name of our Savior, Jesus Christ. Amen."

"Amen," Frau Dostler added as Gunter crossed himself.

Würzburg, Germany
July 21, 1942

Gunter stood in the hallway of the third floor of the science and engineering building of the university, staring at the frosted glass pane on the door. The gold leaf letters were gone, but the shadow of the words they formed could still be read.

PROFESSOR ARZT HANS WERFEL
DIREKTOR, ABTEILUNG FÜR PHYSIK

As Gunter stood there, studying the shadowed letters, a door just down the hall opened, and a man in a white lab coat stepped into the hall.

"Gunter? Gunter Reinhardt, is that you?"

The man was bald and wore rimless glasses, held on by very large ears. Gunter remembered that when he was in class, some aeronautical engineering students worked out lift versus weight ratios and came to the conclusion that, if properly launched in a sufficient headwind, Dr. Schmidt's ears would allow him to glide.

He smiled as he recalled that, and he extended his hand and walked toward the professor.

"Dr. Schmidt," he said. "How are you?"

"I am fine, dear boy, fine," Dr. Schmidt said. "And how are you doing?"

"I'm doing well, thank you," Gunter said.

"You are looking trim. The army must agree with you."

"Yes."

"And are you still working with optics?" Dr. Schmidt asked.

"A little," Gunter answered.

"I know it must be difficult to continue your work while in the army, but you must. Your paper on the use of optics for gathering light is the most brilliant I've ever read. You must keep it up."

"Thank you for your compliment, Doctor. I will do what I can," Gunter replied. He nodded toward the door with the shadowed letters. "What happened to Dr. Werfel?"

"Have you seen our garden? We are quite pleased with it," Dr. Schmidt said. "Come, let me show it to you."

The expression in Dr. Schmidt's eyes indicated that this was more than an idle suggestion.

"I would love to see the garden," Gunter said. "It is one of the things I miss most about the university."

"Oh, you don't miss my brilliant lectures?" Dr. Schmidt said, and they both laughed, more heartily than necessary as they passed a man who was sitting on a bench, reading a newspaper.

Gunter noticed that the man was wearing the same kind of pin-striped suit as Herr Best, the Gestapo agent the wounded soldier had pointed out to him when he was in Wertheim, the day before.

The garden was ablaze with flowers of all hues and varieties, and as they walked through the garden, Dr. Schmidt pointed out each plant, giving its Latin name. When Dr. Schmidt had first mentioned that they should look at the garden, Gunter thought it was a code in order to get them away from the building. But Dr. Schmidt was showing the garden off with such enthusiasm that Gunter began to believe this really was the purpose.

"Whew," Dr. Schmidt said when they reached the far end of the garden. "That's quite a walk for an old man like me. Why don't we have a seat on that bench and rest for a moment before we return?"

"Very well," Gunter agreed.

The two sat on the bench, and Dr. Schmidt removed his glasses and polished them for a long moment before either of them said anything. Finally, Dr. Schmidt put his glasses back on, hooking them very methodically over one ear at a time.

"Dr. Werfel is dead," he said simply.

"Dead? Oh, I didn't know that. I'm sorry to hear it. How did he die?"

"He didn't die. He was killed," Dr. Schmidt said.

"Killed?"

"He was a Jew."

"Yes, of course, he was a Jew," Gunter said. "I don't think there was anyone in the university, certainly not in the department, who did not know that he was a Jew."

"He was deemed a risk to the state."

"But how can that be? Dr. Werfel was an officer during the first war. He was very proud of that. He had a picture of himself in the uniform of an imperial officer, wearing an Iron Cross first class."

"Yes," Dr. Schmidt agreed. "But evidently heroic service during the first war and a brilliant and inquiring mind were not enough to offset the fact that he was a Jew."

"What . . . when?" Gunter asked.

"It has been a year," Dr. Schmidt said. "They came for him one day while he was teaching. They went into the classroom, and right in the middle of a lecture, from in front of his students, they dragged him out."

"Had his lectures become political?"

"His lecture that day was on the atomic weight of elements," Dr. Schmidt said. He was silent for a moment, then he said, "His last words to me were to please see to it that the scores from the last exam were properly posted so that his students would get credit for their course. He was a teacher until his last breath." Dr. Schmidt blinked several times, and Gunter saw that his eyes had filled with tears. Once more he removed his glasses and began polishing them, but he used the handkerchief on his eyes before he put the glasses back on.

"I don't understand," Gunter said. "If he has been gone for a year, why has the door glass not been changed? The gold leaf is gone, but his name can still be read."

"That is my doing," Dr. Schmidt said. "It is my way of protest. It is a small demonstration, I confess, but it is a protest nonetheless." He looked at Gunter. "Gunter, I am putting my life in your hands by such an admission."

"You are in no danger," Gunter assured him.

Dr. Schmidt pinched the bridge of his nose. "I do not know what has happened to this country that I love. We have become a pariah among nations. Our jackbooted soldiers, the epitome of all evil."

"Oh, I'm sure it isn't as bad as all that," Gunter said. "I have seen great hardships among our soldiers. I have also seen great acts of kindness."

"You have seen nothing in your service that would give you pause?" Dr. Schmidt asked.

Gunter was quiet for a long moment, recalling the incident in the village where he saw the young woman and four of her comrades hanged by the SS.

"You have seen something, haven't you?" Dr. Schmidt said, capitalizing on Gunter's extended silence.

"No," Gunter insisted. "No, I have seen the army do nothing that would bring shame upon the fatherland." He was very specific to limit his comment to the army.

Bavarian Luftangriffsschutzhauptquartier
July 30, 1942

"Oh yes, you are the gentleman friend of Karla Maas," the woman in the front said to Gunter when he went into the Bavarian Air Raid Protection Headquarters. "Fraulein Maas said that you would be calling for her today. I believe you are going to a concert tonight?"

"Yes," Gunter replied. He looked around the room. "This building does not look large enough to be the headquarters of the air raid protection for all of Bavaria."

The woman laughed. "Ah, but you are seeing only what is above ground. The real operation is underground, through that door and downstairs. Would you like to see it?"

"Yes," Gunter replied. "Would I be allowed?"

"I will take you," the woman offered.

"Thank you."

The woman opened a door, then led Gunter down a set of stairs to a landing where there was a second door. Opening that door, they went down another set of stairs to a second landing and another door. Beyond that door were one more set of stairs and a third door before they came out onto a platform that overlooked a large, sunken room.

There were several small tables in the sunken room, and at each table sat a woman wearing a headset and microphone, much like that worn by telephone operators. In front of each station, there was a little light projector that the women used to project the planes' positions onto the rear of a translucent map of Europe. Behind the map, others would plot the course of the approaching planes by attaching cutout airplanes.

"Are many airplanes out there?" Gunter asked, looking at the map.

"Tonight, there are several. Each little airplane you see represents ten airplanes," his guide said.

Quickly, Gunter counted the number of airplanes in one of the formations. "Fifty? There are fifty planes. That means five hundred?"

"Yes," the woman said. "It looks as if they are heading toward Frankfurt. It's going to be a hard night there, I think."

At that moment, Karla happened to look up, and seeing him, she smiled broadly and waved. Calling one of the other women over, Karla passed her headset to the new woman, then she came up the stairs.

"Did you have a nice visit to Wertheim and Würzburg?" Karla asked brightly as they left the operations area.

"Yes," Gunter replied. "The doctor's wife was very pleasant."

"And was she beautiful?"

"She was very pretty, yes."

"Not too pretty, I hope."

Gunter laughed. "How can you be jealous of an old woman?"

When they stepped outside, Karla saw her father's Mercedes parked on the street. "You have my father's car?"

"Yes," Gunter said. "He very kindly loaned it to us. He told me that we should have a good time tonight."

"A good time. Yes, that would be nice. Where shall we go?"

"I think to the Wilder Eberweinkeller," Gunter said.

"Yes. I am told they have a good band there."

When Gunter parked in front of the Wild Boar Wine Cellar, two army officers were standing in front of the club. Seeing the Mercedes, they came to attention and saluted, but when a private got out of the car, they were red-faced and embarrassed.

Gunter held the door open for Karla.

"Private," one of the officers said angrily, "what are you doing driving a car like that?"

"The car belongs to my father," Karla said. "Perhaps you have heard of him? He is Reichsmarschall Goering."

At the mention of Goering's name, both officers came to attention and saluted again, this time presenting the extended arm salute. "Heil Hitler! Our apologies, Fraulein," one of them said contritely.

Gunter returned the salute, then escorted Karla inside. Once they were inside, Karla could no longer contain her laughter.

"Did you see how they changed their tune when I told them Goering was my father?"

"Reichsmarschall Goering?" Gunter said. "You had to choose Goering?"

"Well, he was the first name that came to mind," Karla replied. "Come, let's find a table."

The wine cellar was filled with men and women. Practically every man present was in uniform. The music was loud and the conversation and laughter even louder. It was as if all were forcing themselves to have a good time.

The wine and beer flowed freely, and a buxom waitress wearing a Bavarian peasant's costume walked by. She was carrying ten mugs of beer, five in each hand, holding them by their handles.

"It's funny," Karla said. "There is no meat in any of the shops, no fresh fruit, no butter, no eggs, but of the wine and the beer there is no shortage." The tone of her voice indicated that, though she said it was funny, she didn't really think so.

"Maybe the idea is that if the citizens drink enough, they won't notice the shortage of other things," Gunter said.

There were no empty tables, but two Luftwaffe officers at one table invited Gunter and Karla to join them.

"Thank you, sirs," Gunter said as he pulled a chair out for Karla.

"Think nothing of it, Private," one of the officers replied. "For the opportunity to share a table with such a beautiful lady, even for a short time, I would gladly allow a private to join us." He took Karla's hand and kissed it. "Fraulein, I am Todeshandler."

"Your name is Death Dealer?" Gunter asked.

"His real name is Captain Lange," the other officer said. "Todeshandler is his radio call sign."

"I fly the Me-109," Captain Lange said. "And I have shot down sixteen British bombers."

"Hah! He got his kills with the easy ones," the other officer said. "The Blenheims, the Whitleys, the Wellingtons. Wait until the Americans begin their raids. I think their B-17s will not be so easy to shoot down."

"Two of my kills have been against Lancasters," Lange said. "They are quite formidable."

"I am teasing you, Captain. You are the best in our squadron, and I know that."

Captain Lange smiled. "Lieutenant Fromm has to say that. He holds my coat while I do battle."

"Holds your coat?" Karla asked.

"I am his wingman," Lieutenant Fromm said. He looked over at Gunter. "And what about you, Private? What is your job? Do you stand guard around city hall?"

"I think that would be a very good job," Gunter replied.

Captain Lange looked closely at Gunter. "I think you are not a rear echelon warrior," he said.

"I am enjoying a furlough," Gunter replied without further explanation.

"A convalescent furlough," Karla said proudly. "He was wounded."

"Where were you wounded?"

"In Russia," Karla said.

"Russia? That is impossible. No one who has gone to Russia has returned," Fromm said.

"Tell them, Gunter," Karla said.

Gunter forced a smile. "We have come here to have fun," he said. "Let us talk of other things."

"I knew you hadn't been to Russia," Fromm said dismissively. "You shouldn't make such claims, for in so doing, you besmirch the honor of our brave soldiers who are there."

"He is not making false claims," Lange said.

"Of course he is," Fromm insisted. "No soldier has returned from Russia. We both know that."

"Look into his eyes," Lange said.

"What?"

"Look into his eyes," Lange said again.

"I don't understand. Why should I look into his eyes?" Fromm asked.

Lange looked intently into Gunter's eyes, and Gunter returned the captain's gaze with an unflinching stare.

Lange pointed directly at Gunter's eyes. "These eyes have seen death," he said. "And not like us, where death is detached, a flash of fire, an unheard scream in the cold and impersonal sky, followed by a victory roll. This man has seen death up close."

"Please, Todeshandler," Karla said, holding Gunter's arm. "Let us not talk of such things."

Captain Lange looked at Karla with an expression of curiosity on his face. "Have we met?" he asked.

"No."

"I'm sure we have met. I know your voice."

"We have never met," Karla said.

At that moment the band began playing a Bavarian folk song. At all the tables, men and women began singing and waving their beer mugs back and forth in time with the music.

> *Du kannst nicht treu sein, nein, nein, das kannst du nicht,*
> *wenn auch dein Mund mir wahre Liebe verspricht.*

> *You cannot be loyal, no, no, you can't do this*
> *even if your mouth promises me true love.*

The club was warm, the food and drink were plentiful, the music was inviting, the men and women were smiling and happy, and the atmosphere was convivial.

Russia seemed far, far away.

15

New York City
August 2, 1942

Dewey had never seen anything as large as the *Queen Mary*. It looked more like a huge building than a ship, towering as it did over the pier. They had been told that the entire First Infantry Division would be transported by this vessel. That would be fifteen thousand men, plus a crew of about a thousand.

Dewey had a thought, and he laughed out loud.

"What is it?" Travis asked. "What are you laughing at?"

"I was just thinking. You could put every man, woman, and child from Pilot Town and Sikeston on this ship."

"Yes, and with room left over for half the town of Blytheville," Travis agreed.

The pier alongside the ship was crowded with men and their duffel bags. They were boarding by battalions, and Dewey's battalion had not been called. The boarding process was so slow that they were told it would be another two or three hours before they went aboard.

Because Roberto Sangremano was from New York, his family had come down to the pier to see him off. The visitors and well-wishers weren't allowed free roam of the pier, but the army had set aside an area where they and the soldiers could meet. Roberto had gone there shortly after they arrived. When the men looked up, though, they saw Roberto coming toward them.

"Hey, Roberto, what are you doing here?" Aaron asked. "Did your family leave?"

"No, they are still here," Roberto said. "I want you guys to meet them."

At Roberto's urging, Dewey, Travis, Aaron, Alphabet, and José went with him to the visiting area.

"There they are," Roberto said. "My ma, pa, and little sister."

Roberto's father was short and bald with dark, bushy eyebrows. His mother was equally short, with dark hair and dark eyes. She was also very stout. His sister was sixteen years old, very pretty, with dark hair, dark eyes, and a lithe, just-emerging-into-young-womanhood body. Several nearby soldiers had already whistled and called out to her, and it was obvious that she was enjoying their attention because she was smiling and waving back at them.

Roberto introduced his friends to his family.

"I want to extend my admiration to you for adopting someone like Roberto and raising him as your own child," Aaron said to Mrs. Sangremano.

"Adopt?" Mrs. Sangremano replied, confused by the comment. She shook her head. "He's a no adopt. He's a my own child."

"Really? Well, you can understand my confusion," Aaron said. "I mean, you are such a handsome family, and Roberto is so ugly."

The others laughed, but Mrs. Sangremano didn't understand.

"Why you say such a thing? Roberto is a good-looking boy!" she insisted.

The young girl laughed. "Mama, he is pulling your leg," she said.

"Pulling my leg?"

"Dicendo un scherzo," she said, speaking Italian. "Making a joke."

"Pulling my leg. Yes, is very funny," Mrs. Sangremano said. She put her hands on her knee and made a gesture as if pulling, but it was obvious she had no idea what her daughter was talking about.

The young girl laughed with her, but she shook her head, then looked at the soldiers and shrugged, as if saying, "What can I do? Mama is Italian and does not understand."

"What is your name?" Alphabet asked the young girl.

"Maria."

"My name is Ron. Ron Stakowiac."

"Ron? Your name is Ron?" Roberto asked.

"Yeah. What do you think? That my folks call me Alphabet?"

Roberto laughed. "I guess I just never thought of it, one way or another."

"Alphabet?" Maria asked.

Alphabet went through the explanation as well as the correct spelling and pronunciation of his last name.

"Hey, Alphabet, before you get too carried away, she is only sixteen years old," Roberto said.

"Yeah? I'm only seventeen," Alphabet said.

"Seventeen?" Mrs. Sangremano said. She put her hand on Alphabet's cheek. "You are a bambino, seventeen, and you are going to war."

"I am young, yes, but the army says I am old enough," Alphabet said. Then, turning to Maria's father, he said, "Il Signore Sangremano, abbia io il Suo permesso per scrivere a Sua figlia?"

"Lei parla Italiano?" Maria said.

"Yes, I speak Italian. My mother is Italian," Alphabet said.

"Roberto, what did he say?" Travis asked.

"He just asked my father for permission to write to my sister," Roberto replied.

"Ron, I would be honored if you wrote me," Maria said. "And I promise to answer every letter you write." She turned to her father. "Papa, is it all right?"

"Si," Mrs. Sangremano said before Mr. Sangremano could answer. "He's a nice a boy. You, he can write."

"Grazie!" Alphabet said with a happy smile.

"Listen, I don't know about you guys, but I'm getting hungry," Travis said. "I hope they feed us soon."

"I don't see how we are going to get anything to eat before two o'clock or even later," Dewey said.

"Hey," Aaron said, pointing. "There's a vendor over there selling bagels and lox."

"Bagels and lox? Is that some kind of food?" Travis asked.

"Yes."

"It's pretty good," Roberto said. "I've had it before."

"Well, if it's food, I'm willing to try it."

"Couple of you guys come with me," Aaron said. "I'll buy enough for all of us, and you can help me carry it back." He looked at the Sangremanos. "I'll get some for you too."

"No," Mrs. Sangremano said. "Is too much money for you to spend."

Roberto laughed. "Don't worry, Ma. Aaron is rich. Come on, Aaron. I'll help you. Alphabet, you want to come help carry?"

Travis chuckled. "I'd better do it. Looks to me like Alphabet is pretty busy," he said.

Alphabet and Maria had moved a short distance away from the others. They were engaged in an intense and personal conversation, oblivious of any and all around them.

At sea aboard the Queen Mary
August 4, 1942

Every available space on board the *Queen Mary* was filled with bunks, from the grand salon to the theater, the gym, along all the companionways, and in every stateroom and suite. There was no difference between first class and steerage, for the ship was a large floating dormitory.

Although they had been warned of the dangers of German submarines patrolling the North Atlantic, the captain of the great ship put everyone's mind at ease when he announced over the speakers: "We are so much faster than any submarine that they are unable to effect a firing solution. You men just relax and enjoy the voyage. It will be just as if you are riding a bus in London."

"Travis, remind me never to ride a bus in London," Dewey said.

"Why is that?"

"Because if this really is anything like riding a bus in London, I'd get seasick again."

Travis laughed.

"It isn't funny."

"I know," Travis said. "And I apologize."

Dewey had gotten seasick shortly after they passed the Statue of Liberty, and though everyone assured him he would have his "sea legs" by the next day, he was still seasick two and one-half days into the voyage. The only way he could overcome the terrible nausea was to lie flat on his back on the deck of the ship.

"Hey, we're supposed to have fried chicken for supper. You think you might try to eat?"

"No," Dewey answered resolutely. "And don't mention the word *fried* to me again. Ever."

"Okay, okay. What about an orange? Think you could handle an orange?"

"Yes," Dewey said. "I would love an orange if you can get one for me."

"I'll get you one."

For some reason, an orange was the only thing Dewey could eat and keep down. He craved oranges and went to sleep at night, wishing he had an entire sack of oranges. The funny thing was that he usually didn't care that much for oranges.

Bavarian Luftangriffsschutzhauptquartier
August 13, 1942

"Valkyrie?" the Air Defense director's voice said into Karla's headset.

"This is Valkyrie," Karla replied.

"There is a large flight of more than one hundred bombers heading for Mainz. You will handle the fighter operations from your sector."

"Jawohl, Herr Direktor," Karla said.

The Bavarian Air Raid Protection Headquarters was a beehive of activity as the plotting began.

The bombers were at 9,000 meters, approaching on a radial of 250 degrees, at a speed of 300 kilometers. Karla fed all of the information into a plotting device, then selected the fighter squadron that had the best fuel, speed, and distance ratio to make the intercept. Once she had done that she picked up the phone and called the fighter command.

Conn Kaserne, Fifty-Sixth Adlerstaffel

Conn Kaserne was the army barracks that was the school for panzer training. There many of the heroes of Germany's early blitzkrieg victories had trained and had planned their operations. There, too, was the airfield where Hitler had landed on the day he had come to nationalize FAG Kugelwerks. A fighter wing of Messerschmitt 109s, the Fifty-Sixth Eagle Squadron, was stationed here, and the airplanes were lined up on the runway, fueled, armed, and ready to take off on immediate notice. Each yellow-nosed fighter had in yellow silhouette a small, spread-winged eagle with an arrow in its beak, painted just beneath the canopy.

They also had on their rudders black bars indicating the number of enemy airplanes shot down. One had twenty-one such bars, and the pilot of that particular plane, Captain Johan Lange, was sitting in a leather chair in the pilots' ready room, listening to music and reading *Signal Magazine*, a picture magazine published especially for the German military. Over the strains of "Lille Marlene" he heard the call come in.

He looked up as the dispatcher answered the phone. It was the fourth time the phone had rung this morning, and so far none of the telephone calls had been of any consequence. But this one was. Lange could tell by the expression on the dispatcher's face, even before he hung up, that the squadron had just been alerted.

Lange threw the magazine aside, then called to his wingman, who lay sleeping on a nearby couch.

"Fromm," he said. "Come quickly. We have been alerted."

Fromm opened his eyes, then sat up. "Alert? I don't hear the siren."

"You will," Lange said. "Come."

None of the other pilots had responded yet, and they looked at Lange and Fromm in curiosity, wondering why they were leaving so quickly.

By the time Lange and his wingman reached the flight line, the alert siren went off. Immediately thereafter, the other pilots began to respond, hurrying out of the ready room and the barracks toward the flight line.

"How did you know we were about to be alerted?" Fromm asked.

Lange pointed to his ear. "I have a tiny radio in my head," he said. "When there is about to be an alert, the director calls me first."

Fromm laughed as he put his foot onto the assist step, climbed onto the wing, then slipped down into the cockpit of his fighter. Lange's airplane was the next one over, and he got into his as well. A moment later both planes began to move, the spinning propeller blades making shining circles in the floodlights as they taxied onto the runway, getting into position for takeoff, even before the other pilots had reached their planes.

As soon as they took off, Lange came up on the Air Defense frequency and called the controller.

"Air Defense Command, Adlerstaffel is aloft. Todeshandler here," he said.

"Todeshandler, this is Valkyrie. Come to a heading of two-three-five for intercept."

"Thank you, Valkyrie, my lovely. You are lovely, are you not, Valkyrie? Your voice is lovely."

"Bomber stream is at nine thousand meters," Valkyrie replied. "Approach speed is three hundred kilometers."

"All work and no play, is that it, Valkyrie?"

"I have my duty to perform," Valkyrie answered.

Lange chuckled. "Ah, yes, your duty. Interesting that you have the call sign Valkyrie. You do know who Valkyrie is, don't you? She is the Norse goddess whose job it is to visit battlefields and select the warriors who are to be slain. Then she conducts them into Valhalla. Should I be frightened, Valkyrie? Have you selected me tonight for entry into Valhalla?"

"Please attend to the business at hand. We are being monitored," Valkyrie replied.

"Oh? And if the monitor hears me, what will he do to me? Will he tell me I can't fly anymore?"

"Please attend to the business at hand," Valkyrie repeated. "Do you see the bomber stream?"

"There is no moon tonight, so it is very hard to see them."

"They are there. Just continue your present course."

Shortly after that, Lange saw them. It was difficult. The night was dark, and the bombers were showing no lights, but they could not hide the telltale blue flames of their engine exhausts. To an untrained eye, even that would have gone undetected, for at first glance they would look like stars. But Lange could see them moving steadily eastward across the night sky.

"Valkyrie, this is Todeshandler." Gone was the flirtatious cajoling in Lange's voice. He was all business now. "I have the bombers in sight. Commencing the first attack run."

The bombers were slightly higher than he was, so he climbed toward them. Looking to his left, he saw that Fromm was following his lead.

They were British Stirlings, huge, four-engine bombers that could carry exceptionally large bomb loads. Each plane, he knew, could take out several city blocks with its deadly load.

Closing to firing range, Lange pulled the trigger and followed the little balls of fire that leaped from his wing guns and zipped up toward the bomber. The bomber crew saw him as well, and the gunners began firing back.

His tracer rounds and those from the bomber's guns crossed in the darkness between them, and Lange felt strangely detached, as if he were lying on a grassy hill somewhere, watching a lazy fireworks display in the night sky.

Suddenly, the bomber exploded into a huge ball of flame. His bullets had detonated the big airplane's bomb load, and Lange had to react quickly, throwing the stick hard over to avoid the blast effect, peeling off even as fiery pieces of the exploding bomber fluttered down around him.

"That is number twenty-two for Todeshandler," he said.

Karla heard Captain Lange call off number twenty-two, and she breathed a quick prayer for his safety and for the souls of the British airmen. She had never told anyone that she prayed for the souls of the enemy. She was afraid that they might think her unpatriotic.

She had also not told Captain Lange that she knew who he was, that she had met him and his wingman that night she and Gunter had shared his table in the wine cellar. She wished she had never met him. Always before she could maintain a degree of separation between herself and the men for whom she provided attack coordinates. They were only voices in the ether. But Todeshandler wasn't just a voice now; he was someone she had actually met. He was a real person.

She did not have to be told the role that Valkyrie played in Norse mythology. She would have preferred not to be reminded that Valkyrie was a messenger of death. She had not chosen the name Valkyrie and would not have chosen it, had she been able to select something else.

"Valkyrie, are you still there?" Todeshandler asked.

"Yes, Todeshandler, I'm still here."

"We are breaking off from the bomber stream. You can tell the anti-aircraft men that it is their show now."

"Yes, thank you."

"Good night, Valkyrie. I shall dream of you tonight."

"Valkyrie, signing off."

With the fighter squadron phase done, Karla turned control of the bomber stream over to another operator who would handle the antiaircraft batteries. Free of duty, she left her station and climbed the steps.

She stood outside the little building and leaned back against the wall. A refreshing breeze blew across her from the Main River, and she didn't realize until that moment that she had been hot and sweating. She looked around the town of Schweinfurt, at the beautiful old architecture with its arches and columns and spires.

Would Schweinfurt be bombed someday?

Since taking this job, she had tracked the British bombing raids night after night, and she knew that there had been raids as far from England as Schweinfurt was.

She thought of the people in the town of Mainz. Despite the fighters and the antiaircraft batteries, she knew that a significant number of British bombers would get through. In fact, she realized that at this very minute, the first bombs were beginning to fall.

She prayed for the people under the bombs.

16

Langley Field, Virginia
October 5, 1942

S econd Lieutenant Lee Arlington Grant stepped up to the bar of the Officers' Open Mess.

"Something to drink, sir?" the bartender asked.

"I'll have a Coke, please," Lee replied.

"A Coke and . . . ?"

"Just a Coke."

The bartender drew a fountain Coke and handed it across the bar.

"Thank you."

Picking up his drink, Lee walked out onto the patio. Looking east, he saw a B-17 just turning onto final approach, the pilot dissipating airspeed and altitude as he felt his way toward the ground. Lee watched the big bomber approach with flaps lowered and landing gear down and locked.

Lee was meeting his father at the club. He was more than a little nervous about it because their last parting was on less than amicable terms. He had just been granted a West Point appointment, but he gave it up when he received a letter of acceptance from Litchfield College. His choice of a Christian college over the U.S. Military Academy was not well received.

"A preacher!" his father had bellowed. "A namby-pamby preacher!"

That discussion had taken place four years ago, just before Lee's father had left for an assignment in Hawaii. Although they hadn't seen each other since then, Lee had exchanged letters with his parents during the four-year separation, and his mother, who was the correspondent, never failed to end her letters, "Your father sends his love." Lee had no reason to doubt that.

Lee's parents were back from Hawaii now and were at Langley Field. Lee had drawn the same assignment when he was finished with his duties at the Chaplain School, though he hadn't seen either of them yet because today was his very first day at the new duty station.

"Good afternoon, Lieutenant," a voice said from behind him.

Turning, Lee saw a full colonel standing on the patio. He came to attention and saluted. "Sir," he said.

Colonel "Iron Mike" Grant stepped across the patio, extending his hand. "Hello, Son. It's good to see you. Your mother has asked about you already."

"I'll get out to see her as soon as I'm signed in," Lee promised.

"I believe your orders are for the Six-Oh-Fifth Heavy Bomb Group."

"Yes, sir, I believe they are."

"You believe, or you know?"

"I know they are."

"Colonel Grant?" a waiter said, stepping through the double doors that led back into the main dining room. "Your table is ready, sir."

"Thank you." Lee and his father followed the waiter inside. Other diners looked up at the two men, wondering who the second lieutenant was who would have the chutzpah to dine with a full bird colonel.

"I'm proud of you for joining the army," Lee's father said after the two were seated. "I would have chosen some other branch for you, perhaps the infantry, the artillery, combat engineers, anything other than the Chaplain Corps." He sighed. "But at least you are in uniform, and you are here."

"Yes, sir, but I don't plan to stay here long. I hope to get overseas as soon as I can," Lee said.

"You are going to England."

"England?"

"So am I," Mike continued. "I'll be assuming command of the Six-Oh-Fifth as soon as the change of command ceremony can be arranged."

"Then I am to be under your command?"

"That is correct."

Lee was quiet for a long moment. "My coming here wasn't a coincidence, was it?"

"No."

"That's all the more reason I'm going to apply for a transfer."

"It won't do you any good."

"You mean you would stop it?"

"I would."

"Why? I don't understand you, Dad," Lee said. "On the one hand, you are upset with me because I haven't chosen a combat arm. Then you turn right around and get me assigned to your command so you can . . . what? Keep an eye on me? Protect me from all harm?"

"Something like that," Mike agreed. He stared across the table at his son. "Lee, you had an appointment to West Point. Do you know how many young men in this country would give their eyeteeth for an appointment to the military academy?"

"A lot, I'm sure."

"Probably nine out of ten would go if they could. Here you have an appointment handed to you, and you happen to be the one out of ten who doesn't want to go."

"I'm sorry if I disappointed you."

"No, not only disappointed me. You are now flaunting it by choosing to join the army as a chaplain. Is it your mission in life to embarrass me?"

"No, of course not. Dad, I'm as serious about my calling as you are yours."

"Uh-huh," Mike said. "Well, we'll see about that. In the meantime I'm keeping you with me. I intend to keep my eye on you for the duration of the war. I will not let you do anything to disgrace your name or your heritage."

Sikeston, Missouri
October 14, 1942

Clutching her letter, Millie Gates got off her bike in front of the Rankin home, then walked up to the front door, where she rang the bell.

Mrs. Rankin answered the door and, seeing Millie, smiled broadly.

"Hello, Millie."

"Hello, Mrs. Rankin. Is Unity home?"

"Oh yes, she's in the living room with the reverend."

"Oh, well, I wouldn't want to disturb them if they are . . ."

"Oh, don't be silly, dear. We are just listening to *Abbott and Costello*, that's all. Come on in."

"Thanks."

Unity was sitting on the sofa; Phil was in an overstuffed chair. Both were laughing as Millie entered the living room.

"Millie, come, listen to the radio with us," Unity invited. She patted a place beside her on the sofa.

"What are they doing?" Millie asked.

"Costello is about to go out on a date, and Abbott is trying to tell him what he should wear," Unity explained.

"He was going to wear a green jacket, a pink shirt, and lavender shoes," Phil added with a little laugh.

"And when Abbott said with an outfit like that, he might as well wear yellow pants, Costello said he couldn't do that because he didn't want to look like a fool," Margaret said.

Millie laughed at the descriptions, then they grew quiet to listen to the show on the radio.

"I'll tell you what, Costello, I'll let you wear my dinner suit," Abbott said.

"A dinner suit? What is a dinner suit?" Costello asked.

"Don't you know what a dinner suit is?"

"Is it a suit you've spilled your dinner on?"

Laughter from the radio and in the living room.

"No. It is a suit you wear to dinner. In my family, we always dressed for dinner. Didn't you dress for dinner in your family?"

"Of course we did. Do you think we came to the table in our underwear?"

More laughter from the radio audience and those in the living room.

"No, no, I don't mean that. I mean, didn't you wear a suit with tails? In my family, we called a man with tails a gentleman," Abbott said.

"Hah! In my family, we called him a monkey!"

Roaring laughter.

Millie, Unity, and the Rankins listened to the rest of the show. Not until the commercial for Camel cigarettes, which the announcer declared was "the most selected brand for our boys in the army, navy, and marines," signaled the end of the show, did Millie hold up her letter.

"I got a letter from Kenny today."

Kenny was Millie's brother.

"How is he?"

"He's fine," Millie said. She smiled. "He saw Dewey."

"What? Get out of here! Kenny saw Dewey?"

"Yes. Here, I'll read it to you."

Millie opened her letter and, clearing her throat, began to read, moving her lips until she got to the pertinent part.

"Sis, I know you told me you were a bridesmaid for Unity Rankin. Well, guess what? I met her husband. As you know I'm a chaplain's assistant at a big chapel here in London, and Sunday morning I happened to look up, and there he was, big as life, Corporal Dewey Bradley."

Millie looked up from the letter. "Oh, when did he make corporal?"

"Last month," Unity said. "Isn't it exciting? That's twelve dollars a month more."

"I'll bet you can use that."

"I sure can," Unity said.

Millie went back to reading the letter. "I'd only met him a couple of times when he came over to Sikeston, but I recognized him right away, so I went over to introduce myself to him. He's a real nice fella, and after chapel, we went to the Rainbow Corner, a big service club for American GIs. It's about the only place in London where you can actually get a hamburger. I told him I was going to write you and tell you I saw him, and he said to tell you hi."

Millie looked up from the letter. "What do you think?" she asked.

"Oh, I'm glad they ran into each other over there," Unity said. "It's like finding a little bit of home, so far away from home. For both of them."

"Yes, that's what I think too. What do you hear from Dewey? Is he excited about the baby?"

Unity smiled, then rubbed her stomach. She was showing now. "I'll say he is," she said. "He's been coming up with names, girls' names and boys' names."

"Any of them you like so far?"

Unity laughed and wrinkled her nose. "No," she said. "They are awful. Simply awful. Though none could be worse than Unity."

"Here now, I chose that name," Phil said defensively.

"I know you did," Unity said. "And that's exactly why I don't intend to let Dewey just have his way with any of the names he has suggested. Do you know he has actually suggested Dixie Lee if it is a girl? Can you imagine having to grow up with the name Dixie Lee?"

"Oh, I don't think it's such a bad name. In fact, I think it's a rather nice name," Phil said.

"Nice? I think it sounds like a brand of peaches or something," Unity said.

Unity and Millie laughed at the idea, then Unity took Millie back to her bedroom to show her some of the clothes she was making for the baby.

Margaret watched them go back to Unity's room, then turned to her husband. "Oh, Phil, pray extra hard for Dewey and for Kenny. Kenny was such a sweet boy."

"Kenny was a sweet boy?" Phil said. "Are you talking about Kenny Gates? You do remember the time he put fish in the baptismal tank, don't you?"

"Well, yes, but that was just a boyish prank."

"And the time he let the air out of all four tires on Miss Margrabe's car?"

"Yes," Margaret said. "Now that you mention it, I do remember that."

"And the time he ran his sister's unmentionables up the flagpole down at the high school? Is that the sweet Kenny Gates you're talking about?"

Margaret sighed. "Now that I think about it, how in the world did that boy ever wind up as a chaplain's assistant?" she asked.

Phil laughed. "Don't worry. Sweet or not, I keep Kenny and all of our congregation boys in my prayers, along with Dewey."

London
October 18, 1942

"The peace of God, which passeth all understanding, keep your hearts and minds in the knowledge and love of God, and of His Son, Jesus Christ our Lord: and the blessings of God Almighty, the Father, the Son, and the Holy Ghost, be amongst you and remain with you always. Go in peace to love and serve the Lord. Amen," the chaplain said.

"Amen," the congregation responded.

The organist began the postlude as the men started filing out of the church.

Dewey remained seated and was still there after everyone left, and the chaplain's assistant moved through the pews picking up the chapel bulletins. Looking up from his task, Kenny saw Dewey sitting toward the back.

"Hey, Dewey, hi," Kenny called, walking toward him. "It's good to see you. I didn't see you come in. How's it going?"

"Fine," Dewey said. "What about you?"

"You know me. I'm fat, dumb, and happy," Kenny replied. "What are you doing here today? I didn't think you'd be able to get back into London so soon."

"Yes. Well, they gave us one last weekend pass, so I thought I would take advantage of it."

"One last pass?" Kenny asked as he resumed rounding up the pew sheets. "That sounds kind of ominous."

"Yeah," Dewey said. He moved to the pew in front of Kenny and started picking up the bulletins as well.

"Is your unit moving out?"

"It looks that way."

"Do you know where you're going?" Kenny asked as they worked together.

"They haven't told us," Dewey answered. "But I've got a feeling that, wherever it is, I'm going to get seasick."

Kenny laughed. "You say that like you've had experience. Did you get seasick coming over?"

"Oh, wow, did I ever? How about you?"

"Yes, but I only got sick one time," Kenny answered breezily. They moved across the center aisle. "It lasted from the States until we reached England," he added.

Dewey laughed. "Well, we're from the middle of the country for crying out loud. What do we know about ships? We're supposed to get seasick."

"Yeah, that's pretty much my thinking too. Listen, I'm glad you got to come in today because I'll be leaving soon also."

"Oh? Where are you going? Or can you say?"

"Oh, yeah, I can say. I don't think the army is ever going to send me to some secret place. I'm going over to the air corps," Kenny said. "I will be at a base near here called Davencourt."

"You're going over to the air corps? Are you still going to be a chaplain's assistant?"

"Absolutely. Being a chaplain's assistant is the best job in the army," Kenny insisted. He stopped, then looked at Dewey. "By the way, didn't Millie tell me that you turned down a commission as a chaplain?"

"Yeah, I did," Dewey said.

"Man, why did you do that?"

"I don't know. Maybe I was a little crazy."

"Hah, if you ask me, you were a lot crazy. Being a chaplain is even better than being a chaplain's assistant."

"I suppose so," Dewey said.

"And just think. If you were a chaplain, why, I might even have wound up working for you."

Dewey laughed. "Would you really want to work for me?" he asked.

Kenny laughed as well, then shook his head.

"Now that you mention it, that might not be such a good idea after all."

When all the pew sheets were picked up, Dewey handed his to Kenny, who put them in the trash.

"What do you say we go down to the Rainbow Club to get one of those hamburgers?" Dewey asked. "I never thought I'd find myself craving a hamburger. Although you know what I'm really craving?"

"What's that?"

"A barbecue sandwich, like they serve at the Bearcat in Litchfield."

"Or at the Rustic Rock in Sikeston," Kenny said. "Yeah, I could go for a barbecue about now. But a hamburger sounds good too. All I have to do is lock the place up, then I'm free to go."

Dewey followed Kenny to the front of the chapel, where Kenny locked the doors. They walked down the steps, passing a pile of sandbags that were stacked up to protect the building from the blitz, though there had been no German air raids in quite a while. Once on the street, they started toward the USO.

"So, you are going to be in the air corps, huh?" Dewey asked.

"Yep. Air Corps Kenny, that's what you can call me," Kenny replied.

"And where's this place you're going? Davencourt? Have you ever been there?" Dewey asked.

"Nobody has ever been there," Kenny answered.

"What do you mean, nobody has ever been there?"

"I mean nobody has ever been there. Technically, it's not even a real air base yet. It's just being built. Some rich English farmer has turned his land over to the U.S. Army so we would have a place. Can you imagine owning a farm big enough for an air base? I mean in a country this small?"

"He must be a very wealthy man," Dewey said.

"Yeah," Kenny said. "I wonder if he has a daughter. A daughter who just happens to be attracted to American corporals."

Dewey laughed. "Do you know what kind of chaplain you'll be working for? Baptist, Methodist, Catholic?"

"It won't be Catholic. They like to use Catholic boys for that, former altar boys and all. I'll be Protestant. That's all I know. I just don't know what kind of Protestant I'll be. Anyway, for the first couple of months, as I understand it, the only ones there will be the detail getting the base ready. We've got a new air wing coming in. The Six-Oh-Fifth. They fly B-17s."

"B-17s? Those are big airplanes," Dewey said.

"They're big all right. And they'll be bombing Germany. Maybe if we get enough of them over here and they drop enough bombs, we can get this war over with and go back home."

"Maybe," Dewey said. "But like they told us back in infantry training, it's not going to be over until we infantry guys are walking around on German soil."

"Ah, that's just what they tell you infantry guys," Kenny said. "It's us air force guys who are actually winning the war." He put his hand to his left sleeve. "In a couple of weeks I'll be wearing the Eighth Air Force patch right here. Then when I come into town, it'll be different. Just wait and see. Whenever the girls see that patch, they go nuts. They really like pilots."

"Pilots? I thought you were going to be a chaplain's assistant."

"Well, yeah, I am," Kenny said. "But the girls won't know the difference."

Dewey laughed. "Kenny, you are incorrigible."

"Funny you would say that. That's exactly what all my teachers used to say."

"How on earth did you become a chaplain's assistant?"

"Just lucky, I guess," Kenny said. "Say, my sister says you were a big athlete back in high school and college. Is that true?"

"I played football and basketball, and ran track," Dewey said.

"Uh-huh. Well, how are you in Ping-Pong, Mr. Super Athlete?"

"Ping-Pong? Not very good, I'm afraid."

Kenny smiled. "I was hoping you would say that. Come on in. After we eat, I'll play you a few games of Ping-Pong."

17

El Alamein, North Africa
October 23, 1942

Gunter Reinhardt's grandfather had followed through with his promise to send Gunter to North Africa rather than return him to Russia. In fact, Gunter had flown to his new assignment along with his grandfather on board a JU-88, which had been converted from a bomber to a fast executive aircraft assigned to Colonel-General Jakob Reinhardt.

As commandant of the Fifth Light Panzer Division, Colonel-General Reinhardt was the third-ranking general in North Africa, after only Erwin Rommel and Jürgen von Arnim.

As a result of his new assignment, Gunter no longer had the brutal cold to contend with, but he learned that the desert had its own kind of horror.

The Germans called it a *ghibli*, from an Arab word referring to swirling sandstorms that could blot out the sun, raise temperatures by as much as thirty-five degrees, and sap the strength of the strongest individual. When the wind roared in, it swept up sand and sent stinging grains into the skin at speeds of up to 130 kilometers per hour. Visibility dropped to less than 2 meters, and soldiers had to wind scarves around their faces to breathe. Telephone poles were ripped from the ground; compasses and delicate instruments were driven crazy by electrical disturbances that often were a side effect of the whirling sandstorms.

Gunter already had experienced such conditions, but tonight was nothing like that. Tonight was quiet, with only a soft warbling of night birds to break the silence. On this quiet Friday night, Feldwebel (Sergeant) Gunter Reinhardt leaned against a pile of sandbags, his arms folded across his chest. The moon, gold in color and exceptionally large, made the desert so bright that, even from his position, which was ten meters away from a stack of wooden crates, he could clearly read the writing on the crates and see the symbol of the Afrika Korps, a swastika superimposed over a palm tree.

Because the sand reflected the moonlight, Gunter was able to use an optical device he had been working on. He had modified a pair of binoculars to use mirrors, which gathered the available light and almost tripled the effectiveness of binoculars at night.

As sergeant of the guard, Gunter checked his watch and saw that it was 9:40 P.M. In twenty minutes it would be time to turn out the new relief. He lifted the binoculars and searched the horizon.

He saw something that looked a little like a field of wheat, waving on the distant horizon. Lowering the binoculars, he saw nothing, but when he raised them back to his eyes, he saw the waving wheat once more.

Puzzled by what he was seeing, he adjusted the binoculars, then had another look.

They were British soldiers!

Quickly, Gunter grabbed the field phone and twisted the crank.

"Ja," the radio operator said at the other end.

"British soldiers are advancing on our positions," Gunter said.

"Wait."

Gunter waited a long moment, then the radio operator came back. "We have checked with all our lookouts. No one else is reporting such a thing."

"But I see them," Gunter said.

"How is it that you see them and nobody else does?"

Gunter started to explain the binoculars he had modified, but he knew it would be useless to try. Instead, he said, "I will look again."

Gunter studied the distant soldiers through his light-gathering binoculars. Oddly they didn't seem to be moving. It was as if they were waiting for something.

Suddenly, he saw flashing light all up and down the eastern horizon. That was followed a few seconds later by the swooshing sound of hundreds of incoming artillery rounds.

"Ankommendes Artilleriefeuer!" Gunter shouted, diving into a trench behind the sandbags.

Explosions burst all up and down the German lines, sending out shards of hot shrapnel, rocks, sand, and whirling jagged bits of barbed wire.

Gunter grabbed the phone and twisted the crank to inform command headquarters. They would have to believe him this time. The incoming artillery was all the validation he needed. Twisting the crank a couple of times, Gunter realized that he was wasting his time. The first barrage had chewed up the telephone wires, and he wasn't equipped with a radio.

The barrage continued throughout the night, the flashes of light illuminating the desert. Under the sustained barrage, German blockhouses were destroyed, and sandbag revetments caved in. Soldiers were killed not only by the shrapnel but also by the concussion of the explosions.

The barrage lifted just before dawn, and Gunter knew that it meant the infantry he had seen last night would be coming in. He knew now what they had been waiting for. They had been waiting for the massive bombardment to open the attack.

Moving quickly up and down his own area of responsibility, he got his men into position, ready to repel the assault.

"How are we going to hold them off, Sergeant?" one of his men asked, his voice quaking with fear. "We've lost half of our platoon."

"Then fire your weapon twice as fast," Gunter replied. "Each of us will have to do the work of two men."

"Are you frightened?" one of the others asked Gunter.

"Yes," Gunter replied. "But at least I am not cold."

"Not cold? Ich verstehe nicht."

Gunter's chuckle was sardonic. "You don't have to understand," he said. "Just stay ready."

At that moment, General Georg Stumme and Colonel Walter Buchting came out of what was left of the command bunker. Like Gunter, Stumme was a veteran of the Russian campaign. The men in the ranks sometimes referred to General Stumme as General Schwein because he was considerably overweight.

Despite his physical condition, Gunter remembered him from Russia and knew that he was a very capable general. In fact, precisely because of that, Gunter had requested to be assigned to Stumme.

"Sergeant Rienhardt! We are cut off from every regiment!" he said. "Get a staff car! I'm going to the center of the line."

"Jawohl, General."

Gunter brought the Kubelwagen, the little open staff car, around, and Stumme and Buchting climbed in. Buchting took the front seat beside Gunter, and General Stumme, with some effort because of his girth, climbed into the back.

"Go! Go!" Stumme ordered, waving his hand forward.

Gunter drove away, going as fast as the little car could cross the desert, bouncing furiously through holes and over bumps and ridges. The British continued the artillery firing, and though it was not as heavy as it had been, Gunter had to continuously maneuver to avoid the burst radius.

Suddenly, a machine gun opened up on them. Several bullets slammed into the side of the little car, and Gunter could hear them whistling by his head. Beside him, Colonel Buchting let out a grunt, and Gunter saw a spray of blood on the dashboard. Buchting fell forward.

"Back! Back!" Stumme shouted.

Gunter threw the car in reverse, then drove backward for some distance, steering with one hand while firing his MP-40 machine pistol over the front of the car. As he backed, he whipped the steering wheel back and forth, causing the car to zigzag. His success in avoiding the machine-gun fire was evident by the tracers that zipped first to one side of the car, then to the other, but not into the car. Finally, he was able to turn the car around. Retracing his path, he raced back toward the command bunker.

"General, shall I try to find another way to get to the center of the line?" he shouted.

When Stumme didn't answer, Gunter looked into the backseat. He saw the general gasping for breath, his face ashen. He was holding his hands over his chest.

"Are you hit?" Gunter shouted.

"My heart," Stumme gasped, barely managing to get the words out. He tried to stand, then he fell back, his mouth slack, his eyes open, but sightless.

Gunter was some distance from his headquarters, with the commanding general and chief of staff in the car, both dead.

Returning to the headquarters, he found that even the captain who had remained behind was dead, and the soldiers were cowering in the bottom of the trenches, their heads covered with their arms.

"Who is in command?" he shouted.

"Dead!" a corporal replied. "All dead!"

Looking east, Gunter saw the British soldiers coming toward them, line upon line of steel-helmeted figures. Their rifles were held out in front of them, bayonets glistening in the morning sun, as they advanced across the desert.

"Get up!" he shouted at the men, running up and down behind the trenches. "The British are coming! Get up! Get ready!"

With shouts, curses, and cajoling, Gunter finally managed to get what was left of the company on line. He jumped down behind one of the machine guns and, clearing the headspace and operating the bolt to throw the first round into the chamber, opened fire. He saw several of the advancing soldiers go down under his fire. His men saw it, too, and that emboldened them to open fire as well.

For several minutes the heavy fighting continued until finally the Brits withdrew.

"Cease fire, cease fire!" Gunter shouted. "We must conserve our ammunition!"

"What do we do now, Sergeant?" one of the men called.

"Half of you rest. The other half stay on alert," Gunter said.

Taking his helmet off, Gunter slid down to the bottom of the trench and leaned his head back. He breathed a prayer of thanks for surviving the battle.

Shortly thereafter, a staff car arrived behind them.

"Brilliant!" an officer shouted, getting out of the car. "Thanks to the resistance of this sector, enough time has been bought to allow a strategic withdrawal. Stumme, come!"

Standing up to see who it was, Gunter recognized General Ritter von Thoma. He saluted.

Von Thoma returned the salute. "Where is General Stumme?" he asked.

"Dead, sir."

"Dead? Then Buchting? Where is Colonel Buchting?"

"He is dead as well, General."

"Then who is the officer in charge?"

"General, our officers are dead," Gunter said.

"Then who organized the resistance?"

"Sergeant Reinhardt did, General," one of the other men said. "He is in charge here."

"Sergeant, this is true? You are in command?" General von Thoma asked.

"I suppose so, sir."

"You are to be congratulated. Keep your men together until I can get an officer here to help with the strategic realignment."

"Yes, sir," Gunter replied.

General von Thoma climbed back into the staff car, then it drove off, leaving a plume of dust in its wake.

"Sergeant Reinhardt, what is a strategic realignment?" a soldier asked.

"Strategic realignment is what generals call a retreat," Gunter explained.

Sikeston, Missouri
February 7, 1943

Millie Gates had been invited to the Rankins for Sunday dinner so, after church, she rode home with them. Unity promised to take her to her own home later in the afternoon.

Sunday dinner was baked hen, the chicken a gift of one of the congregation who raised his own. Margaret made dumplings and cornbread dressing to go with the chicken.

"Oh, wouldn't Kenny love this, though?" Millie said as they were eating. "Chicken and dumplings are his all-time favorite meal."

"What do you hear from him?" Margaret asked as she passed around the green beans.

"Well, he seems to like his new chaplain. He's Episcopalian, but Kenny says he doesn't hold that against him."

Phil chuckled. "I would hope not," he said.

"Oh, and get this," she said, looking over at Unity. "Guess where he went to college?"

"Where?"

"Litchfield."

"You don't say," Unity replied. "Well, this is a small world, isn't it? What's his name?"

"Some sort of army name."

"Army name?" Unity chuckled. "Well, there are several million in the army now. What do you mean army name? GI Joe?"

Millie laughed. "I don't think it's that army," she said. "But it's like a general's name or something. Wait, I brought his latest letter to read to you. I'll see what his name is."

Millie excused herself from the table for a moment while she fished her brother's letter from her purse. She opened the little V-mail envelope, then pulled out the letter.

"Here it is," she said. "It's Lieutenant Grant. I knew it was some kind of army . . . wait, here's his whole name. Lee Arl—"

"Lee Arlington Grant!" Unity said quickly, finishing the name before Millie did.

Millie looked up in surprise. "You mean you know him?"

"Yes, I know him," Unity said. "Why, he is one of Dewey's best friends! He ran track with Dewey and cross-country. He was quite good too."

"Is he married?"

Unity laughed. "Married? No, I don't think so. No, in fact, I'm sure he isn't."

"What's he like?"

"He's a very nice guy," Unity said. "I think Kenny is going to like him."

"Kenny already likes him. I mean, Kenny has actually started listening to his sermons, and he wrote me a part of the last one."

"Kenny Gates taking notes on a sermon?" Phil said. "Well, either this fellow is very good, or Kenny has grown up a lot."

"I'd like to hear what he said," Unity said. "I mean, if you are a chaplain, what kind of things can you say to comfort men who are in battle?"

"All right," Millie said. She scanned the letter until she found the part she was looking for. "Here it is."

Millie began reading: "You are being asked to do something that no man should ever have to do. You are being asked to go out into a terrible arena where you must kill or be killed. How can any man of God find it within himself to do such a thing?

"And yet, consider the alternative. Hundreds of thousands, perhaps millions of men, women, and children have died at the hands of the evil that we fight. If we don't stop the Nazis, who will? And if they aren't stopped, then hundreds of thousands, perhaps millions more, will die not only in Europe, but eventually even in our beloved United States.

"When you shoot down airplanes, people will die. When you drop bombs, people will die, including innocent people. But you must not think of it in that way. You are fighting the immorality, not the people, and you are killing the evil, not the individuals."

Millie looked up from her letter and saw that the others had quit eating and were staring at her intently.

"You say you know this young man, Unity?" Phil asked.

"Yes. He was in school with Dewey and me."

"I would like to meet him someday. He is a remarkably mature and well-spoken young man."

18

Sidi Bou Zid, North Africa
February 13, 1943

Dewey was reassured by the sight of the six armored half-tracks that occupied the hill with them. One of them was just above where his squad was dug in. Equipped with twin-barrel .30 caliber machine guns, all six trucks were positioned in such a way as to allow their weapons to have interlocking fields of fire in the direction of the Germans. They could put out a tremendous amount of fire, and it was good to know that they were there to support the squad in case they needed them.

As the sun sank in the west, it spread the horizon with blazing color. Corporal Dewey Bradley, who was now assistant squad leader, checked the deployment of his men. He, Travis Logan, Aaron Weintraub, Alphabet, José Montoya, and Roberto Sangremano made up six of the nine-man squad. On a couple of occasions reorganization had almost separated the men, but so far they had managed to stay together. John Haverkost, Paul Cooper, and Roy Tinker, who had been with them since Camp Shelby, were still in the First Battalion, but were no longer in Able Company.

"Ain't nobody goin' to break up the Double Musketeers," Alphabet insisted.

The squad leader was Sergeant Ward Hornsby. Their Browning automatic rifleman was PFC Timmy Drake. The ninth rifleman was Fred Ryder. Hornsby, Drake, and Ryder had joined the company in England.

Drake was from Cleveland, a pipe fitter before the war.

Ryder, from Wyoming, was a cowboy—the only genuine cowboy Dewey had ever met. Ryder often sang to himself, a habit he said he had picked up by riding fence. His favorite song was "Buffalo Gals," and sometimes when Dewey, as corporal of the guard, checked the relief, he heard Ryder singing in the middle of the night.

"You're supposed to be standing guard," Dewey told him once.

"Yeah, I am standing guard."

"Well, if I could hear you singing, don't you think the Germans could?"

"Oh. Sorry, Corporal," Ryder said. "I do it so much, I don't even know when I'm doing it anymore."

Of their new replacements, Dewey decided that Sergeant Hornsby was the most valuable. He was regular army and a World War I veteran. He had been a member of the First Division in that war and claimed to know the soldier who had taken the red stripe from the collar tab of a dead German soldier to put it on his own left sleeve, thus creating the first "Red One" shoulder patch.

Hornsby didn't smoke because he said that the temptation would always be there to light up sometime when the flare of a match could make you an easy target for an enemy sniper. But he did chew, or "chaw," as he called it in his Georgia accent.

The battalion was dug in on the slopes of a hill named Djebel Lessouda, and Sergeant Hornsby had walked out along a little spine, where he stood on a rock, looking down toward the little village of Sidi Bou Zid. After checking the position of all the men, Dewey walked out along the little spine to stand alongside Hornsby.

Hornsby pulled out a square of Brown Mule tobacco and, using his pocketknife, sliced off a piece of it.

"Chaw?" he offered.

"Thank you, no," Dewey said. Hornsby always offered a chew, and

Dewey always turned him down. Once Dewey asked why he always offered, knowing it would be turned down.

"A long time ago my pappy told me you could always tell a gentleman by the fact that they was generous with their terbaccy," Hornsby said. He stuck the chew in his mouth, then put the knife and plug of tobacco back in his pocket. "Did you check 'em out?"

"Yes, Sergeant. They're all in good positions," Dewey answered.

"No, they ain't," Hornsby said.

Surprised, Dewey looked back toward the men. "Sergeant, they've all got overlapping fields of fire and they've all—"

"Ain't your fault," Hornsby said. "From what you got to work with, you done good. The men is in good shape. It's us, I'm worried about."

"What do you mean?"

"Look at this," Hornsby said, pointing to the plains below. "We're supposed to be guardin' that pass, right?"

"Right."

"Half of us is over here, and the other half is over there on that other hill."

"Djebel Ksaira," Dewey said.

"Yeah, whatever it's called," Hornsby continued. "But the thing is, if the Germans decide to come through that little village down there, we ain't strong enough by ourselves to stop 'em. And them fellas over there on the other hill, well, they ain't strong enough either, and we're too far apart to support each other. What General Fredendall has done is, he's split up his forces. If the Germans want to, they could come right over here and wipe us out, then go right over there and wipe them fellas out, and there wouldn't be a blessed thing we could do about it."

"Oh, surely Fredendall knows what he's doing," Dewey protested.

"Uh-huh," Hornsby said. He spit a wad of tobacco. "Custer figured he know'd what he was a-doin' too, and you seen what happened to him whenever he split up his forces."

"Well, shouldn't we tell somebody?" Dewey asked.

Hornsby spit again.

"You're the only one I can tell. I'm a sergeant and you're a corporal. I can tell corporals. I can't go 'round tellin' generals."

Dewey chuckled, though he couldn't help feeling a little uneasy about what Hornsby had just told him. The uneasiness came from the fact that Hornsby's assessment of their situation made sense to him.

"You a papa yet?" Hornsby asked.

"No, not yet," Dewey said. "You've got children, don't you, Sergeant?"

Hornsby was quiet a moment. "Yeah, I got a boy," he finally said. "But me 'n' his mama split up when Tyler was but a tyke, and she took 'im off to California. She's a good woman, deserved better 'n I coulda give her. And she done a lot better for the boy. He got hisself a good education and a good job." He chuckled. "You ever seen any of them Walt Disney movies?"

"Yes, of course."

"Before the war, Tyler, he worked for Walt Disney, drawin' pictures for him and all. His mama says he's just all broke out with talent."

"You said before the war. Where is he now?"

"He's in the navy," Hornsby said. He laughed. "I reckon him havin' a pa in the army, even one he didn't grow up with, was enough to keep him out of the army. Anyhow, he's on a submarine out in the Pacific."

Hornsby reached into his shirt pocket and took out a piece of paper, then unfolded it. "He done this here picture that they put on the side of the submarine."

The picture was of a fish with a determined scowl. Standing on the fish's back, holding reins in his left hand and a broadsword in his right hand, was the archangel Michael. Thunderbolts emanated from the tip of Michael's broadsword.

"What do you think of this here picture? The submarine is called the *Angelfish*."

"That's good," Dewey said. "That's really good. I know you're proud of him."

"Yeah, I am," Hornsby said. Folding the paper carefully, he put it back in his shirt pocket.

Hornsby didn't extend the conversation, so Dewey turned and walked back to the squad area. Before getting into his own hole, he filled his canteen at the Lister bag. Then, while there was still enough sun to allow him to read, he pulled out his latest letter from Unity.

My dearest,

I know you couldn't tell me before, but we read in the papers and heard over the radio about the Allied troops, including the First Infantry Division, landing in North Africa. They are calling it Operation Torch, and they said that at first the French fought against you. Everyone here is mad at the French. Don't they know you were just trying to help them? I'm glad they finally came to their senses.

I am so proud of you, Dewey, but I also worry about you and pray for your safety every night. Daddy has you, Kenny, and all the boys from our church on the prayer list, and we pray for you every Sunday morning, Sunday night, and Wednesday night.

I'm glad you can't see me now. I'm as big as a house. Millie says that after the baby is born, maybe we can make some money by renting my maternity smock to the circus for use as a tent. Ha, ha.

What am I saying? I'm not at all glad you aren't here to see me. Of course I want you here. I would want you here even if my face was covered in warts and I had green hair! I just want you here.

The baby kicks almost all the time now. I don't know if it is going to be a boy or a girl, but if it is a boy, I'll just bet he will be a wonderful athlete. Maybe a runner, like your friend Lee, because this baby sure moves his or her legs a lot.

I love you and I miss you terribly. Every night I look at the moon and think that you can see the same moon, though I know not at the same time. Then I pray that God will protect and keep you in His loving care.

Your loving,
Unity

Dewey was awakened the next morning by a very loud wailing sound. When he first opened his eyes, he looked around in confusion, unsure of what he was hearing.

"Dive-bombers!" Hornsby shouted.

Dewey's first reaction should have been to dive for cover. Instead, he looked up and saw Stuka dive-bombers coming right for them. He had seen the gull-wing planes in newsreels, but this was the first time he had ever actually seen one in the field.

The first plane released its bomb, and in total fascination, Dewey watched it start arcing down.

Suddenly, Dewey was hit with a jarring body block that took him back to his football days. He and the man who hit him wound up in the bottom of Dewey's foxhole, and it was good that they did. At almost that precise moment, the first bomb hit one of the half-tracks. The armored car went up with a whooshing roar.

Rolling out from under his blocker, Dewey saw that it was Hornsby who brought him down.

"Thanks, Sarge," he said sheepishly.

"I know you wanted to see that, Son," Hornsby said. "But this here ain't the movies."

Five more explosions rocked the hill, then the planes flew off, leaving behind six burning half-tracks.

"Get ready!" Dewey shouted to the others.

"No hurry," Hornsby said, crawling out of the hole and dusting himself off. "They'll be going after those fellas down in the village now."

Another wave of Stukas came in, but as Hornsby had predicted, they went after the American tanks arrayed around the village, not the infantrymen who were dug in on the hills.

By the time the second wave of Stukas left, three American tanks were burning in the valley below. Then rumbling toward the American tanks, the clanking, squeaking sound of their tracks audible even above the din of battle, came scores of German tanks.

"Whoa, look at that," Travis said. "Their tanks are bigger than our tanks."

Like a string of flashing lights, there was a ripple of fire from the muzzles of the panzers, and almost instantly a half-dozen American tanks were hit. All six erupted into flame.

One American tank fired at a German tank and hit it, but the shell careened upward, bursting about nine meters over the tank.

"Hey, did you see that?" Alphabet called. "That shell bounced off the German tank."

For the next several minutes there was a growing cloud of dust as the American and German tanks scrambled through the desert trying to find some advantage. Through the smoke and dust of battle, though, Dewey could see that the Germans were quickly gaining the advantage. One after another American tank went up after being hit by German fire, and with the exception of a couple of panzers that had been detracked, the Germans were relatively unscathed. And even those tanks could, and did, continue firing.

By midmorning, the Germans were obviously in control of the situation, and the Americans had begun to withdraw.

"Look! Our guys are pullin' out!" Travis said, pointing to the retreating Americans.

"Okay," Sergeant Hornsby said. "Now is the time to get ready. They'll be coming after us next.

Dewey leaned against the side of the half-track, fighting the nausea and dizziness.

"Corporal Bradley, get your C's and hurry back!" Hornsby called.

There were several C ration cans in the blackened bottom of the truck. The boxes were all burned away, and heat had blackened the outside of the cans so that nothing was legible. He grabbed four cans, with no idea of what he was getting, then he hurried back to his hole.

"You all right?" Hornsby said.

"Yeah," Dewey replied. He had just learned that Tinker had died in the most recent artillery barrage.

"Sorry, I should've told you about Tinker. I thought you knew."

"I'll get over it," Dewey said.

Hornsby and the other half of the squad hurried back to fill their own canteens and grab C ration cans, then they, too, returned to their holes to wait for the next German attack.

"Hey, Sarge! Look! Our guys are coming back!" Alphabet called.

Hornsby raised his binoculars to his eyes and studied the valley floor.

"Oh no," he said. "What idiot is in command of that operation?"

An entire battalion, the tanks lined up as if in parade formation, moved across the open plains toward the village.

"Don't they know the Germans are lying in ambush for them?" Dewey asked.

They watched helplessly as the Americans continued their precision-like approach. Then the Germans opened up.

For the next hour the battle raged. Shell after shell from the German tanks found their targets, and the American tanks went up, sometimes with such force that the entire turret was blown clear. At the same time, they could see American shells bouncing off the German tanks.

"They better get out of there," Dewey said. "If they don't, they're going to be completely annihilated."

Then, as if they had heard him, Dewey saw four tanks breaking out of the din, dust, and smoke of battle, running fast to get away. The only advantage the American tanks had over the Germans was that the American Shermans were faster than the German Panzer IVs.

On the battlefield just abandoned, fifty American tanks were either afire or disabled. Already, German infantrymen were rounding up American prisoners.

Within a very short time a small American spotter plane flew low over the hill where Dewey and the others were dug in. A long yellow ribbon fluttered behind a small canister as the pilot dropped something.

Dewey watched someone from one of the other companies run out, retrieve it, then run back. A moment later the call came down for all company officers to gather at the battalion CP.

"What do you think is going on, Sarge?" Dewey asked.

Hornsby spit out a wad of tobacco. "I reckon we'll find out soon enough," he said.

Fifteen minutes later, Dewey's company commander issued a call for all NCOs to gather at the company CP.

"Come on, that's us," Hornsby said.

"Me too?"

"You're an NCO, ain't you?"

"Yes."

"Then it means you too. Logan," Sergeant Hornsby called, "you're in charge 'til Corporal Bradley and I get back."

"Don't you worry about a thing, Sarge. You left 'em in good hands. Okay, boys, all passes canceled. Inspection in five minutes," Travis teased.

The company CP was nothing more than another hole in the ground, though it was marked by the company guidon. Captain Kirby, their company commander, had joined them since Torch. Their original commander was promoted to major and assumed a staff job at another battalion.

"Anybody got a cigarette?" Kirby asked when all the NCOs were gathered.

"Yes, sir, here you go," one sergeant said.

"Thanks," Kirby said, taking the cigarette. He lit it, inhaled deeply, then let out a long cloud of smoke before he began speaking.

"Our guys can't come for us," he finally said. "So we've been ordered to withdraw."

"Withdraw?" one of the lieutenants asked. "Captain, how are we going to do that? We're sitting on a hill in the middle of the Germans. They know we're up here. When we come down, they're going to see us."

"Do you propose surrendering, Lieutenant Fuller?" Kirby asked.

"No, sir."

"Then it looks to me like we have only three options. Stay here and be killed, surrender, or try to get out of here. Now, which of those three do you want?"

"I want to get out of here if we can," Lieutenant Fuller said.

"Good. At least we are in agreement there. Now, does anyone have any ideas on how we might accomplish that?"

"Captain," Hornsby said, holding up his hand.

"Yes, Sergeant, go ahead."

"If we try to leave as a company-sized unit, we're going to stand out like a black roach crawling across a white carpet. Besides which, you won't be able to exercise any command and control over the whole company."

"So what is your suggestion?"

"That we break down into platoons. Or, better yet, into squads. Everybody here knows that our guys are west, the Germans east. I say we withdraw by squads and head west."

Kirby thought a moment, then nodded his head. "All right," he said. "That's the way we'll do it."

"When do we start?" Lieutenant Fuller asked.

"As soon as it's dark. We'll start with the first platoon. Release your squads one every half hour—"

"Captain," Hornsby interrupted. "If we are going to get the whole company out of here, we'd better release the squads closer together than that."

"What would you say? Fifteen? Ten?"

"Five minutes."

"All right, five minutes. The rest of you, take your lead off the first platoon. Keep the squads going out, one every five minutes. Lieutenant Fuller, the first sergeant, and I will divide up and go out with one of the squads," he said.

"Captain, what if the Germans don't wait until nightfall? What if they send infantry after us today?" the first sergeant asked.

Almost as if punctuating the first sergeant's question, the distant rattle of gunfire sounded. Sergeant Hornsby, who was wearing his binoculars around his neck, stood up and looked in the direction of the gunfire.

"I don't think we're going to have to worry about that, First Soldier," Hornsby said. "Looks like they're going after those boys on the other side of the valley."

"Yeah, well, better them than us," Kirby said. "All right, get back to your men. Wait until it's dark. Then if you know any prayers, say them."

Dewey and Hornsby returned to their squad, which was dug in just in front of Tinker's half-track.

"What did they say?" Travis asked.

"We're going to try to get out of here tonight," Hornsby replied.

"Hah! You had to have an NCO and officers' meeting to decide that?" Travis asked. "All you would've had to do is ask me. I was ready to run yesterday."

19

With the Germans at Sidi Bou Zid
February 15, 1943

The Afrika Korps swept the Americans from the field at Sidi Bou Zid. Not since the heady days of the war in Poland and France, and the early successes in Russia, had Gunter been a part of a victorious operation.

When Feldwebel Gunter Reinhardt awoke at sunrise, he was greeted with the welcome smell of coffee. Taking advantage of their victory on the previous day, the Germans had been able to move in a field kitchen, and Gunter took his kit over where he got a cup of coffee and a piece of bread.

"Would you like some marmalade, Sergeant?" the cook asked.

"Yes, please," Gunter replied. "And some bratwurst would be nice."

"Of course it would. And perhaps a nice chocolate torte as well?" the cook teased.

Gunter held his bread out for the marmalade, then he left the kitchen to find a place where he could sit while he enjoyed his breakfast. It was good to see the men smiling again.

Gunter had overheard his grandfather discussing the current operation with Generals Arnim and Rommel. Rommel had been in the hospital, back in Germany, during the disaster at El Alamein. Gunter was convinced that his return was all that had been needed to turn the fortunes of war around, and the action of the two previous days seemed to be proving him right.

What Rommel intended to do, Gunter knew, was to sweep through the American-defended passes of the Eastern and the Western Dorsals, then turn north toward the Algerian coast. If successful, the operation would capture Allied airfields and supply depots. The supply depots, rich with fuel and food, were particularly valued prizes.

Finishing his coffee, Gunter stood up and walked a few meters to toss the grounds into some shrubbery. That was when he saw them. Dozens of men were moving across the valley floor, trying to sneak from bush to rock to shrub.

They were Americans, and at first, he thought they might be attacking. But there were far too few of them to actually launch an attack against a position as strong as that held by the Germans. Then he realized that they were the Americans on the hill! They were trying to sneak away.

Without giving any indication that he had seen them, Gunter walked almost casually back to the company headquarters.

"Good morning, Sergeant," Captain Dumey said. Dumey was the company commander, having been brought in to replace the one who was killed during El Alamein. "How is Germany's newest hero this morning?" He was referring to the fact that Gunter had recently been awarded the Iron Cross for his defense during that same battle.

"I am good, Captain, thank you," Gunter said. "Don't look toward them now, but the Americans are trying to escape from the hill."

"What? Where?" Dumey asked.

"They have come through our panzers and are in the field between us and our tanks."

"How many?"

"I saw at least ten, but I'm sure there are many more."

"Very well. Take half the company to the left, I will take half to the right, and we will surround them," Dumey said.

"Jawohl," Gunter replied.

Moving quietly through the men, Gunter told them to get their weapons and follow him. Dumey was doing the same thing, and in what would have looked to the Americans like an unhurried maneuver with no relationship to them, Gunter's company spread out a long net. With the net in place, they encircled the Americans.

At that moment the Americans realized what was going on, and they began firing, trying to fight their way out of the encirclement.

"Return fire!" Gunter shouted.

For the next several minutes, there was a fierce firefight between the Germans and the Americans.

Whether called or attracted by the firing, Gunter didn't know, but when he looked up, he saw German tanks hurrying toward them in support. As one of the tanks passed him, he jumped onto it, then directed the driver to take him directly into the circle. He was standing on the tank, exposing himself to enemy fire, but it was his hope that the Americans would realize the helplessness of the situation.

An American colonel was standing in the center of the defensive circle, and he watched the tank approach. The American colonel was holding a pistol, but he didn't fire.

"Colonel, you surrender!" Gunter called.

With a curse, the American colonel turned his back and started walking away. Gunter waved the tank on, and it came right up to the colonel, swerving at the last minute to keep from running him down.

"Your situation is hopeless," Gunter said. "Do you want all of your men to be killed?"

"You are a sergeant, aren't you?"

"Yes."

"I'm a colonel. I prefer to surrender to an officer."

Gunter smiled and waved to Captain Dumey. "Yes, sir," he said. "I'm sure that can be arranged."

On the other side of the plain, about five kilometers away from Djebel Ksaira, Dewey's battalion started their own escape attempt. For maneuvering purposes, Hornsby and Dewey divided the squad into two groups, with Hornsby taking half and Dewey the other half. That way, one group could advance while the other covered them, and in a leapfrog fashion, they made it down the hill and out onto the plain.

Dewey and his men moved into position to cover Hornsby, then Hornsby went forward. Suddenly, the night erupted with machine-gun fire. Tracers zipped toward Hornsby and his men, and Hornsby went down.

"Return fire!" Dewey shouted, and he and his group opened up. Dewey had no specific target, but he fired his M-1 toward the muzzle flashes of the machine gun, the spent shell casings flipping out of the chamber, followed by the empty clip holder. Dewey pulled a fresh eight-round clip from his cartridge belt, pushed it down into the rifle, slammed the bolt home, and began firing again. The German machine gun stopped firing.

Some of Hornsby's men came running back, but Hornsby didn't. Travis Logan stayed out with him.

"Sarge! Sarge!" Dewey heard Travis call to their sergeant. "How bad are you hit?"

"Get out of here," Sergeant Hornsby called.

"Come on, I'll help you back."

"No. Get out of here! Get back!" Hornsby called.

Despite Hornsby's warning, Travis started to pick him up, and Drake ran over to help. Then with one man on each side, they managed to pull Hornsby to his feet. They started back when suddenly a German half-track roared up beside them. Six German soldiers jumped down from the track with their weapons pointed toward Hornsby, Travis, and Drake.

Hornsby and the other two put their hands up in surrender. The German in charge ordered them down on their knees.

"Where are the others?" the German demanded.

"What others?" Hornsby asked.

"The other Americans who are trying to escape from the hill. Do you take me for a fool, Sergeant?"

"Yeah," Hornsby said. "Yeah, I do."

"We know there was at least a battalion of Americans on the hill. Where are they now?"

"I don't know. We scattered. Every man for himself," Hornsby replied.

"Every man for himself? But there are three of you."

"They just happened by and saw that I was hurt," Hornsby said. "I need to get to an aid station. According to the Geneva Convention, you're supposed to take care of your prisoners."

"Yes," the German in charge said. "Yes, we will take care of you." He made a jerking motion with his hand, and the other German soldiers began firing their MP-40s, the automatic weapons flashing and bucking as they held the triggers down.

It happened so quickly and unexpectedly that Dewey was totally shocked by what he saw. One moment Sergeant Hornsby, Travis Logan, and Timmy Drake were kneeling on the ground, with their hands behind their heads. The next moment their bodies were jerking convulsively under the impact of the German bullets.

"No!" Dewey shouted. Without thinking about what he was doing, he leaped to his feet, then started charging toward the Germans, screaming at them at the top of his lungs.

Shocked by his sudden appearance, the Germans turned toward him, and two of them pulled the triggers on their weapons. To their surprise, they discovered that they had expended all their ammunition as they were murdering their prisoners.

Dewey started shooting. His first three shots dropped three of the Germans, and two of the others were dropped by shooting from behind him because the rest of his squad had followed him.

By the time Dewey reached the scene, only one German was still standing, and with his eyes wide with fear, he was trying desperately to put a new magazine into his weapon. Dewey took him down with a vertical butt stroke of his rifle.

With the six German soldiers down, Dewey looked at Hornsby, Travis, and Drake. All three were dead.

Dewey leaned his head against the side of the German track, breathing heavily.

"Wow, Dewey, you were something," Alphabet said.

Dewey didn't answer for a long moment, then finally he turned away from the track and looked at the six Germans. "What about them?" he asked.

"They're dead," Aaron said.

"All of them? Even the one I hit?"

Aaron chuckled. "Let's put it this way. If his head had been a baseball, you would've knocked it out of any park in the league," he said.

"What'll we do now, Dewey?" José asked.

Dewey glanced at the bodies of Sergeant Hornsby, Travis Logan, and Timmy Drake.

"I don't want to leave them behind," he said.

"I don't either, but it's going to be hard to carry them with us," Roberto said.

Dewey looked at the track. "José, you're good with vehicles. You think you could drive this thing?"

"What are you saying, Dewey? You thinking of taking the track?"

"Yeah," Dewey said. "Can you drive it?"

José nodded. "Yes, I can drive it," he said.

"Get the shirts and helmets off those Germans, then put them on," Dewey instructed the men. "We're going to use this car to get out of here."

"Dewey, not that I'm trying to protest or anything," Aaron said. "But you do know what will happen to us if we get caught wearing German uniforms, don't you? We will be shot as spies."

"You mean like Hornsby, Travis, and Drake were shot as spies?" Dewey asked.

"Well, no, they weren't spies or anything. They were just . . . ," Aaron started, then he stopped and nodded. "Yeah," he said. "I see what you mean." He pointed to one of them. "Since you're in charge, you may as well put that shirt on. He was the only officer of the bunch."

"You can tell German rank?" Dewey asked.

"Yes."

"Can you speak German?"

"As a Jew, I am pained to admit it, but ja, ich spreche Deutsch."

"All right, José, you drive. Aaron, you've just been promoted to . . . what's the rank?"

"Major."

"Right. Well, you've just been promoted to major. If we're challenged, tell them we've been ordered to scout ahead."

"What about when we get closer to our own lines? What'll keep our guys from shooting us?" Roberto asked.

"Well, there is an antenna here, which means this thing has a radio," Dewey said. "As soon as we can, we'll contact our people."

"How will we know what push to use?" Alphabet asked.

"I have an SOI," Ryder said.

"You have a signal operating instructions booklet? How come you've got one?"

"First platoon is commo backup to HQ platoon, remember?" Ryder replied. "And I'm backup radioman."

"You think you can use this Kraut radio?" Roberto asked.

"Yeah, sure I can. There's not much difference between them. A radio is a radio," Ryder said.

"Okay, Ryder, you're the radio. José, you're the driver. Aaron, you're the major. Let's get out of here."

"Hey, Dewey, you think this will work?" Alphabet asked. "I mean, it sounds pretty screwy to me."

"You got a better idea, Alphabet?" José asked as he began putting on the German uniform shirt.

"No."

"Then it will work."

Even before the others had finished changing, José started the armored personnel carrier. It slipped into gear easily, and he drove away with no problem. Inexplicably José chuckled.

"What is it? What are you laughing about?" Aaron asked.

"Man, I'm uptown now," José said. "I'm driving a Mercedes."

When Gunter saw the armored car coming toward them, he pointed it out to his commanding officer.

"Captain, someone is coming," he said.

"Probably someone wanting to interrogate our prisoners," Dumey said. "Take charge here, Reinhardt. I will go see what they want."

"Hey, Dewey, there's some Kraut coming out to wave us down," José said. "You want to just keep on going or what?"

Dewey stood up and looked ahead. He saw the soldier coming out to stop them, and he also saw the tanks that were in position all around the German soldier.

"No, you'd better stop," Dewey said. "If we run, we'll be sitting ducks for their tanks. Let's see if Aaron can talk us out of it first. If he can't, then be ready to go because we will try to make a run for it."

"Okay," José said.

"Hey, Dewey, there is something I forgot to tell you," Aaron said.

"What's that?"

"I speak German all right, but I speak it with a Yiddish accent."

"What does that mean?" Ryder asked.

"It's a Jewish accent," Aaron explained.

"Oh, wow, that's just great," Roberto said. "We are going to speak Jewish to a German officer."

"Buffalo gals won't you come out tonight . . . ," Ryder started to sing nervously.

"Ryder, hush," Dewey said.

"Yeah, sorry."

"Hey, wait a minute, we might be getting a break here," Aaron said. "I outrank him. These Kraut heads are so rank conscious, he'll be more concerned about my rank than he will be about my accent."

"I do like your confidence," Dewey said with a sigh. He patted Aaron on the shoulder. "I just hope it isn't misplaced."

José stopped when they reached the German officer.

"Wo gehen Sie?" Captain Dumey challenged, stepping up to the personnel carrier.

"Mein Rang ist das von Major! Wer sind Sie, um mich herauszufordern? Stehen Sie entfernt, Kapitan! Wir suchen nach dem Feind," Aaron said in as arrogant and gruff a voice as he could muster.

Captain Dumey clicked his heels and saluted. "Entschuldigen Sie mich, Major. Sie gehen vielleicht," he said, clearly chastised by Aaron's scolding.

Nodding disdainfully at the German officer, but not actually returning the salute, Aaron signaled José to go, and José stepped on the gas. Not until they were at least half a kilometer away did Aaron turn around and look into the back of the vehicle at those who had sweated through the encounter.

"Oh," Aaron said with a wide smile on his face. "Oh, you don't know how good that felt."

"Okay, what happened? What did he say, and how did you answer him?" Dewey asked.

"He wanted to know where we were going. I told him I was a major and he had no business challenging me. Then I ordered him to stand aside so we could look for the enemy."

"I wish your father could've seen that," Dewey said. "The way you pulled that acting job off, why, you could've starred in any picture he ever produced."

"Yeah, I could've, couldn't I?" Aaron said. "You know, maybe growing up in Tinsel Town had its advantages after all."

For the next fifteen minutes, the armored scout car bounced across the terrain between Sidi Bou Zid, controlled by the Germans, and Kasserine Pass, where the Americans had stopped their retreat and were planning to make a defensive stand.

"Okay, guys, let's get out of these German jackets," Dewey said, stripping off his tunic. "If we've got observation planes up, I don't want them calling in artillery on us."

"Good idea," Aaron said.

"Hey, Dewey, shouldn't we be flying a white flag or something?" Alphabet asked.

"Yeah," Dewey said. He took off his T-shirt, then climbing up on the seat beside José, he reached for the top of the whip antenna.

Just as Dewey was at his most extended and vulnerable, the half-track hit a hard bump, and Dewey pitched over the edge. He would have fallen from the vehicle if Roberto and Aaron hadn't grabbed him by the legs and pulled him back.

"Thanks," Dewey said. "Hold on to me."

With Roberto holding one leg and Aaron the other, Dewey managed to tie his T-shirt to the antenna, thus making an acceptable white flag.

"Okay, hope that works," Dewey said, climbing back down. "Now, Ryder, see if you can get anyone on the radio."

"Okay."

Ryder took the signal operating instructions book from his pocket. The SOI would give him the command frequencies for every unit in the II Corps. It would also provide the authenticators for each day.

"Hey, what is today's date?" he asked.

"February 16," Dewey answered.

"Okay, here we go," Ryder said. He turned on the radio, and as he did so, they heard someone speaking in German. Ryder started to switch frequencies.

"No, wait," Dewey said, holding his hand out to stop him. "Aaron, what is it? What are they saying?"

"This can't be right," Aaron said.

"What?"

"They say they've got more than two thousand American prisoners."

"Well, now you know they're lyin'," Alphabet said. "There's no way they've got two thousand prisoners."

"I believe them," Dewey said.

"No, that's not true, man! You know it isn't true!" Alphabet said.

Aaron shook his head, then put his hand on Alphabet's shoulder. "Look around us, Ron," he said quietly. "Have we passed any of our men?"

"No," Alphabet said.

"Well, if we haven't passed any of them, where do you think they are? I mean, I'd rather them be POWs than be dead."

"But what about our battalion?" Alphabet asked. "The guys we trained with, took weekend passes with. Are you saying they are either prisoners or dead?"

"Yes," Dewey said. "That's exactly what I'm saying."

Hanging his head, Alphabet chewed on his lower lip as tears began to slide down his cheeks, leaving tracks across his sand-covered face.

"You okay, Ron?" Roberto asked.

Alphabet nodded. "Yeah," he finally said. "Yeah, I'm all right."

"Hey, Dewey, can I come up to our push now?" Ryder asked.

"Yes."

As Ryder searched the SOI, he began singing nervously, but no one stopped him. Finally, he found the frequency he was looking for and retuned the radio.

"Good Nature, this is Able One, Able One, over," Ryder called.

There was no answer.

"Good Nature, this is Able One. Able One. Come in, over."

"Hey, maybe this thing isn't working," Alphabet suggested.

"No, it's working all right," Ryder said.

"How do you know?"

"Listen to that," Ryder said, pointing to the speaker. "That sound you hear is the squelch."

"The what?"

"The carrier wave."

"Try it again," Dewey said.

"Good Nature, Good Nature, this is Able One. This is Able One. Do you read me? Over."

The squelch was broken, and for a moment there was absolute silence. Then a voice, obviously American, came over the air. "Able One, I authenticate Vexation."

"What's that mean?" Alphabet asked.

"He's challenged us," Ryder said. "Now I have to respond. That way they'll know we are legit."

Ryder looked at the SOI for a moment, then he looked up at Dewey, his face drawn up in confusion. "I don't understand this," he said. "There's no response in the SOI for a challenge of Vexation."

"Yeah, I was afraid that might be the case," Dewey said. "All the SOIs have been compromised. Let me have the mike."

Ryder handed the microphone to Dewey.

"Good Nature, this is Corporal Dewey Bradley," Dewey said.

"Vexation," the voice said again.

"Look," Dewey said in exasperation, "I know the SOIs were compromised when the Germans came through, which means all the authenticators were changed. We have an old SOI, so we can't authenticate. I say again, this is Corporal Dewey Bradley. We are Americans from the First Battalion. Our hill was overrun by the Germans, and we are trying to get away. We are coming toward you in a captured German armored car, and we'll be flying a white flag. Don't shoot."

"Wait one," the voice said.

"Wait one? Wait for what?" Roberto asked. "It's not like we told him we were coming for dinner or something."

Suddenly, an artillery round went off in front of them.

"Dewey, you better get up here and do something! Our guys are already shooting at us!" José called down.

Dewey stuck his head up and looked around. Then, from behind, he saw a flash. A moment later, another artillery round exploded just in front of them.

"That's not our guys shooting at us," Dewey said. "It's the Germans."

"They must be monitoring this frequency," Aaron said. "They heard us."

Dewey keyed the mike button. "Hey, Good Nature," he called. "Do you see these rounds exploding out here? That's the Germans shooting at us. They believe us. Why don't you?"

The voice came back on the air.

"Corporal Bradley, on Thanksgiving Day of 1941, what was the score of the football game between Litchfield College and Washington University?"

"What?" Dewey asked. "Why would you want to know such a thing?"

"What was the score?" the voice asked again.

"Uh . . . let me think. We . . . that is, Litchfield won, twenty-one to twenty, I think."

A new voice came on the air. "And who threw the block that let you make the winning touchdown?"

Dewey laughed out loud. "Don! Don Mitchell! Is that you?"

The new voice laughed. "It's Lieutenant Mitchell to you now, Corporal. Bring your boys on in. We'll be looking for you."

20

Kasserine Pass with the Americans

A ble Company lost four men, including Fred Ryder, but the next morning, they were still in place.

When Lieutenant Colonel Merkh, the battalion commander, called a meeting of his officers and NCOs, some of them were pretty full of themselves, talking about their victory over the Germans.

"Victory over the Germans?" Colonel Merkh asked. "What victory would that be?"

"Well, last night, sir," one of the junior officers said.

"Last night was a probe," Colonel Merkh said. "I doubt that it was battalion strength, and even so, it was all we could do to hold them off. Scarcely a victory, but it was helpful in that it gave our men experience and perhaps a little confidence. Just don't let your men get too sure of themselves because no one can break faster than a man who suddenly realizes things aren't as rosy as he thought. There's no middle ground for such people. They go from overconfidence to self-doubt with no stops in between. I'm counting on you officers and noncommissioned officers to provide the dampening they need."

After the meeting, Dewey found the opportunity to look up his old college friend who had spoken to him over the radio during their mad dash back to the Western Dorsal. Lieutenant Don Mitchell was a tank platoon leader for one of the tank companies. Dewey found him standing by a tank. A couple of mechanics were sitting on the tanks, their arms stuck down in the open engine compartment. At six feet four, Don didn't need football padding to be a big man.

"If I called seventeen blast, red, freeze, would you know what to do?" Dewey called.

"Pull right, take out the defensive end," Don said, smiling and coming toward Dewey with his hand extended. "Only you would probably trip over your feet getting out of the backfield. How are you doing, Dewey?"

Dewey smiled. "Uh-uh, that would be, how are you doing, Sergeant, to you . . . sir," he said, setting the *sir* apart from the rest of the sentence.

"Here, let me introduce you to some of my guys," Don said, and he introduced Dewey all around.

"Did you lose anybody last night?" one of the men asked.

"Four," Dewey said.

"That's tough."

The men went back to working on the tank, while Dewey and Don started talking about their time together in Litchfield.

"Wouldn't you like to be at the Bearcat Den right now?" Don asked. "I'd crawl a mile on my hands and knees for a hamburger, onion rings, and a 7-Up."

"Huh-uh," Dewey said, shaking his head. "A barbecue, French fries, and a vanilla milkshake."

"And a quarter to feed the jukebox," Don said. "Hey, I want you to tell these guys how you managed to make the winning touchdown against Wash U."

"What's there to tell them?" Dewey replied. "I just swiveled my hips and stuck out my hand and stiff-armed my way through the tacklers," he said.

"Whoa, Lieutenant, that's not the way you've been tellin' us it happened," one of Don's men said.

"Yeah, to hear the lieutenant tell it, he knocked down every tackler, then came back and picked you up, put you on his shoulders, and carried you across the goal line."

"Okay, I'll admit, that's pretty much the way it did happen."

"I hear you are about to be a papa," Don said. "Or are you already?"

"Not yet," Dewey answered. "But it's getting close. What about you? Did you and Barbara get married?"

"Yes," Don said. "Oh, I wish you could've been there. We had a military wedding right after I graduated from OCS. Ha, I'll bet you never figured your old lineman would be an officer."

"No, I'm not all that surprised," Dewey replied. "How do you like being an officer?"

"You know what, I may just stay in this man's army after the war is over," Don said.

"I'll bet you are a very good officer."

Shortly after Dewey returned to his own area, Lieutenant Robison called his NCOs together to brief them on their defensive position against the expected German attack.

"I wish we had three times as many men, or one-third of the territory we were responsible to defend," Robison told his four NCOs. "But we don't, which means we're going to have to make do with what we've got."

Dewey returned to his squad and got them into position, making certain that they had overlapping fields of fire. That done, he got into his own position. Dewey loaded his rifle, then took out ten more clips of "ammunition ball, caliber .30," and laid them on a little piece of canvas. The canvas would keep them from getting dirty and fouling the chamber.

As he sat quietly in his hole, he thought about the firefight last night when he had killed so many German soldiers that his barrel was smoking with the heat of expended rounds.

How many men had he killed since this war began?

He didn't think he had killed anyone during Operation Torch. He had fired his weapon in the general vicinity of the French lines, but he hadn't taken specific aim. Although he was not a policy maker, it had seemed somehow inappropriate to him to be killing Frenchmen.

But he had killed four men during their escape from Djebel Lessouda. And he had killed again last night.

When he thought of Travis Logan and Sergeant Hornsby, of Privates Drake and Ryder, he felt no remorse over the killing. He was vaguely aware that he should feel some remorse, or at least, he should feel guilty that he felt no remorse.

But he didn't. God forgive him, he felt nothing at all.

Trying to force such thoughts out of his mind, he thought of Unity. Closing his eyes, he pictured himself walking up the front steps of the Rankin house and being greeted by Unity. He could picture that scene, the welcome home scene, but he couldn't comprehend anything beyond that one moment. He couldn't even look behind Unity to see the baby.

He leaned forward in the hole and looked across the floor of the basin. The floor was filled with daisies and scarlet poppies, and he marveled at how a place of such beauty could also be a place of such evil.

Dewey closed his eyes to pray . . . but no prayer would come!

He was shocked by the realization that he could not pray. He could think only of the words of anguish that Jesus had called out from the cross.

"Eli, Eli, lama sabachthani? My God, my God, why hast thou forsaken me?"

Almost as if in answer to that tormented thought, the pass suddenly echoed with the scream of rockets being fired from the six-barreled launchers the Germans called Nebelwerfers. A massive artillery barrage followed the rocket bombardment. Then coming in behind the rocket and artillery fire were thousands of ghostlike forms moving through the daisies and poppies, and the smoke and dust. The German infantry was attacking in force.

Before Dewey could fire one round, Lieutenant Robison told him that word had come down, they were withdrawing to the Tebessa Road.

"Why are we going back?" Dewey asked.

"We're going to dig into stronger positions back on the road," Robison answered. "Or at least, so they say."

"Seems to me like we've done nothing but retreat, ever since we got into this war," Alphabet said when Dewey carried the word to the rest of his squad.

"You want to be the only one up here?" Aaron asked.

"No."

"Nor do I. If everyone else is going back, I am too."

Waiting until all of his men were out of their holes and on the way back, Dewey brought up the rear. The Germans were pressing the attack, and though their infantry was firing at relatively long range, Dewey could hear the bullets whistling past his ears.

For reasons that nobody could understand, the Germans interrupted their attack once Kasserine Pass was abandoned, and that night, after digging into new positions on Tebessa Road, the Americans were heartened by the addition of fresh new artillery battalions from the Ninth Division.

The Germans had been gone twenty-four hours before the Americans realized it. Because the Germans left, there was some discussion that, though the early engagements had been lost, the Americans actually won the battle. The validation of this logic was the fact that they had fought the Germans off in the last day of the campaign.

Dewey had no idea how history would record the Battle of Kasserine Pass, but in his mind, it always would be a bad memory. Here, he had lost his friends Travis Logan, Ward Hornsby, Timmy Drake, and Fred Ryder.

Lieutenant Don Mitchell also had been killed, though Dewey didn't learn about that until late that night when he went to Mitchell's company to look for him.

"His tank caught a direct round from an eighty-eight," Mitchell's commanding officer told Dewey.

Dewey let out a long sigh, then bowed his head. As before, no prayer would come.

"We were college classmates," Dewey said.

"Yes, the Bearcats," the captain replied.

"Yes, sir."

"I know all about you, Sergeant. What a great quarterback you were and, to hear Don tell it, almost as good at basketball. Here, you might be interested in something we took from his personal effects."

"What is it, sir?"

There was a manila folder on the captain's olive-drab field desk, and opening it, the captain took out what appeared to be a newspaper clipping. He held it out to Dewey.

Wash U Loses to Litchfield College
By *St. Louis Globe* Sportswriter, Glen Page.

APNov271941/Litchfield, Ill.-A capacity crowd of 10,000 fans filled Litchfield College's Shackleford Jackson stadium yesterday, to watch the 36th annual Turkey Day Classic.

The game was a thriller, bringing the crowd to its feet several times, causing the stadium to live up to its nickname, Shaky Jake.

Wash U took the lead in the first quarter with a sustained drive that culminated in a six-yard touchdown run from scrimmage. But Litchfield responded with two unanswered touchdowns, one, a pass from quarterback Dewey Bradley to Bob Dyer, and the next, a 36-yard touchdown run by Tom Murchison. Then, with but 1 minute and 22 seconds remaining, Wash U's Buddy Cox hit Bill Lewis with a perfect pass, and once again, Wash U held the lead. But Mickey Thomas's try for point went wide.

Then, disaster struck for Wash U. Dewey Bradley took the ensuing kickoff and <u>with Don Mitchell providing the springing block,</u> the Litchfield quarterback carried it all the way for a touchdown. The extra point was good, and Litchfield held on for the win.

The sentence about Don Mitchell throwing the block that sprung him was underlined.

It was a shame, Dewey thought. Don Mitchell had been an outstanding ball player, a very good lineman who had contributed greatly to Litchfield's conference championship that year. And yet, as was the case for many an unsung lineman, Dewey was certain that was the only time Don's name had appeared on a sports page.

Dewey handed it back to the captain. "Please send that to Barbara, his wife," he said.

"Yes, we intend to. Listen," the captain said, "I'm sorry you lost your friend."

Dewey didn't answer the captain, but as he started back toward his own position, he couldn't put away the thought that kept crowding to the front of his mind.

I've lost more than my friends. I've lost my soul.

21

Sikeston, Missouri
March 14, 1943

T he Sikeston General Hospital was only marginally larger than the
other houses that were in the same block. It was at the corner of
Gladys and New Madrid Streets in a residential area that, by coincidence,
was just across the street from the parsonage of the First Baptist Church.

Because of the hospital's location, when Unity went into labor early
that Sunday morning, there was no panic about getting her there.

"But it's Sunday morning," Phil said. "We've got church services."

"Maybe you had better tell this baby that," Margaret said. "I'm taking the car. When you are ready to go to church, you can just come
across the street and pick it up."

"How will you get to church?"

"I won't be coming to church, Phil. I'm going to stay at the hospital
until all this is over."

"Oh yes, of course," Phil said. He kissed his wife and then his daughter. "I'll be praying for you," he said.

Margaret helped her daughter down the front steps and into the car. It was merely a matter of backing out of the driveway, then going less than half a block down the street until she was at the hospital.

"Oh, dear," the nurse on duty said when she saw Unity and Margaret coming in through the front door. "I expect I had better call Dr. Urban."

"Thank you," Unity said.

The nurse picked up the phone and held it, waiting for the operator. "Mildred, this is Joyce. Down at the hospital? Get me Dr. Urban."

It took but a moment, then Joyce said, "Dr. Urban, I expect you'd better get on down here. It's Unity Rankin."

"Bradley," Unity said.

"Bradley," Joyce corrected. "Okay, I'll tell her." She hung up the phone and smiled at Unity. "He said he'll be here as quick as he can, and for you not to start without him."

Unity laughed. "I'll try."

Joyce and Margaret walked Unity down the hall and into a little room. Joyce helped Unity out of her clothes, into a robe, and onto the bed. Unity shivered.

"Are you all right?" Joyce asked anxiously.

"I'm cold," Unity answered. At that moment another contraction hit her, and she winced hard against the pain.

"I'll get you a little more heat in here," Joyce promised. She stepped over to the radiator and turned the knob. There was a hissing sound as steam came up. After that, the nurse set a little oscillating fan on the windowsill just above the radiator and turned it on. It hummed, rattled, and squeaked as it moved back and forth, directing a current of warm air through the room.

Margaret sat in a chair beside her daughter and held her hand.

Unity had one more contraction before Dr. Urban showed up. Urban was very thin, with a small mustache, glasses, and a prominent Adam's apple. He was wearing a bow tie and a broad smile as he came into the room.

"Well, it's about time you had this baby," Dr. Urban said. "You've been walking around town, putting on a big front for almost nine months now. Let's see what it is you're so proud of."

Dr. Urban took off his coat and put on a white hospital jacket.
Unity was hit with another contraction.

Tebessa, Tunisia
March 16, 1943

It was Wednesday, and except for motor stables and weapons cleaning,
Company A was on stand-down.

"Sergeant Bradley to the CP!" Cleaning his rifle, Dewey heard the
word being passed down. "Sergeant Bradley to the CP!"

"Hey, Sarge, Cap'n Robison wants to see you," someone said from a
couple of tents down.

"Yeah, thanks," Dewey answered. He stuck his rifle into his sleeping
bag, then walked to the far end of the bivouac area to the command post,
which was a somewhat larger tent, called a "tent, squad, four sided."

The CP also served as quarters for Robison, who was now a captain,
and First Sergeant Braxton Todd. First Sergeant Todd, who had recently
joined them when Able Company was brought back up to strength,
looked up from the little field desk where he was working on the morning report.

"Bradley," he said by way of greeting.

"Top," Dewey replied.

Captain Robison was sitting on a little camp stool just under the open
flap of the tent. He had his .45 pistol apart, and pieces of it were lying
spread out on his cot. The company commander and first sergeant had
canvas cots to sleep on, a luxury no one else in the company enjoyed.

Dewey saluted and reported. "You wanted to see me, Captain?"

"Yes," Captain Robison replied. He held up the slide assembly and
blew on it before continuing. "There's going to be some bigwig powwow
down at the schoolhouse. I want you to take your platoon down there
and provide security for the meeting."

"Yes, sir," Dewey said. "When?"

"They asked me to send someone right away, so I'd say right away,"

Robison replied. Holding the slide assembly up for a close examination, he blew on it again.

"Very well, sir." Dewey started back toward his tent.

"Sergeant Bradley?" Captain Robison called.

"Yes, sir?"

"This meeting is between General Patton, General Allen, and who knows who else. So, if you pick up any scuttlebutt, share it with me, will you?"

"Yes, sir."

It was nearly dark before Patton and his command and staff officers held their meeting. Under the auspices of seeing to the position of his men, Dewey managed to listen through an open window of the schoolhouse, which was dimly illuminated by a kerosene lantern.

"We've been given a very important mission," Patton said. "We are to attack the enemy at Gafsa so as to relieve the pressure on Montgomery. Now, so far, the II Corps has not exactly covered itself with glory. But I intend for that to change. Do you understand that?"

"Yes, General," the others replied.

"Good, good, I'm glad that you do," he said. "Because, gentlemen, tomorrow we attack." Patton paused for a moment, then looked dramatically into the face of every officer present. "If we are not *victorious*," he said, his voice rising on the word *victorious*, "let no man come back alive."

The advance began almost as quickly as Dewey was able to get back to report to Captain Robison with what he had heard. They moved easily back over the same ground they had abandoned a month earlier, unopposed through the little village of Gafsa. They drove on to El Guettar, where they paused in a vast green valley, filled with date-palm trees. Then just when it appeared that they would be able to push all the way to their objective, they encountered stiff resistance and were held in check for three days.

While his men dug their foxholes, Dewey went back with the other NCOs and officers for a briefing at the CP.

"I just got back from Battalion. Colonel Merkh says we've just gotten word that the Germans are sending one-half of their army against us," Captain Robison said. "It looks like we're in for another fight, but this time, according to General Allen, we're going to stay."

"It's about time," First Sergeant Todd said. "I don't mind tellin' you, Cap'n, I've been gettin' a little tired of haulin' out of here with my tail between my legs every time the Krauts so much as spit at us."

"Yes, well, I don't think you will have to worry about that, Top. General Patton wasn't born. He was issued from an army motor pool, and they only put one gear on him," Robison said. "Forward, at full speed."

Everyone chuckled appreciatively.

"Make sure all the canteens are full before nightfall. Make certain rations and ammo are distributed. Lieutenant Clemmons, have we got the land lines down?"

"Yes, sir, all phones are up from every platoon back here to the CP, and from our CP to Battalion," Clemmons replied.

"Good job."

Clemmons smiled nervously. Second Lieutenant Vernon Clemmons had graduated from OCS only last month. He had recently arrived as part of a mass influx of replacements.

According to the Table of Organization and Equipment (TO&E), Clemmons should have taken over one of the platoons, but he had no combat experience. Because he was an untried commodity, Captain Robison decided to keep his experienced NCOs as platoon leaders.

"You platoon sergeants, if you hear anything coming up during the night, ring up the CP and let us know. Any questions?"

The NCOs looked at one another, then back at Captain Robison.

"No questions, sir," Sergeant First Class Shell said. After the first sergeant, Shell was the ranking NCO in the company.

"Good. Get back to your platoons and set up your final defensive fire perimeter."

"Final defensive fire?" Clemmons asked, saying the words not in fear, but in awe.

The term *final defensive fire* had lost its impact with Dewey. He had already put them up several times and once had even been forced to use it. He knew, though, that to someone fresh from infantry training, the term *final defensive fire* still had a frightening connotation. It was literally a last-ditch desperation ploy whereby all remaining weapons were fired not at individual targets, but at a preselected zone. It was to be implemented only when a position was about to be overrun.

"Yes, Lieutenant," Captain Robison said. "Final defensive fire."

By the time Dewey got back, nearly everyone had dug his hole, and Roberto and Alphabet had teamed up to dig Dewey's hole for him. Roberto and Alphabet were still PFCs. José was a corporal, and Aaron, like Dewey, was a sergeant.

"Hey, Dewey, you know what? I was looking at a globe one time, and I believe I've got this all figured out," Alphabet said. "If I could do all my digging in one hole, instead of a lot of holes, why, I believe I could just dig right through to Chicago."

"Chicago?"

"Yep, and I'd come right up in Grant Park. That's only about six blocks from where I live. I could just brush off my clothes and walk home."

Dewey laughed. "I'm going to check with the other guys. Thanks for diggng my hole."

"You bet."

"Hey, Dewey," Private Woodward said. "You want to check mine out?"

Dewey looked at Woodward for a long, silent moment, then he nodded. "Yeah, I'll check it," he said as he walked away.

"That's Sergeant Bradley to you, kid," Alphabet said. Alphabet was at least three years younger than Woodward, but he didn't flinch at calling the replacement soldier a kid.

"Wait a minute. You guys call him by his first name," the confused new private said. "Why can't I?"

"Because we're friends," Alphabet explained.

"Well, we're in the same platoon, so it looks to me like we could all be friends," Woodward said.

"It doesn't happen that way," Alphabet said.

"Yeah. Get your own friends," Roberto said.

With Dewey's hole finished, Roberto and Alphabet knocked the dirt out of their entrenching tools, then returned to their own position. With a pained expression on his face Woodward watched them walk away.

"Don't let what they said get you down, Woodward," José said.

"I don't understand. I haven't done anything to them."

"It's not you."

"Then what is it?"

"You're new. Too many new guys get killed. If you live long enough, you'll be an old guy, then you'll be one of us and you'll see what I mean."

"If I live long enough?"

"Yes," José said. "If you live long enough."

At dawn the next morning, the Germans attacked, led by fifty tanks from the Tenth Panzer Division. Behind the tanks were self-propelled artillery pieces and armored troop carriers filled with infantrymen. But even before the tanks arrived, Messerschmitts swooped down to strafe the entrenched men of the First Infantry Division.

Bullets kicked up dirt all around, and Dewey fired back at them with his M-1. Up and down the line a few of the other, older men were also firing back, but most of the new men were in the bottom of their holes, covered up.

"Don't just cover up!" Dewey shouted. "Shoot back at them!"

"Shoot at airplanes with rifles?" one of the newer men questioned.

"Rifles, BARs, machine guns, pistols . . . throw rocks if you have to," Dewey shouted. "Don't let them have free run at us!"

At least six Messerschmitts were operating. They swung around and, once again, started a strafing run, with flashes of fire lighting up the leading edge of their wing.

"Don't shoot right at them. Give them a lead," Dewey shouted as he began shooting again. "It's like bird hunting, really fast birds!"

This time fire erupted all up and down the line, and when one of the planes pulled up, it was trailing an almost pencil-thin line of smoke.

"I got 'im!" Woodward shouted excitedly.

The others laughed at him.

"Well, okay, *we* got 'im," Woodward amended sheepishly.

The six fighters withdrew, including the one that was trailing smoke. But the smoke began to grow heavier and heavier until they saw the pilot bail out. The fighter nosed over, then crashed on the desert floor about three kilometers in front of their lines. It sent up a huge flash of fire, then a billowing tower of black smoke. The pilot drifted down under a greenish brown parachute, and they saw one of the troop carriers stop to pick him up.

The panzers closed to within range and began shooting. Their shells were exploding all around the men, and one of the newer guys started shouting, "We've got to get out of here! We can't hold against tanks!"

"Stay where you are!" Dewey shouted.

"Are you crazy? They'll grind us up like hamburger!" The soldier crawled out of his hole.

"Soldier, get back in that hole!" another voice shouted. "If you try and run, I'll shoot you."

Looking around, Dewey was surprised to see that it was the new, young, still untried Lieutenant Clemmons who stopped the fleeing soldier.

"Way to go, Lieutenant!" Dewey shouted.

Lieutenant Clemmons smiled back at him and nodded.

Suddenly, there were several different-sounding explosions from the area of the approaching panzers. They had run into an American-laid minefield.

The first several tanks were stopped by the mines, and the remaining tanks turned to withdraw. The infantry had already dismounted and come through the minefield that, because they were antitank mines, couldn't be set off by foot troops.

"Fire!" Dewey shouted.

Not only his platoon, but every man along the entire line of the First Infantry Division began shooting. They poured a withering amount of fire into the advancing Germans, who, because they were on foot, made good targets.

In addition to the small arms fire, American artillery opened up. The Germany infantry wavered and thinned, then the attack broke. The

Germans withdrew, leaving several of their dead and wounded on the battlefield behind them, along with burning tanks, half-tracks, and one airplane.

With the field before them cleared, the Americans renewed their own attack. On April 7, the American II Corps and the British Eighth Army met on the beach near the Tunisian port city of Sfax.

That night the men of Able Company received a message from Patton: *The German army is through in North Africa. Well done, men of the II Corps.*

22

Sfax, Tunisia
April 8, 1943

L ieutenant Clemmons, having proved himself in battle, was now
Dewey's platoon leader. Captain Robison asked Dewey to take the
new lieutenant under his wing. A few of the other NCOs teased Dewey
a little about having to babysit a second lieutenant, but Dewey and
Clemmons actually got along quite well.

Once more, Able Company was in stand-down, and the kitchen was
brought up to provide hot meals. In addition, a shower had been built,
which consisted of an airplane wing tank mounted on stilts. The water
in the tank was warmed by the sun and operated by pulling a rope that
allowed the water flow through a manufactured showerhead.

Having just taken a shower, Dewey walked back toward his tent. A
Jeep stopped alongside him with Lieutenant Clemmons driving.

"I was just down at battalion," the lieutenant said. "They broke out
the mail, and I saw this one for you." Clemmons handed the envelope

to Dewey. "From the return address, I have a hunch this might be the one you are looking for."

The return address read:

> Mrs. Unity Bradley & Daughter
> Patricia Leigh Bradley
> 815 West Gladys
> Sikeston, Missouri

"Patricia Leigh!" Dewey blurted excitedly. "I'm a father!"

Dewey tore open the envelope. Inside was a picture of a smiling Unity, holding a baby. The baby stared directly at the camera with shining eyes.

Dear Papa,

Allow me to introduce you to your daughter, Patricia Leigh Bradley. She arrived at 11:13 on the morning of March 14. She weighed 6 pounds 12 ounces, and is 19 1/2 inches long. Her hair is light brown and her eyes are blue. And she has a dimple! Oh, Dewey, she is absolutely the most beautiful thing you have ever seen! I can't wait for you to hold her.

You should see Daddy. He is strutting around so much over the fact that he is her grandfather that Mama says he needs to preach a special sermon on the sin of pride and listen to what he preaches.

I miss you, darling, more than I can say, and now, more than ever. Oh, I pray that this war will end soon, and you can come back home and we can have the life that we used to plan when we were back at Litchfield College.

Litchfield, oh, that seems so long ago now.

Speaking of Litchfield, I was saddened to hear about Don being killed, and of course, Travis and your other friends, including your sergeant. I know you thought the world of Sergeant Hornsby.

I pray every day for your safety. Please come home to us, Dewey.

> Your loving wife,
> Unity

"Your baby?" Lieutenant Clemmons asked.

"Yes, sir," Dewey said, proudly showing the picture.

"Beautiful baby and beautiful wife."

"Thanks."

Clemmons returned the picture, then turned the Jeep around and drove it back toward the motor pool.

Dewey showed the picture to Aaron, then to José, Roberto, and Alphabet. He saw Woodward looking at them, but Woodward made no overture.

"Here, Jim, what do you think of my daughter?" Dewey handed the picture to the young private.

Eager as a little puppy, Woodward smiled broadly, pleased at being included, and especially pleased that the sergeant had called him by his first name. "She's beautiful," Woodward said as he examined the photo. "She's the most beautiful baby I've ever seen."

Shortly thereafter, the others got their mail, and they lay around for several minutes, reading and enjoying their mail.

"Hey, Roberto," Alphabet said, looking up from his letter. "Your sister says she has my picture on the table by her bed, and every night, before she goes to sleep, she kisses it."

"You better watch it, Roberto. Alphabet is going to wind up as your brother-in-law," José said.

"Ouch!" Roberto teased. "I can see right now, I need to write Maria a letter and put a stop to this. Say, what is that girl's name down in Alabama that Alphabet is also writing to? Tammy or something like that?"

Alphabet looked up in surprise. "What are you talking about? I don't know anyone in Alabama named . . ." When he saw the big smile on Roberto's face, he threw a boot at him.

"Hey, hey!" Roberto laughed and put his hands up to block the boot. "You keep that up, I really will start telling my sister lies."

"Caramba! Fantástico!" José said, looking up from his letter. "Papá says that Mr. Patterson has bought a race car, and he is keeping it for me to fix up and drive when I get back home."

"You can drive a race car?" Private Woodward asked.

"Jimmy, my boy, José can drive anything on wheels," Aaron said. "You should've seen him driving that Kraut armored car."

"Yeah, hadn't been for him, we'd still be walking across the desert," Alphabet replied.

"Or in a Kraut prison," Roberto added.

"That's neat," Woodward chimed in. "I mean, the way you guys have stories you can share. Maybe one day I'll have stories to share with you too."

The others looked at him, and for a moment, Woodward thought that perhaps he had overstepped his bounds. But Aaron smiled at him. "As long as you remember, Woodward, it's not just José. We're *all* heroes," he teased.

"Yeah, Sarge, you bet," Woodward said.

In the Pacific theater—underway replenishment for the submarine
Angelfish
April 23, 1943

It was just before sunset, and the *Angelfish* cruised on the surface with lookouts aloft. In the west the sun spread color through the heavens and painted a long smear of red and gold on the surface of the sea. The *Angelfish* had rendezvoused with the destroyer *Patterson* as it came alongside for underway replenishment. The destroyer also delivered and picked up mail.

Pat Hanifin, officer of the deck as the destroyer came alongside, looked up at the bridge. He recognized the ensign on duty as his roommate from officer candidate school. Pat raised the bullhorn.

"Paul Griffin, how are you?" he called.

Griffin, who had been supervising the transfer, hadn't seen Pat, so he looked around in surprise at being called by name.

"Pat, how's it going with you?" Griffin called down to him.

"Fine, fine," Pat replied. "What movie do you have?"

"Abbott and Costello in *Keep 'Em Flying*. What about you?"

"*Kings Row* with Ronald Reagan and Ann Sheridan."

"Sounds good. Send it over."

"What do you hear from Tim Hawthorne and Jack Hayes?" Pat asked, referring to the other two roommates.

The smile left Griffin's face. "You mean you haven't heard?"

"Heard? No, heard what?"

"They were in *Barton*. Their ship went down at Guadalcanal. Eighty percent of her crew went down with her. Tim and Jack were lost."

"Oh," Pat said. "I am really sorry to hear that."

"Yeah, well, we're losing a lot of good guys in this war. So you take care of yourself, you hear?"

"Yes, you too."

The boatswain's call sounded in *Patterson*.

"Well, I guess we'll be going now," Paul called down to Pat.

Half an hour later, the boatswain made an announcement over the 1MC: "Now hear this. Mail call. Now hear this. Mail call."

For the next several minutes, the sailors whooped and shouted as they read their letters, sharing passages of them with one another. But Seaman Tyler Hornsby was strangely subdued. Unlike the mail the others had received, Seaman Hornsby's mail had not brought joy.

Sitting at the table in the men's mess, Tyler drank a cup of coffee and read the letter again.

Dear Seaman Hornsby,

My name is Sergeant Dewey Bradley. By now, you have already been officially informed that your father was killed in action. I hope that is the case because notification of the next of kin is neither my job nor something I want to do. But I do want to share some thoughts about your father with you.

I know that you and your father were not very close. He told me about the separation between himself and your mother when you were very young. As I understand it, you probably got to see him only once or twice during all the time you were growing up. I know that was not your fault, but I think you should also know that you are the poorer for not knowing your father any better than you did.

Sergeant Hornsby was one of the finest men I have ever known, and every man in his squad loved him. He died while trying to lead his squad out of a German ambush. I am convinced that if I survive this war, it will be because of what I learned from your father. Indeed, anyone with whom your father ever came in contact will, if he survives this war, owe his survival to your father.

Sergeant Hornsby was very proud of you, Seaman Hornsby. He was proud of what you had accomplished as an artist for Disney Studios, and he was proud of your service with the *Angelfish*. You may not know this, but he carried your drawing of the *Angelfish* insignia with him at all times and would take it out at the drop of a hat to show it proudly to any and all.

I will miss him very much. I just wanted you to know that.

Sincerely,
Sergeant Dewey Bradley

Folding the letter closed, Hornsby sat at the mess table, staring straight ahead. A young black man sat down across the table from him, and when Hornsby looked up, he slid a sweet roll across.

Mess Steward Leon "Choirboy" Jackson was practically the chaplain of the boat. Known as a very religious and highly moral young man, he read the Bible all the time and could quote chapter and verse on just about anything. He also had a reputation for honesty and had become an unofficial Solomon-like arbitrator, settling disputes for others on the boat. His decisions were so respected that even the losing party never questioned him.

Hornsby wasn't surprised to see him. "My dad," he said, answering the unasked question.

"Your father is in the army, isn't he?"

The crew of the submarine was so small that everyone knew just about everything about everyone.

"Yes." Hornsby sighed. "He was killed in North Africa."

"I'm sorry."

"You know, Choirboy, I didn't even know him. And to be honest, I used to say that it wasn't my fault that I didn't know him. He and my mom were divorced when I was very young. But after I got older, I could have made an effort. I could have, but I never did." He shook his head. "Funny," he said. "Now, I feel very much like I just lost something I never had."

"Rejoice the soul of thy servant: for unto thee, O Lord, do I lift up my soul.

"For thou, Lord, art good . . . and plenteous in mercy unto all them that call upon thee.

"Give ear, O Lord, unto my prayer."

"Is that a prayer you made up?"

"Not me—David."

"David?"

Choirboy Jackson smiled. "It's from the Eighty-sixth Psalm."

"Thanks," Hornsby said. He put his other hand on Choirboy's shoulder and squeezed. "I mean it."

Djebel Tahent, Tine River Valley, Tunisia
April 30, 1943

Dewey sat near the top of the hill looking down on the valley. The tanks and trucks destroyed during the battle just completed were still smoking on the floor below.

Able Company was in position on the military crest of a hill the Tunisians called Djebel Tahent. On U.S. military maps, though, it was Hill 609. Dewey knew that meant the hill was 609 feet high. Not very high perhaps as hills go. But it had been necessary to fight for every inch of territory.

The Americans had won the battle, but it was a very costly victory. The losses were 200 dead, 1,600 wounded, and 700 missing. Among the dead were two men from Dewey's platoon: Corporal José Montoya and Private James Woodward.

Davencourt Air Base, England
May 14, 1943

C haplain," Kenny said, shaking Lee gently. "Chaplain Grant?"

"Yes," Lee said, opening his eyes. "Yes, Kenny, is something wrong?"

"No, sir. There is a mission laid on. They are waking the aircrews."

Lee sat up and rubbed his eyes. Quickly, he got out of bed and dressed, then walked through the darkness with Kenny toward the mission mess hall. There, Lee had breakfast with the mission aircrews, a privilege allowed only to the chaplains and flight surgeons. All others on the base, including the airmen who would not be flying this day, took their breakfast in a separate mess hall.

After breakfast, the crews went to the mission briefing hut where they learned all the details of their target. Today, they would be bombing Würzburg. The announcement met with several groans, for Würzburg was deep into Germany, which meant that a great deal of their mission would be without fighter escort.

When the briefing was finished, Lee took his place on one side of the briefing shack, while a Roman Catholic chaplain took his place on the other side. On the way out a sizable number, though not all, of the pilots and crew stopped in front of the chaplain who represented their particular faith.

Lieutenant Mark White, who, like Lee, was a graduate of Litchfield College, and who had become one of Lee's best friends, stood at the back of the little assemblage. He was not a part of Lee's prayer group, but not totally detached from it either.

Mark's copilot, Paul Mobley, and Lieutenant Carradine, pilot of *Lusty Gal*, stood beside Mark. Lieutenant Carradine, who went by the name of Dusty, had transferred into the Six-Oh-Fifth shortly after they arrived. Dusty already had flown several missions before he transferred to the Six-Oh-Fifth, thus he was bringing some much-needed experience to the wing.

When all were gathered and ready, Lee began his prayer: "O most gracious Lord God, who lives in heaven but sees all things below, look down, we beseech Thee and hear us, preserving us from the jaws of death that threaten to swallow us up. Save us, Lord. The living shall praise Thee.

"Send Thy word of command to rebuke the raging winds and the roaring fire of our enemies, that we, being delivered from this distress, may live to serve Thee, and to glorify Thy name all the days of our lives. Hear, Lord, and save us for the infinite merits of our blessed Savior, Thy Son, our Lord Jesus Christ. Amen."

"Amen," the men said.

Fifteen minutes later, Lee was standing on the tarmac in front of the operations shack. The sun had just come up, and there was a bright, golden haze on the fields adjacent to the air base. He heard the whine and cough of the first engine, followed almost immediately by so many more that he quickly lost the first one as all blended into one heavy, sustained roar.

With propellers spinning, the almost endless line of B-17s trundled out the taxiway somewhat like a parade of elephants, trunk to tail, toward the end of the runway. The first airplane to taxi by was his father's airplane, the *Truculent Turtle*. Colonel Iron Mike Grant looked over at his son and nodded as he passed by, and Lee, though he felt guilty in doing so, said an extra prayer for his father's plane. As each subsequent airplane passed by, Lee could see the young men in the cockpits and the gun ports, their faces intent as they started their mission. He said a prayer for each of them, then added an extra prayer for *Gideon's Sword*, Mark White's airplane, and *Lusty Gal*, Dusty's ship.

The *Truculent Turtle* was the first one to start down the runway, all four engines roaring as it quickly gathered speed. Because of the weight of its bomb load, it stayed glued to the runway until the very end, then lifted from the ground as if reluctant to abandon this place of relative safety. Even as it broke free, the one just behind it was starting its own takeoff run.

It took nearly an hour for all the planes to take off, and Lee said an additional prayer for each one until finally the last one was airborne. He remained rooted to his spot until the thunderous roar of engines was a distant rumble and the planes indistinct black spots in the morning sky.

Bavarian Luftangriffsschutzhauptquartier

"This is Todeshandler aloft."

Karla heard Captain Lange's familiar voice in her headset.

"Todeshandler, this is Valkyrie."

"And, so, it is the lady with the beautiful voice who, once again, will attempt to conduct me into Valhalla," Captain Lange said.

Karla envisioned Lange in the close quarters of a Messerschmitt 109, somewhere in the cold, upper reaches of the sky over Germany. Although she forgave Captain Lange his bravado, even encouraged it, she had never told him that she knew who he was, that they had once met.

He was up there alone facing death, and yet there was a vitality, a buoyant air to his voice that she had to admire. How could he do it? How could he go up, day after day, knowing full well that each day might be his last?

"I have a bomber stream report," Karla said.

"Ah, yes, the nasty business at hand. Now, tell me, my sweet, lovely Valkyrie, what are the coordinates of the bomber stream?"

"Come to 230 true. Altitude 8,000 meters, speed 350 kilometers. There is a very large dispersal pattern."

"The Americans and their B-17s," Todeshandler said. "They are interesting planes to shoot down. They can take so much punishment."

Karla had two light guns in front of her, and she projected the bomber stream's position with one and Todeshandler's position with the other on the large map in front of the room. As she plotted the course of the converging flights, assistants moved felt cutouts across the map, bringing them closer and closer together.

There was a long moment of silence, then, once more, she heard Captain Lange's voice.

"Valkyrie, say again the bomber stream's altitude."

"Eight thousand meters," Karla said.

"Eight thousand meters, thank you."

Karla heard the roar of Captain Lange's engine over the voice of the pilot. Her stomach tensed, and she could almost imagine that she was there in the plane with the brave young officer who was Todeshandler.

Gradually, the dots grew closer together on the large map, then Karla heard from Todeshandler.

"Valkyrie, we have contact."

At 7,600 meters over Würzburg

What had been a quiet, almost pleasant flight in a clear blue sky changed dramatically when a gunner's high-pitched, excited voice alerted everyone on board *Gideon's Sword*: "German fighters, ten o'clock high!"

"I got 'em. They're comin' around," the top turret gunner said in a low, calm voice, contrasting sharply with the excited outcry.

"Okay, boys, keep your eyes on them," Mark said.

The German fighters, Me-109s, flew ahead of the Fortress formation, then turned and came back toward them, attacking head-on.

The bombardier on the nose guns and the top turret gunner opened up. The combined speed of the B-17 and the German fighters created a closing rate of more than 950 kilometers per hour. Mark could see winks of light flashing on the leading edge of the fighter's wings.

"He's going to crash into us!" Paul, Mark's copilot, shouted in alarm. "Do something, Mark!"

"Take it easy!" Mark said.

The fighter screamed straight toward them in a colossal game of chicken. There was nothing Mark could do to avoid collision. For the moment there existed an unholy partnership between Mark and the German pilot. Both knew that only the German pilot was quick enough to avoid impact.

"Do not lose your nerve, American pilot," Lange said. Because he had not keyed his microphone, his words were lost in the rubber cup of the oxygen mask he wore.

He headed straight for the plane, firing as he did so, but watching, with disgust, as his tracer stream fell away from the plane. To avoid wasting any more ammunition, he stopped firing, then pushed the stick forward slightly and flashed by underneath.

As he passed beneath, he saw another Messerschmitt closing on the B-17 from the rear of the plane, firing as he made his approach. Lange whipped his plane around in a G-producing turn, and as he completed the turn, he saw that the second Messerschmitt was caught in the middle of several converging streams of glowing tracer rounds. Between every glowing round, Lange knew, there were four other rounds, which meant that the airplane was being badly hammered.

Smoke streamed from the engine cowl, and the blur of the propeller disk slowed to the point that Lange could nearly count the revolutions.

The plane was fatally hit. It flipped over onto its back, and its pilot fell clear, rolling himself into a little ball for the long plunge down.

Lange knew that getting out of the plane didn't mean that the pilot was out of danger. He would have to pass through another bomber formation fifteen hundred meters below this one, where more than one hundred spinning propellers waited for him.

Breaking right, Captain Lange found himself lined up on another B-17. He moved in closer, so close that he could see little lines of oil streaming back over the top of the wing from all four engine nacelles. On the nose of the airplane was the drawing of a woman, filling out a sweater and a tight skirt. It was more of a caricature than an attractive rendering; the woman's breasts were well out of proportion, and her face was slightly distorted, as if viewing her through flawed glass. The name of the airplane was painted in yellow: *Lusty Gal.*

For just a second, Lange held his fire. There was something very human about someone who would put such nose art on his plane and name it *Lusty Gal.* Someone who was very human and very much like Lange himself.

Lange had shot down bombers before, but they had never been anything more than targets to him, huge mechanical things that he tried to knock down. There were people in this airplane.

"No!" Lange shouted. He put his ring site over the cockpit windows, then opened fire with his 40 millimeter cannon and watched as the explosive tracer rounds slammed into the cockpit, right above the little line of tiny, painted bombs, which he knew signified the airplane's previous bombing missions.

He saw a flash of fire momentarily light up the inside of the cockpit, then he saw the B-17 nose down. At first, it went straight down, then he saw it spin, twisting into a tighter and tighter spin.

"Fighters, disengage now," Valkyrie's voice said. "You are in the anti-aircraft artillery zone."

Lange flew in a long, lazy orbit as the bomber stream continued toward Würzburg. While the other fighters returned to their base, he continued to watch *Lusty Gal,* which now seemed a very tiny toy airplane far below. He followed it all the way to the ground, where it erupted in a flash of fire, followed by a billowing column of smoke.

Ordinarily after shooting down an enemy plane, Captain Lange executed a victory roll in celebration. But as he watched the oily smoke billow from the fire eight thousand meters below him, he had no desire to celebrate. For the first time in his life, he felt a sense of uneasiness about what he was doing.

"Todeshandler?" Valkyrie called.

Lange didn't answer.

"Todeshandler?" she called again.

Lange still didn't answer.

"Captain Lange, are you there?" Valkyrie called again, her voice clearly showing her anxiety.

Lange was shocked to hear her call him by name. How did she know who he was?

"Lange, is it?" he asked.

"Todeshandler," Valkyrie said. "I . . . you didn't respond. I thought you were—"

"I know what you thought, Valkyrie." The uneasiness he had felt a moment earlier fell away. "You were worried about me."

"No, I . . ."

"Admit it, Valkyrie. You were worried. Who are you that you know me?"

"This is Valkyrie, turning you over to Falcon Vector," Valkyrie said.

Fifty-sixth Adlerstaffel

Even as Captain Lange climbed down from the cockpit, the ground crew was already working on his plane, refueling it, rearming it, checking the engine, searching the skin for bullet holes.

"Captain, you were lucky." His crew chief pointed to a hole in the wing. "A few centimeters more and this would have hit your fuel tank."

Lange made no direct response. He watched as one of the crew removed the exposed film from his gun camera and replaced it with new film. The exposed film would provide a record of his kill.

His kill. Funny, how they called shooting down an enemy airplane a kill. Funny perhaps, but he wasn't laughing. Today he had killed not one B-17, but ten men. It wasn't just a word anymore.

"Captain Lange, we just got word," Lieutenant Fromm said to him. "You will be pleased to know that Lieutenant Metz has been picked up. He is uninjured."

Lieutenant Metz was in the plane Lange saw get shot down.

"Thank you," Lange replied.

"I saw that you got a bomber today."

"Yes."

"So did I," Fromm said happily. "Let us go to the club and celebrate."

"Thank you, no, I would rather not," Lange said, giving no further explanation as he walked toward his quarters.

Davencourt Air Base, England

The Wing had lost fourteen Forts on the Würzburg mission. Six of the fourteen were from Mark White's element, including *Lusty Gal,* Dusty's airplane. Mark hadn't seen *Lusty Gal* go down and didn't even know it was lost until he got back and Dusty didn't. Then he heard what happened from those who had been flying close to Dusty's ship.

"It caught an explosive round right in the cockpit. Dusty and his copilot must've been killed instantly because it nosed over and dived straight for the ground."

"See any chutes?"

"No, none."

Not just Mark, but the entire group took the loss of *Lusty Gal* hard because it was supposed to have been the last mission for Dusty and his crew. After this one, they would have gone home.

That night, the post-mission interrogation seemed endless: "What kind of fighters did you encounter? How heavy was the flak? What sort of damage do you think your bombs did? How many aircraft are you claiming killed? How many aircraft are you claiming damaged?"

Afterward, Mark borrowed a bicycle from the operations Nissen hut and rode into the night. At first he had no particular place to go. He just felt the need to be alone in the open and the quiet under the brilliant spread of stars.

Although he hadn't consciously planned it, Mark realized that he had ridden out to the hardstand where, just last night, Dusty's airplane had sat.

The hardstand was empty, but the ropes that had tied the bomber were neatly coiled, awaiting a return that wouldn't happen. The engine tarps and the pitot tube covers were still here. So, too, were the APU, or auxiliary power unit, the generator that supplied electrical power for starting, and the fire extinguisher. The yellow wooden wheel chocks were here as well, the ones that kept the wheels from rolling when the airplane was tied down.

Mark mounted his bicycle and rode all the way around the perimeter, feeling the tears stream down his face. By the time he returned to the BOQ, he was all cried out, but he had not overcome the pain.

24

Tunis
June 1, 1943

I 'm sure all of you can understand," explained Captain Felder, the army liaison officer who was assigned to the troupe. "The enemy would like nothing better than to capture one of our USO groups. If they did that, it would devastate the morale of our fighting men."

"To say nothing of our morale," Donnie Fritz said, eliciting a laugh from the comment.

Captain Felder had just informed the troupe that no advance announcement could be made of their arrival in Tunis. Marika Fletcher, the biggest thing in movies, was disappointed because she very much wanted to see Aaron Weintraub. Emily Hagen was also upset because she had a brother, Sergeant George Hagen, whom she hoped to see. Marika soon learned, though, that several others were in the same boat because nearly all of them had someone they wanted to see.

Marika knew Maurice Felder. Before the war he had been a press agent in Hollywood. She didn't know him all that well, but she knew him by reputation, and she knew that he was very good at his job.

As soon as the two C-47s, into which the USO troupe had transferred from the Clipper, landed, Felder went to work. He contacted every performer in the USO troupe, soliciting names and units of the men they wanted to attend the show.

Company A had won the First Battalion softball championship. Colonel Jonathan Merkh decided that his champions could beat anyone in the division and arranged a tournament. They had worked their way up to the final game, playing a team from one of the armored battalions.

In the last half of the last inning Able Company was up by one run, and the team from the armored battalion was up with its best batter at the plate.

Alphabet was pitching, and Aaron played first, with Dewey at second base and Roberto at shortstop.

"Come on, Larry, don't try to kill the ball. Just meet it," one of the armored battalion players coached.

"No batter, no batter, no batter!" Roberto chanted.

Larry swung at and missed a second pitch.

"There's a hole in the bat," Roberto said.

"Come on, Larry. What are you doing? Just get on base," the armored battalion coach shouted.

"Sergeant Hagen?" Captain Felder called.

"Not now!" Hagen was the armored battalion coach at first base, urging his team on.

"Are you Sergeant Hagen?"

Alphabet pitched the ball, and Larry swung. He hit the ball hard, but Dewey scooped it up on the short hop, stepped on second, then pivoted and threw to first, doubling the batter up. That ended the threat and the game.

"No!" Sergeant Hagen shouted in frustration.

"Yea!" Roberto shouted, running toward the pitcher's mound. Roberto,

Aaron, Dewey, and Alphabet started a celebration that was joined by the other players from the team.

"Sergeant Hagen?" Felder called again.

"What do you want?" the sergeant shouted angrily. Turning to see a captain, he quickly added, "Sir?"

While Captain Felder spoke with the first base coach, the other players ran over to congratulate Dewey and his team.

"Hey, Alphabet, are you going to tell my sister how you won this game?" Roberto asked.

"Yeah, why, you aren't going to try to tell her I didn't, are you? You know it was my brilliant pitching that carried the day."

"I can't believe Maria is still writing to Alphabet," Aaron said. "Hasn't she gotten him figured out by now? Roberto, you better do something. This might be getting serious."

"Yeah," Dewey said. "Could you see you and Alphabet as brothers-in-law?"

"Aargh, you mean my sister's name would be Alphabet?" Roberto teased.

"Aaron Weintraub, I've been looking for you," Captain Felder said, walking over to the group.

Aaron looked around then, and seeing Captain Felder, he laughed. "Well, well, if it isn't Maurice Felder. I thought you were too smart for the army." He stuck out his hand for a handshake, and when Felder stuck his out as well, Aaron jerked his back, then saluted.

Felder let his hand hang there for a moment, then, joining in the laughter, returned Aaron's salute.

"Boys, if you are ever in Hollywood and need a date, Captain Felder here is the one to see. He specializes in starlets. He's the one who fixed me up with Judy Garland."

"What about Susan Hayward?" Roberto asked. "Can you fix me up with Susan Hayward? Sir?"

"I'm afraid not," he said. "I'm not a romance broker. The dates I arrange are strictly business."

"What brings you to North Africa?" Aaron asked.

"I'm escorting a USO troupe around," Captain Felder replied.

Aaron chuckled again. "That figures," he said.

"Marika is with the troupe," Felder said. "And she wanted to make certain you were there." He gave Aaron a yellow card. "This will get you down front."

"I'll need three more," Aaron said.

Felder shook his head. "No can do. The front row seating is very restricted. Too many high-ranking officers."

"Push three colonels back a row," Aaron said.

"Come on, Aaron, you know I can't do that."

"Then give my ticket to someone else, and tell Marika I'll see her when I get home."

Felder looked stricken. "No, I can't tell her that. She asked specifically for you to be there."

"Yeah, and from what I've been reading in the trades, she is red hot right now."

"That's true."

"And unless you plan to make a career of being in the army, you won't be wanting to get on her bad side."

Felder pointed an accusing finger at Aaron. "You are trying to blackmail me."

"Really?" Aaron said, smiling at the captain. "Now, what gives you that idea?"

"I'm a captain. You're a sergeant. I don't know much about the army, but I know a sergeant can't blackmail a captain."

"You are probably right. In fact, I'm sure you're right," Aaron said. "So, just tell Marika I'm sorry."

Felder looked around and, seeing that nobody else seemed to be paying any attention to them, handed Aaron his yellow ticket, plus three others. He held his finger in Aaron's face.

"When this war is over and we're back in Hollywood, you are going to owe me for this, Aaron Weintraub. And you are going to owe me big."

"Thanks, Maurice," Aaron said, taking the tickets. "I'll see you at the show."

"Ha!" Alphabet said. "I knew you weren't going to let him break up the Double Musketeers."

Nobody bothered to remind Alphabet that two of the Double Musketeers were now dead.

Five thousand servicemen gathered in a large field just outside Tunis. The men sat on backpacks, helmets, or the ground, though up front there were a few rows of wounded who were sitting on benches and, in some cases, in wheelchairs. MPs were directing the arriving soldiers to areas where they could be seated. "Sit, don't stand!" they told the men.

Aaron and the others showed their yellow cards, which allowed them to go down front. The stage had been built by the engineers just for this show. It stood about one and a half meters off the ground and was flanked on either side by large general purpose tents, which were clearly marked as men's and women's dressing rooms. Canvas screens stretched from each dressing room to the stage. A large white canvas formed the stage backdrop. On the canvas were the words II CORPS AND UNITED SERVICE ORGANIZATIONS SHOWS PROUDLY PRESENT DONNIE FRITZ'S HOME FRONT REVIEW.

Captain Felder came down front to see Aaron. "Marika wants you to come backstage and see her," he said.

"Come on, guys. You want to meet a movie star?" Aaron invited.

"She didn't invite . . . ," Felder started. Then realizing there was nothing he could do about it, he shrugged his shoulders. "Yeah, okay, go ahead."

When Aaron and the others went behind the screen, they saw Marika and three other girls standing there, already in costume, waiting for their time to go on stage.

"Aaron!" Marika said, smiling broadly and rushing toward him. She embraced and kissed him.

"Wow," Roberto said when the kiss was done. "Aaron, don't wash your lips for the rest of the time you're here. From time to time I might want to just reach up and touch them."

Marika laughed, then said, "Oh, heavens, I can do better than that." She kissed Roberto, then Alphabet.

"Don't even start on Dewey," Aaron said. "He's married, and we've all met his wife."

"Yes, and we promised to look out for him," Alphabet said.

"Which means we can't be letting him kiss any pretty girls," Roberto added.

"Well, then how about shaking hands?" Marika said, taking Dewey's hand. "Oh, and let me introduce you to my friends."

Marika introduced Emily, Betty, and Norma Jean. During the next few minutes of conversation, Aaron learned that Emily had a brother in North Africa and a boyfriend in England.

"Maybe you know her brother," Marika said.

"You know how many troops we have in North Africa?" Aaron asked.

"No, how many?" Marika responded.

"Well, I don't either, but there are a lot."

"His name is Sergeant George Hagen," Emily said. "He's in the Third Armored Battalion."

"Hey, how about that? We do know him!" Aaron said. "Or at least we've met him. We just played a ball game against him."

"Beat him too," Alphabet said.

"My, I'll bet he's not happy about that," Emily said, laughing.

"Well, Emily, so you've got one down and one to go," Marika said.

"What do you mean?" Aaron asked.

"Emily has a brother here, and a boyfriend in England, a flier, that she is hoping to see when we get there. What's his name again?"

"White," Emily said. "Lieutenant Mark White."

"Wait a minute. Did you say Mark White?" Dewey asked. "Did he happen to write a book called—"

"*Man's Heavenly Quest*," Emily said, answering before the question was finished. "You've heard of the book?"

"I've got an autographed copy," Dewey said.

"Do you know Mark?"

Dewey shook his head. "No, not really. But I have met him, and I took a class from his father."

"Litchfield College?"

"Yes."

"Oh, this is just too wonderful!"

"You men better get back out front," Captain Felder said. "General Patton is here."

With waves of good-bye, the men hurried outside and sat down just as Patton took the microphone. The men cheered until Patton held out his hands, calling for silence.

"When General Eisenhower asked me what I thought would improve the morale of the Second Corps," Patton began, "I told him the best thing we could do is, kick the Germans out, and bring a few pretty American girls in."

The crowd laughed.

"So, I'm happy to tell you, that is exactly what we've done. We've kicked the Germans out, and we've brought some pretty American girls in."

More cheering and laughter.

"I know it's been a long time since you men looked at anything but the ugly faces of your sergeants, and the even uglier tails of the Germans who are running from you . . ."

Again, the crowd laughed.

"But that's all changing today because today we are proud to bring you some of the most beautiful young women in America. So, sit back and enjoy the show, men, because when it's over, we're going to go to Italy to kick some more German . . . ," he paused and looked toward the wings of the stage. "Well, there are some ladies present, so I'll just say we're going to kick some German rear ends!"

Patton left the stage to thundering applause and was replaced by a man wearing slacks and a sport shirt, swinging a golf club. He stepped up to the microphone.

"I'm Donnie Fritz," he said. "Who did you expect, Bob Hope?"

The audience laughed, then Fritz introduced the first act.

25

Rome
June 12, 1943

Gunter walked along the Via Tiburtina Vetus, not far from the most ancient ruins in the city. On his left stood the Colosseum, while ahead of him the specially braced Arch of Constantine bridged the road. He had been in Rome for just over a month now, and the remnants of the mighty Roman Empire still impressed him, not so much with their individual magnificence as with their collective reminder of man's transient status on this planet. Countless generations had been born, made their puny efforts, then turned to dust while the structures stood by in haughty grandeur.

A poster, faded by weather and torn on one side, decorated a kiosk on the corner. It featured a picture of the face of Mussolini with his jaw thrust out and his lower lip rolled down, snarling and staring into infinity like a man who could envision the future. Behind Mussolini's face was the ghostlike image of a Caesar from the days of the Roman Empire, and beneath the picture the words: *Il Duce and Caesars of old: a wondrous past, a glorious future!*

On the streets, black-market vendors were displaying their wares. At a nearby stand, someone was selling eggs, and though the price of the eggs was much higher than the price authorized, he was doing a brisk business.

As Gunter walked by the vendors, they turned their backs to him. Black-marketing was against the law, and violators could be arrested and shot. However, food was in such short supply that the law was sporadically enforced.

"German swine," Gunter heard someone mutter.

Allies, Gunter thought. The Italians were supposed to be Germany's allies. He had seen them run from battle in Africa and sometimes abandon their positions before the battle began. And now, the Anglo-Americans were poised to invade Italy, but the Italians clearly were not up to defending their own country.

And yet, despite the constant undercurrent of hostility between Germany and Italy, and his disdain for the Italian army, Gunter rather liked the Italian people. They bore up under the hardships with a stoic determination that spoke well of their two-thousand-year history. It was as if the people, like their ancient monuments, were determined not to be changed by the temporary insanity that had overtaken the world. They would survive with their personality and nationality intact.

Gunter remembered a conversation with a dignified-looking older man in an art gallery. Gunter had been genuinely interested in striking up a conversation with him, but the man, while not rude, was distant.

"You don't like me very much, do you?" Gunter asked.

"You are a German soldier, and as such, you represent everything I dislike," the man said.

"You hate the military?"

"No, I don't hate the military. I served in the army during the first war. I don't like the German military."

"But we are allies," Gunter reminded him.

"Allies? You have stolen our food, looted our art treasures, and gutted our industries. You have taken Italian citizens off the streets and shipped them to concentration camps in Poland."

"That is not our military. That is the SS," Gunter said. "And they take only the Jews."

"Jews who were Italian citizens," the art dealer said. "And the most terrible crime of all, you have robbed every Italian of his dignity, his self-respect, even his soul. Now, Sergeant, if that is what you do to your allies, what do you do to your enemies?"

"But I have come to like and admire the Italian people," Gunter said. "I wish everyone could see everyone else as I see the Italians. If we Germans could see the Poles, and the English could see the Germans, and the Americans could see the Italians as family—cousins, brothers, aunts, and not as alien cultures—there would be no war."

"And the Jews?" the art dealer asked. "Would you see the Jews that way as well?"

Gunter was silent a long moment.

"We Germans are going to have much to answer for," he finally said. "We are all guilty, if not by commission, then by omission, because we have not done anything to stop it."

"Are you saying you do not approve of your country's policy toward the Jews?"

"No, I do not approve," Gunter said. "But I have done nothing to stop it."

The art dealer was silent, then he put his hand on Gunter's shoulder and looked directly into his eyes. Gone was the hate he had seen earlier. The hate had been replaced by a sense of sadness.

"What can you do?" he asked with a knowing sigh. "What can any of us do? The whole world is guilty of the crime of omission. You Germans aren't alone."

Troina, Sicily
August 12, 1943

The town of Troina was built high on the side of a cliff located in a system of ridges and peaks. The road was rocky, precipitous, and broken, cut by mountain streams and laced with mines. A company marched toward the town while the men sweltered in the heat and the exhaustive effort. As Aaron pointed out, even if it had been a Sunday afternoon stroll, it would have been hard going.

But it wasn't a Sunday afternoon stroll. It was an advance against German troops who were well dug in and stubbornly determined to defend their position.

Suddenly, there was the familiar whooshing sound of incoming artillery, and the shell burst on the road, right in the middle of A Company. Two men went down.

"Medic! Medic!" someone screamed.

Turning to look behind him, Dewey saw a medic dart out to the middle of the road to check on the two men. Another round came in, and the medic threw himself on the ground, actually covering the two wounded men. The second round hit somewhat up on the side of the hill so that rock shards were added to the shrapnel that whistled down onto the road.

The word came up the road. "First platoon, locate and take out that gun."

"Sergeant Bradley," Lieutenant Clemmons called.

Dewey smiled. Clemmons was no longer the hesitant young second lieutenant in North Africa; he had become hardened, experienced, tough enough to commmand. "Take a detail and find that gun," Clemmons ordered.

"Yes, sir," Dewey replied.

Leaving the road, Dewey led them up the side of the hill until they reached the cutback at a higher elevation of the same road they had been on. There, they were surprised to see three young boys. The boys started to run.

"Roberto! Stop them!" Dewey called.

"Alt! Noi abbiamo cibo per Lei!"

The boys stopped running.

"Come," Roberto said, beckoning them toward him. Then to Dewey, "You have any food?"

"I have some K rations. Why?"

"Because when I yelled at them to stop, I promised them food."

"Okay, but only if they tell us where the gun is," Dewey said.

Slowly, cautiously, the three boys returned. "Dove è cibo?" the oldest asked.

"What does he want?" Dewey asked.

"He asked, 'Where is the food?'"

Dewey took out three K ration packets. "Okay, but if I get hungry, I'm going to eat yours." He showed the K rations to the boys. "Tell them, first, they must tell us where the German gun is."

"Prima Lei deve dire dove e cannone tedesco?" Roberto asked.

The three boys looked at one another, then the oldest tugged on Roberto's sleeve and led him across the road. He pointed up the hill.

"I see it," Roberto reported.

Dewey gave the three boys the food. "Tell them to scram."

"Vada via, rapidamente." Roberto signaled with his hand. The boys ran back down the road.

"If we climb up that way, we can get above and behind them, I think." Roberto pointed to a long ridge.

"All right, let's go."

All the while they were climbing, they could hear the gun firing, about one shell every half minute.

"Our guys are catching it pretty good down there," Dewey said.

"Yeah," Roberto answered between gasps for breath.

It took about fifteen minutes for them to get into position. Then Dewey held up his hand.

About ninety meters downhill from them, they saw the German gun crew. There were four men manning the .88, and a fifth, giving the orders.

"We've got ten men," Dewey said. "Roberto, Cooper, Haverkost, I know you guys can shoot, so each of you will take one man. Who, among the rest of you, is the best shot?"

"I fired expert on the KD range," one of the new men said.

"All right, you take him," Dewey said, pointing to one of the others. "The rest of you, team up. We'll put two of us on each one of the Krauts. That will increase our chances of getting the job done."

After some whispering, the firing teams were selected, and each of them picked out a target.

"I'm going to count to three," Dewey said. "Fire on three. One . . . two . . . three."

The ten M-1 rifles cracked as one, and all five Germans went down.

"Okay, Haverkost, Cooper, you come with me. We'll go down there and disable the gun before they can get another crew on it. Roberto, you take the others and get word back to our guys that they can come on up now."

"You got it," Roberto said.

One hour later, with the Germans at Troina

Gunter stood just below the crest of the hill and looked out along the road that unwound in a series of curves before him. Advancing up this road, he knew, was the American army.

The Americans, Gunter thought. They had bombed all of Germany's cities, and it didn't look as if they were going to stop until there were no longer two bricks standing together anywhere in Europe. They had all the artillery in the world and dry socks and hot coffee. They had bullets and toothpaste, gasoline and soap, tanks and ham. They had a supply system that was so untaxed that Gunter had found homemade cookies and record players among the American dead, and that was proof that there was enough room to ship nonessentials into the war zone.

He contrasted that with his own situation. The Germans were limited in everything. The lack of gasoline meant that they had to plan every move. Infantry, which in the glory days of the war used armored personnel carriers for their movements, now marched. Even their ammunition was limited.

"Sergeant Reinhardt," a voice called from behind Gunter.

"Yes?" Gunter turned and saw a soldier on the crest of the hill, standing in a way that caused him to be outlined against the sky. "Don't you know better than to stand on top of a hill?" Gunter asked sharply.

"I'm sorry, Sergeant," the soldier said, coming down from the crest. "I have a message for you."

"What is the message?"

"It is from Captain Dumey. He says you are to report to him immediately."

"He does, does he?"

"Jawohl, Feldwebel."

Gunter raised his binoculars and looked over to a nearby hill. "I told Horst to bring up six tanks," he said disgustedly. "He has only four. Get a radioman for me."

"Sergeant?" the soldier said, surprised at Gunter's reaction. "Aren't you going to report to the captain?"

"I'll report to the captain when I am ready," Gunter said.

"But, Sergeant—"

"I told you to get a radioman for me," Gunter ordered.

"Yes, Sergeant."

Gunter raised his binoculars to his eyes again and searched the road. Far off, he could see some movement, and soon he saw the American army coming into view. They were being led by a tank, then a double column of troops that marched down each side of the road, then another tank and another double column of troops, stretching on back nearly to the horizon. *There are so many of them,* Gunter thought, *all laughing and wisecracking and chewing gum.*

The radioman reported to Gunter a moment later, and Gunter used the radio to contact Horst and order the other two tanks to be brought into position on the other hill.

"The other tanks are disabled," Horst replied.

Gunter paused a minute. "All right, be ready to fire on my command."

Gunter looked through the glass again. "Heibler," he called.

Heibler came up to him.

"Have you put explosives on the bridge?"

"Yes, Sergeant."

"Wait until the first tank has crossed the bridge, then set off the charge. The tank will be trapped on this side, and the others won't leave him. We'll have the Americans in our killing zone for as long as possible."

"Yes, Sergeant."

"Do we have a motorcycle?"

"Yes."

"Have it standing by. I must report to Captain Dumey."

"When, Sergeant?"

"Right now," Gunter answered. "But I intend to wait until we have trapped the Americans in our killing zone."

"I'll get the motorcycle ready," Heibler said.

"Tell all the tanks to be ready to fire on my command," Gunter said to the radio operator, and the radio operator passed on the message.

"Just one more moment," Gunter said softly as he watched the approaching Americans. "Are your bellies full of ham and Coca-Cola?"

The first tank rumbled across the bridge. Gunter waited until it was across and the first column of infantry was on the bridge.

"Blow the bridge," he said.

Heibler gave the signal, and a German engineer pushed down the plunger, setting off the charge. The bridge came down, spilling several infantrymen into the chasm below. Even above the sound of the explosion, Gunter could hear them screaming in pain and fear.

"Tanks, fire!" Gunter ordered.

The radioman repeated the order, and instantly the German tanks opened fire. The ground shook with the guns booming all at once, and Gunter, watching through the glasses, saw the black arc of the projectiles as they slammed into the troops on the road. When the smoke cleared away, the remaining infantry had dispersed to either side of the road. The tank that had already crossed fired back, but it had no idea where the rounds had come from, so the American shells exploded harmlessly on a hill a full kilometer away from Gunter's position.

"Fire into the killing zone," Gunter ordered, and across the road, the tanks began to fire again, dropping shells right on the American troops. Within thirty seconds two of the American tanks were burning.

"The motorcycle is here?" Gunter asked.

"Yes," Heibler said.

Gunter gave Heibler his binoculars. "You are in charge," he said.

"For how long?"

"For as long as it takes," Gunter replied. Even as the fighting was going on behind him, Gunter straddled the motorcycle, kick-started it, and started toward Messina.

Gunter stopped in front of the command headquarters in Messina. Here, as the trucks were being loaded, Gunter saw that they were carrying out as much loot as matériel.

"Here! Careful with that painting," a major shouted to two privates loading a crate into a truck. "That is a masterpiece, and it is priceless."

Gunter hurried up the polished marble steps of the headquarters building. It had been a museum before the German army took it over.

"Oh, Sergeant, good, you have come. What I want moved is in there."

The man who was speaking didn't have on his tunic, but his trousers had wide red stripes down each leg, which meant he was a general.

"I'm sorry, General, but I have an urgent message for General Kesserling," Gunter answered. Gunter didn't know who the general was, but he did know Kesserling by sight, and he knew this general would be outranked by Kesserling.

"Oh yes, well, you will find him on the second floor, I believe," the unnamed general answered. "I do wish that sergeant from transportation would hurry. I must get out of here."

Gunter hurried up the stairs to the second floor, which was also the floor where he knew he would find Captain Dumey.

"Sergeant, good, good, you did come," Dumey said.

"Captain, what is going on?"

"What is going on? Why, we are retreating, Sergeant. We are abandoning Sicily."

"Do the men in the field know this?"

"Of course not. Do you think they would cover our withdrawal if they knew that we were leaving?"

"But that's not right," Gunter protested. "I left my men in battle."

"Did you leave someone capable in charge?"

"Yes."

"Then your men are just as well off without you as they are with you. Come, there is transport down at the dock. We must hurry."

"I would prefer to get back to my men," Gunter said.

"Yes, well, you aren't being asked to withdraw, Sergeant. You are being ordered. You can leave with me willingly, or you can leave in restraints."

"Why am I being ordered to leave?"

"Let's just say your military experiences in Poland, Russia, North Africa, and Italy are too valuable for the fatherland to lose," Dumey said. "Now, come, we must get to the docks."

"There won't be any room by the time we get there. I must have seen a hundred cars heading that way."

"Ha," Dumey said. "The funny thing about that is, none of them will be allowed to put their cars on the transport. They must go aboard on foot or not go aboard at all."

"Are we going to defend Rome?"

"Oh, the rest of these fellows are," Dumey said with a dismissive wave of his hand. "But you and I have an even more important job."

"More important than the defense of Rome?"

"Yes. You and I are going to join Rommel and your grandfather again. We are going to prepare for the defense of Europe. Paris, my boy, Paris."

"How is it that we got such orders?" Gunter asked. "Everyone else is staying for a fight to the finish, while you and I are going to Paris."

"Well, my boy," Dumey said. "If you can't have a grandfather who is a colonel-general, then the next best thing is to have a sergeant under your command whose grandfather is Colonel-General Jakob Reinhardt."

"I see. So, it isn't my experience, is it? It is my family connections."

"How can I put this delicately?" Dumey asked. He smiled a Cheshire cat smile at Gunter. "Yes."

26

Davencourt Air Base, England
October 14, 1943

After breakfast the crews gathered in the Nissen hut for their briefing. Though it was cold and raining outside, the furnace orderlies had the two coal stoves blazing, and that, plus the body heat of the assembled men, caused the temperature inside to rise to a comfortable level.

The men sat on wooden benches or in chairs as they waited for the briefing to begin. They spoke with their neighbors, dozed, or stared straight ahead with the glazed look of individuals who were trying hard to put all feeling, fear, hope, thoughts of home, and plans for a future out of mind.

Colonel Iron Mike Grant stepped onto the platform in front, and all conversation came to a halt. He jerked aside the black curtain that covered the map. Those in the back couldn't see the target, but those in front could, and someone gasped aloud, "Schweinfurt!"

"Schweinfurt," another said, and the word was repeated several times until even those in the very back row knew the grim truth.

"That's right, Schweinfurt," Colonel Grant said.

There were several groans. Schweinfurt was very deep inside Germany, and the strike route would take them within attacking range of more than eleven hundred German fighters.

Grant remained silent a moment, allowing it to soak in, letting the men prepare themselves mentally and emotionally for the ordeal ahead of them.

"Schweinfurt is the city where the Germans make all their ball bearings, and everything they use in the war against us depends on those ball bearings, from their fighter planes to their tanks, all the way down to the Führer's desk chair."

"Well, by all means, let's take out Hitler's chair," someone shouted, and the others laughed nervously.

"Takeoff at 0600. Lead element will be at 20,000 feet. Second element at 25,000. Third element at 30,000. Course is 080 degrees until checkpoint Able, then 115 to IP. Return 250. Command push is 121.9, but keep the communication to a minimum."

Pilots, navigators, and radiomen began writing the pertinent information on the backs of their hands.

"We'll pick up FW-190s and Me-109s on the way in and on the way out. They stay on station and are radar-vectored to us. We may also get some of the twin-engine Me-210s as well."

"What about fighter escort, Colonel?" one of the pilots in the front row asked.

"We are supposed to have P-47s take us halfway in, then they'll meet us again about halfway back, but we may not. Right now, they're socked in worse than we are, and there is a very good chance they won't even get off the ground."

"Tell 'em to give us a call when they're ready," someone quipped.

Grant said nothing, but his prolonged silence indicated his displeasure at being interrupted.

The men grew quiet once more.

"It doesn't matter whether we have fighter escort or not," Grant said. "Because with or without them, we're going to take out this target."

The meteorology briefing followed, given by a bespectacled captain who told them that, though the weather was bad over England, it would be clear over the Continent.

Then Grant retook the stage. "Today's authentication code is Buster," he said. "I say again, Buster. And if you are diverted and have to use smoke to signal the tower, the color of the day is green." He looked at his watch. "Time at my hack is 0525."

Every pilot in the room pulled the stem on his watch and set it to exactly 0525 and waited, with hand poised.

"Hack," Colonel Grant said. Every watch showed exactly the same time.

After the briefing, the aircrews came to Lee, who prayed with them. Though Mark White was not one of those who came to Lee, Lee prayed for him as well.

Bavarian Luftangriffsschutzhauptquartier
October 14, 1943

Karla felt a sickening hollowness in the pit of her stomach. They were coming for Schweinfurt!

"Controller-Director, this is Valkyrie," she said, her tongue so thick with fear that she wasn't certain she could even make the words.

"Go ahead, Valkyrie."

"I have a plot on the incoming bomber stream. Their target appears to be Schweinfurt."

"Very well, I shall notify the Schweinfurt antiaircraft batteries and Eagle Squadron."

Karla waited for what seemed an eternity until she heard Captain Lange's voice.

"This is Todeshandler. I'm aloft with all my chicks."

"Todeshandler, I have a large bomber stream. Turn to three-zero, no, wait, make it, uh, two-nine-five. Yes, two-nine-five true."

"Coming to course two-nine-five," Todeshandler replied calmly. "Valkyrie, what's wrong with you today? You sound nervous."

"The bombers, Todeshandler. They are coming here to Schweinfurt. I'm frightened."

Lange chuckled softly. "Welcome to my world, my dear. I am always frightened. Say now their altitude."

"Six thousand, five hundred meters."

"Six thousand, five hundred," Lange repeated.

"Oh, Captain Lange, stop them, please."

"Don't worry. I shall do my best."

Karla projected the bomber stream and Eagle Squadron flights onto the large map in front of the room, then watched with the others as the bomber light source moved slowly, but inexorably toward Schweinfurt.

FAG Kugelwerks

Viktor Maas was on the assembly line of the .32-inch extruder machines. The line was temporarily shut down because of an errant stator guide, and he was working with the technicians, trying to get it started again.

"Herr Maas! Herr Maas!" someone called from the catwalk above.

Viktor looked up. "Yes?"

"The bombers! They are coming to Schweinfurt!"

"Sound the alarm," Viktor said. "Everyone to the bomb shelter!"

The plant workers scurried to get out of danger.

"Stefan, have my car brought around," Viktor ordered. "I'm going to the antiaircraft battery."

"Jawohl, Herr Maas."

Viktor's car was waiting for him in the drive in front of the building, and his driver was sitting behind the wheel, nervously tapping it with his fingers.

"To the number one gun position. Hurry," Viktor said, slipping into the front seat beside his driver. The car was moving, even before Viktor closed the door.

Viktor thought of his family. Karla was safe, he was sure of that, because she was on duty in the plotting room. The plotting room was an exceptionally well-fortified underground bunker that could survive a direct hit from a bomber. His wife, Olga, was at home, and he could only hope and pray that the house would not be hit. It was far enough away from the factory, which he knew would be the primary target, that he believed she would be safe.

When Viktor arrived at the antiaircraft battery, the gun captain reported to him. Because the batteries were there to protect the factory, Viktor had been given the rank of oberst, or colonel.

"All guns are manned and ready, Herr Oberst."

"Good," Viktor said. He put his hand over his eyes and stared high into the northeast. In the distance he could see hundreds of black dots and the long white scars of contrails across the sky. "Get ready, Captain. Here they come."

"Altitude seven thousand meters!" a soldier called. He sat behind some kind of sighting device.

"Set fuses for seven thousand meters," the gun captain said.

"No, altitude six thousand meters! Wait, six thousand five hundred meters!"

"Schmidt, which is it?" the gun captain asked in irritation.

"I . . . I . . . ," Schmidt stammered.

Viktor put his hand on the young man's shoulder. "Take it easy, Schmidt," he said calmly. "We are all equal in our danger."

"Jawohl, Oberst," Schmidt said nervously.

"Now, what is the elevation?"

"Six thousand five hundred, Herr Oberst."

"You are sure?"

"Jawohl."

"Reset the fuses. Six thousand five hundred," the gun captain said.

Quickly, the gun crews adjusted the pressure-operated fuses on the noses of the projectiles. The loaded gun was then moved into position.

Now, Viktor could see the smaller dots flitting around the larger ones, and he knew they were German fighter planes, nipping at the bomber squadron as a wolf pack would nip at a herd of deer. One of the bombers in the formation fell away from the others, then disappeared in a brilliant flash of light.

Viktor heard the thump of the farthest gun. Other thumps followed, moving closer and closer as the huge bomber squadron approached until finally the gun nearby him opened up with a stomach-shaking roar.

The sky above filled with metal, the sheet metal of the giant four-engine airplanes and the darting, deadly German fighters and the white-hot metal of exploding shell fragments. The sound of the engines beat down upon the ground now, and they could be heard even above the ear-splitting sounds of the rapid-firing antiaircraft guns. The fighter aircraft and the antiaircraft guns were exacting a heavy price from the raiders, and the bombers began falling like rain. At one time Viktor saw as many as eleven bombers spiraling down at the same time, and some of the black dots had blossomed into white puffs as scores of men were coming down in parachutes.

The bombers made a slight turn and headed for Schweinfurt, then Viktor saw the bombs beginning to tumble out. There were thousands of bombs, and he watched in morbid fascination as they hurtled down across the six and a half kilometers of vertical space that separated the city from those who would destroy it.

"Listen," someone said. "What is that strange sound?"

"It's the bombs," another said. "They whistle as they fall. I've heard them hit before."

The first bombs hit then, and Viktor saw the white flash, then the smoke, followed several seconds later by the roar of the explosions. After that the bombs continued to rain down and explode in one never-ending roar for nearly fifteen minutes. Finally the last bombs had fallen, and the planes turned away, heading back in the same direction from which they had come. Once more, the fighters engaged them while, below and behind the bombers, Schweinfurt burned.

Viktor's wife was not at home. Olga had chosen this day to go down-town to do volunteer work for the War Relief. When the first bombs exploded in the city, about three thousand meters from Olga's location, she dived to the sidewalk next to the wall of the building and put her arms over her head. She heard the steady thump of explosions as the bombs fell. After several minutes of constant explosions, she heard the roar and lick of flames.

When finally the bomb bursts stopped, Olga stood up and brushed herself off. She looked down the street toward the apothecary and saw a wall of fire. The apothecary was on the other side of the fire, so there was no way she could get there.

Dazed and not knowing quite what to do, she sat down on the steps in front of the building beside which she had taken shelter and watched almost disinterestedly as people began running through the street, screaming in panic. She saw one figure running from the wall of fire, then collapse on the street, and only then did Olga realize that the person was burning.

A fire truck passed by in front of her, its siren sounding, its firefighters hanging on to the side. *What a puny, insignificant sight it is,* she thought, *one fire truck and six men against a blazing city.*

The explosions started again, and at first she thought they were explosions set off by the fires. Then she realized that it was a second wave of bombers. All the fires had merged into a howling firestorm. The firestorm superheated the air around the flames, and the air rose, creating a suction that drew more air into the inferno, feeding it with fresh oxygen, making it even hotter and sucking in even more air.

At first Olga felt the heat that warmed what had been a chilly fall day. But the heat increased, becoming uncomfortable and then nearly unbearable. She had to twist around on the steps and turn her back to the approaching wall of flame to shield herself from its scorching effect. Several minutes later Olga actually realized the true danger of her situation, and when she did realize it, time had run out for her.

To the crackle of flames and muffled explosions was added the whistling rush of wind, which blew in a hurricane fury. But even the wail of the wind could not shut out the sounds of a dying city . . . the screams of terror, cries of pain, and here and there, a last, blasphemous oath of anger.

Finally a crash, then a roar unlike any sound Olga had ever heard. She looked toward the noise and saw a giant wave of fire, shooting up from the building against which she had taken shelter. The building collapsed, and everything went black.

Fromm could not believe it. Captain Lange was invincible. He had proven his invincibility in countless sorties against the enemy. And yet the Todeshandler's airplane, a flaming torch, spun out of control.

"Todeshandler! Todeshandler!" he called. "Jump! Jump!"

Captain Lange's airplane exploded into a white-hot ball of flame.

Viktor returned to the plant as quickly as possible. Amazingly the plant was relatively undamaged. Only seven bombs had fallen within the plant compound, and only two of them had hit the main assembly building.

One of the two bombs had been a high-explosive bomb, which the Allies believed would destroy the tooling equipment. It did nothing but knock over a couple of the machines, which Viktor's men reset.

However, the plant did not escape serious consequences. An incendiary bomb, intended by the attacker to be used as a nuisance factor only, set fire to the oil baths. That fire raged for quite some time before they were able to bring it under control, and though the machinery looked unharmed, all the rollers, which were set to the most delicate of tolerances, were warped. That, Viktor knew, would bring production to a standstill.

Viktor went to his office, which remained unscathed as it had been when he reported to work that morning. "Have you been able to reach my wife yet?" he asked his secretary.

"No, sir," the secretary replied. "The phones are still out. Would you like me to send someone to check on her?"

"Thank you, no," Viktor said. "I will check myself."

When Viktor got home, he saw Karla sitting in the parlor.

"Karla," he said, pleased to see her. "Thank God, you are safe."

Karla had a pained expression on her face.

"Where is your mother?" Viktor asked. "Olga!" he called. "Olga, come!"

Without a word, Karla handed a note to Viktor.

Karla

    I have gone to work with the War Relief today. I made a nice cabbage soup for you and your father.

Viktor looked up, a confused expression on his face. "What does this mean?" he asked.

"Papá, the War Relief building," Karla said in a frightened, weak voice. "It was in the center of the bombing. It was completely destroyed."

27

Davencourt Air Base, England
December 22, 1943

Kenny Gates met Dewey at the entrance to the airfield, vouching for him to the guard.

"A staff car?" Dewey asked as he got into the black Buick.

"Well, why walk when you can ride?" Kenny asked. "And why ride in a truck or a Jeep when you can ride in a sedan?"

Kenny took Dewey to the chaplain's quarters, where Lee greeted him warmly.

"Lee, or should I say, Chaplain Grant? It's good to see you," Dewey said, shaking Lee's hand.

"I'm hurt you would even ask such a thing," Lee said, though the smile on his face indicated that he wasn't really hurt.

"Are you still running?"

"No, it's not all that smart to be running on an air base. Some nervous guard may take a shot at you," Lee replied.

"I know what you mean."

"So, how long have you been back in England?" Lee asked.

"We were pulled out of Italy last month," Dewey replied.

"You've been here for more than a month, and you haven't come to see me before now?"

"They've been pretty tight on allowing us out."

"Why?"

"Well, there's been no official word, but everyone says, and believes, that we are getting ready to go to France. The way we've been training certainly suggests that. And I guess they are trying to make sure nobody talks about it."

Lee looked at Dewey's shirt. He was wearing his class A's, as required when going on pass. Above his pocket he had two rows of ribbons, including the Silver Star. The ribbons were topped by the combat infantry badge.

"From the looks of all that cabbage, you've already seen your share of combat," Lee said.

"Most of this stuff is just 'I was there too' ribbons," Dewey said dismissively.

"The Silver Star is hardly an 'I was there too' type of medal. How did you get that?"

"I helped take out a gun," Dewey said.

When he didn't elaborate, Lee didn't press. He knew from his experience of dealing with the aircrews that there were some things the men just didn't want to talk about.

"Hey, Dewey, you want some ice cream?" Kenny asked, interrupting the moment of silence.

Dewey looked at Kenny in surprise. "You've got ice cream?"

"Yep. And Coke," Kenny said. "If you'd like, I'll make you an ice-cream float."

"If I'd like?" Dewey smiled. "I'll tell you the truth, Kenny. About the only thing I'd like more would be to see Unity coming through that door."

"Listen, you know Unity was just a little brat when she was growing up, don't you?" Kenny said. "She and my sister were always trying to tag along."

Dewey laughed. "From what I've heard, Kenny, it was to keep you out of trouble."

"Yeah, so they say," Kenny said.

"Kenny and I have been keeping up with your baby," Lee said. "She's a beautiful child."

"Oh?"

"The chaplain is sniffing around my sister," Kenny said as he opened the freezer compartment to the refrigerator and removed a box of ice cream.

"Kenny!" Lee said.

"Well, aren't you sniffing around her?" Kenny asked as he dropped a scoop of ice cream into a glass. He added Coke and, as it started fizzing, handed it, with a spoon, to Dewey.

"I'll have you know that chaplains don't sniff. We approach courtship with dignity and aplomb."

"Courtship?" Dewey took a bite of his float, then made an expression of pure joy. "Oh, this is good." He smacked his lips. "Pure heaven."

"I thought you might like it," Kenny replied with a broad smile.

"I didn't know you had met Millie."

"I must confess that I have met her only through letters," Lee said. "But she seems like a delightful person, and I am taking great joy in our exchange of mail."

"Unity thinks the world of her, so that's good enough for me," Dewey said. "And I can vouch that she is a very pretty girl . . . though, of course, to look at Kenny, you would never know that."

"I'll have you know I'm considered quite handsome in some circles," Kenny said.

Dewey held up the float. "If you can produce these, I can see why."

"Kenny has a remarkable talent for, uh, obtaining the unobtainable," Lee remarked. "Take the car, for example."

"Yes, I noticed that. Everyone else is driving around in Jeeps or three-quarters, and here Kenny is in a Buick. How did that happen?"

"They took the chaplain's Jeep away from him," Kenny said. "So, I went to the navy motor pool in London and convinced some chief there that I was going to provide transportation for a navy captain. He jumped through hoops to give me the car."

"I did chastise Kenny for lying." Lee sighed. "Though there have been times when having this car was a godsend."

"And it's not entirely a lie," Kenny said defensively. "I mean, if I ever see a navy captain in need of a ride, I will pick him up in a heartbeat."

Dewey and Lee laughed.

"Listen, I've got some things to take care of. I know you two are old friends from college, so I think I'll let you visit."

"Thanks, Kenny," Lee said.

"I met Mark White's girlfriend," Dewey said. "She was with a USO troupe down in North Africa. Did she connect with Mark while she was here?"

"Yes, barely. There was some, well, let's call it, missed communication. But they got it worked out and had a grand reunion. They are, in fact, engaged to be married."

"Good for them," Dewey said.

Lee walked over to the coffee pot, poured himself a cup, then looked over at Dewey. "Coffee?"

"No, thanks, I'm still working on this," Dewey said.

Lee brought his coffee over and sat down. "Dewey, I was a little surprised when I learned you had turned down a chaplaincy."

"Yeah, I probably should've taken it. But it's too late now."

"Never too late," Lee said. "I'll bet if you put in for it, you could still get it."

Dewey looked up from his Coke float, and Lee found himself looking into eyes that were deeper and more full of pain than any he had ever seen.

"No, I don't mean that, Lee. I probably could get a chaplaincy. But it's too late for *me*."

Lee studied Dewey over his cup of coffee for a long moment before he finally spoke.

"Funny that you would mention Mark White. I would like to tell you something about him."

"What is that?"

"Like you, Mark has seen a lot of combat. He has the Distinguished Flying Cross, among other medals, and he was recently promoted to major. Both the medal and the promotion happened as a direct result of the Schweinfurt mission."

"Mark is a major already? Good for him."

"But if you were to ask Mark, neither the medal nor the promotion is the most significant thing about the Schweinfurt mission."

Dewey smiled wryly. "Now, why do I think you are going to tell me what the most significant thing about that mission was?"

Lee said, "Mea culpa. For Mark, the most significant thing about that mission was that he found Jesus."

Dewey blinked in surprise. "Wait a minute. What do you mean he found Jesus? He is the author of *Man's Heavenly Quest*. That is one of the most brilliant theological tomes I've ever read."

"Oh yes. Mark has always been the theologian, but he wasn't a truly religious man. That is, not until he opened his heart and let the Lord come in."

"And you say all that happened during the Schweinfurt mission?"

"It did. I don't know what you know about the air war over Europe, but our losses are high. Staggeringly high. And Schweinfurt was one of the worst. During that mission Mark needed a miracle from God to get home safely. God not only brought him home, but saved his soul."

Dewey went back to studying his float, staring at the little lump of white at the bottom of the glass. He made no response to Lee's comment.

"Dewey, what did you mean when you said it was too late for you?" Lee asked.

Dewey didn't answer.

"Because no matter what it is, you know you can always talk to me about it," Lee invited. "I don't put my life on the line the way you have and the way the aircrews here have. But I do put my sanity and my soul on the line, and so far both have survived."

"You are lucky, Lee. You are very, very lucky." Dewey continued to stare into the bottom of the glass.

"Talk to me, Dewey. I can't help you if you don't talk to me."

"You can't help me at all," Dewey answered.

"How do you know if I don't try?"

"Your job is to save souls." Dewey put his hand over his heart. "I have no soul to save. Do you understand that?"

"No, I don't understand that. Everyone has a soul," Lee insisted. "Maybe yours is battered, bruised, and in great pain. But it is there."

"Do you know how many men I've killed, Lee? I don't mean dropping bombs from five miles high so that all you see below are little puffs of smoke. I'm talking about watching the life leave the eyes of men whose blood and guts you have just spilled. Men who are carrying pictures in their billfolds, pictures of wives and babies, of mothers and fathers, and friends. Do you know how many of those human beings I have killed?"

"I know it must be hard."

"No!" Dewey shouted. "You don't understand, do you? It isn't difficult, Lee. It's so easy that I can kill someone without giving it a second thought. They are targets, shadows, nonentities. They are there one second and gone the next. I kill them, and I feel nothing."

Dewey stared with an intensity that unnerved Lee. Finally, Lee got up and removed the empty glass from Dewey's hand.

"When you write to Unity, do give her my regards," Lee said, changing the subject.

One of Lee's most valuable assets as a chaplain was his perceptiveness. He accurately perceived that Dewey needed time to think about what he was going through. Dewey claimed that he felt nothing over killing German soldiers, but Lee knew that he felt each incident personally and deeply.

"Lee, what am I going to tell Unity?" Dewey finally asked. "She still tells me all the church news that's going on, and she is making plans for our life after the war with me as a pastor somewhere and her as a schoolteacher."

"You haven't shared any of this with her?"

"I can't. She would never understand. No offense to you, Lee, but for all your counseling of these guys," he made an inclusive motion with his hand, taking in the air base, "you don't know what it's like."

"God understands—" Lee started, but Dewey interrupted him.

"There is no God, Lee!" he shouted, slamming his fist down on the desk. "I am a fraud! Everything about me is a fraud!"

Lee remained quiet a long moment, then he took a deep breath. "God is there, Dewey. I can't find Him for you, any more than I could find Him for Mark. Or my father, for that matter. They had to find Him for themselves, just as you will. God is there, and I will tell you this. You may have turned away from Him, but He has not turned away from you."

"You really believe that?"

"I believe it with every ounce of my being." Lee smiled. "So, why don't we leave that little task in His hands. Tell me, does your pass last through Christmas?"

"Yes. I don't have to be back on duty until Monday, the twenty-seventh."

"I have it on pretty good authority that the Six-Oh-Fifth will be on stand-down until the twenty-seventh. And since my father is the CO, that authority is pretty good. What do you say we go to London for Christmas? I've always wanted to find that shop where the goose hangs."

"What goose?" Dewey asked.

"You know, the goose in Dickens's *Christmas Carol*."

Dewey laughed with his friend. "With all the rationing, they probably took him down for the duration. But we can go look for him."

Schweinfurt, Germany
December 24, 1943

Lieutenant Gunter Reinhardt, still unused to his new rank, returned the salute of three soldiers as they debarked from the train. The young soldiers appeared self-conscious in their field-gray uniforms.

Gunter's duty station was Calais, where he commanded one of the infantry companies assembled for the defense of Europe. The Germans had fortified the entire coast, from the Netherlands all the way down to Spain.

Von Rundstedt remained overall commander, while Rommel was his field chief. Gunter's grandfather served as Rommel's assistant. Von Rundstedt was absolutely certain that the attack would come at Calais, since that was the closest place to England, and he wanted to concentrate most of the defense there.

"He who attempts to defend everything, defends nothing," von Rundstedt quoted Frederick the Great.

Debate still raged when Gunter asked for and was given Christmas leave.

"You'll be seeing Karla?" the colonel-general asked. "It is a shame about her mother. But her father has done miracles, keeping the factory open."

"Yes, Grandfather," Gunter agreed.

"Germany has suffered much from the constant air raids, British by night and Americans by day," Colonel-General Reinhardt said. "But if they think that, by their bombing alone, they can beat Germany, they are badly mistaken." Gunter's grandfather held up his index finger to make a point. "No country has ever occupied another country without putting its infantry on the ground. And so far, not one of our enemy has set foot on German soil. If we can turn back the invasion, we will assure Germany of its final victory."

"I'm sure we can prevent their landing," Gunter said.

Suddenly, Colonel-General Reinhardt smiled at his grandson, and he opened a desk drawer. "I have a gift for you to take to Karla and her father." He pulled out two flat, oval-shaped tins. "Norwegian sardines. Quite good."

"Thank you, sir. I will tell them they are from you. I'm sure they will appreciate them."

"Well, with rationing I know it is sometimes difficult to obtain some of the finer things," the colonel-general stated.

Gunter left feeling sanguine about Germany's chances. Historically and militarily he felt that his grandfather was right. Germany could not be beaten by aerial bombardment alone. And he believed that the German defensive positions at Calais, should the Allies try to land there, were impregnable.

As Gunter had traveled across France, then across Germany, he was stunned by what he saw. France was the conquered country . . . Germany occupied Paris and manned defensive positions on the French coast. Yet the difference between the two countries was striking. There was some isolated bomb damage in France, but in Germany entire cities lay in waste.

Gunter witnessed bombed-out buildings, piles of rubble, charred, smoking timbers, and rerouted rail lines around trains that lay as heaps of burned-out, rusting metal still on the track on which they were attacked.

When he reached Schweinfurt, he did not detrain in the beautiful old train station from which he had departed four years ago. The depot lay in ruins, like much of downtown Schweinfurt, and the trains arrived and departed on the far side of the marshaling yard.

Outside, on the street, Gunter found a taxi that operated not on gasoline, but on gas generated from a large charcoal burner attached to the back of the car.

"Nach Niederrwerrn, bitte. Friedrichstrasse Seventeen."

"Jawohl," the driver said.

There were no streets, as such, in Schweinfurt—just cleared pathways through the rubble. Gunter sat in the back and looked out the window. They drove past the Wild Boar Wine Cellar, or what once had been the Wilder Eberweinkeller. The night club where he and Karla had gone during his last leave was, like all the other buildings in the city center, rubble.

Funny, when he was here last, it had seemed so far away from the war. Now the war had come home to the German citizenry. They faced dangers that were, in some ways, greater than the danger he knew at the front.

"Are you home for Christmas?" the driver asked. He looked to be in his mid- to late sixties.

"Yes."

"I hope you brought food."

"I beg your pardon?"

"Food is very scarce right now," the driver said. "If you are going to be staying with someone, I hope you were able to bring something to eat."

Niederrwerrn, a suburb of Schweinfurt, lay far enough from the city and was small enough not to have suffered any direct damage. It was refreshing to see houses and buildings standing as they had before the war. There were, however, two sites where American bombers had crashed.

Typically neat and orderly people, the Germans had left the wreckage where the planes fell as symbols of their defiance against the ceaseless air raids.

"Seventeen Friedrichstrasse." The driver stopped in front of the Maas home.

"Thank you," Gunter said, handing money across the backseat.

"I'd rather have food if you have enough to spare."

"I'm sorry, I don't," Gunter said.

"Hardly anyone does," the driver replied, taking the money.

Gunter got out of the car and stared up at the house. There was something different, but he couldn't quite figure out what it was. The house was still as impressive as ever, but now the grandeur was more fortresslike than inviting. The garden, once the pride of Olga Maas, was dead, and the leaded windows were boarded over.

Phone and telegraph service were reserved for government and military use, so the only way he had of letting them know he would be here for Christmas was by letter. There had not been enough time for them to respond.

Hefting his bag, Gunter walked up to the front door. He pulled the bell cord and heard the echo inside. He hoped they were home, and he hoped they had received his letter.

The door opened just a crack, revealing a safety-chain lock on the other side.

"Yes?" It was Karla's voice, Gunter was certain, but muffled, and she did not show herself, so he couldn't see her.

"Karla? It is Gunter."

For just a moment, Karla's face appeared in the little crack of the door. She closed the door, and Gunter heard the chain latch being removed. Then she opened the door. "Gunter!" she exclaimed, her arms wide in welcome.

Gunter held her. He would have kissed her, wanted desperately to kiss her, but she clung to him too tightly. They embraced in the open door for a very long time.

"Oh, come in, come in!" Karla finally said. She closed the door and smiled at him. "You look wonderful."

"So do you," Gunter replied.

In fact, Karla didn't look good at all. She had the same dazed look he had seen in other war-weary women. Worse, she had an expression that he recognized in old soldiers, men who had seen the horrors of war from its beginning. One of his friends had once called the look "the stare without a soul."

"My, my, a lieutenant now," she said. "When did that happen?" In the cold, clouds of vapor came from her mouth as she spoke.

"A short while ago. Our army has formed many new infantry companies to aid in the defense of Europe. They needed experienced men for officers. I am to command one of the companies."

"I'm very proud of you. And what a happy surprise it is to see you here."

"You did not get my letter?"

"No, but it doesn't matter. You are here, and we will have a wonderful Christmas. Come, Papá is in the library."

As Gunter followed Karla from the foyer into the library, he was acutely aware of how cold it was. Karla was dressed for the cold, wearing an old, ragged coat. That, as much as anything, contributed to her defeated look.

"Are you cold?" she asked.

"Uh, yes, a little."

"We have some blankets and a nice, warm fire in the library."

Although he didn't ask, Gunter wondered why, if there was a warm fire, they would need blankets.

He discovered the answer as soon as they stepped into the library. It was only marginally warmer than the rest of the house, and for a moment, it reminded Gunter of Russia.

The library had been Viktor's pride and joy. It had shelf after shelf of books, printed in German, French, and English. He had German translations of Tolstoy, keeping them even though they were among the books banned by the Nazis. He had French writers Hugo, Balzac, and Zola; English writers Walter Scott, Joséph Conrad, and Ford Madox Ford. He had Mark Twain, Hemingway, Fitzgerald, and even Westerns by Zane Grey and Owen Wister from America.

It seemed so natural to see Viktor sitting in his beloved library, and yet Gunter sensed that something was wrong. This was not the man he remembered. If Karla looked bedraggled, Viktor looked defeated. Wrapped in a blanket, he sat in a rocking chair, drawn close to the little fire, and stared straight ahead. He did not react to Gunter's arrival.

"Papá, look who is here," Karla said.

There was no response.

"Papá? Look, it's Gunter. He is a lieutenant now."

"How long has he been like this?" Gunter asked quietly.

"Almost two months now. It happened shortly after Mamá was killed. The doctor said he suffered a stroke."

"You told me about your mother." Gunter took in her father with a little motion of his hand. "But I didn't know anything about this."

"I hoped he would come out of it. Or maybe I just didn't want to face up to it. Regardless, there was no need to burden you with it. There was nothing you could do."

"No," Gunter said. "I suppose not."

"But it has caused a problem," Karla continued. "He is no longer able to work, so he has lost his position. And I get paid practically nothing at the Air Defense headquarters. I've been selling some things from the house to help us get by. I've sold a couple of sets of silver, a few pieces of furniture." A tear came to her eye. "Gunter, I had to sell Mamá's clock, the one from her great-grandfather."

"I am so sorry. I didn't know things had gotten this bad. I had no idea."

"I curse Hitler for this war!" Karla said.

"You mustn't say such things."

"In my own house I can't say this? Gunter, you have been out there. You have seen the war for four years. Can you tell me that you do not want this war to end?"

"Of course I want the war to end. Everyone wants the war to end."

"Everyone but Hitler," Karla said. "Don't you see? Hitler and those around him have no place to go. They can only hang on until they die, and they are determined that everyone in Germany shall die with them. Someone should—" She stopped in midsentence.

"Kill Hitler?" Gunter said.

"Yes. God help me, Gunter, for wishing someone dead. But if killing Hitler can prevent thousands more from dying, then, yes."

Gunter pulled her close and embraced her once more, but said nothing. He could say nothing because the plan was too new, too terrible in its consequences if it failed. But he knew that some generals, including his grandfather, and possibly Rommel, were planning the very thing Karla had just mentioned.

"Oh," Karla said, brightening. She wiped the tears from her eyes. "We have a Christmas tree."

"You do?"

"Yes. At first, I wasn't going to have one, but I thought, *One should always have a tree at Christmas.* So, I cut one down from our backyard and brought it in. Would you like to see it?"

"Yes, I would love to see it."

Gunter followed Karla out of the library, down the hall, and into the great room. There, in front of a boarded-up window, stood the tallest, most beautifully decorated Christmas tree he had ever seen. Sparkling with hanging ornaments, resplendent with tinsel, it was crowned by an angel with outstretched arms. Beneath the tree lay a beautifully carved crèche.

"We've had the decorations for years, but we haven't had a tree since the war started. Mamá said that somehow it didn't feel right for us to have a tree. She thought Christmas should be a time of prayers. Maybe she was right. But, oh, Gunter, is it wicked of me to have it?"

"No." Gunter put his arm around Karla and pulled her to him as they stood there. "Looking at this tree can do nothing but give one hope. It's as if God Himself has come down in all His glory to assure us that this terrible time will pass."

They stood there a moment longer. "Well, we have the tree, but I'm sorry to say that we won't have much of a Christmas dinner. All we have is a bag of brötchens. But Meuller's Bakery still makes very good bread."

"Ah!" Gunter said. "Grandfather sent something as a present for you. Wait, and I will get it." He went back into the foyer where he had left his kit. Digging through the bag, he took out the two tins, then went back to Karla. He held the two tins behind him.

"What is it?" she asked. "Oh, Gunter!"

"This." He held out the two tins in front of him. "Norwegian sardines."

"Oh!" Karla squealed in excitement. "Oh, I love sardines. With our brötchens, we will have a feast!"

Sikeston, Missouri
December 31, 1943

Trisha slept soundly, but Unity could not. She lay in bed, listening to the sounds of the house at night. It was cold in the bedroom. The coal fire in the furnace, downstairs in the living room, had been banked for the night, but was putting out very little heat.

Unity looked over at the clock on the bedside table. The radium dial was glowing a soft green in the darkness. It was five minutes until twelve.

Unity smiled. She could remember, back in college, when she and Dewey had gone to parties to celebrate the coming of the new year. No doubt there were parties going on in Sikeston tonight, where there would be song and laughter, drink, and noisemakers, all the traditional trappings of a New Year's celebration.

It was already 1944 in England. Dewey was not only in a different country, he was in a different year. Somehow, that seemed to make the separation even greater.

Unity got out of bed and walked over to look down at her daughter. She was sleeping on her back, but her head was turned to one side. The moon was in its first quarter, just bright enough to let her look at Trisha's face. How cute she was, with her eyes closed, her mouth pursed, almost as if puckered for a kiss. Her hand was beside her face, the fingers curled into a fist.

Unity adjusted the covers, then she put on a warm robe and went downstairs into the living room. The Christmas tree was still up, and she turned it on. All of the lights were blue, and it created a soft blue glow in the room. She turned the radio on, tuned it in to WREC in

Memphis, then sat back in the chair and listened to the music. The soothing tones of the announcer came on.

"It is one minute before midnight, one minute before 1944. Many of you, I know, have loved ones in the armed forces, and whether they are in the Pacific or European theater, in Alaska or at the Panama Canal, at sea or in the air, or at some army or navy base here in the good old United States, the prayers and well wishes of this radio station are with them tonight. Counting down now, five, four, three, two, one. Happy New Year, folks! Happy New Year!

"And now, here is Guy Lombardo's orchestra with 'Auld Lang Syne.'"

Unity leaned her head back against the chair, and as she listened to the music, tears began to slide down her cheeks. She closed her eyes. When she opened them, her father was there, standing between the radio and the blue-glowing Christmas tree.

"Do you want me to build up the fire?" her father asked quietly.

"No. I'll be going back to bed now."

Unity stood up, and when she did, Phil opened his arms. She went to him, and he stood there, embracing his daughter, feeling her tears against his cheek. He stroked her hair.

"I don't think we've done this since you were a little girl and Kenny hit you with a rock," he said.

Unity chuckled with him. "Kenny was an awful child."

"Are you going to be all right?"

"Yes. Oh, Daddy, I know it is childish of me to cry. I'm not the only one separated from my husband right now, and he isn't the only one who has not yet seen his child. But I miss him so."

"Of course you do. And you have every right to miss him," her father said as he continued to hold her and stroke her hair. "But as long as we keep him in our prayers, he'll be kept in the bosom of the Lord."

"What? A New Year's celebration and I wasn't invited?" Margaret asked.

Unity turned toward her mother and smiled. "What makes you think we are having a New Year's party? How can we have a party without noisemakers?"

"Don't worry. Wake up the baby, and we'll have all the noisemaker we need," Phil joked.

From outside, they could hear car horns being honked and even a few firecrackers going off.

"Any pie left in the icebox?" Phil asked.

"You want apple pie in the middle of the night? Why, it'll be so heavy on your stomach, you won't be able to go back to sleep," Margaret scolded.

"And melt some cheese on it," he said.

28

Normandy, France—the Americans
June 6, 1944

T he invasion had been scheduled for the fifth of June, but weather conditions were such that the whole thing was called off. Then after much soul-searching and weather prognostication, the invasion fleet put back to sea the very next night. On the morning of June 6 at 0630 hours, the Americans landed on the south part of the landing area, at beaches designated as Omaha and Utah. They were on the beaches one full hour before the British and Canadians, who hit the beaches farther north, in areas designated as Gold, Juno, and Sword.

Dewey stood on the deck of the USS *Samuel Moore* in the predawn darkness, looking at the other men who had been shuffled up on deck, their station and boat numbers written in chalk on their helmets. They had actually been brought up on deck at 0100, and many of the men, including Dewey, hadn't slept a wink the entire night. Dewey couldn't sleep because his adrenaline was flowing too freely.

Suddenly, the heavens were lit with brilliant flashes, and streaks of light sped through the night, heading toward the shoreline. A moment after the light came the roar of explosions.

"Would you look at that?" Aaron said. "I sure wouldn't want to be on the other end of all that."

"Yeah," one of the new men said. "I hope they leave something for us."

Dewey, Aaron, Roberto, and Alphabet looked at him, then shook their heads.

The navy continued with the bombardment, and the sky all around took on the illusion of a horrendous thunderstorm, complete with brilliant flashes and stomach-shaking roars. Each time one of the navy ships unleashed a salvo, Dewey could see the silhouette of the hundreds upon hundreds of ships that lay at anchor off the Normandy coast.

"Now hear this. First serial, to your debarkation stations. That is, first serial, to your debarkation stations."

"All right, listen up!" Dewey shouted to his men. "Remember, keep your hands on the vertical ropes, not the horizontal. That will keep you from being stepped on by the man above you. When you go over, keep the upper part of your body leaning in toward the ship. Push out with your feet. If the upper part of your body should lean outward and your feet come in, you may find yourself parallel with the sea, and you'll have to hang on for dear life."

The men had practiced going over the side for several months now, using specially constructed towers and cargo netting. He wasn't giving them new information, but his saying it again made it seem more like one of the many rehearsals than the real thing, and he thought that might have a calming effect for them. And in truth, it was calming to him to be able to say it.

"Be very methodical as you climb down," he continued. "The ship is rolling, so you may take a step and find there's no rung there. Most of your weight should be borne by your hands. Your hands are for support, your feet for transportation. Don't look up and don't look down. If you look up, the upper part of your body will swing out. If you look down, you can become disoriented. Now, and this is very important, when you get to the bottom of the netting, there will be net holders, men assigned to keep the net away from the side of the ship. They'll tell you when to disengage. You must disengage the moment they tell you, for what with the rolling of the ship and the landing boat, the last step can sometimes be as much as ten feet. Don't go before they give you the word, and don't hesitate for one second after they do."

"First serial into the boats! That is, first serial, into the boats!"

Captain Clemmons was one of the first five over the side. Dewey, now a sergeant first class, was right by his side. The boat was filled quickly, then it pulled away from the side of the ship.

The next three hours were agony. Waiting for all the other boats to be filled, the landing craft sailed in large circles, contending not only with the roughness of the sea, but also cutting back through its own wake. In addition, the orbiting path never let it get free of its exhaust fumes.

The men were loaded down with seventy-three pounds of personal equipment, and there was no place for them to sit. They stood crowded together while their own shells passed overhead and German shells burst all around them. They couldn't see the beach, the boats next to them, their ships, or the bursting German shells. They could see only the gray inner walls of the little craft, the back of the neck of the man in front of them and, by looking up slightly, the flak-jacketed, helmeted coxswain who, eyes straight ahead, steered the little boat.

They threw up on the floor, on themselves, and on one another. The seasickness had a domino effect, and even those with the strongest stomachs found themselves overcome with nausea at the motion, sights, and smells.

Then the circling stopped, and the little boat started in a straight line. The sound of the engine grew louder, and the roll of the boat became flatter and choppier.

"We're going in now!" the coxswain shouted.

Dewey looked into the faces of his three best friends. Aaron was now a staff sergeant, Roberto a sergeant, and Alphabet a corporal. Roberto was mouthing a prayer, which he ended by crossing himself. Alphabet was staring straight ahead. Feeling Dewey's eyes on him, Alphabet looked back and forced a smile. Aaron was slowly unpeeling a piece of chewing gum, working hard to project the expression of someone who was riding on a city bus.

"Get ready!" the coxswain shouted.

The ramp went down.

"Let's go!" Captain Clemmons called, leading the way off the ramp.

The men had been instructed to depart from each side rather than the front of the ramp. That way, if the surf caused the ramp to pop up, there was less chance of its tripping them.

The beach was filled with large concrete tank obstacles and strewn with barbed wire.

"Out of the surf, onto the beach!" Dewey shouted to the men around him.

Holding his rifle at high port, he ran through the surf, lifting his knees high. For a moment, he had a flashback to his days as a football player because he was running the way he had done in practice when the coach would have them run through automobile tires.

Machine-gun bullets snapped and popped around him, some of them passing so close he could feel the concussion. Suddenly just to his right, Alphabet went down.

Dewey reached down to grab Alphabet by his shoulders, but even as he did so, he saw Alphabet's eyes roll back into his head.

"Sergeant Bradley, get out of the surf!" Captain Clemmons shouted.

Leaving Alphabet, Dewey sprinted up to the beach. Machine-gun fire was pouring onto them, and he saw two more men go down. One of the men was new, having just joined them last month. But the other was First Sergeant Todd. Todd had been with the company since the early days in North Africa.

Looking around, Dewey saw that most of the men were stopping on the beach and taking shelter behind the tank obstacles. These were concrete tetrahedrons, called dragons' teeth. Each one was almost two meters high and two meters across the bottom.

"No!" Dewey said. "We can't stay here! We have to get off the beach! Come on, move!"

Dewey, Captain Clemmons, Lieutenant Peters, and Aaron started running from dragon's tooth to dragon's tooth, trying to motivate the men. Lieutenant Peters went down.

The Germans

Gunter stood in the back of one of the heavily fortified concrete bunkers, staring into a small hanging mirror as he shaved.

"Gott im Himmel!" he heard his sergeant say.

"What is it?" Gunter asked, looking around. Although he had on his trousers, he was shirtless, and his face was half covered with shaving cream.

"Lieutenant, the invasion! It has come!" the sergeant said.

Gunter stepped up to the firing slit in the thick concrete bunker and looked out to sea. Without another word, he reached for the phone.

"This is Lieutenant Reinhardt. Get me Major Dumey," he said. Dumey, now a major, had managed to wrangle a staff position back at Chartres.

"Dumey."

"Major, this is Reinhardt. Call Rommel! The invasion has begun."

"The field marshal has gone home for a short leave."

"Then call von Rundstedt! We must bring up the reserves!"

"Take it easy, Gunter," Major Dumey said. "It's too early to call Paris. I doubt if the field marshal is even awake yet."

"Then wake him."

Dumey chuckled. "My dear boy. A major does not awaken a field marshal, except in the case of the gravest emergency."

"This *is* the gravest emergency," Gunter shouted into the phone. At that moment, the first heavy rounds from the naval bombardment crashed all around him. Though no damage was done inside the bunker, the concussion raised the dust and made Gunter's ears ring. "Do you hear that?" Gunter shouted.

There was another crashing barrage of naval artillery.

"Get hold of yourself, Gunter," Dumey said. "You are in no danger there. The Allies are merely making a feint. The real invasion will be at Calais. If you are still convinced, one hour from now, that the invasion is real, then call me back."

"If I wait an hour, I won't have to call you back," Gunter said. "I'll send the message by an American courier, you idiot." Angrily Gunter slammed the phone down. "Tell all positions to engage," he said to the sergeant.

The Americans

It was midmorning, and most of the First Division was still pinned down on the beach, including Company A of the First Battalion. The company had more than twenty killed and even more who were badly wounded. Lieutenant Peters was dead, the first sergeant was dead, Haverkost and Cooper, two of the men who had been with the company since Camp Shelby, also were dead.

"Sergeant Bradley, as of right now, you are the acting first sergeant and executive officer," Clemmons said. "And if anything happens to me, you're going to be the company commander. You got that?"

"Yes, sir."

"We've got to get off this beach," Clemmons continued. "We've got LCTs circling out there that can't come ashore because it would just put more men in the killing zone."

"We need some close-in artillery," Dewey said. "But we lost most of our guns trying to get them ashore."

"We'll use the navy," Clemmons said.

"Captain, that won't do any good. They're two or three miles out to sea. We need in-close, direct artillery fire."

"Yes." Clemmons signaled for the radioman, then he called Battalion. "Colonel Merkh, you think we can get some of those ships to come in close enough to give us direct covering fire?"

Dewey couldn't hear Colonel Merkh's response.

"Yes, sir, I know, but if you can get them to steam in closer, I'll direct the fire."

Clemmons looked at Dewey. "He's going to try to get some of the destroyers to come in closer."

"I don't know how shallow they can come," Dewey said.

"Yes, well, I don't either, but that's their problem, not ours." He looked at the radioman. "Give me the radio," he said.

"Beg your pardon, sir?"

"Give me the radio," Clemmons said again. He pointed up the beach, beyond the barbed wire. "I'm going to call in the fire mission from up there. There's no sense in both of us risking our lives."

"Uh, you sure, sir? I mean, I am your radio operator. I should go where you go," the RTO said, though it was obvious that he didn't want to go.

"I'm sure," Captain Clemmons said, strapping the radio onto his back. "Okay, Dewey, you've got the company. When the shelling starts, I'm counting on you to get them off this beach."

"Yes, sir," Dewey said.

Captain Clemmons ran from the dragon's tooth to the concertina wire. There, even as bullets whipped around him, he picked his way through. After that, he darted up through the dunes until he reached a German pillbox. Crawling up to the pillbox, he tossed a grenade inside. When the grenade was tossed out, he picked it up and tossed it back in. He barely got it out of his hand before it went off. Then he began calling in artillery.

The destroyers came in close, closer even than the circling LCTs. Watching them, Dewey felt nothing but respect for the captain and crew; they couldn't possibly have more than a few inches of clearance between their hull and bottom there. If one of them went aground, it would be easy pickings for the Germany artillery. Then he noticed something. The destroyers had actually come in so far that the Germans could not depress their heavy guns enough to bring them to bear. By their very daring, the destroyers had taken themselves out of danger from the really big guns.

Captain Clemmons called in the first barrage on the rolls of barbed wire, chewing it up to make a path for the men on the beach to get through. He called the next barrage on his own position.

For a moment, until the smoke cleared, Dewey thought Clemmons had been killed. But when the smoke of the first barrage drifted away, he saw that Clemmons was still there, still calling in artillery.

"All right, men. Let's go!" Dewey called out. "We have to clear this beach!"

Dewey got up then and started running toward the break in the barbed wire. The men followed him in twos and threes, building to squad strength, then in platoon strength, until all of Able Company left the beach and gained the high ground.

But the surge forward was not without cost. At least thirty more men lay dead between the dragons' teeth and the high ground, some shot down as soon as they stood, others on the sand, still others hung up in the concertina wire.

Looking back at the men he had lost, Dewey saw Aaron and Roberto. Of the six men that Alphabet once called the Double Musketeers, only he remained.

Carentan, France—the Germans
D-day plus 6

Although the Germans had inflicted heavy casualties against the Americans on Omaha Beach, the savage fighting had cost them dearly as well, draining their morale and exhausting their resources. Twenty-five panzer divisions were still in reserve, still uncommitted, because Hitler still believed that the real invasion would be at Calais.

The 352nd had been pulled back to defend the town of Carentan. If they could hold Carentan, they could prevent the Americans who had landed at Utah Beach from linking up with the Americans who had landed at Omaha.

Shortly after dawn on the morning of June 12, Gunter was surprised to see his grandfather's staff car drive up. He was further surprised to see that there was no one in the car but the driver.

The driver reported to Gunter and saluted. "Lieutenant Reinhardt?"

"Yes."

"I am driver for Colonel-General Reinhardt. He asks that I bring you to see him, sir."

"Very well," Gunter said, wondering what it was about.

Gunter's grandfather had his headquarters in a farmhouse about sixteen kilometers east of Carentan.

"Have you had your breakfast, Gunter?" his grandfather asked.

"No, sir."

"Then join me."

"Thank you, sir," Gunter said, sitting down at the table.

The general's orderly served them, and Gunter was spreading butter on his bread when his grandfather spoke.

"I know I should be asking this question of General Bayerlein or one of his staff officers," Colonel-General Reinhardt said. "But from you, I think I will hear the truth. How long do you think we will be able to hold Carentan?"

"Not long, General, unless we can bring up the reserves," Gunter replied.

"I still have no permission to commit them, but will two hundred and sixty panzers help?"

Gunter smiled and nodded. "If we can get them there in time, it will," he said.

"I'm ordering up Panzer Lehr."

"Thank you, sir."

Colonel-General Reinhardt stroked his chin. "Of course, the Allies control the air. So we have to face the possibility that the tanks won't even make it there."

"I understand," Gunter said.

Gunter's grandfather walked outside with him, and the two men sat on a low stone wall. Birds were singing in the trees, and in a nearby field, a cowbell clanked as a cow grazed. In comparison with the Sturm und Feuer of war at the front, the scene was surreal.

"Hitler must go," Colonel-General Reinhardt said quietly.

"I beg your pardon, sir?"

"Hitler has ordered the burning of Paris," Gunter's grandfather said. "And I know that he has secret plans to completely destroy Germany if we lose the war." The colonel-general laughed bitterly. "That is, assuming the Allies leave anything for him to destroy."

Gunter didn't reply. For a long moment, there was no sound save the chirping of birds and the clanking of the cowbell.

"What I am about to tell you could, if it falls in the wrong hands, be the death of many good men—including you if you are privy to the information. Shall I go on?"

"Do you have a role for me to play, Grandfather?" Gunter asked.

The colonel-general said, "Not unless we are successful. I would rather you be completely out of it at this point. But if we are unsuccessful, and if it is discovered that I am a part of it, I will surely be killed." He put his hand on Gunter's shoulder. "I would want you to know why. And I would want you to know that I would prefer such a death than to stand by and do nothing while Hitler continues with his madness."

"I understand, Grandfather," Gunter said.

"You had better get back now."

The two men stood, and Gunter saluted. For the first time since the war began, his grandfather didn't return the salute. Instead, he embraced him.

The cowbell continued to clank in the field behind them.

Returning to his own headquarters, Gunter rode in the backseat of his grandfather's staff car. Three American fighters passed over them, but they made a wide, 180-degree turn.

"They are coming after us," the driver said.

"I doubt they would waste ammunition shooting at a lieutenant and a corporal," Gunter replied.

"Lieutenants don't ride in BMW staff cars," the driver said. "They can't see your rank. They see only this car."

The corporal's observation was correct because the planes peeled off, dropped down to no more than thirty meters, then came screaming up the road toward the car. The corporal slammed on the brakes.

"Out of the car!" he shouted.

Gunter jumped from the car, dropped into a ditch, then crawled into a concrete culvert alongside the road. He managed to get into it just as the first plane opened fire.

The BMW went up with a whoosh. The second and third planes

fired into the ditch. The bullets slammed into the dirt and chipped away concrete from the edge of the culvert.

The airplanes did not make a second pass. Gunter lay in the culvert for a moment longer, listening to the receding sound of the engines as they flew away. Finally, he crawled out of the culvert and dusted himself off.

"Corporal?" he called. "Corporal, are you all right?"

He saw the corporal, belly down in the ditch, about eighteen meters away from the culvert. The corporal was lying very still with three bullet holes in his back.

Gunter had seen them all over France, the little grottoes in churchyards, town parks, and even the fields. This one was in a hedgerow, stones piled up and mortared together to make a small cave. There was a cross on top of the grotto, with the cruciform hanging from it, Jesus' eyes looking up toward heaven, as if saying, "Father, forgive them, for they know not what they do."

Gunter lay down his MP-40, took off his helmet, then knelt before the cross. Clasping his hands in front of him, he began to pray.

His rifle ready, Dewey picked his way through a small gap in the hedgerow. Seeing the German on his knees, he raised the M-1 to his shoulder, then with the front of his trigger finger, he pushed off the safety lock.

The German heard the click of the safety and looked toward Dewey. At first there was an expression of surprise on his face. Looking toward his own gun, he knew that he couldn't get to it in time. The expression of surprise turned to one of resignation. The German crossed himself, then bowed his head, waiting to be shot.

It wasn't until that moment that Dewey realized that the German soldier had been praying. He lowered his weapon.

"Do you speak English?"

"Yes."

Dewey saw the Iron Cross on the German's jacket. But more than that, he saw the weariness in the German's face.

"How long have you been in the war?" Dewey asked.

"Three and a half years."

"And after all this, you still believe in God?"

"Of course. Don't you?"

"God has abandoned us."

The German shook his head. "No, God has not abandoned us. We have abandoned God."

Dewey made a motion with his rifle. "Go," he said. "Return to your own lines."

The German picked up his helmet, then reached for his MP-40. "No," he said with a smile. "I think I should leave it here."

"I think that's a good idea."

The German stood, started to walk away, then turned back toward Dewey. "Do you know what I was praying for, American?"

"No."

"I was praying for forgiveness."

"I wish I had the strength of faith to believe that forgiveness is still attainable."

"The Lord will give strength unto his people; the Lord will bless his people with peace." With a little wave, the German turned and walked away.

Dewey recognized the words. They were from the Twenty-Ninth Psalm. He had killed more Germans than he could count, and the Germans had, in turn, stripped him of all his friends. Could it be that a German would show him the way?

Suddenly, he heard the word of God as if in the roar of thunder heard by Jeremiah. He felt as Paul must have felt on the road to Damascus. Like the German before him, Dewey fell to his knees. "Thank You, God," he prayed. "Thank You for lifting the scales from my eyes."

Dewey's life might still be in danger, but his soul was no longer in peril.

Epilogue

Harmony Baptist Church, Gulf Shores, Alabama
October 24, 2004

A hardworking committee had spent many days cleaning up the mess left by Hurricane Hannah. The fellowship hall had been condemned and would have to come down; so for now, sawhorses and yellow tape prevented unauthorized entry.

Out in the parking lot, cars were parked in such a way as to allow part of it to be used as a picnic area. The women did what they could to make it festive, putting checkered cloths on the tables and decorating the tables with flowers and balloons. They also brought side dishes, such as potato salad, baked beans, green beans, black-eyed peas, and coleslaw. Cobblers, pies, and cakes were placed on a dessert table.

Toward the back of the lot, the men, many of whom were wearing aprons boasting "World's Greatest Grandpa" and "King of the Grill," worked at smoking grills and bubbling deep fryers. The aroma of fried amberjack and mullet, grilled tuna, boiled, fried, and barbecued shrimp blended with hot, freshly baked bread and permeated the church grounds.

The men were almost evenly divided in their loyalties between Alabama and Auburn. Many wore caps representing the school of their choice, and as they cooked, they tossed barbs back and forth, remembering games from many years past. One of the cooks, however, who had only recently transferred his letter to Harmony Baptist from Prestonwood Baptist in Dallas, wore a Baylor cap.

"Now, Ralph, we're going to let you get away with that cap this time," Greg Tobin said. "But next time we do anything like this, you're going to have to declare whether you are for the greatest football team in America, the Crimson Tide of Alabama, or you support those weak sisters from Auburn, who can't even make up their minds whether they are called War Eagles or Tigers." Greg was wearing an Alabama hat.

"But I went to school at Baylor," Ralph replied.

"And Ernie Westpheling went to West Point," Greg said. "But you see what he's wearing, don't you?"

Ernie also wore an Alabama cap.

"Yeah, but that's 'cause his wife's from Alabama and she browbeat him into wearing it," Pat LoBrutto said. "If he had enough gumption to stand up to her, he'd be wearing this." Pat tipped his Auburn cap.

Pat's response drew laughter, and as they worked, the men continued their good-natured barbs toward one another. Despite the fact that they were doing it in the very shadow of their destroyed fellowship hall, it was a gala event. Reverend Carl Baumgartner and the members of his congregation had resolved not to let a little thing like a hurricane get in their way. The Loaves and Fishes Dinner was a genuine celebration.

A red Jeep SUV drove up, parking in one of the remaining designated areas.

"Well, it's about time the reverend showed up," Greg said.

"What are you talking about?" Ralph asked. "Brother Carl is over there. He's been here all morning."

"I'm talking about Brother Bradley. He was pastor before he retired."

"He was the pastor here? I didn't know that. I've seen him here, but

I thought he was just a member of the church."

"Looks like Brother Dewey's got the general with him," Pat said.

Two men and two women got out of the SUV.

"The general?" Ralph asked.

"Yes, that fella with him is General Clemmons," Greg said. "He lives over in Mobile, but one weekend, he and Emma were down to the beach and they came to church. Turns out, he and Dewey were together during World War II. So, about once a month, the general attends church here. We almost count him as a regular."

"Yes, and he does come to our men's breakfasts," Pat said.

"Isn't that neat, them getting together again after all these years?" Ralph said.

"General Clemmons won the Medal of Honor in Vietnam, didn't he, Ernie?" Greg asked.

"No, he won it during World War II," Ernie replied. He was a retired colonel.

"I don't think I've ever met anyone who got the Medal of Honor. How did he get it?" Ralph asked.

"I remember reading about it in a military history class at the Point," Ernie said. "It happened on D-day. He charged a German bunker single-handedly, called artillery down on himself, then held off an entire platoon of Germans until his company could get off the beach. And he did all that with a broken mess kit knife."

The subject of their conversation came toward them.

"I smell something good around here," Clemmons said.

"I don't know, General. I think you're going to have to supervise this bunch," Pat said. "I mean if someone doesn't keep an eye on them, this stuff may not be fit to eat."

"You've got a colonel watching over things. If he can't handle it, what makes you think a general can?"

"My only experience with the military is as a two-year draftee, back in the fifties," Ralph said. "From my perspective, sergeants ran the army."

"From my perspective too. Wouldn't you say so, Ernie?"

"You got that right, sir," Ernie replied.

"And speaking of sergeants, in thirty years of military service, World

War II, Korea, and Vietnam, I never served with a better one than your own Dewey Bradley."

Carl and Dewey came back to join the cooks. "Hey, guys, the crowd is getting restless, and I'm getting hungry," Carl said. "How much longer?"

"We've about got it in the bag here," Greg answered. "I think in a minute or two, you can zap a blessing on this and we can eat."

"I wonder who that is?" Pat looked toward the front of the parking lot.

A stretch limousine was just turning off Fort Morgan Road. It drove up as far as the sawhorse that was blocking the way, then the uniformed driver got out of the car and opened the back door.

A young, very attractive woman stepped out of the limo. By then everyone had seen the arrival, and all conversation halted as they stared in unabashed curiosity at the woman.

"Dewey, Vernon, would you come with me?" Carl asked as he started toward the woman, who had advanced only as far as the sawhorse blockade.

When they reached the sawhorse, the woman smiled and stuck her hand out toward Carl. "You would be Pastor Baumgartner?" She had a slight accent.

"Yes."

"General Clemmons, it is good to see you again," the woman said. She offered her hand to him as well.

"Mrs. Helgen," Vernon said, shaking her hand.

Dewey looked at Vernon in surprise.

"Then you must be Pastor Dewey Bradley," the woman said, offering her hand to Dewey.

"Yes," Dewey said, still curious as to what this was all about. "I'm retired now, but I was a pastor."

"I am very pleased to meet you, Mr. Bradley," Karla Helgen said. "Especially since my grandfather told me that if it weren't for you, I wouldn't be here."

Dewey was even more confused. "I don't understand."

"During the war, my grandfather was in the German army. The two of you had a momentary encounter in a field in France. To use my grandfather's words, you had him at a disadvantage, but you spared him. Do you remember that?"

"Yes, I remember it quite vividly, in fact," Dewey said. "But I don't understand. How does your grandfather know who I am? We never exchanged names."

"His name was Gunter Reinhardt. Have you ever heard of Colonel-General Jakob Reinhardt?" Mrs. Helgen asked.

Dewey shook his head. "No, I'm afraid I haven't."

"You know about the German generals' attempt against Hitler, don't you?" Vernon asked.

"You mean the one that involved Rommel?"

"Yes. If you recall, Rommel was given the option of committing suicide. Colonel-General Reinhardt, who was also involved, wasn't as lucky. He was executed," Vernon explained.

"Colonel-General Reinhardt was my grandfather's grandfather," Karla Helgen said. "My grandfather learned, very soon afterward, that the Nazis were after him as well. He actually had nothing to do with the plot, but he was the grandson of one who did, so he knew the Nazis wouldn't have believed him."

"He and about one hundred of his men surrendered to us in early August," Vernon explained.

"At the time of his surrender, my grandfather saw you," Mrs. Helgen explained. "But he thought it best not to approach you. He wasn't sure how your army would accept the fact that you could have killed him, but let him go. However, he did remember Captain Clemmons, and because he became a general, it was easy to keep up with him. A few years ago, he gave me the task of keeping up with the general, and through the Internet, it was amazingly easy to do so. My grandfather wanted this so that, when the time came, he would be able to find you or someone in your family."

"When the time came," Dewey said. "I don't know what you mean."

"When my grandfather died," Mrs. Helgen said. Then before Dewey could respond, she continued. "After the war, he returned to Germany where he started a small company, making telescopes and binoculars. As many companies do, Reinhardt Optics grew and diversified, night vision technology, fiber optic transmission, various other products. Gunter Reinhardt became a very wealthy man, and in his will, he left you ten thousand shares of Reinhardt Optics." She opened her purse, took out an envelope, and handed it to him. "As of close of trade today, it was worth fifty-six American dollars per share."

"Fifty-six . . . ? That's over a half-million dollars!"

"Yes," Mrs. Helgen said, smiling broadly.

Dewey was silent a long moment. "Mrs. Helgen," he finally said. "This is such a bolt out of the blue that I don't know what to say, except thank you."

"No thanks are necessary," Karla Helgen said. "I told you, if you had not spared my grandfather that day, I wouldn't even be here."

"Would you and your driver like to join us?" Dewey asked. "We are celebrating the miracle of the loaves and fishes."

"Yes, I would be pleased to join you."

As they started back toward the others, all of whom were still looking on in curiosity, Dewey saw Unity coming toward him. She could barely contain the smile that was spreading across her face.

"Well, I'll be. You knew about this, too, didn't you?"

"Yes, but I didn't know until this afternoon," Unity said. "Carl told me. I've practically chewed my tongue off, biting it to keep from telling you."

"Did everyone in the world know but me?"

Unity laughed. "What difference does it make? You know now, and that's all that's important," she said.

"Come inside with me for a few minutes," Dewey said, heading toward the church.

As the congregation enjoyed their dinner, they also enjoyed talking about the good fortune that had just fallen upon Dewey, and that was the conversation at all the tables. They were nearly half-finished with the meal, and Dewey and Unity had not come back outside, so Carl went in to see about them.

He saw Dewey and Unity, sitting together in the fourth pew from the front, left-hand side, nearest the aisle. It was where they sat every Sunday, and now, even though every pew was empty, it was where they chose to sit.

"Dewey?" he called.

"Come on down, Carl. Unity and I have something to tell you."

Carl walked down to their pew, then sat just across the aisle from them.

"How are the fishes and loaves?"

"Great," Carl replied. "Everyone is having a wonderful time."

"I hope there is some left."

"There is. We're waiting for you to join us."

"Unity and I have just been sitting here, thanking God for our lives, our children and grandchildren, and our good fortune. And we want to share that good fortune. Put the roof back on the fellowship hall, Carl. We'll pay for it." Dewey held up the envelope.

"Dewey, you don't need to do that. We can have a fund drive and—"

Dewey waved his hand. "I know we don't need to do it, but we want to do it. I don't believe it is a mere coincidence that this money would come to me on this day of fishes and loaves. I believe, with all my heart, that this miracle is a part of His plan."

"I don't know what to say," Carl said. "Except I think I can speak for all of us when I say thank you for sharing your miracle of the money with the church."

"Oh, the money isn't the miracle," Dewey said. "You want to know the real miracle?"

"Yes. I would love to know the real miracle."

"Gunter Reinhardt thought that I saved his life that day. What he didn't realize was that for me, he saved something much more important than my life. He saved my soul."

About the Author

R obert Vaughan is a retired Chief Warrant Officer–3. He entered military service in 1953 as a member of the Missouri National Guard. Transferring to active duty, he attended the Aviation Maintenance in Fort Rucker, Alabama. After serving a tour of duty in Korea as crew chief on an H-19 helicopter, he returned to the Army Aviation flight school at Ft. Rucker, where he became a warrant officer.

After receiving his appointment to warrant officer, Robert was posted to the 101st Airborne Division at Ft. Campbell, Kentucky. His next assignment was the Seventh Calvary in Germany, "Custer's Own." While in Germany he was historical officer for the Seventh Calvary, and in that capacity, he was custodian of the Custer memorabilia (such as Custer's field diaries, saber, hat, and so on). That assignment created a fascination with Custer, which eventually led to four published books.

From Germany, Robert went to Ft. Riley, Kansas, where he accompanied the 605th Transportation Company to Vietnam for the first of what would be three tours in Vietnam.

In Vietnam, he was a recovery officer (when an aircraft would go down, Robert would take a rigging crew to the site and rig it so it could be sling-loaded by helicopter, back to base; on several of these missions the crew would encounter intense and accurate enemy fire). Later, he would serve in the same job for the Fifty-Sixth Transportation Company. His last assignment in Vietnam was with the 110th Transportation Company, where he was chief of the Open Storage Depot. During his three years in Vietnam, he was awarded the Distinguished Flying Cross, the Air Medal with "V" device and 35 oak-leaf clusters, the Purple Heart, the Bronze Star, the Meritorious Service Medal, the Army Commendation Medal, and the Vietnamese Cross of Gallantry.

During his military service, Robert was selected by *Army Aviation Digest* as having written the "Best Article of the Year" for six consecutive years. He also wrote and produced several training films for use in the Aviation Maintenance Officers' Course. His last assignment was as Chief of the Aviation Maintenance Officers' Course.

As an author, Robert sold his first book when he was nineteen. Today, he has over 30 million books in print. Writing under thirty-five pseudonyms, he has hit the *New York Times* and *Publishers Weekly* bestseller lists twice: In 1981, *Love's Bold Journey* and *Love's Sweet Agony* each reached number one on both mass market lists, with sales of 2.2 million each. His novel *Survival* won the 1994 Spur Award for best western novel, *The Power and the Pride* won the 1976 Porgie Award for best paperback original, and *Brandywine's War* was named by the Canadian University Symposium of Literature as the best iconoclastic novel to come from the Vietnam War. In the 1970s Vaughan was an on-air television personality with "Eyewitness Magazine" for WAVY-TV in Portsmouth, Virginia, and later, doing a cooking show for "Phoenix at Mid-Day" on KPHO-TV in Phoenix, Arizona. He is also a popular speaker at several colleges and has appeared at numerous writers' conferences throughout the country. Each winter he runs the "Write on the Beach" writers' retreat in Gulf Shores, Alabama.

Robert lives on the beach of Gulf Shores, Alabama, with his wife, Ruth, and his dog, Charley. A lay eucharistic minister, Robert is a past warden and vestry member in the Episcopal Church. He is currently very active in the Holy Spirit Episcopal Church.

Also Available from Robert Vaughan

TOUCH THE FACE OF GOD

In this moving novel, Lt. Mark White, a B-17 bomber pilot, meets Emily Hagan only weeks before he ships out to England. They fall in love through letters but will the war and a misunderstanding tear them apart forever? This powerful story is about a man's love for a woman, the soldiers' love for their country, and the love of God for each of His children.

0-7852-6627-5

WHOSE VOICE THE WATERS HEARD

The romance between Patrick Hanifin, son of a famous novelist, and Diane Slayton, the daughter of an American missionary in Japan, bears the hardships of World War II—separation, death of loved ones, and near-death experiences—but ends with miraculous survival.

0-7852-6315-2

HIS TRUTH IS MARCHING ON

This third WWII novel from best-selling author Robert Vaughan follows the physical and spiritual journeys of an American soldier who is disillusioned with his faith and the German soldier who helps to restore it. With painstaking historical accuracy, Vaughan weaves a story of intrigue and passion, offering readers a suspenseful glimpse into WWII—from both a military and human experience.

0-7852-6185-0

Also Available from Robert Vaughan

0-7852-6235-0

CHRISTMAS PAST

John and Madison Carmichael's success in their careers has come at a high price at home: they are on the brink of divorce. To soften the blow for their two children, they decide to spend one final Christmas together as a family. Responding to a travel brochure, they set off, but tensions only worsen when their car breaks down. A horse-drawn carriage arrives and delivers them to the home of Judge Andrew Norton and family, where their Victorian Christmas begins. John and Madison rediscover each other and the love they once felt. But upon their return to "modern civilization," the Carmichaels learn that the nineteenth-century house has been empty and boarded up for more than thirty-five years. Could it be that a miracle from "Christmas Past" has brought their family together again?